RATTLE SNAKE BLUFF

A SAM RIVERS MYSTERY

CARY J. GRIFFITH

adventure PUBLICATIONS

Cover design: Travis Bryant
Text design: Annie Long
Author photo: Anna McCourt
Editors: Mary Logue, Jenna Barron, and Emily Beaumont

Library of Congress Cataloging-in-Publication Data
Names: Griffith, Cary J., author.
Title: Rattlesnake bluff / Cary J. Griffith.
Description: Cambridge, MN: Adventure Publications, 2025. |
  Series: A Sam Rivers Mystery
Identifiers: LCCN 2024059799 (print) | LCCN 2024059800 (ebook) |
  ISBN 9781647554743 (pbk.) | ISBN 9781647554750 (ebook)
Subjects: LCGFT: Detective and mystery fiction. | Novels.
Classification: LCC PS3607.R54857 R38 2025 (print) | LCC PS3607.R54857
  (ebook) | DDC 813/.6—dc23/eng/20241220
LC record available at https://lccn.loc.gov/2024059799
LC ebook record available at https://lccn.loc.gov/2024059800

Copyright © 2025 by Cary J. Griffith
Rattlesnake Bluff: A Sam Rivers Mystery (book 5)

Adventure

Published by Adventure Publications
An imprint of AdventureKEEN
310 Garfield St. S.
Cambridge, MN 55008
800-768-7006
adventurepublications.net

All rights reserved
Printed in the USA

PRAISE FOR *RATTLESNAKE BLUFF*

"Special Agent Sam Rivers finds himself on the endangered species list in this rollicking page-turner."

—Jeffrey B. Burton, award-winning author of *The Second Grave, The Dead Years,* and the Mace Reid K-9 Mysteries

"Cary J. Griffith is a master of suspenseful and rugged outdoors adventures. In *Rattlesnake Bluff,* his latest Sam Rivers Mystery, he pits the U.S. Fish & Wildlife Services special agent against a ruthless killer who will stop at nothing to keep a 25-year-old cold case buried. The author's knowledge of both his setting and endangered wildlife—this time, deadly rattlesnakes—is once again on full display. Lovers of wildlife mysteries will not be disappointed."

—Lois Winston, best-selling and award-winning author of the Anastasia Pollack Crafting Mysteries

"In *Rattlesnake Bluff,* Cary J. Griffith presents readers with his most provocative and fascinating villain—a man who, as a teenager, likes to call himself 'Der Fuhrer.' Still infatuated with Nazism as an adult, he is remarkable for his ability to rationalize in his mind his horrific acts while appearing to be a constructive member of society. After arriving in Bluff Country to investigate the discovery of an endangered species of rattlesnake, Sam Rivers and Gray, his wolf dog, track the murderer. And rattlesnakes provide justice. Griffith's knowledge of flora and fauna, along with his understanding of the psyche of an American devotee of Hitler, enables him to masterfully tell this story that will resonate with many readers. *Rattlesnake Bluff* is Griffith's finest novel."

—Brian Duren, award-winning author of *Whiteout, Ivory Black,* and *The Gravity of Love*

PRAISE FOR *RATTLESNAKE BLUFF* (continued)

"Cary J. Griffith is a master creator of edge-of-your-seat outdoors mysteries. *Rattlesnake Bluff* kicks off with a haunting cold case that will rattle the reader. When two children go missing, all the leads are dead ends. No one knows the truth about what happened to the kids except the twisted murderer. Twenty-five years later, U.S. Fish & Wildlife Special Agent Sam Rivers and his sidekick, Gray, a wolf-dog hybrid, are drawn into the haunting case when a rare rattlesnake is discovered in an area ready for development. The snake will lead Rivers and Gray to more sinister murders as the past comes full circle and ends with ultimate satisfying karma for a cold-blooded killer."

—Kathleen Donnelly, Retired K-9 handler and award-winning author of the National Forest K-9 series

"In this tightly coiled fifth Sam Rivers mystery, Cary J. Griffith proves he's on par with C.J. Box and Craig Johnson. *Rattlesnake Bluff* takes readers on a thrill ride with U.S. Fish & Wildlife Special Agent Sam Rivers and his wolf dog, Gray, as they poke around Minnesota's eerie Driftless area looking for an endangered rattlesnake. These isolated caves and bluffs hide something worse than a snake bite: human remains. Griffith's fast-paced storytelling immerses the reader in equal parts landscape, wildlife, and danger."

—Sara E. Johnson, *New York Times* Readers' Pick author of the Alexa Glock Forensics Mysteries

*For Benjamin Waldron,
native son of Minnesota's bluff country*

PROLOGUE

July 17, 1998

"I'm Der Führer," he said to his buddy Paul.

At the start of his 18th summer, Der Führer discovered the Golden Gar, a ramshackle bar in the Wisconsin river-bottom woods. The bartender, Frank, had a pirate's beard and mustache, stained yellow like his teeth. His tattooed arms stuck out of a black leather biker vest. Frank was their new best friend because he served anyone with the necessary cash, no questions asked.

Der Führer and Paul had been perched on a couple of the Golden Gar's barstools for the last 2 hours, sipping Harvey Wallbangers and talking about the start of their lives.

"Der what?" Paul said.

"Der Führer. The main guy. The leader."

"Der Dink, you mean," Paul said, happy with his joke.

"The guy who almost had it all. Should have, for Christ's sake. Adolf Hitler, man." Der grew wistful.

"I'll just call you Der Dink," Paul laughed.

Der Führer looked at his buddy, sitting at the bar beside him, both of them bleary-eyed and tottery. *Der fuck off*, came to mind. Instead, he said, "If you're too illiterate to pronounce Führer, just call me Der."

The Golden Gar was getting busy. Frank thought the kids were entertaining, until they weren't.

"I believe you boys have had enough," Frank said.

Der thought about it. "I disagree, Frank."

"Kid, I don't give a fuck what you think. Get the hell outta my bar."

Paul's leg kick snapped Der back to reason.

On the way to their vehicles, Paul said, "Sleeping it off in Winona." Paul's grandparents liked to watch *Jeopardy* on Friday nights, so he could stumble up to bed unnoticed.

Der nodded and said, "Catch you back at the Hole."

The Hole was Owen's Gap, where both boys had grown up, gone to school, and graduated—Der with honors. He was headed to the university in the fall. The previous week he'd gotten his dorm assignment. He couldn't wait to get out of the Hole.

Der's old man was spending the weekend in La Crosse, no doubt with his mistress-cum-legitimate squeeze Bonnie Sorenson. That left Der alone till Monday. Time to take another ride down County Road 8. The remote blacktop was straight and hilly. When he pushed his Range Rover, taking the hills at top speed, he could get his whole chassis airborne. Der Führer loved to fly.

A half hour later, he spun his wheels onto the black road. His tires made a satisfying squeal. He dropped the visor to block the setting sun and told himself, *Watch the road, check your speed, keep an eye out for deer.*

But he wasn't feeling it.

He was feeling quittin'-time-at-4-o'clock-Friday and more Harvey Wallbangers than he could remember.

The previous weekend, he'd struck a doe and fawn. He'd been startled by the blow. Their gristle, blood, and fur had gnarled the Rover's grill work. His dad told him to get it power washed and fixed. But when Paul saw his front end, he said, "Two deer with one shot. You the man!"

Der dragged his feet on the repairs, considering the Rover's crumpled front end a bloody badge of courage. His old man was too busy with work and Bonnie to notice.

Der's tire squeal notwithstanding, he reminded himself to take it slow. Especially when he passed the sign for the Low Valley Trailer Park, the start of the roller-coaster road.

His dad called the park "the barracks for wetbacks, scofflaws, wannabes, and everyone else who does our dirty work." It was also a favorite haunt of the Owen's Gap police force and county sheriff's patrols.

The Wallbangers gave Der an invincible edge. But he wasn't so dead-drunk stupid as to speed past the park. He kept his wheels straight and an eye out for the law. He had time.

He continued down the blacktop, visor lowered, heading west, straight into the setting sun.

His mom had died the previous year, a loss Der thought he should have felt more keenly than he did. At the funeral, he tried to summon tears, but his eyes were stubborn. Ditto the old man's, who attended to all the necessary arrangements with a sober, proper countenance, but never anything resembling sorrow.

Afterward, when it was just him and his dad, the old man took him out to the barn for what felt like a rite of passage.

"It's time I introduced you to the Lair," his dad said.

Der had grown up playing in that barn, which was mostly storage for some of the old man's toys. He was stunned when his dad raked hay across a false floor, revealing a lock and iron pull ring the boy had never seen.

"Your mother wasn't partial to my interests," his dad said. "Her time on the town council and as mayor forced me to keep my hobbies to myself. I guess she had a point."

His dad lifted the hatch to his underground room. A short ladder descended to an 8x8-foot space with headroom. There was a workbench against a side wall. Over the bench hung several pistols, World War II vintage German Lugers, and a sniper rifle. They were clean, carefully placed, and well-oiled. There was a red flag with a black swastika hanging on a back wall. Beneath hung a portrait of Adolph Hitler, *Der Führer*.

It was a small room, to be sure. His dad called it his Lair because Hitler had called his eastern front military HQ the Wolf Lair.

Der was thrilled to be introduced to the old man's secret world. His father had always been reticent, strict, and disciplined—all attributes Der had gradually come to appreciate.

Now he knew why.

Der followed his father into the woods behind their house and they shot the Lugers at tin cans and bottles. The pistols bucked, hard, but the lethal weapons fit into the boy's hand like a custom-made grip slipping into a glove.

Der's father told him his grandfather had started the collection. Der's old man expanded it. And even though there were still some who considered Der Führer and the Third Reich a step in the right direction, it was best if, for the time being, they kept the Lair to themselves.

Then the old man was in La Crosse every weekend, banging Bonnie, leaving Der to fend for himself.

On one of those weekends, Der discovered joyriding down County Road 8. The number had never been lucky. But liftoff was too glorious to ignore.

At this hour of the evening, filled with liquid courage, he didn't care about luck. He cared about the roller coaster's heady rush of weightlessness.

Two miles west of the trailer park, he began his gradual acceleration. He had never seen anyone on the road. But he needed to keep an eye out for wildlife.

Der adjusted the visor, getting ready to push his speed and feel the thrill. There were six hills, and he took the first one going 50. When he reached the top, the sun was briefly in his eyes. Going 50, his body barely shifted out of its seat.

Once over the rise he accelerated, speeding down the first descent. By the time he hit the second hill, his speed had increased to 67. He dropped over the rise with a momentary thrill of weightlessness. Enough to make him aim the car straight down the hill and hammer the pedal to the floor.

The Rover roared ahead, accelerating through the climb, the kid feeling the speed like a lightning bolt. When he hit the hill's top, he lifted wholly out of his seat and let out a whoop. The Rover dropped over the rise and bottomed out on the blacktop with a screech, sending the tires sideways, and Der, struggling to hold on, skidding to the right. But he kept his pedal to the floor. Because he took chances for the thrill, and he knew the next rise was going to be a freefall that would make him happy to be alive.

He neared the rise dangerously close to the shoulder, almost out of control. The speedometer breached 90, certain to make him free.

The Rover roared ahead, summiting the peak, and for just one second, maybe a millisecond, the sun was blinding.

And then he felt a sudden impact and the ugly, unexpected jolt of something alive, something of flesh and blood. Knocked off course, Der waited for his wheels to touch down. He skidded sideways, and there was a moment he was certain he'd topple. The car pitched and he thought he was going to tip and roll, end over end, into the weeds.

At the bottom of the hill, he regained control and braked hard to stop.

His pulse was rocketing. He had no idea what he'd hit. There had been the flash of something that hadn't looked like a deer. It looked like boots. White boots. But he was speeding so fast into the sun he'd only caught a glimpse of something that shouldn't have been there.

He put the Rover in reverse and backed up the hill. He felt sick and drunk and afraid.

Near the hill's crest he parked, cut the engine, and swung open his door, stepping onto the shoulder. The weeds were tall and thick and, when he looked down, hoping to see the brown body of a deer, he saw something else entirely: high-top, white roller skates.

He walked over and saw a body lying face down in tall grass. Long black hair. A girl. Young. She was crumpled beyond recognition. Her head was misshapen and turned at an unnatural angle. Her legs were twisted and broken, red, purple, and ugly. Her white skates were crazily pigeon-toed. Amazingly, her body hadn't broken open. But what was left looked like a miscolored leather bag filled with bones. A body that was not breathing now and never would again.

Fuck! Goddamn it.

The previous year, a drunk driver in Winona struck and killed a grandma. He'd been sent to prison. It'd been all over the news. You drink and drive, you pay.

The sickening reality of Der's predicament caused the bile in his stomach to rise. He backed away long enough to bend over and vomit. The air filled with the stench of partially digested pizza, Wallbangers, and fear.

He was in trouble. Goddamn it, he was in trouble.

The girl was dead.

He searched around, looking into the nearby woods, as though he might find answers among the trees. He glanced down the road. For the moment, he was alone.

What to do? What to do?

Call someone, he knew. Drive back to the park and find a pay phone and call someone.

But his dad was in La Crosse. Paul was passed out at his grandparents' house in Winona. And the law... the law would put him in jail. He was drunk and he'd killed someone. A girl.

He looked around, panicked and uncertain. He glanced farther into the ditch weeds and saw another pair of skates. Black. Smaller.

He stepped deeper into the weeds. A boy, on his back, his eyes closed and his body still. He was less crumpled, but clearly hurt, either dead or unconscious.

He'd killed two kids! He was going to prison. He peered down and stared at the small boy to be certain his nightmare was real.

And then he recognized him. He'd seen the kid around the Hole, maybe in a store? He and this other kid, the one near the shoulder, the slightly older girl. He'd seen them walking around town. He guessed a brother and sister.

Then he remembered, before his mom died, he'd been riding in her car and she'd seen them and said, "Those are Ginny Dickinson's kids."

Garcia. They were the Garcia's kids. He didn't know their first names. They lived in Low Valley. The trailer court. Their dad was a foreigner. From south of the border. Der remembered his dad saying, "Any foreigner who marries a white girl is after a Green Card."

Ginny Dickinson's kids. A woman his mother knew.

The boy lay 10 yards to the right of the girl. He wore black skates that were splayed out and, at first, Der was sure he was dead. He kept looking and, in the waning light of day, he watched the boy's small chest rise and settle. *Still breathing.*

The girl was struck first, full on. The boy must have been to the right and in front of her. She was thrown into her brother and, while the girl was knocked into the nearby ditch, her brother had been hit so hard he'd caromed 10 yards farther into the high weeds and now lay there, unconscious.

He looked again to be certain. The kid was alive.

Goddamn it!

What to do, what to do, what to do . . .

Get the kid into the Rover and rush him to the clinic. Fifteen minutes . . . he could be there.

But the other one.

Leave her. Out here, with no traffic . . . he could leave her in the weeds.

But his future. The university. The dorm.

He was drunk. He'd killed someone.

He hadn't meant to. It wasn't his fault. They shouldn't have been on the road. The goddamn kids, trailer park kids, shouldn't have been out roller-skating in the middle of the road.

But they were on the edge of the road. And he was going 90. And he was drunk!

Think.

Vehicular homicide. He'd read about it in the papers, heard someone talk about it. The new laws. That man in Winona who struck and killed the grandma. He was in prison now.

His dad would get him out of it. His dad would . . .

But the old man was in La Crosse! It'd take him 2 hours to get here. He'd be in a holding cell in the Hole's jail. And what could . . . would . . . the old man do?

Think!

They never should have been there.

The trailer park was home to wetbacks and scofflaws. Ronnie Garcia, their dad, had married Ginny Dickinson for a Green Card. For these people, Der thought, life was cheap. Hadn't his dad always said that? What kind of future did they have? No prospects. Their old man wasn't prominent.

Der's family had money. He was going to college!

No way Der should go to prison. Nothing in his future of getting out of the Hole involved prison. Not a cell. He was 18! His life was in front of him. Four years in a prison or four years at the university.

He looked at the boy, thinking. The boy was practically dead. If not dead, he'd be a cripple. Der could help him. Maybe Der should help him.

Think!

There had been a case a couple of years ago, when Der had entered high school. A kid up north had gone missing and was never found. He'd disappeared. End of story. It happened all the time. Kids went missing. Especially trailer trash.

Der could make the bodies disappear.

It was bluff country. Bluff County. It was a place of rolling hills and high outcrops and dense woods. Lots of dense woods. The country around Owen's Gap was full of them. But not here. Too near the park. Not here.

But the boy . . .

Make them disappear. They could disappear and be like that kid up north. People would search, but they'd never be found. He knew a place he could put them. Where no one would ever find them. A place the old man said would never be developed because it wasn't suitable for anything except looking out over bluff country. A remote corner of the woods. It was a nothing place. A nowhere-ever-to-be-seen place. A place nobody would ever walk. Too crowded with bush and trees. Too rocky to farm. The cliff too near to build.

If they disappeared, everyone would assume they'd been taken. Taken, and carried from here. Far away.

Kidnapped.

Vanished.

In the waning light of day, Der saw what could be done. What must be done. He could bury the problem. Make it go away. It took nerve. Der Führer's nerve.

The girl was dead. The boy, an obvious cripple, had no future.

Der needed to take care of the boy, and then hustle both of them into the Rover's rear cargo hold. He had construction plastic from the job. Black. In back. Wrap them in plastic and get them the hell off County Road 8. Drive to the remote place. Bury them in bluff country.

But the boy was breathing.

Do it! He could hear his dad's voice. *Do what needs to be done.*

And then something else took over. Something fateful, awful, reaching for the future he knew was his. Reaching for the boy . . .

He hid the two bodies in the black plastic folds and stuffed them into the Rover's cargo hold. Then he took side roads back to the farm. He pulled a spade from the barn. He waited until midnight and took more back roads until he pulled onto a remote gravel road. A long strip of field spread out to his right for 50 yards. Beyond it was a rise of trees, the bluff edge. The left and right sides of the pasture were bordered by dense woods.

Der parked half in the ditch. The grillwork had a few more dents, but no more blood, fur, or gristle than had already been there from the doe and fawn. More dents. There had been two pieces of cloth he'd pulled off, like pulling a thistle burr off a pant leg. And then he hauled the two black-plastic-covered bodies into the north edge of the woods. There was a limestone shelf partially buried. Like lots of places in bluff country, it hid a small opening, a cave-like crevice large enough to hold the bodies of two kids wrapped in heavy plastic. He'd dug a wide, narrow hole, wide enough for each of them, side by side, skates and all. A tight fit. He piled rocks over the entrance and then buried the rocks so no coyotes or wild dogs would dig them up.

And then he took the shovel and started back to the Rover, trying to think of nothing. Fifty yards and he'd be in his SUV heading down the road. Just another late-night driver.

An engine . . . the noise a distant whine, like insects. The sound made him stop at the tree edge as it grew louder.

There was a bend in the road a half mile away. Der glanced through branches and thought he saw something, a flicker of distant light. Headlights.

As the headlights turned the corner, the sound grew louder, coming at him.

Der crouched.

Fuck. Fuck, fuck, fuck, fuck, fuck . . .

But his Range Rover was off the road. Even if it was someone local, somebody who knew the vehicle and knew it was his, Der was nowhere near it. They'd think he'd stalled and gotten picked up.

Stay low. Out of sight.

The headlights neared. Another minute and they approached the Rover. Then slowed.

Der held his breath and stayed out of sight.

It was a truck. F-150. Blue. Joe Smiley's truck. He had a dairy farm a mile down the road, in the valley. He was the nearest neighbor to the bluff site. His farm was at the bottom of a steep decline.

Smiley was behind the wheel, his wife in the passenger seat. They slowed and peered at the Rover. They looked around. And then Joe Smiley kept driving, accelerating as he continued down the road, following the white cone of his headlights.

Der waited until the lights turned the corner and the engine's sound diminished. He waited until he couldn't hear it at all.

Then he returned to his Rover, turned the ignition, and steered away from Smiley's farm. He waited until he was 50 yards down the road before turning on his headlights.

If the Smileys ever asked him about his Rover by the side of the road in the middle of nowhere, Der would tell them he'd broken down, got a ride from a buddy, came out and jumped it later. It was a bad battery. He played out the comments in his head in case the Smileys ever saw him and asked.

But they never did.

CHAPTER 1

Tuesday, Present Day

Julio Vargas Ortega loved Minnesota's Driftless.

Ever since he was a young boy, Julio—Jules to his friends and colleagues—rose before dawn. Even with the windows shut to birdsong and the blinds pulled, Jules could feel first light. Didn't matter if the previous evening he'd been out past midnight at a tequila fest, doing the Marimba two-step, hoping to snag a partner, beating out a rhythm all his own. When the eastern horizon grew pale, Jules shuffled into his galley kitchen to brew coffee, his tighty-whities tented by his tumescence and the hope for better luck getting a girlfriend ahead.

At 27, Jules liked his coffee black. He was 5'8", built stout and thick-muscled, with jet-black hair and a tan patina he claimed was from his mother, Esmerelda, who was one-quarter Mayan. Apart from a taste for occasional tequila, Jules lived clean. And even though Jules missed his mother, there wasn't a morning that passed without Jules feeling lucky he lived in southeastern Minnesota's bluff country.

He stared at the kitchen calendar, admiring the photograph. It was a morning shot in July, looking out across the only place in Minnesota that escaped the Ice Age glaciers. The Driftless extended from southeast Minnesota into southwestern Wisconsin and northeastern Iowa. It featured green land undulating in sweeping ridges all the way to the horizon. In the calendar photo, taken east of Rochester, Minnesota, the mists hung over the verdure like the treetops of an Amazonian rain forest.

Today was Tuesday, July 11. He had always believed Tuesdays were the most productive day of his week. Similar to his instinctual sense of first light, he felt certain today was going to bring something special.

He was usually on a construction site an hour before anyone else, especially on a Tuesday. He enjoyed sitting in the company's Silverado, sipping double-strength. By 7:00, the sun was off the horizon, turning the fields of bluestem golden. And on this morning, his first on Alta Vista, a new construction site, he loved watching the goldfinches flash their yellow regalia, trolling for mates, getting ready to nest when, later in the month, the mullein and thistle seeds would start to come in. Whether they were calling for the girls, or just 'cause the morning was blue, clear, and warm, it didn't matter to Jules. Things were going great for him. The beautiful midsummer morning in the heart of resplendent country, filled with birdsong and sunlight, seemed like the perfect accompaniment to his mood, which on this day was ebullient.

Yesterday, Leslie Warner, owner of Warner Construction, had made him foreman on this site.

"You're the best man for the job," Leslie said.

At 40, she had been in the business long enough to recognize an excellent worker when she saw one. With an equally excellent demeanor. Jules always did exactly what she asked. She also appreciated the fact that, unlike most men on the site, Jules always looked her in the eye instead of scanning her body.

The previous afternoon, she and Jules had walked to the tree edge of the proposed Alta Vista development, where scrub brush was perched atop a limestone bluff. They'd bushwhacked through 10 feet of undergrowth until they were right at the cliff edge.

The limestone-topped escarpment dropped more than 100 feet to the valley below. When they stood on its edge, the panorama unobstructed, they were blessed with a view as fine as the one on Jules's kitchen calendar. The hills, undulating in front of them, took their combined breath away.

"I'll be bringing out some potential partners this week," Leslie said. "The first one tomorrow, over the lunch hour. Can you make sure and clear out some of this brush? Doesn't have to be a lot. Just enough so he can see this."

"Of course," Jules said. "I'll get the Bobcat this afternoon and start on it first thing in the morning. I'll make sure there's a view by 11."

"Perfect," Leslie smiled, already thinking about the words she'd use to sell the site to her new investors. *From here you can see across the Driftless to the Mississippi River. And you're only 45 minutes from Rochester.*

The setting was bucolic, the vista magnificent, and its proximity to the medical complex practical. Her potential partners were doctors who wanted all three. Leslie had a good feeling about this, her most ambitious project. It was going to sell out fast. And it was going to be lucrative, providing they didn't run into any snafus.

Unfortunately, Leslie had been working in construction long enough to know unexpected issues always arose. Her first issue had been getting the county to agree the site could be developed. She hired a surveyor to mark off the site. Then she worked with an architect to address the potential issue of building on an area bluff. She'd expected Henry Fields, the zoning commissioner, to balk at the site, and he had. But she was ready for him, threatening to complain to the other county commissioners if he didn't greenlight her project.

If everything had as few hiccups as the site's start, she could expect clear sailing.

But she knew bumps in the road were inevitable. She just hoped they didn't slow her down.

On Monday afternoon, Jules drove 45 minutes to the Warner Construction Equipment lot outside Winona. The yard was near the Mississippi, and like everything in bluff country, Jules liked to pause and admire the flow of big water.

He was back at the bluff site by 5:00. It took another 15 minutes to position the flatbed on the gravel shoulder and unhitch it, making sure the Cat was still chained to the bed and secured for the night. The trailer had a rear black metal gate that doubled as a ramp. Jules unhitched the rear gate and dropped it to the ground, making it ramp-ready for his early morning work. Then he returned to his truck, anxious to tell his friends about his promotion.

Before Jules pulled away, a pickup came up beside him. A man rolled down his passenger-side window, nodded to Jules, and said, "What's goin' on?" indicating the trailered equipment.

He looked like a local farmer, Jules thought. Maybe in his seventies, with what sounded like the hint of an English accent. He seemed friendly enough, but you could never tell.

"Doing work for Warner Construction," Jules said.

"What kind a work?"

Jules knew enough to play dumb. Leslie Warner never wanted others knowing her business, until it was well enough along for them to figure it out on their own.

"Clearing land."

The man seemed to think about it. Then, "I always thought, remote as this is, but still being close to Rochester, it'd be a bonny site for a row of townhouses, or maybe a big house," the man said. "Providing you're a multimillionaire." He smiled.

Jules smiled back. "I guess," he said. "Definitely a nice view."

"Once you get beyond those trees," the man said.

Jules agreed. "You live around here?"

Jules knew he'd tell Leslie about the man, and his questions. He knew she'd be curious.

"Down the road about a mile. Name's Joe Smiley. Got a dairy farm in the valley."

"Jules," Jules said, shaking Joe Smiley's hand.

In the winter, when Warner Construction work slowed, Jules sometimes worked dairy.

The two talked cows for a while. The man was interested to know that Jules knew dairy. It was hard work, and he was always looking for help, which he didn't mention, wondering if the man with tan skin and an accent was legal. Must be, he guessed, working for a construction company. He didn't know Warner Construction, but he made a note of the name and would look it up when he got a chance.

They finally said their goodbyes, and Jules headed back to Rochester, excited for the evening's entertainment.

By 7:30 a.m. on Tuesday, Jules stepped out of his cab, fully caffeinated and ready to take on the day. It felt like he could lasso the sun and ride it into the heavens, if need be, so much was going so well for Jules these days. His work as a foreman meant more money. And he had the oddest premonition good things were about to happen on the girlfriend front. He'd had several dance partners at the festival, though he hadn't felt "bitten" by any of them.

Bitten was his mom's term for when he would meet someone who would strike him like a hammer blow in the heart, filling his veins with love. He missed his mom, who often said crazy stuff to which he only half listened. He had not seen her for three years, and it was hard. Super hard for Jules, who loved his *mamá*. If he was worth anything, it was because of her. And his father. But his father had passed when he was a boy. And his *mamá* had never remarried. Thankfully, there was plenty of family around Llanos, a dirt-poor community less than 2 hours southwest of Ciudad Juárez. The area was destitute, with little work and no future.

So, Jules came north.

He sent his mother money and Facetimed her the Sundays she could borrow a phone. But it was a poor substitute for being at her table and enjoying hot tortillas off the stove with *huevos* from her free-range chickens, and *queso, frijoles,* and pimientos out of her garden.

It was hard not giving his *mamá* a hug or being hugged by her. But it was one of the sacrifices you made when you crossed the border in search of better fortunes.

Jules walked down through the bumpy pasture, thinking about how his raise would give him enough money to send his mom a bus ticket here so they could spend some time together.

Before offloading the Bobcat, he scanned the tree line ahead of him. If he was going to finish before noon, he needed to hustle.

The trailer's ramp was already down. When he circled in back to step onto it, he noticed a boot print in the gravel dust. The print looked fresh, though the weather had been sunny and calm the last few days, so it could have been made anytime. He glanced over his equipment, but everything appeared fine. And there was only the one print.

Jules thought no more about it. He stepped up onto the bed and unlocked the chains, pulling them from the Bobcat's four wheels.

The day was beginning to warm. The Cat had been sitting all night, so its front handle was cool. Jules turned the door's handle and swung it open. Before twisting and hoisting himself onto the cab's seat, he glanced down and noticed something different, something unexpected. It looked like a thick, colorfully patterned coil of rope.

Then it rattled.

It was a sound he hadn't heard since the day he'd left home. A rattlesnake. Dangerous. The sound and its appearance made him scream and spring back, cat-like, onto the trailer bed.

Once he was certain he was at a safe distance, he breathed. The unexpected shock of seeing a rattlesnake rocketed his pulse.

"¡Mierda!" he said. *Shit.*

In northern Mexico and Texas, rattlesnakes were commonplace. There were several kinds, all of them easily recognized. When he was young, he and a friend had killed a 4-foot timber rattler, skinned it, and roasted some of its meat over a fire. It smelled good over the flames. They'd taken a few bites, the flavor a cross between frog legs and turtle. A little gamey, but tasty. And filling for a couple of kids who seldom had enough to eat.

Then they tossed the entire carcass—less its head, where the venom was stored—to the hogs.

When Jules's mother found out, her eyes turned fearful, then angry. Esmerelda's Mayan heritage always made her think a little differently. Especially about things in nature. Whenever she encountered snakes—any snakes, but especially rattlesnakes—it was an omen.

"No good comes from killing Kukulkan," Esmerelda said. "Killing any snake."

Kukulkan was the Mayan serpent-god, bringer of rain and sun, the intermediary between the living and the dead.

Esmerelda instructed them about giving the rattler a wide berth or using a long stick to shoo it out of their path. They should never kill it.

But this snake was on the front seat of his Cat. And Jules needed to get on with his Tuesday morning. He needed to get that tree line cleared by 11:00, so Leslie could show her client the view.

The rattlesnake wasn't moving. The inside of the Cat was cool, so even though the snake had rattled, it wasn't ready to slither away anytime soon. Jules couldn't imagine how it had gotten into the Cat. Or why, for that matter. Probably following a rat, he guessed. Though none of that made any difference.

He fetched a long-handled shovel from the cargo hold of his truck and returned to the flatbed.

When the snake saw the shovel blade, it made a quick rattle. Jules said a prayer, for his mother. Then he brought the metal down flat and hard, whacking the reptile. It writhed and rattled, and he struck it again, twice. Then it stopped.

Jules had encountered lots of rattlesnakes. But he had never seen a rattler like this one. It was covered with beautiful dark-brown splotches. There was a pattern to the splotches, along the top of the back and around the sides. The top splotches were the largest, separated by tan skin. Its head was in the shape of an arrow point. He watched it for a full minute, making sure it was dead. He regretted killing such a beautiful creature.

He recalled the scolding he'd gotten from his mom. She was always using herbs, not only to spice their food but also for native rituals she remembered from childhood. After the boys had killed the rattlesnake, eaten part of it, and thrown the rest to the hogs, she'd pulled down a bundle of dried sage. Then she made the boys go out to the livestock tank and wash their hands and faces. When they were finished, she lit the dried sage and waved the smoke around their heads, hands, and upper bodies, saying some kind of incantation Jules had never heard before. To cleanse them.

Jules wished his mother were here to help him. But this morning, Jules didn't have time for a ritual. Jules was a foreman, and he needed to get into his Bobcat and use its front loader to plow up the bush edge, then cut the last part by hand. The boss needed her view.

Once he was certain the snake was dead, he used the shovel blade to scoop it up. He dropped the snake on the road's shoulder, well away from his truck and trailer. Then he returned to the Cat and checked it for more snakes. Not finding any, within five minutes he'd backed it off the trailer and was motoring to the bluff edge.

He knew he'd clear a view for his boss well before noon. It was his job.

But it was hard not to recall his mother's voice.

"Snakes are omens. No good comes from killing a snake."

CHAPTER 2

Wednesday

Sam Rivers and Carmel Rodriguez sat at her kitchen table, finishing breakfast. Between them lay a pile of returned wedding RSVPs. A list with more than 100 names rested beside the small stack of postcards. Most names had a Y next to them. There were fewer than 10 with an N, those who indicated they could not attend Sam and Carmel's late-fall wedding. There were maybe another 20 without any mark, nearly all Sam's invitees. The unmarked were people who had not yet responded, a lack of communication Carmel considered rude.

"You need to reach out to these people," Carmel said, tapping the sheet like a drum. "We need to know if they're coming."

Sam frowned, chewing slowly, buying time.

"You know," Carmel said, "some psychologists believe managing the wedding details is the couple's first real relationship test."

Sam kept chewing. And thinking. Then he swallowed and said, "I thought the first real test of the relationship was, well . . . the first time you slept together."

"Is that a joke?" Carmel said.

Clearly, she didn't think so.

Sam paused. "Sort of."

"Not funny, Rivers. The wedding is in two months. We need to let the caterers know how many people are attending. We also need to let the lodge know how many rooms to reserve. Why haven't your people responded?"

They were getting married at Gichigami Lodge on Lake Superior's North Shore.

Sam loved Carmel and admired her work as a veterinarian. And he was looking forward to getting married up north. He even enjoyed working on some of the wedding details, time permitting. It was Sam who nixed the salmon dinner option in favor of Minnesota's favorite fish, walleye, even though it was more expensive. And the Gichigami Lodge was Sam's suggestion. But he didn't have the bandwidth to track down every person on his list who hadn't responded. He figured, given a little more time, they would respond. But he knew reminding Carmel that patience was a virtue would be poorly received, given the heat of the moment.

Fortuitously, his phone buzzed. It was his boss, Kay Magdalen. It was 7:30 a.m.—6:30 for Kay, who worked out of the Denver office.

"I gotta pick up," Sam said. "She wouldn't call this early unless it was important."

Carmel understood, as long as he understood they weren't finished.

"Rivers," he said, picking up the list of wedding invites and seeing Kay was one of those who had not responded. "I hope you're calling about our wedding?"

"What?"

She sounded irritated. Was he pissing off everyone this morning?

"Our wedding invite," Sam said. "You haven't RSVP'd."

There was a pause. Then, "Goddamn it, Rivers. That's not why I called. Now's not the time."

Carmel begged to differ, but he wasn't going to say so.

"Okay," Sam said, looking at Carmel and shrugging. "What's up?"

"How do you feel about southeastern Minnesota?"

"The Driftless?" Sam said. Sam knew it as a place of caves and trout streams, and the only part of Minnesota glaciers didn't plow over and drop rocks on. But to Kay, he said, "It's an interesting place. Why?"

"Did you know they have rattlesnakes down there?"

"I think I heard that," Sam said. "Timber rattlesnakes. But they're rare. A threatened species, as I remember. Nothing like where you live."

When Sam and his first dog, Chance, lived in Denver and roamed Green Mountain and the Hogback, they often encountered rattlers. Chance had enough sense to give the snakes a wide berth. He was a good dog, Sam remembered.

Gray, Sam's current dog—a wolf-dog hybrid—seemed to read his thoughts. He came out of his sit and approached, looking for a head rub. Sam obliged, and Gray's eyes squinted appreciatively.

"Well, a rare one in Minnesota just rattled," Kay said. "Apparently, this kind isn't threatened, it's endangered. At least in Minnesota, crazy as that sounds. Mass-something."

"A massasauga?"

Sam had always been interested in snakes. As a boy he had only seen the occasional garter snake, snakes being uncommon on Minnesota's Iron Range, where Sam grew up. But when he moved to Denver, he grew accustomed to their presence and often searched for them in the foothills around town. They could be deadly, but they were also startlingly beautiful and exotic.

Once in Minnesota, working for the U.S. Fish and Wildlife Service (USFW), he had familiarized himself with the state's threatened and endangered species. He had seen the eastern massasauga (pronounced "ma·suh·sau·guh") rattlesnake on the list. He recalled reading that they were extremely rare in Minnesota and could only be found in bluff country, usually down by the river.

"About the only thing I know is the name," Sam said.

"And how to pronounce it."

"And that if you find one it's likely to be in southeast Minnesota."

Sometimes Sam Rivers impressed Kay Magdalen, a perspective she kept to herself. Kay believed Sam was indulged in ways other agents were not. His status in Minnesota, for instance. Over the last three years he had been called back to the state for a variety of reasons, mostly official. During one of those visits, he'd met Carmel Rodriguez. Then he'd fallen in love, for God's sake. That prompted him to finagle a temporary liaison position, hobnobbing with Minnesota law enforcement. And now he and that wolf dog Gray were kind of settled in the state.

The dog, mind you, was a wolf dog and had no business being involved in the Service. It sent the wrong message, Kay knew. And on this score—involving a wolf dog in his cases—she happened to agree with her USFW superiors. No one in the Service would allow a wolf dog to be part of the K-9 staff.

And yet Sam Rivers and his wolf-dog sidekick were still in Minnesota, liaising with state law enforcement and solving crimes. It was their success at crime-solving that caused Kay to indulge her spoiled agent.

She reminded herself that he was one of the best agents in the Service, maybe *the best,* and had a wide-ranging knowledge of wilderness and wildlife issues, including, apparently, rattlesnakes. But the last thing Sam Rivers needed was praise from his boss. What Sam needed was a short leash. Preferably held taut.

"Maybe you have a future as a host for *Wild Kingdom,*" Kay said.

Sam, familiar with Kay's sarcasm, said, "I've got a job. Besides, the show's never been the same without Marlin Perkins."

Kay was old enough to remember Marlin Perkins, who started hosting the show in the 1960s, before Sam Rivers was born.

"I'd love to talk TV history, but we've got a problem with a rattlesnake."

From Sam's experience, snakes weren't the problem, people were. "What happened?"

"Some guy . . . a worker using a Bobcat to clear ground," she said.

Sam heard papers shuffling.

"Here," she said. "It was outside a town called Owen's Gap."

"Did he run over it?"

"No. Got there yesterday morning and found it on the Bobcat's seat."

That sounded odd. There was a pen beside their guest list. Sam picked it up, flipped over the paper, and scrawled *Owen's Gap*.

"Looks like it's due east of Rochester, Minnesota," Kay said, about the town. "Aren't they known for some medical thing there?"

"The Mayo," Sam said.

"Sandwich spread?"

"No. The Mayo Clinic. It's a big deal."

"In Minnesota?"

"Internationally," Sam said. "In fact, it's a medical destination for the world's elite. Not saying I agree with that kind of thing, being a member of the serf class, but royalty is a regular at the Mayo."

"Whatever," Kay said, unimpressed. "The rattlesnake was about 45 minutes east of there. A developer was breaking ground. The guy found the rattlesnake in his Bobcat and killed it. Then he tossed it to the side of the road, but an anonymous caller phoned the sheriff."

"An anonymous caller phoned in about a dead snake?"

"I know. Sounds a little odd. But maybe it was one of those environmentalists. Heard there are a lot of them in Minnesota."

"You mean, people who care about the land and everything in it? People like us?"

"I'm nondenominational," Kay said.

Sam knew Kay Magdalen kept her politics to herself. "Your profession belies your perspectives," Sam said.

"It's a job, Rivers. My perspectives are a closed book."

Kay Magdalen had been Sam's boss for nearly a decade. Whatever else she was, he knew she was a closed book. She was married to Clarence, a man Sam had never met. He was hoping that might change with the wedding.

"The sheriff sent a deputy," Kay said. "Deputy Rosie Miller." More paper shuffling. "The deputy called the DNR. The DNR sent out a conservation officer, Bob Greene. Bob wasn't sure what he was looking at, so he called my niece, Gina Larkspur. Gina works for the DNR. Some kind of non-game wildlife specialist, but she's always been interested in reptiles."

"A herpetologist," Sam said. "I didn't know you had relatives in Minnesota."

"By law," Kay said. "Clarence's sister's kid. Gina Larkspur. You know her?"

"Never heard of her. I don't know a lot of the DNR non-game wildlife people."

"Turns out she was the lead researcher in a DNR paper on the timber rattlesnake in Minnesota. She tells me timber rattlesnakes are threatened in Minnesota, 'cause you can't find them. More or less. But this other rattlesnake," Kay paused, thinking.

"The eastern massasauga," Sam said.

"That one. Yes. It's unheard of, according to Gina. They have not seen one in Minnesota for more than three decades. It's not threatened in Minnesota. It's endangered."

"You said that." Endangered was a whole new level of classification. If a species was endangered, the USFW got involved.

"Gina told the developer she had to stop developing, for the time being, because of the snake. You can imagine how that went down."

Whenever an endangered species was discovered, the authorities needed to investigate. All development needed to cease, at least until a survey was done of the property. If the species could be removed or relocated, the site could reopen. If not . . .

"I understand," Sam said. "How big's the development?"

"Ten acres."

"Shouldn't take long to do a survey."

"We need you down there this afternoon. There's a meeting with the local sheriff, the DNR folks, the developer, some doctors, I guess . . . investors in the project. Might even be a lawyer or two."

"Uh-oh," Sam said.

"The USFW needs to let them know about their options," Kay said.

"That they can't bulldoze an endangered species?"

"That," Kay said. "But we don't want to be obstructionists. If there's a way to clear the site so development can continue, it's a win-win."

Sam knew it was true. If they stopped a development on account of an endangered species, especially if it was a reptile, the press would have a field day, giving anti-environmentalists plenty of ammunition. Sam recalled the heated controversy surrounding snail darters, a fish the size of a minnow, halting the construction of a Tennessee dam. And the northern spotted owl preventing the logging of old-growth forests.

Coincidentally, Sam was supposed to meet with some legislators this morning, to review and discuss the state's wolf-management plan, another perennially controversial topic. If he had to choose controversies, he'd much rather be hunting rattlesnakes in the Driftless. And postponing his need to check up on wedding invite laggards.

"Just so you know," Kay said. "The guy who found this rattlesnake killed it. But he didn't know it was endangered."

Sam wasn't surprised.

"And as far as I know, they only found the one."

"We'll need to make sure," Sam said.

Sam mentioned his morning meeting, and Kay told him to reschedule, it could wait. It was a sentiment Sam was glad to hear.

"Can you send me the name of the people who will be there, and their phone numbers? Whatever you have?" Sam said.

Kay assured him she would.

She was just about ready to hang up, when Sam said, "You still haven't RSVP'd to our wedding yet. You and Clarence coming? It wouldn't be a party without you."

"Have you ever seen me party?" Kay said.

"It's my wedding. You're my boss. You should be there."

There was a pause, during which Kay must have realized she couldn't get out of at least a partial response.

"Gotta see if we can move some stuff around."

"Kay," Sam said. "This is serious. I'm getting married."

"Isn't this your second wedding?"

"Yes, I've been married before. But that wasn't much of a wedding. And as I recall, you ignored that one too."

"I had a hunch it wouldn't last."

"You might have said something."

"You were in no position to hear reason."

Sam paused, not sure what to say. "This one's going to stick," he finally said. "It would be good to see you there."

There was a pause. "Keep me posted on the rattlesnake," she said, then hung up.

CHAPTER 3

Sam was told to be at the Alta Vista development site by 4:00. Because the site had no address, he entered Owen's Gap in his app and saw it was a 2½-hour drive. Kay had texted him the names and numbers for Deputy Rosie Miller; DNR Conservation Officer (CO) Bob Greene; Developer Leslie Warner; and Kay's niece, DNR herpetologist Gina Larkspur. She had also told him the sheriff for Bluff County was Betsy Conrad. He would call the people with numbers on the way down. But county sheriffs, Sam knew, could be great partners or impediments. He needed to know where Sheriff Betsy Conrad fell on the continuum. And he knew a good source to help him figure it out.

Vermilion County Sheriff Dean Goddard picked up on the second ring. "I mailed it yesterday," Dean said.

Sam remembered his morning conversation with Carmel. "You're coming?"

"Of course. Wouldn't miss it. Me and the doctor and John Michael will be there."

The doctor, Sam knew, was Susan Wallace, Dean's wife. "Carmel will be happy to hear it."

Vermilion County, where Dean was the sheriff, was in northeastern Minnesota, near where Sam had grown up. Four years ago, Sam and Dean had worked on a case in Vermilion County, becoming friends over crimes they helped solve.

They made small talk, asking about each other's families. Then Sam explained where he was headed and why.

"I need some background on one of your colleagues. Bluff County Sheriff Betsy Conrad."

"I know her. But not that well. I know she's been in the job for . . . just a sec."

Sam heard clicking.

"She's been the sheriff since 1996. Damn. That's a long time for a sheriff."

"Do you know anything about her?"

"I've seen her at conferences. But I don't really know her. I can tell this much, though. Any sheriff who has survived in office for more than 25 years must be pretty good at her job and one hell of a politician. Why do you want to know?"

Sam also mentioned the USFW had already told the sheriff's office and the developer the site needed to be closed. At least temporarily.

"Then you're walking into a hornet's nest," Dean said.

"You think so?" Sam said.

"I know so. You're a federal agent and you're closing down some kind of development because of a snake?"

"It's an endangered species."

"A poisonous creature."

"I think the term is 'venomous.'"

"Sam, you can split hairs all you want. But if there was a developer in Vermilion County who had to shut down their site because of a snake, you can bet there'd be fireworks."

Sam suspected Dean was right. Especially since he was pretty sure there were populations of the eastern massasauga rattlesnake in other states.

"You're the fed," Dean said. "So, by law you can shut it down for a while. But if I were you, I'd have a Plan B. Something that'll reopen the site sooner rather than later."

Sam thought about it. "Maybe relocation," he said, thinking out loud.

"That'd work."

Sam told him the site was 10 acres and it shouldn't take more than a couple of days to survey it.

"Gray could find them." Dean knew Gray and had been impressed by the wolf dog's keen nose and work ethic.

"Not sure I want him to look," Sam said. "Gray would get there first and either get bit, or kill it, or both."

"Use a leash," Dean said. "All I know is, if it was me, and you closed a development up here, I'd commiserate with the developer, then let the feds take the heat. Let *you* take the heat."

"Gee, thanks, sheriff."

"Just sayin'," Dean said. "I live here. That developer would be one of my constituents. You're an out-of-towner and don't mean jack to me. Figuratively speaking."

"I appreciate your candor," Sam said.

"Don't mention it," Dean said. "I just wish I was down there to watch the fireworks."

Sam thought about the call. The truth was, he did not have a Plan B. If they looked for more rattlesnakes and found them, especially a den, the DNR and his colleagues back at the USFW would want the place sealed off. At least long enough to study the animals. Sam could see the site becoming a long-term academic research project. He didn't know what kind of development it was. But if it was a plot of land with woods and fields and bluffs, 45 minutes from Rochester, he suspected residential.

Sam dialed CO Bob Greene. After Sam introduced himself, Bob said, "I wondered if it might be you. I saw the 303 area code."

Colorado, Sam knew. "Given the circumstances, I guess I should feel good you took my call."

Bob Greene laughed. "You've definitely rattled some cages."

"Rattlesnakes will do that."

As a DNR CO he was familiar with Sam Rivers. Last fall, Sam had investigated the murder of DNR CO Charlie Jiles, who was found submerged in a fishing net on Lake Vermilion. As a CO, Bob had heard things about Charlie, none of them good. But he hadn't really known him. When Bob learned USFW Agent Sam Rivers was coming to look into the Alta Vista site, he Googled him. In addition to the poaching fiasco on Lake Vermilion, he found other incidents, including one involving drug smugglers and scorpions.

Sam asked him about the site, and Bob told him what he knew. They were building high-end townhomes, and yes, the site was quite beautiful. It was an ideal location, being an easy commute from the Mayo. They were going to start breaking ground when they found the snake, sitting on the seat of a Bobcat. The worker killed it with a shovel and tossed it on the side of the road. Somebody saw it, some guy, and phoned it in.

"9-1-1?" Sam said. A 9-1-1 call would be recorded.

"Nah. It wasn't an emergency. The snake was already dead."

"Called in to the switchboard?"

"Yes," Bob said. "It was kind of . . . odd. You see a dead snake on the side of the road . . . a common enough sight . . . and you report it to the sheriff?"

"I'm surprised you guys looked into it."

"That's part of what was odd. The caller said he thought it was a rattlesnake. That's why Rosie called me."

"The deputy?"

"Yes. Rosie Miller."

It was Deputy Miller who went out and placed the dead snake in a plastic bag. She and CO Bob Greene were friends, and she knew Bob would want to see it. Bob knew they had rattlesnakes in the area, though they were rare—he'd never seen one. Bob dumped the one onto the ground, took a photo of it, and texted the picture to DNR Non-game Wildlife Specialist Gina Larkspur, a herpetologist.

Kay Magdalen's niece, Sam remembered.

"Gina freaked out," Bob said. "She came right over. She identified the snake. An eastern mass-something."

"What'd she do with it?"

Bob chuckled. "She picked it up and said she was going to take it home and put it in her fridge. For safekeeping."

"Smart girl," Sam said. At least Gina recognized the value of the serpent.

Sam told Bob he would arrive at the site around 4:00, if he could meet him there. Bob told him he'd call Gina and see if she could make it too. And he suggested Sam call Deputy Miller. And the developer, Leslie Warner.

"Yup," Sam said. "They're on my list. How's the developer taking it?"

"I wasn't around when she got the news. I guess the sheriff called her. Said it was a federal matter and, until they spoke with you, they'd need to halt all work on the site."

Sam knew Kay Magdalen had made the call. She was the one who shut it down, at least long enough for Sam to investigate. And Sheriff Dean Goddard had been spot-on. The politically savvy Sheriff Betsy Conrad was blaming the feds. Sam understood. He'd probably do the same thing.

"So," Sam said. "I'm walking into a hornet's nest."

"Probably a piece of cake for someone who is used to scorpions."

Sam phoned Leslie Warner. She didn't pick up. An unknown number from an out-of-state area code. Sam wouldn't pick up either.

Then he called Deputy Rosie Miller.

When she picked up, he introduced himself and told her where he was headed, hoping she could join him.

"Of course," Deputy Miller said. "We will meet you out there at 4:00. Me and Sheriff Betsy Conrad."

So, it was going to be a party.

CHAPTER 4

Sam had worried about finding the place. But when he turned a corner in the remote gravel road, he saw several vehicles parked on the shoulder. As he approached, he passed a couple of trucks, one trailering a Bobcat. Both trucks had *Warner Construction & Development* on their sides. He also passed a Lexus SUV, a Tesla, a Minnesota DNR truck, and a sheriff's patrol car. He saw four people on the side of the road, standing next to the trailered Bobcat, talking. None of them were in uniform. He also noticed two officers sitting in the sheriff's cruiser, while two others waited in the DNR truck. As Sam and Gray passed by, everyone—those out of their vehicles, and those in—took note.

Sam pulled his Jeep Wrangler in front of the line of cars and trucks and parked. Gray was in the back seat, returning the spectators' stares.

Sam looked at Gray and said, "Show time," and opened his door.

As soon as Sam exited, the DNR folks got out of their truck. Sam opened Gray's door, leashed him, and led him down to the road's shoulder, where he sniffed and pissed.

Sam introduced himself to CO Bob Greene and DNR Nongame Wildlife Specialist Gina Larkspur.

Greene wore the CO's familiar khaki uniform. Sam guessed he was in his fifties, with short, gray-black hair. He was maybe 5'11" and thin. Gina Larkspur was short and sturdy, dressed in tight jeans and a simple faded work shirt, tucked in. She was maybe in her late twenties.

"And this must be Gray?" Bob said.

"Yup." Sam introduced them.

"You're Kay Magdalen's niece?" Sam asked Gina.

"Yes," Gina smiled.

"She's my boss," Sam said.

"I heard that. She speaks highly of you."

"I usually hear the not-so-highly stuff," Sam said.

Gina laughed. "Sounds like Aunt Kay. My mom says Uncle Clarence has got his hands full."

"As do those of us who work for her," Sam said. "But don't tell her I said that."

Gina smiled.

Sam glanced behind them and watched two officers get out of their patrol car. The younger woman was tall and thin, like CO Greene, with jet-black ponytailed hair. Deputy Rosie Miller, Sam guessed. The deputy's companion was older, probably in her fifties. She had short silver hair and was pudgy around the middle, probably from too much desk time. She also moved like someone in charge. Sheriff Betsy Conrad, Sam guessed. The younger officer turned and started walking toward them. The sheriff turned to the group standing beside the trailered Bobcat.

First, she's going to meet with her constituents, Sam guessed. Smart. She was, as Dean Goddard suggested, a politician.

The woman in the group of four—Sam assumed Leslie Warner, the developer—looked about Sam's age. There was a young man. Maybe the guy . . . Jules, he remembered . . . was the one who found the snake? Sam definitely wanted to speak with him, and examine the Bobcat, if this was where the rattler was found. And killed.

The other two must be the Lexus and Tesla owners. Maybe investors?

Deputy Rosie Miller approached. She nodded to CO Greene, friendly. Clearly, they knew each other. Bob introduced the deputy to Gina Larkspur and Sam. And Gray.

"That's a handsome dog," the deputy said.

"Thanks," Sam said.

The deputy nodded and reached out a hand so Gray could sniff her.

"Bob mentioned he was a wolf dog," the deputy said. "I was curious. Never seen one before. He looks pretty friendly."

"He's a cross between an arctic wolf and a malamute," Sam said. "Gray has a lot of wolf in him. At least physically. But his temperament is more malamute. Providing you're not breaking the law."

"Glad he's on our side," the deputy said.

Sam returned Gray to the Jeep. Then he walked over and met the large group. Sam knew he was going to have trouble remembering everyone and their roles in the Alta Vista site, so he took a moment to greet each and settle them in his head.

From county law enforcement there was Sheriff Betsy Conrad and Deputy Rosie Miller (who he had already met).

The people working to make Alta Vista a reality were developer Leslie Warner and her foreman, Jules Ortega. The guy with the money, an investor, was Dr. Dick Blare. From the DNR there was Bob Greene and Gina Larkspur. And from the county there was County Commissioner Cab Teufel.

Leslie and Jules were dressed in jeans and denim shirts with *Warner Construction & Development* logos. Leslie's sleeves were pulled down and buttoned. It was a hot day. Sam guessed Leslie had spent it in an air-conditioned office, behind a desk. Jules, who Sam thought was a little nervous, or maybe shy, had his sleeves rolled up. His arms were well-muscled and darkened, like his face and neck, from working outside. Jules was probably in his late twenties.

The doctor and Leslie were around Sam's age, 37, or maybe in their early forties.

County Commissioner Cab Teufel appeared to be in his mid-forties.

"Are you the one who found the snake?" Sam asked Jules.

Jules nodded. "In the Bobcat," he said, indicating the trailered machine.

Deputy Rosie Miller, CO Bob Greene, and Wildlife Specialist Gina Larkspur all gathered behind Sam. The five people in front of Sam were decidedly less friendly than the three at his back.

As if they didn't already have enough people at the site, a black VW sedan pulled up and parked behind the row of vehicles along the road. A short, heavy-set man with sandy hair and a matching complexion got out of the car.

"I did not know the snake was special," Jules said.

While the new guy approached, Sam turned to Jules and said, "Endangered." He thought Jules was apologetic, which he appreciated. Killing an endangered species was a felony. And while ignorance was no excuse for breaking the law, Sam recognized the extenuating circumstances. "I can completely understand how you were surprised," Sam said. "Rattlesnakes can be dangerous."

Jules nodded.

The new arrival, probably in his mid-forties, wore pressed jeans and a light-green, short-sleeved golf shirt tucked into his pants. His belt was pulled tight, navel high.

"I thought it'd be useful to have our zoning commissioner here," Cab said, as the man approached and nodded. "This is Henry Fields, who knows just about everything there is to know about the ins and outs of zoning."

"Don't know about that," Henry said.

"He's shy too."

Henry shrugged.

"Hi, Henry," the sheriff said.

"I think you know everyone except maybe these three," Cab said, pointing to Sam, Gina, and Bob. "And Dr. Dick Blare?"

Henry shook hands with the people he didn't know and nodded to the rest.

"I hope I don't have to remember any names," Henry said, after the introductions.

"Copy that," said CO Bob Greene.

"So, what's it mean for us?" Leslie said, bringing Sam back to the moment. "That the snake's endangered?"

"It means the animal is nearing extinction," Sam said. "Under the Endangered Species Act, we're responsible for protecting them and keeping them from becoming extinct, if possible."

"I get that," Leslie said. "Nobody wants an animal to go extinct. But what does it mean for our development?"

"Hopefully not much," Sam said. "Maybe an idle couple of days while we figure out if there are any other snakes around."

"And if there are?" Leslie said.

Sam thought about it. "It would depend on what we found. If there were some kind of nest, or a colony, that could be a problem. But I suspect we won't find any more snakes. These guys are rare."

"In which case we can get back to work?" Leslie said.

"That's the plan. If you can give us some time to look around."

Leslie looked at the doctor, Dick Blare. Dick frowned. Leslie told him about an investor, a gastroenterologist from Dr. Blare's practice who had been out yesterday and was excited about the project.

"Said he was in," Leslie said. "Wanted me to draw up the paperwork."

"Doesn't surprise me," Dr. Blare said. "Who wouldn't be?" He turned to admire the view Jules had cleared earlier.

"I'd hold off on the paperwork, Dick," Cab Teufel said. Cab's face was a little pudgy, like the rest of him. But he wore a loose-fitting knit shirt and slacks that hid it. His clothes, like his car—given that he was driving a new Lexus or Tesla—were expensive.

He also had the demeanor of someone who is used to calling the shots.

"Why?" Dick wanted to know.

Leslie ignored Cab, but turned to Dick and said, "Because we'd need to note this snake thing on the paperwork. But I'm not so sure, given the snake wasn't found right on the property."

"This could be significant," Cab said. "Any potential investors would need to know. Isn't that right, Henry?"

"If it was me advising you," Henry said, "I'd suggest you make a full disclosure. Just to be on the safe side."

"Technically, the snake was found on the road," Leslie said. "Right, Agent Rivers?"

Sam thought about it and turned to Jules. "Where did the Bobcat come from?"

"From our equipment yard in Winona," Jules said.

"Was the Bobcat already on the flatbed when you trailered it up here?"

Jules nodded.

"But you didn't see the snake when you trailered it up?" Sam said.

"No," Jules said. "But I didn't look inside the cab."

"Maybe it was inside the Cat when you moved it?" Leslie said.

Jules shrugged. "Maybe."

They all considered it.

"But as I understand it, you found the snake here yesterday morning and then killed it?" Henry said.

"That's right," Cab said.

Jules nodded. "When I started to get into the Bobcat."

"Then you should probably report it," Henry said. "It was the first place the snake was found, so it's most likely from around here."

"Not if it came up from Winona," Leslie said.

Henry didn't say anything.

"If that's the case, we shouldn't find any other signs of them here," Sam said. "And no other rattlesnakes. But we need to look."

"Maybe somebody put it there," Leslie said.

Sam thought about it. "Why?"

"To stop the development."

"Do you think somebody wants to stop it?" Sam said.

"Could be environmentalists?" Leslie said.

"I'd be the first to admit we have some people in Bluff County with a few screws loose," the sheriff said. "But I'm not sure any of them are crazy enough to use a rattlesnake to stop a development."

Sam agreed, it sounded far-fetched. It would require someone to find an endangered creature, a dangerous one, and then sneak it into a Bobcat. And then the snake would need to stay put.

"But what I'm hearing you say, Henry," Cab said, "is that it doesn't make any difference where it came from. Since it was found here, it should be disclosed to any potential investors."

"That's right," Henry said.

"We still need to look around and see if there are others," Sam said.

Dr. Blare looked at the sheriff and Sam, thinking about it. "Postpone the paperwork," he said to Leslie.

Sam assumed Dick Blare was the primary investor. At least he seemed like the one in charge. He and the county commissioner, Cab Teufel.

Leslie's eyes darkened. "I can do that," she said, though she wasn't happy about it. "And I can reschedule the other showings I had set for this week."

"Who?" Dick wanted to know.

"Those other two in your practice. OBGYNs."

Dick considered it, briefly. "Definitely reschedule them," he said.

Cab glanced at Sam and the sheriff. "This will remain confidential?"

"Of course," the sheriff said. "Nobody's gonna find out from the sheriff's office."

"Or mine," Sam said. "At least until we're done with the survey. We'll need to reach out to our colleagues who are more familiar with the species. They might be able to help us ID the snake. At least where it came from." Sam looked at Bob and Gina.

"We don't want any press on it," Cab said.

"Of course not," Bob said.

"I know a colleague in Wisconsin who works with their eastern massasauga population," Gina said. "She might be able to help us."

"First, we need to spend some time surveying the site," Sam said.

"How long is this gonna take?" Leslie said.

"Depends on the size of the site and the terrain," Sam said. "It's 10 acres?"

"Yes," Leslie said. She pointed to some distant survey markers, farther north. And then to others farther south. "Those flags up by the road and those at the opposite end mark the northern and southern boundaries. And if you walk into those woods, over by the bluff," she pointed due east, "you'll find a 100-foot drop that marks the eastern side of the property. This road marks the western side. You could probably walk it all in an hour."

Sam considered it. "There's a lot of mixed terrain," Sam said. "This field by the road, those trees, and then the limestone bluff. When you're looking for something as rare as an endangered species, a venomous snake who can wriggle into a pretty tight space, you've got to be careful about how you search."

"A day?" Leslie asked. "Two days?" Sam could tell she was disappointed about the delay but was trying to be reasonable.

The sheriff considered Leslie and, with a sober countenance, said, "I understand how you feel about this, Leslie. And I have to say I'm a little surprised myself that these townhomes could be held up by a dead snake."

She looked at Zoning Commissioner Henry Fields for concurrence.

"That's right," Henry said. "I don't understand the Endangered Species Act well, but I think Agent Rivers is correct. They need to figure out what's here and whether it needs to be protected."

Sam nodded.

"So at least for the moment, whether or not I agree with you guys," the sheriff continued, nodding to Leslie and Dick, "doesn't really make much difference. The federal law supersedes state and local jurisdictions. So, Agent Rivers can take the time he needs. But he can't take forever."

Then she paused and turned to Sam and said, "I can't believe it'll take you more than two days."

The sheriff was being sensitive to the needs of her constituents. Especially prominent ones like these. Politics.

"We should be able to do it in two days," Sam said.

"Good," the sheriff said, as though she'd won some kind of victory.

"I'm hoping you guys can assist?" Sam said to Gina and Bob.

They both agreed, and Gina said, "I love a snake hunt."

Sam smiled, but no one else did.

"And I can loan you Deputy Miller," the sheriff said.

"Sure," Rosie Miller said, not nearly as excited as Gina.

"That'd help," Sam said. To the sheriff, he said, "But if we find another snake, or snake habitat, or any other signs of them, we might need more time."

Sam didn't think they'd find anything, but he wanted to manage expectations. And he wanted to send a message; when it came to endangered species, the USFW didn't cut corners or dodge confrontation. Building new townhomes was, of course, important. But when it came to making sure an endangered species did not go extinct, Sam was glad a venomous snake could stop development. At least for as long as it took to find a fair and viable solution, like relocating any rattlesnakes they found. Though Sam knew relocation wasn't always the best solution.

"Can you start now?" Leslie said.

It was nearly 5 p.m. Sam still needed to find a place to stay. He'd Googled Owen's Gap and found The Bluff Country Inn, on the town's outskirts. But he needed to get Gray out on a walk, and he figured this would be a good place to do it. He could get a feel for the site and plan their morning snake hunt.

"If Jules has a minute, I'd like to talk with him and check out that Bobcat. Then Gray and I can walk the property and get a feel for how best to start on a quadrant search, first thing in the morning. You can probably help with that, Gina."

"We could survey it the way we canvas other sites," Gina said.

Sam said, "Good." Then he looked at Jules. "Got a minute?"

Jules nodded.

And Leslie said, "Just get it done, please. We're already on a tight schedule. I don't want to lose any more days than I need to."

"We'll get it done as soon as we can," Sam said. "Shouldn't take too long."

They settled on meeting here at 7:30 tomorrow morning. Then everyone began returning to their vehicles, except for Jules.

Leslie walked up to her truck, accompanied by Cab, Dick, and Henry.

"Good to see you, Cab," Dick said.

"If we can help in any way," Cab said, indicating Henry, "Just let us know." He paused to take one last look at the view. "Gotta say, it's a sweet location."

They all paused, looking out over the Driftless.

"You did a good job getting approvals," Cab said to Leslie.

Leslie appreciated the comment because it was true, and because she wanted Dick Blare to hear it. And if she didn't know

Cab as well as she did, she would have considered the praise a compliment. But a man like Cab Teufel, who was not only a county commissioner but also a developer, always had a personal agenda.

"Henry was a big help," Leslie said, turning to Henry.

"When you bring us plans like you did," Henry said, "it makes my job easy."

She still didn't know how Cab had been invited to this meeting. When she'd proposed the development to Henry Fields, she knew Cab Teufel was out of the country, though no one was quite sure where he was. Somewhere in Europe, but apparently out of cell range, or at least not returning messages. That was the perfect time to submit her plans for the development to Henry, for Zoning to sign off on them. With Cab *persona non grata,* Henry wouldn't be able to share her plans with him. Leslie had worried that if Cab found out about her project, he would somehow interfere with it. And she knew Henry and Cab seemed tight, but not in a good way.

Now, she wondered if Dick Blare had called Cab, because they'd worked together in the past, building some apartments in Owen's Gap. Or maybe Cab had somehow gotten wind of the project (probably from Henry) and just happened to stop by for a look?

When Leslie brought her development idea to Dick, looking for an investor, Dick had asked if Cab was involved. When he found out Cab wasn't, he still moved forward with Leslie. But Leslie didn't know Dick as well as she knew Cab. Maybe Dick Blare called Cab because he was hedging his bets or he wanted a county commissioner to weigh in on the project or he didn't think Leslie, a woman, could manage a development as big and expensive as Alta Vista.

Regardless, if Dick wanted Cab and Henry along to weigh in with their opinions, that was fine. But no way was she going to let Cab Teufel in on her project. Especially because she and Cab had a past, one she would just as soon forget.

Dick Blare and Henry Fields turned and started walking toward their cars.

When Leslie turned away, Cab followed her.

Sam turned to Jules and said, "Can you show me where you found that rattlesnake?"

CHAPTER 5

After the plan was made to meet the following morning, Sam turned to Jules, wanting a tour of the trailered Bobcat and the location where the rattlesnake was found. The flatbed's off-ramp had been dropped to the ground. It rested at an angle behind the truck and trailer.

Jules confirmed he'd dropped the ramp down the evening before he found the rattlesnake. If the ramp was down all night, the rattlesnake could have used it to crawl up onto the flatbed. Sam still thought it was unusual for a snake to have found its way onto the trailer, and then into the Bobcat, curling up on its seat. Unusual, but not impossible. Snakes are contortionists. They can stretch, twist, and squeeze through holes that appear impossible to pass through, given their girth. A snake wouldn't need much of an opening to get into the Cat, and it could have been attracted by the heat of the dark vehicle sitting in the sun, or the relative cave-like darkness of its interior, or more likely the heat signature of a field mouse.

Rattlesnakes are pit vipers. They have pits near their eyes that they use to follow the heat trail of their favorite prey, typically small rodents, like mice. They also use their tongues to smell. If a snake is following a field mouse and caught up in the hunt, it will go just about anywhere.

"Where's that equipment yard in Winona?" Sam said. "The one where you got the Cat?"

"It's a big lot down by the river."

"And the trailer and Cat were both there?"

Jules nodded.

Winona, Sam knew, was directly across the Mississippi River from Wisconsin. Before leaving to come down here, Sam had done a little research on the eastern massasauga. There were isolated populations of the endangered rattlesnake in Iowa, Illinois, and in southeastern Wisconsin, across the river from Winona. It was conceivable the eastern massasauga rattlesnake floated across the river on a log, or swam it, and ended up near the Warner equipment yard. And then made its way up into the yard. And then what? It followed its favorite prey into the Bobcat?

"When did you put the Cat on the trailer?" Sam said.

"It was already on the trailer," Jules said.

Jules explained the Cat had been on the trailer in Winona for nearly a week. Then late Monday, he'd driven it to this site and parked it, dropping the ramp so he'd be ready to work first thing Tuesday morning. That's when he opened the Cat's door and found the rattlesnake on the seat.

Sam spent a couple of minutes examining the narrow cab. There was very little space around the bottom of the seat. Sam still didn't see how the snake could have gotten up onto the seat. But he guessed the black leather seat was probably the warmest place in the cab. From that perspective, it made sense that the snake might be attracted to it. Maybe if it somehow found its way into the Bobcat, it got stuck and couldn't find its way back out and crawled onto the warmest place. And if it tracked and killed and ate a mouse, it could have been sleeping off its feast.

When he looked around the base of the seat, he noticed something tucked back behind it, in a crevice, something loose.

Sam had some baggies in his pocket, in case they saw something he wanted to retrieve. Now he pulled out one of the baggies, opened it, and carefully used a second baggie to pick up a piece of loose gray plastic from behind the seat. It looked like it had broken off something, some piece of equipment. He thought it looked like part of a handle to something. He dropped it into the open baggie and then came out of the cab to examine it.

He showed the piece of plastic to Jules and asked him if he knew what it was.

"No," Jules said. They examined the inside of the Cat for anything resembling the piece of gray plastic, anything from which it might have broken off. But everything inside the cab was black or glass.

Probably nothing, Sam knew. But if someone dropped the snake on the Bobcat's seat, they had to transport it. Crazy, Sam knew. Why would anyone put an endangered species on a Bobcat's seat? Made no sense. But since it didn't appear to be part of the Bobcat, he double bagged it and dropped it in his shirt pocket.

CHAPTER 6

When Leslie Warner paused at her driver's-side door to let Cab pass and continue to his Lexus, he didn't. Obviously, he wanted to talk, a conversation Leslie was hoping to avoid.

"What's up?" Leslie said. The best way to deal with Cab Teufel was head on.

"You worried about building townhomes this close to a 100-foot cliff?" Cab said.

Leslie considered the comment. "No one's mentioned it," Leslie said.

"The county wasn't concerned?"

"When I showed Henry the plans and told him what we were going to do and how we were going to do it, he blessed it," Leslie said. "Especially when the county figured out the potential tax base. They were more excited than anything else."

"It's awful close to the bluff," Cab said.

"The townhomes won't be," Leslie said. "According to Henry, we need to set them back at least 75 feet."

Cab thought about it, and with a slight grin, said, "You must have had a good architect."

"I did. A firm in the Cities."

"I wondered about that," Cab said.

Leslie knew that if she'd used a Rochester firm, given Cab's contacts and the fact he was a county commissioner, he would have heard about her project before anything was filed. She wasn't sure he would have done anything about it. But just in case, she'd waited to submit it to the county because she'd wanted the site to fly under the radar. So far, she had been successful. At least until the appearance of a rattlesnake.

"I meant what I said to Dick," Cab said. "If there's anything I can do. Any way I can help out, just let me know."

"I appreciate the offer," Leslie said. She didn't, but there was no reason to cause unnecessary friction.

Cab grinned. "I can see you've got things under control. I'm not surprised. You were always a fast learner, Les."

Ten years earlier, when Leslie Warner started her company, she and Cab Teufel had worked on two projects together. Cab was a little older than Leslie and had been in the business for nearly two decades. He took an interest in Leslie and her company. At first, Leslie was flattered. She thought it was because of her construction acumen, which Cab clearly recognized and praised. In time, she let herself be seduced by his compliments and attention. The man had lots of contacts and, from what she could tell (at least back then), a good reputation. And he was married. Leslie had met his wife, Becky. A little meek, Leslie thought. But nice enough. And pretty.

Leslie was young and knew enough in the business to recognize that a man like Cab could help her open doors. They spent a lot of time talking about the male-dominated construction business. They sat over a lot of tables, almost exclusively in Rochester, which Cab claimed was the only place to find decent food. The venues were always pricey and usually involved excellent fare and expensive bottles of wine. Despite Leslie's protests, Cab Teufel, like a gentleman, always paid.

Leslie considered Cab an older-brother type, a kind of senior partner knowledgeable in the business, helping to guide her career. He brought her in on a residential project, a six-plex he was building on Rochester's east side. She'd worked hard on that project, carrying the load for him. Cab wasn't stingy with the praise or the profit. He appreciated her help, and she wasn't surprised when he proposed a second venture. To celebrate, they dined at Ringover's Supper Club, near downtown. Cab ordered two bottles of wine, and they got a little carried away.

Cab wasn't the most attractive man, but he had a kind of swagger Leslie found endearing, as though he didn't care what anyone thought. Maybe a little pugnacious.

So, after coming in to assist Cab with a second project, and then after too much wine, she didn't say "no" when Cab came onto her. She'd been too drunk for the sex to be decent. Frankly, she was more interested in keeping the man happy. From what she remembered, he enjoyed himself.

Afterwards, they both agreed it had been a mistake, Cab being married. Also, getting naked with another person and having sex gave you a perspective you couldn't get in any other way. Leslie felt terrible about sleeping with a married man. And the memory of his touch left her feeling slightly repulsed.

Then, at the end of the second project, Cab invited her, their foreman, and his accountant out to celebrate. Given it was a crowd, Leslie figured it was safe. After her three-drink maximum, she went to the bathroom. She returned to a fourth drink sitting in front of her empty chair. The accountant and foreman had conveniently departed. Cab sat alone at their table.

She had a sudden recollection of the infamous movie producer Harvey Weinstein, who would engineer gatherings at which he would eventually be left alone with a starlet. And then he'd rape her.

Cab didn't rape her, but when she refused his suggestion they check into a hotel, the prick told her lucrative projects like the one they'd just completed "didn't grow on trees."

His meaning was obvious. If she wanted more work, she could expect a periodic summons to his bed.

She considered going public with the affair (if you could call it that). By the time she figured out she wasn't the only woman who had been part of Cab's extracurricular activities, she understood that the male-dominated industry not only turned a blind eye to Cab Teufel's indiscretions, but there were some in the industry who admired his transgressions. Further, she understood there had been enough of them that Becky Teufel knew her husband was a snake. Becky, Leslie guessed, tolerated the man because he was rich and successful.

Leslie told the man to fuck off, politely, and decided against making a scene.

Cab never gave her any more work.

Regardless, over the last 10 years, Leslie had been successful in her own right, Alta Vista being her most ambitious and largest project to date.

"Thanks," Leslie said, about his compliment that she was a fast learner.

Cab looked at her, paused, and then said, "What happened to us?"

She was startled by his comment.

"There was no 'us,'" she said, folding her arms across her chest.

"I mean," he backtracked, "our working together. We did some good work."

She didn't think that's what he meant. But she could play along.

"I got busy on projects of my own," she said.

"Like this one."

"Yes," she said. "Like Alta Vista."

"Good name."

"I thought so."

"If you run into trouble with this snake stuff, I have bluff property almost exactly like this less than 5 miles away, as the crow flies. I'd make you a deal."

"I appreciate that," Leslie said. She didn't. "First, I'm going to see what happens with this survey."

"You might run into some trouble building on that bluff."

"We can manage it," Leslie said. To make sure he understood there was no room for him on this project, she added, "Just being honest here, Cab, but I don't think your wife, Becky, would appreciate another partnership."

"I guess you haven't heard," Cab said. "We're separated. She's been living in Rochester for the last six months."

"Sorry to hear it," Leslie said. But she wasn't. She was happy to hear the woman had finally left him. She hoped Becky would take half his fortune with her.

Cab glanced over to where Jules and Sam Rivers were in conversation, up ahead by the trailered Bobcat.

Cab had spoken with Jules earlier, when he'd first arrived.

"Seems like a pretty handy kid," Cab said.

"Jules? He's great. Hard worker. Smart."

"And you got paper on him?"

"Of course," she said. "You know me. I'm a cross the T, dot the I kind of employer."

Cab smiled. "You are. I guess Dick called me because he wanted another pair of eyes on the project. Someone with ties to the county and plenty of experience dealing with state and federal issues."

Leslie had wondered if Dick had called Cab. She'd need to speak with him about it. But she didn't let her irritation show.

"He thinks the USFW and the DNR are filled with tree huggers," Cab said.

Leslie shrugged but didn't comment.

"I told him about the *Gazette's* coverage of that trout stream runoff."

The *Gazette* was the local Owen's Gap newspaper. A couple of recent articles had covered a fish kill on one of the region's trout streams. Agricultural runoff was blamed, though they never figured out the source. An op-ed decried the kill and quoted a DNR fisheries representative, who said, "When we value agricultural production over the health of a trout stream, we've lost our way."

"Won't be an issue up here," Leslie said.

"Still, Dick mentioned he'd appreciate it if I could keep an eye out."

Leslie thought about telling Cab that wouldn't be necessary, that she and her team could manage whatever issues arose. But given his new marital status and obvious interest in the project, she knew that would only embolden him. So, she looked away and said, "Another pair of eyes never hurts."

CHAPTER 7

While Sam examined the trailer and Bobcat, he had noticed, more out of his peripheral vision than through direct observation, Leslie Warner and Cab Teufel talking. If Sam had to guess, it looked like the two knew each other but were more cordial than friendly. Maybe even tense.

Interesting.

While he and Jules were still bent over, examining the trailer's undercarriage, Cab and Leslie ended their conversation and returned to their vehicles.

Leslie sat in her truck, thinking. The idea Cab was going to be hanging around her project irritated her.

After Cab's Lexus was a half-mile distant and had turned around a bend, she started her truck and pulled out. She drove up beside Sam and Jules, stopped, and called out to Jules.

Jules stepped over to the open window.

"How would you like to help out on that snake hunt tomorrow?"

"Sure," Jules said.

"That okay with you, Agent Rivers?" Leslie asked.

"Sure," Sam said. "We could always use the help. As long as he doesn't kill another rattlesnake."

"I promise not to kill any rattlesnakes," Jules said.

"I'll stop by in the morning to check on progress," Leslie said.

"We'll be here," Sam said.

Leslie put the truck in gear and started down the road.

As soon as Cab rounded the bend and could no longer see Alta Vista or the vehicles beside the road, he called Henry. The zoning commissioner's phone jumped to voicemail, which meant the man must be on a call. Cab checked the time and saw it was well after 5:00, so Henry could have turned his phone to "silent mode," but Cab didn't think so. The man was savvy enough to know he should expect a call from Cab, given recent events.

At Henry's voicemail beep, Cab said, "Call me," and hung up.

He thought about his conversation with Leslie Warner. He'd managed to keep his calm, even though she was pissing him off. First, she'd pushed through her Alta Vista project while he was out of the country.

Cab had been in Europe. It was a trip he'd planned a year ago with Becky. He'd planned the trip while they were still living together and civil, Cab thought, if you could call no sex and rare conversation civil. But then she moved out and filed for divorce.

No matter. He'd gone to Europe without her. On a sex holiday, as it turned out.

Becky had surprised him. He didn't think she had it in her. Over the years, she realized who Cab was and what he did. He had a reputation. Frankly, it was a certain standing he enjoyed. He thought Becky tolerated his affairs because of his business.

Leslie Warner had been fun, as long as she had the common sense to play along. It had taken longer than normal to bed her. But that one time had ended her willingness to play.

Then, over the last 10 years, she'd been successful without him. And she'd been smart about Alta Vista.

Henry Fields could have put the brakes on the project when he had the chance. Henry didn't always think on his feet.

Leslie Warner was smart and definitely a worthy competitor.

Cab's cell phone buzzed.

"Henry," Cab said.

"Got your call."

"You were probably lining up a squeeze for next weekend," Cab said. Henry was a bachelor farmer. Cab had never seen him with a woman. He'd never seen him with a man, either, which Cab appreciated, considering they lived in a rural part of the state and if Henry did have that inclination, he was smart to keep it quiet.

"Try Burt the plumber," Henry said. "Kitchen-sink leak."

Cab knew Henry well enough to help him get the zoning commissioner job and to know he'd be thankful for it. And smart about it. Unlike Leslie Warner, Henry was good at playing along.

"You think you can use this rattlesnake business to stop the development?"

"Sure, for the time being."

"What about that law that guy from the feds mentioned?"

"The Endangered Species Act?"

"Yeah, whatever. That."

"Maybe," Henry said. "But why don't we let Sam Rivers take the heat? If he finds another snake, there's a good chance he'll close it."

Cab thought about it. "Wish I knew where to find some," he said.

Henry chuckled. He knew the commissioner was joking. But he said, "They're rare, Cab. Even if you found one, it's against the law to mess with it."

There was a long pause, before Cab added, "Who knew a rattlesnake had so much power?"

Henry agreed.

"One of the reasons I backed you for the zoning job was because you're creative," Cab said. "Even if they don't find another rattlesnake, it would be helpful if you could figure out anything else that might at least slow the project?"

Cab didn't really think Henry Fields was creative. But if Henry could figure out a way to slow the project, Cab might be able to entice Leslie to buy his bluff property. And no doubt about it, the project was sweet.

"I'll try to think of something," Henry said.

Henry had never been partial to Cab Teufel. But he recognized Cab's usefulness in county politics, and the role Cab played in landing Henry his job. It was a good job, and Henry wanted—needed—to keep it. So helping slow down or close the Alta Vista site could be good for both of them.

"Give me a little time," Henry said. "Zoning regulations are complicated. I suspect we can find something."

Cab thanked him and hung up.

CHAPTER 8

As dusk came on, Adder Musgrave sat beside his smoldering firepit, picking his teeth with an oak splinter, contemplating his next stroke of good fortune.

Adder believed good luck came in threes. His first gift from the universe had been the appearance of one of his favorite wild marsh meals.

Last Sunday, he'd been walking along the edge of the Sweet Marsh and stumbled across a possum playing dead. Some, like Adder, whose cosmology was firmly planted in the marsh, might have considered it a bad sign, a harbinger of death. But Adder knew what to do with a possum.

Half of Adder's diet came from an assortment of tinned meat and canned beans, what could be had for cheap at the Sumner Dollar Store. The other half came from the marsh. Turtles, muskrats, beavers, racoons, fish, crawdads, birds of all kinds, rabbits, occasional deer, groundhogs, possums, and just about any other wild animal that dared to crawl, fly, amble, or slither within Adder's purview, in season or out. He also fed on cattail roots, dandelion greens, day lily buds, young burdock greens, and an assortment of the marsh's plant life. At one time or another, they all found their way into Adder's pot.

So, when he walked the marsh to survey the turtle population (the trapping season just around the corner), he was startled to find a possum playing possum. And he was happy. He grabbed the burlap gunnysack affixed to his belt, opened it, and lifted the possum by its rat-like tail, depositing it into the black maw. Its only indication of life was a snarl in the rodent's upper lip, exposing a row of needle-like teeth. Too little, too late.

"My lucky day," Adder said. To the possum, "Yours, not so much."

When he finished with his turtle survey—it was going to be another good year—he placed the still-unmoving marsupial into a crude metal cage. Possums eat anything, Adder knew. The rodent might have just dined on desiccated rat or a rotting carp. Adder scattered a fistful of corn kernels across the cage bottom. In the varied estimation of Adder's palate, few delicacies measured up to a cornfed possum slow-roasted with sweet potatoes and bacon grease.

He placed the cage in an outside shed, where it would reside in darkness (possums preferring the night). It would take about two days to clean out and fatten up.

As soon as he closed his shed door, his second stroke of luck had arrived like a thunderbolt. His phone startled him with a rare ring. He saw the area code was 507. He had shirttail relatives up near Rochester, the heart of the 507 area.

"Yeah?" Adder said.

"Adder Musgrave?" the man said.

"Who's this?" Adder said, suspicious.

"I understand you're a wildlife expert."

Adder had never been called expert at anything. He guessed he was expert at making a living from the marsh, but he'd never use that word to describe what he did to survive.

"You know that area down there," the man said. "The Sweet Marsh."

After a long pause, Adder said, "Yeah."

"I suspect you might be able to help me," the man said. "And I would make it worth your while."

The hair on the back of Adder's neck bristled like a treed racoon.

Adder's past involved occasional skirmishes with the law, game violations, and petty theft. He had been cited four times for taking animals out of season. Once, he had been caught stealing a leghold trap from McCutcheon Hardware. He appeared in local court, and pleaded guilty to a misdemeanor. Since it was McCutcheon and Adder was known to live at or below the poverty line, he was fined $100, which he took six months to pay off.

Most of Adder's illegal activities passed quiet as a blue-winged teal in cattail reeds. But there were enough known game violations and petty crimes so that anytime something untoward happened involving animals in and around the marsh, Adder was a "person of interest."

When Adder got a call from a stranger wanting help, and willing to pay for it, he was wary. Adder was a skilled enough trapper to know something didn't smell right, something that required a lot of sniffing before he stepped into it.

"How did you get this number?" Adder said.

The man chuckled. "You've got a record, Adder. Enough to tell me you might be the kind of man who could help me acquire something . . . special. Something that might get you some cash."

"Not interested," Adder said. But he didn't hang up.

"Would you be interested in $1,000?"

The question stunned Adder Musgrave. Adder cut and sold firewood, helped farmers lay tile, plant, and harvest. He could get good money for coyote, fox, and weasel pelts, in season. During various times of the year, he drove to Waterloo greenhouses and sold them birch branches, cattail reeds, pussy willows, and the like. But he'd never sold anything for $1,000. What little money he had passed through his hands like swamp water. He kept spare change and dollar bills in an old coffee can above the stove, which at the moment held $184.72.

"You can at least hear me out," the caller said.

When Adder didn't hang up, the caller continued.

"I assume you're familiar with the eastern massasauga rattlesnake?"

Adder knew all about the rattlesnake. He'd had numerous opportunities to kill the beast. And eat it. And he would have, except the last thing he needed was for a local deputy or conservation officer to stop by while he was roasting the animal over his spit. Or nose around his place and find a massasauga snakeskin and its rattle.

The marsh had animals aplenty, including that rattler. Which is why Adder Musgrave never understood why the government took particular interest in a rattlesnake. Endangered, was what they said. But the only thing endangered about the massasauga was the life of whatever it bit.

"I know it," Adder finally said.

"Do you know where you can find a couple? Two I can buy?"

Adder knew a boggy area near the marsh edge where he felt certain he could find two rattlesnakes. But he didn't visit there often, on account of the snakes.

"You a scientist?" Adder said. He knew a guy out of the University of Iowa who was also interested in the massasauga. Barry Vander. Barry had interviewed him in the past, about the marsh and its wildlife. Especially its rattlesnakes. But also other animals the government considered special. In fact, the man kept massasaugas in cages where he studied and bred them, and then let them go. Over near McCutcheon. Crazy stupid, Adder thought, to study rattlers so he could help them survive. And increase in number. And, of course, the government paid for it. Sometimes the government had as much sense as a rabid skunk.

"Not a scientist," the man said. "Just . . . interested."

"What do you want with rattlesnakes?" Adder said.

"Does it matter, if I'm paying $1,000 for them?"

The man had a point. It was the most commonsense thing the man had said. Adder had no interest in adding another line to his lengthy record. Especially since messing with an endangered animal was a felony. Bigger fines and probably jail time, given his past.

But $1,000 was $1,000.

"You the law?"

The man chuckled again. "No," he said. "But if I was, this would be entrapment. The law can't trick people into committing a felony. That's illegal. Even if you did what I'm asking, you wouldn't be prosecuted. *If* I was law, which I am not."

There was a long silence. Clearly, Adder was thinking about it.

"If you did get me two eastern massasauga rattlesnakes and I gave you a thousand dollars for them, we'd both be breaking the law. I'd be prosecuted along with you."

More silence, as Adder considered the sense of it.

"The turnoff to your place is down a remote rural road," the man said. "We could see or hear the law coming a mile off. No way we'd get caught. And you'd be $1,000 richer."

"You been here?" Adder said.

"I like to know what I'm walking into," the man said. "I'm careful that way."

Adder didn't like an unnamed stranger knowing him and where he lived and his phone number. But for $1,000, he was willing to make allowances.

"I can find them," Adder finally said. "Two of those rattlesnakes. When do you want them?"

"Tomorrow afternoon," the man said.

"Whoa," Adder said. "Not sure I can find them that fast."

"Fifteen hundred if you can get them by tomorrow afternoon."

Goddamn, Adder thought. Whoever it was must have buckets of money. And a hard-on for rattlesnakes. "Okay," Adder said. He could play along. "How do I let you know I got them?"

"Call me at this number if you *don't* get the snake. Don't bother if you do."

"What do I call you?" Adder at least wanted to know the man's name.

"Der," the man said. "Just Der."

"Der?"

"Der."

What kind of fuckin' name was Der? Adder wondered. But he didn't really care.

"How do I get you the snake? And how do I get my money, Der?"

Tomorrow afternoon at 3:00, Adder should walk up his drive to the last bend before it hit the road. There was a big stump, set back from the rutted drive, on the right side, if Adder was walking away from his cabin. There'd be an envelope on top of the stump. Adder should bring the rattlesnakes in a container with a lid, something big enough so the snakes couldn't escape. He should set the container behind the stump.

"Then you can take your money and walk back to your cabin," Der said.

The whole thing sounded crazy, Adder thought. The guy could sit in the weeds, or in a nearby tree, and shoot him, if he wanted. But why would he go to all this trouble? And besides, killing a guy over a snake was, well, crazier than anything even Adder Musgrave would have done. And if he approached the stump, saw the envelope with the cash, and opened it, he could count it. He could make sure all that money—$1,500—would be in hand before he left the snakes.

He had an old plastic container with a clampdown lid he used to keep perishables from the rodents, moths, and hungry ants. He could leave the rattlers in it. For $1,500, he could afford to replace it.

"You'll git your rattlers," Adder said.

And then he spent the rest of the day and the following morning beating the marsh edge for eastern massasauga rattlesnakes. Midmorning, he rolled over a log and found a 2-footer startled enough to coil and rattle. Adder used a forked stick to pin its head to the ground, pick it up from behind its neck, and drop it into the plastic bin. He placed some swamp grass and sticks in the bottom. The opaque bin was deep enough to keep the snake corralled until he could affix its lid.

A hundred yards farther he stumbled onto a second rattlesnake, sunning itself near the base of a boulder. A 3-footer. It coiled to strike, which was when Adder pinned its head to the ground with his stick.

Then everything had gone as planned.

By 3:00 in the afternoon, he carried the bin up the drive to the boxelder stump. He found the envelope stuffed with 15 $100 bills. More money than he had ever seen. Or held. He looked around, but he couldn't see anything except familiar woods and the double rut of his driveway, bending just ahead and running up to the gravel road.

A red-winged blackbird trilled from a cattail patch. A locust buzzed in the heat. Overhead, a crow cawed, twice, on its way to the marsh. Otherwise, nothing stirred.

Seeing nothing was good enough for Adder, who suddenly found himself rich. He'd been so busy finding the rattlers he hadn't thought about how he might spend the money. But as soon as he held the envelope in his hand, an image popped into his head of the Axis 500 camo-colored ATV he'd seen in a dealership over in Waverly. List price: $2,300. The ATV looked rugged enough to drive just about anywhere in the marsh, any season. And starting next week, it would make this year's turtling season a breeze.

Counting the $184 and change in his coffee can, he'd still be short more than $600. Maybe they'd give him a deal, he wondered. He'd have to think about it.

After the excitement of the last two days, he finally checked on the possum. It still played dead, even though the corn was almost entirely eaten and the water down to dregs. Adder knew it was time.

He built up a bed of coals in his firepit. Then he fetched the possum from his cage and used a thick oak club, smacking it hard enough across its head to make it actually dead, not fake. Next, he skinned, gutted, and cleaned the animal. Finally, he'd placed him into his passels pot—the one with a locking lid—adding quartered sweet potatoes and two heaping spoonfuls of bacon grease. He hung the pot a foot above the coals. Throughout the afternoon, he'd kept the fire fed and banked, the aroma of slow-cooked possum ratcheting his hunger.

Finally, the smell of cooking vittles was too powerful to ignore. He shoveled some of the pot's contents onto his plate and sat down to feast.

Whether it was the bacon grease or the corn-fed quality of the possum, it always reminded him of pork. The slow roast caused the rodent's flesh to fall off the bone. The sweet potatoes gave it a starchy, brown-sugar goodness.

He finished three plates before he finally retired to a crude Adirondack chair beside his pit, picking possum flesh and sweet potato skins out of his teeth, wondering how his good fortune could possibly improve, luck coming in threes and getting bigger with each stroke.

Then his phone rang. The 507 caller again.

"Yeah," he said.

"Adder?" Der said.

"Mr. Der," Adder said.

"Looks like I need another massasauga rattlesnake," Der said.

Adder remembered taking half a day to find the others. "When?"

"Tomorrow afternoon, same time and place."

"They aren't exactly common as red-winged blackbirds," Adder said. As soon as he said it, he remembered that wildlife lab over near McCutcheon, where Barry Vander kept some in cages, for breeding and study. Adder had driven by the place. It was in a stand of trees outside of town, secluded. But he wasn't sure if he could get in. What if they had those cameras?

Adder used a couple of cheap camouflaged game cameras around the marsh. They were easy to set up and took reasonably clear photos when he was looking for something special. Maybe Vander set up some kind of surveillance?

But the low-hung, cement-block building didn't seem like the kind of place with security, given it housed mostly rattlesnakes. He suspected Barry Vander never guessed anyone would try and steal a rattlesnake, so it probably just had a locked door. Easy enough for a man with Adder's skillset to break in.

"I understand," Der said. "Given the extenuating circumstances, I'll make it another $1,500."

Adder didn't know what Der meant by *extenuating circumstances*, but he certainly understood $1,500.

The man had rattlesnake fever, Adder thought. And money. Who was Adder to argue with crazy. Besides, once he delivered the snake, he could head over to Waverly with his flatbed. He could already hear the rumble of the Axis 500 cruising around the marsh.

They agreed on the same time and place, the next day.

Thinking about game cameras gave Adder an idea. He'd never liked not knowing who the hell Der was, never having met him. He was pretty sure he could conceal a game camera in the upper branches of a nearby juniper. One that took in the stump and everything around it. At least he'd have a picture of Der. Insurance, just in case.

After Adder hung up, he realized this third stroke of luck had been bigger than the last, which satisfied his perspective about good fortune. He just hoped, once everything was delivered and he was riding his new ATV with his pocket full of money, the universe didn't conspire to correct the imbalance of earning a half-year's salary in three days.

CHAPTER 9

Owen's Gap had a HyVee grocery store on the outskirts of the city's limits. Across the blacktop from the grocery, a welcome sign declared, "Entering Owen's Gap: Home to 1,754 good eggs, and a few stinkers." At least they acknowledged not everyone in town was perfect, Sam thought. Usually, small-town people could identify the bad eggs. Though sometimes they got it wrong.

Sam was tired and it was getting late, and he didn't want to sit in a local café, review a menu, order something, and wait for his meal. And he needed to get Gray fed.

He walked into the grocery and visited the deli, buying a sandwich and a couple other items for dinner.

The motel was a long, straight line of rooms tucked against the bottom of a bluff that marked the western edge of Owen's Gap. Sam had driven down through the bluff, the "gap," to get into town. He'd found the inn, saw there were plenty of vacancies, checked into his room, got Gray his dinner, and finally sat down at a table in front of his motel room's window.

Through the window, he had an expansive view of the town, such as it was. While he ate, he noticed two church steeples and a typical downtown with a gas station, an Owen's Gap Hardware, and various other small-town shops. There was a Gap Café within walking distance of the inn, a place Sam guessed would be good for breakfast, providing they opened early enough.

After finishing his dinner, including half the bag of Cheetos, Sam walked Gray onto a flat strip of freshly mowed grass in front of the bluff. Then he called Carmel.

She picked up on the first ring.

"Where are you?" Carmel said.

"Owen's Gap. A small town about an hour out of Rochester."

"I think I've heard of that town," she said.

"I don't know why," Sam said. "It's a nice enough town, but not very big."

"It'll come to me," she said. "You miss me?"

"Does a rattlesnake rattle?"

"I'm not sure what that means," Carmel said.

"It means, of course, I miss you. That's what rattlesnakes do. They rattle. Wish you were here."

"Rattlesnakes rattle when they're pissed," Carmel said.

Sam started laughing. "I miss you, is all."

"You should be pissed, 'cause another day has passed with none of your wedding invitees responding."

Sam told her about his conversation with Sheriff Dean Goddard and that he, his wife, and their kid were all coming.

"Did they send in the RSVP?"

"He said it's in the mail."

Carmel wasn't placated. Sam had held off on eating the rest of his Cheetos. Now he put one in his mouth and crunched.

"What are you eating?" Carmel said.

"Cheetos."

"You're eating Cheetos?"

"And some tea, a ham-and-cheese sandwich, and some potato salad," Sam said. "Don't tell me you've never enjoyed Cheetos."

"I've enjoyed a lot of things that are bad for you."

Sam considered a few lurid responses, but settled on, "Not everything that's enjoyable is bad for you."

Long pause. Then, "Rivers..."

She sounded exasperated, and Sam thought she was going to lecture him.

But then she said, "I wish you were here so you could give me some good enjoyment."

Sam laughed. And then they embarked on the banter of intimates who were old enough to know themselves but young enough to feel a hunger for each other that could only be satisfied by touch.

Finally, Carmel said, "We still need to hear from your outstanding invitees."

"You really know how to throw a cold blanket onto a hot conversation."

"We need to hear from these people," Carmel said, ignoring his comment. "Sooner rather than later."

"Just," he said, "give them another day, and if we still don't hear from anyone, I'll start making calls. Promise."

That night, when Sam finally got Gray settled in his dog bed and turned out the lights, he didn't think about RSVPs. He thought about rattlesnakes.

CHAPTER 10

Thursday

Thursday morning, Sam and Gray rose around dawn. July 13 was near enough to the summer solstice to make it one of the longest days of the year. Sam parted his window curtains and admired the sky beginning to turn a beautiful burnt orange over the next bluff east of town. He checked his weather app and saw it was already 76 degrees, and the high by this afternoon would be in the 90s. And humid. Perfect for carefully stepping through beautiful country in search of a snake. Or two.

Sam brewed himself some motel-room coffee. While he drank a couple of cups, he answered emails. The only one that counted was from his boss, Kay Magdalen, reminding him to keep her posted on progress.

"This shouldn't take long," she wrote.

That depends on what we find, Sam thought. But he told Kay he agreed and said he'd send an update after they searched the field. Maybe end of day tomorrow.

After Gray was fed, watered, and walked, it was nearly 7:00. Sam got Gray into his Jeep and they started off for Alta Vista, stopping off at the HyVee deli for a breakfast sandwich, some chips, and another sandwich for lunch.

He pulled down a second bag of chips, thinking Carmel would place chips for breakfast and lunch in the same category as Cheetos for dinner. But there were occasions he'd seen her buy and eat potato chips, so he knew she wasn't a complete food Nazi, her perspective about Cheetos notwithstanding.

By the time Sam and Gray pulled up at the site, all the day's snake hunters were assembled: Deputy Rosie Miller, CO Bob Greene, DNR Non-game Wildlife Specialist Gina Larkspur, and Jules Ortega. The officials were in a huddle, standing outside Bob's official DNR truck. Everyone had driven separately. Jules was still sitting in the cab of a vintage Ford truck.

As Sam pulled up and parked in front of the line of vehicles, a new Dodge Ram blue pickup drove up and parked beside Jules's beater. It was an old guy, Sam could see. There was printing on the truck's side door. When Sam got out of his Jeep and turned around the ditch side to let Gray out of the back seat, he read: "Bright Horizons Dairy" on the truck.

Sam listened as the farmer rolled down his window and Jules, in response, got out of his truck, stepping over to the man's passenger-side window.

"Top of the mornin'," the farmer said.

Clearly, he'd had his coffee, Sam thought. The dairy farmers Sam had known were all clean-living, hardworking, early-rising types. This guy had that look, that he'd been up since 4 a.m., when he did the first milking.

"And to you, Mr. Smiley," Jules said. "It's beautiful out."

"Joe," the man said. "Call me Joe, Jules."

Jules nodded and said, "Joe."

"You know, around here it's not easy finding people who know dairy," Joe said.

"It's a hard business," Jules said. "The dairy guy I worked with in Texas always said 'feed, water, waste, and then you gotta find a market for your milk.' He worked hard."

Joe laughed. "That guy knew his business," he said. "It ain't getting any easier, and I ain't getting any younger."

Jules laughed.

"But I manage," Joe said.

They talked a little about milk prices, and the farmer mentioned he was part of a dairy co-op in the valley that helped make his farm profitable. Then there was some talk about Venita, Joe's wife, who wanted to go on a cruise this winter. Joe wondered if, when the construction business slowed down, Jules would be interested in helping out.

Jules seemed to brighten at the prospect. "I like dairy," he said. Then, thinking about the old couple getting away, he said, "It's nice to go someplace warm in the winter."

"You should stop by when you get a chance," Joe said. "Check out the operation."

Jules told him he would, and Joe gave him directions. It was less than a mile down the road, then a turn into the valley below. As soon as he reached the bottom of the hill, he'd see the drive and sign for Bright Horizons Dairy. Jules had driven that route before, since it was the best way to get to the Warner Construction lot in Winona. He'd noticed the sign.

By the time they finished talking, Sam, Gray, and then Jules had walked back to Bob Greene's DNR truck and said hello.

The sun was out, and it was already warm and muggy. There were intermittent clouds on the eastern horizon, but they appeared to be moving due west. There was almost no wind. It was a beautiful, still morning.

"Perfect day for a snake hunt," Sam said.

"It is," Gina Larkspur said. Enthusiastic. "It's a great day for reptiles."

"And humans," Bob Greene said.

Everyone agreed.

Last night, thinking about his tour of the 10-acre site, Sam had drawn a crude map on an 8.5x11 piece of notebook paper. The others crowded around to look at Sam's sketch.

"I think we should start on the northern side, where a slight downhill grade starts heading south," Sam said. He pointed to the line of trees beside them. "Ideally, we should spread out in an even line across the site, west to east. Gray and I can take that thick patch of woods along the east. And maybe Gina?" Sam said.

Gina nodded.

"I'm thinking if we find any snakes, they'd be down in that area, close to the bluff," Gina said. "Where there's more cover and more places along the bluff edge for hidden dens."

"Good," Deputy Rosie Miller said. "You guys search there. Because I'm hopin' I don't see a snake."

Sam smiled and explained that if any of them saw any snakes—not just rattlesnakes, but any snakes at all—they should call out for him or Gina. Gina had brought along two snake hooks—4-foot-long aluminum poles with flattened hook ends. She said she preferred them to snake poles with a scissors grip and closeable tongs, which could harm the animal. The flattened hooks could be used to pin the snakes or pick them up by their middle and drop them into a bucket or a bag. She handed one of them to Sam and kept one for herself.

Earlier, Sam noticed Jules had a pair of thick leather work gloves in his back pocket. When he'd spoken to Jules yesterday, the kid told him he'd dealt with plenty of rattlesnakes in northern Mexico, where he was from, and in Texas, where he had worked.

Given Rosie's reluctance to get involved with snakes, they positioned her near the road, where she'd be walking primarily in pasture, near the ditch. Sam positioned Jules next, maybe 20 feet from Rosie. And then Bob, then Sam and Gray, and finally Gina, who loved snakes and would be in the trees near the bluff where she thought she was most likely to find one.

Sam reminded them all to keep their line straight, and to not get ahead of Gina, who had the toughest area to traverse.

And then they spread out and began searching.

Throughout the morning, they moved slowly, zigzagging across the 20 or so yards each of them had to cover. They'd taken more than an hour to move less than an acre, when Deputy Rosie Miller screamed.

"Snake, snake, snake!" she said, backing away from the place she pointed.

Jules hurried over, donning his gloves. Before Sam and Gray could get there, Jules bent and, quick as a snake himself, came up out of the grass holding a 4-foot garter snake by the neck, behind the head. He grabbed the base of the writhing snake with his other hand, to stop its whipping back and forth.

A pungent musk filled the air.

Rosie kept backing away, trying to get up onto the road.

"It's okay," Sam called out to Rosie, but she didn't stop until she got to the road.

Gina, Sam, and Jules admired the garter snake, which was large and beautiful. It was mostly black with yellow lines down its sides and spine. It wasn't only the interesting designs embedded in its scales, but the scales themselves looked like they had been carefully woven into an intricate, interlaced pattern that helped protect and camouflage the snake. The snake's scales, Sam knew, were made of keratin—the same substance in human hair and fingernails. Sam had always considered physiological similarities between humans and animals—in this case between human fingernails and a snake's scales—to be another example of how all creatures on the planet are connected.

Jules, holding the snake comfortably, also admired the animal's design, despite the musk scent the animal was giving off as a defense mechanism.

"The smell isn't so bad, once you get used to it," Gina said.

Both Sam and Jules agreed. The others, standing well away, weren't so sure.

Gina spent a moment taking some photos and noting the snake's measurements. She thought this was a female because males have longer, thicker tales. She thought this one might be a female with young.

"These guys are viviparous," Gina said.

"They give birth to live snakes rather than lay eggs?" Sam said.

"That's right. So is the eastern massasauga rattlesnake. The little ones are pretty much ready to go off on their own as soon as they come out."

"That creeps me out," Rosie said.

"That's interesting," Jules said. "I did not know that."

Sam reminded Rosie that if she saw anything else, she should call out just like she did, except that she shouldn't worry about it, because they'd take care of whatever she found.

She nodded once, reluctant but willing to continue.

After Gina recorded her observations, Sam told Jules to let it go.

"Not here," Rosie said.

Jules walked back 10 or 20 paces. Gina followed to watch.

When Jules set it down in thick pasture grass, he said, *"Ve con dios."*

That made Gina smile, and when Jules saw it he said, "My mom thinks snakes are sacred."

"So do I," Gina said.

They continued their slow search. Midmorning, they all took a break and returned to their cars. Some of them went to their vehicles and pulled out water bottles. The day was growing hotter; even though they were moving very slowly, they had all begun sweating.

"Best to stay hydrated," Gina said.

Gina was young and obviously spent time outdoors, but perspiration was already beading on her forehead and along her neck and under her arms. She appeared used to it. She was a head shorter than Sam, similar in height to Jules.

Sam walked back to his Jeep, pulled out a portable bowl, and filled it with cold water. Gray, who was feeling the heat, appreciated the cool drink.

Jules came over to admire Gray, who liked the attention and the young man.

Sam and Jules walked back to Gina's Prius.

"How do you think that massasauga got into the Bobcat?" Sam said.

Jules was eating an apple, listening.

"It's strange," she said. "I really wondered about it. Very bizarre behavior for any snake. Last night, after we left, I called around. We've got some other snake people in the DNR. First, they were excited we found a massasauga. Then they were surprised we found one all the way inland, up on this bluff."

"Why?" Sam said.

"Not their habitat. They're typically in lower, marshy areas. They like to use crawdad holes for burrows. When they breed, they'll come to higher ground, but it's unusual they would come this high and this far from water. I found a *Federal Register* note that listed these snakes as extirpated from Minnesota."

The *Federal Register* was the official daily journal of the federal government, including regulations.

Sam was surprised.

"What does extirpated mean?" Jules said.

"Basically, exterminated," Gina said. "Not surprising, given the hatred some people have for snakes. Especially venomous ones. It means the massasauga has been completely eradicated from Minnesota. Not supposed to be any trace of them in the state."

Gina explained how she led the official DNR group who did a survey of timber rattlesnakes in the region. They had not found many timber rattlesnakes, but there were still some of them around. Timber rattlesnakes preferred rocky outcrops next to open forest land or pasture. They preferred holing up in small crevices and caves, for protection. During the day, they ventured into the surrounding country to hunt and warm themselves. Timber rattlesnakes were also endangered in Minnesota.

During a pause, Gina opened up the driver's side of her Prius, reached over to the front seat, and brought out the page from the *Federal Register* that talked about the eastern massasauga rattlesnake.

She'd highlighted the section—"Endangered and Threatened Wildlife and Plants; Draft Recovery Plan for the Eastern Massasauga Rattlesnake"—and Sam noted the date at the top of the page: "Wednesday, February 26, 2020."

Jules and Sam read the rest of the highlighted section:

"It is believed that populations have been extirpated in at least two states (Minnesota and Missouri). The species is impacted by a number of threats. The loss of habitat was historically, and continues to be, the threat with greatest impact to the species, either through loss of habitat to development or through changes in habitat structure due to vegetative succession. Poaching, either by persecution or illegal collection for the pet trade, is also a continuing threat."

Sam knew the USFW's effort to create a "Recovery Plan for the Eastern Massasauga" would shock many Minnesotans who were probably happy the rattlesnakes were no longer around. Like the assistance given to wolves, there were lots of people who thought the absence of wolves and rattlesnakes was a good thing. From Sam's perspective, it was much more complicated. If the rattlesnakes made a comeback in an area they had once inhabited, it would mean man's footprint had for the moment reversed itself and expanded its wild country enough to provide a place where indigenous species could thrive.

There was a Thoreau quote Sam had always appreciated: "In wilderness is the preservation of the world." The natural world was worth saving because we were part of it, and its health was intrinsically part of human health.

Sam asked about massasauga populations in other states.

"There are pretty viable populations right across the river in Wisconsin. And in Illinois and parts of Iowa. My main contact in Wisconsin is a herpetologist who's using DNA to ID their population. All of these populations are isolated, so each of them are a little different, at least genetically."

Sam immediately understood. "We've got to get our snake tested."

Gina, who was a step ahead of Sam, had their snake in a cooler and was taking it to Wisconsin, just across the border, during lunch, to get it tested.

Sam wanted to see the snake. He was familiar with rattlesnakes, but he had only seen pictures of the eastern massasauga. So did Jules, who still felt bad about killing it.

Deputy Rosie Miller and CO Bob Greene had come over to rest with Sam, Jules, and Gina.

"Must we?" Rosie said, about seeing the snake.

Gina was excited. "Yes. You can see what we're looking for."

CO Greene was also excited. Everyone but Rosie, who didn't really care to look at snakes and was hoping she wouldn't find another.

Gina fetched the small cooler from her back seat. The massasauga was double bagged in two gallon-size, plastic zip-top bags. The snake was stiff and cold under the clear plastic. Sam peered at the creature, admiring its design. The snake had large, dark-brown, nearly black symmetrical blotches set into a light-brown background, as though they'd been painted onto the snake's skin. Its head was in the shape of a modified arrowhead. There was a deep cut on top of it, where Jules had bludgeoned it with the shovel blade. Its underside was lined with universally black scales. Unusual, Sam thought. The underbelly of the garter snake had been light yellow.

"I can see how it would blend into the ground. But the pattern's so beautiful it would be hard to miss," Sam said. "It's like looking at a piece of art."

"If you say so," Rosie said.

The others agreed.

"When I first saw it on the Bobcat, I thought it was some kind of colored rope," Jules said. "Until it moved. And rattled."

"It's like . . . a miracle to find one in Minnesota," Gina said.

"Rattlesnakes are common in Texas," Jules said. "They are beautiful too. I mean, nice patterns and color. My mom thinks they are omens."

"Omens?" Gina said.

"My mom was raised in the Yucatan. She's part Mayan," Jules said.

"Kukulkan?" Gina said.

"Yes!" Jules said. "The snake god."

"Snake god?" CO Greene said.

"Kukulkan was a serpent god to the Mayans and Aztecs," Gina said. "They worshipped the serpent god, the creator of wind and rain. Like real snakes, the serpent god lived above and below ground, so it was connected to the living and the dead."

"They worshipped a snake?" Rosie said.

Jules shrugged. "My mom has a lot of ideas like that. About nature. She would be very unhappy I killed a snake. She would tell me to be careful."

"Doesn't seem like you had a choice," Sam said. "That was a tight space and I'm not sure you could have easily coaxed it out of that Bobcat."

Gina sensed Jules's concern and said, "You didn't really know you were dealing with an endangered species."

"My mom says all snakes are part of Kukulkan," Jules said. "No good comes from killing a snake." Clearly, he was worried.

"I agree with your mom," Gina said. "But not because it's a bad omen or it's going to wake the dead. They're an important part of our ecosystem."

"How long will it take to get the DNA results back?" Sam said.

"If I can get the Madison lab to fast-track it. We should have the results in a day or two."

"It's gotta be from Wisconsin," CO Greene said. "I bet it swam over or came over on a log. Landed near Warner's equipment lot and crawled up and got into the cab."

"It's the most logical choice," Gina said. "Given this bluff isn't the right kind of habitat."

CHAPTER 11

They all broke and returned to the field, strung along the line in the same positions they'd had when they stopped. Sam exhorted them to step carefully and make sure they covered every inch of the property. They continued moving, slowly, throughout the rest of the morning, north to south, slightly downhill.

Near the bluff, Gina found another garter snake. Given her comfort with and interest in snakes, she picked it up, carefully measured it, documented its size and where she found it, and let it go.

Not long after Gina's garter snake, Jules found a fox snake. Its pattern was like a rattlesnake, but its head was narrower, and it had no rattles. Jules thought it looked like a bull snake, and Gina agreed, a common misidentification. Before he grabbed it by the neck, behind its head, it had coiled and rattled its rattle-less tail.

"They do that," Gina said, grinning. "If one is in leaves, it makes a rattling sound and mimics its more dangerous cousin. It probably thought you were going to eat it." Gina had come over to measure and document the snake, a healthy, 2-foot-long teenager.

Jules, quiet by nature but especially so with this many officials around, only nodded. He was tempted to tell Gina he had already tasted snake, rattlesnake, and that it tasted like a cross between frog legs and turtle. But he doubted Gina would appreciate his dining experiment.

Near noon, they paused long enough for lunch.

Gina told Sam she was going to run the rattlesnake across the river. Sam reminded her to plead with her contact to fast-track the analysis. The sooner the massasauga was confirmed to have come from Wisconsin, the better. At least it would support their hypothesis of how the snake got into the Bobcat, improbable as it seemed.

Then Sam turned to his sandwich, chips, and bottled water. He'd just finished giving Gray more water and a chew stick when Leslie Warner drove up in her truck and parked in front of Sam. She was talking on the phone.

It was getting hot. Sam was in shorts and a sun shirt, and he wore one of those safari hats. He and Gray stayed well hydrated, but it was hard not to perspire in heat and humidity like this.

After a couple more minutes with Leslie still talking on the phone, Cab Teufel drove up in his Lexus and parked in front of Leslie's truck. Sam wondered if they'd coordinated the visit. But given what he'd thought he'd witnessed the previous evening—a tense interaction—he didn't think so.

The sight of Cab getting out of his Lexus appeared to hasten the end to Leslie's call. They nodded in greeting and then both walked back to where Sam and Gray were leaning against his Jeep.

"Find anything?" Leslie said.

"Two garter snakes and a fox snake," Sam said.

"But no rattlesnakes?" Cab said.

"No," Sam said.

"Good," Cab said. "Doctor Blare'll be happy to hear it."

"Yup," Leslie said. "Dick'll be happy."

It was subtle, but Sam picked up Leslie's use of the doctor's first name.

"Are you done?" Cab said.

"God, no," Sam said. "We just got started."

Sam retrieved his crude map to show them. Sam figured the irregular rectangle of 10 full acres measured approximately eight football fields, set side by side. It was approximately 100 yards wide and 400 yards long. He showed them where they started, at the north end, and where they were headed.

CO Bob Greene was across the field, sitting on a fallen tree, eating his lunch in the shade.

"We got to where Bob is," Sam said.

Leslie considered it and said, "Looks like it's going to take you into tomorrow?"

"I'd guess. Probably be finished by around noon, maybe? Or early afternoon."

"Unless you find something," Cab said.

"Even if we find a massasauga, all we'd do is capture it and document it. Then we'd keep searching."

"What would that mean?" Leslie said. "If you find another one."

Sam considered it. He was hoping his theory about the snake swimming the river was true, because if they found another one of the rattlesnakes up here, on the bluff site, they'd need to spend more time searching. The land on either side of the 10-acre site was owned by the county. They'd probably expand their search into the neighboring land. Sam suspected it would tie up the site, at least for another week or so, while they tried to figure out if relocation was an option.

But to Leslie Warner and Cab Teufel, he said, "Sorry to say it would probably mean further delays."

"Permanent delays?" Cab said.

"Depends what we found. It's possible," Sam said. He didn't want to suggest there wasn't a chance. "But unlikely. We'll just need to see what we find."

Cab thought about it. Then, "Damn, it's hot out here."

He was wearing a red knit golf shirt with black slacks and a black baseball cap with Titleist across its bill. His graying hair feathered beneath the cap, over his ears. His shirt was tucked, and a belly lip hung over his belt. The guy looked like money, Sam thought. He looked like he was getting ready to go on the PGA tour. Sweat marks were starting to form under his armpits. If he was a developer, other people did the work.

"I believe this kind of heat calls for AC," Cab said, and smiled.

Leslie, who was dressed in tan hiking pants, a white long-sleeved work shirt, and an REI hiking cap, said, "I hear you."

It appeared to Sam as though Leslie was one of those developers who liked to get her hands dirty, liked to roll up her shirt sleeves and do whatever it took to move her project forward. Digging dirt, hammering nails, or meeting with county commissioners.

"I've got some bottled water on ice in the car," Cab said, to Leslie, "if you'd like one."

It was an invitation for Leslie to join him, Sam thought. In his Lexus.

"Thanks, but I'm fine," Leslie said. "And I still gotta make some calls."

"Well, if you get thirsty," Cab said.

Leslie thanked him again and Cab started back to his car.

She looked out onto her site and seemed to take it all in. But Sam noticed she was keeping an eye on Cab Teufel. Once she saw him enter his car, start the engine, and presumably turn the air conditioner up full blast, she turned her body so Cab couldn't see her face, and said, "Give me more details about what you mean by 'delays.'"

By this time, Jules had gotten out of his truck and joined them. He'd waited, giving the three principals on the site time to finish their discussion. His cab windows were down, and the shade of the cab felt good, but it was still hot and he was happy to get out into a slight breeze. Also, he knew his boss wasn't partial to Cab Teufel. Frankly, the man seemed overly interested in his boss and her project.

Leslie greeted Jules and smiled. She told Jules what they were discussing and that he should listen in because it would impact how he was going to continue working on the site, either hunting rattlesnakes or clearing land.

Sam shared everything he thought or knew about how their work on the site might change if they found another rattlesnake. He also told her he believed the snake probably came from Wisconsin, and they should know by tomorrow, Friday, if that was the case. If it came from Wisconsin, and if they didn't find any other signs of massasauga, she could probably get back to clearing the land by the weekend.

"You could give us the go-ahead by Saturday?"

"Yes. It could be approved by tomorrow afternoon," Sam said. "*If* we don't find anything."

"You might be working this weekend," she said to Jules.

Jules was fine with working weekends. Saturdays, time and a half. Sundays, double time. And now he was foreman.

"But if you do find a rattlesnake, all bets are off?" Leslie said.

"Not exactly. We'd work as quickly as possible to do another survey and catch and relocate any other snakes we found. I can't believe that'd take us more than a couple of days."

"Into next week?" Leslie said.

"I can't imagine we'd be holding up your work more than by the end of next week," Sam said.

"That's the worst case?"

"Well," Sam said, pausing. "Worst case is we find more snakes and an obvious den—or dens—and relocating them is not an option."

"Then what?" Leslie said.

"We'd need to close the site down. If there turned out to be a breeding population of endangered snakes, for the first time in decades, we'd need to preserve the land as-is. But I don't think that's going to happen."

She looked away. "I sure as hell hope that doesn't happen."

Sam told her it was extremely unlikely, and that if it did the federal government would pay her for the land, full market value.

She frowned. "Would the federal government pay me to find a new site? Would they pay me for the architects to come up with a new plan? Would they help me get it through zoning?"

Sam told her she could try, but he was doubtful those claims would be honored.

"Goddamn it," she said.

Sam understood.

Complicating her efforts to remain optimistic was the man sitting in his Lexus behind her. *If* her site was closed, she might need to work with Cab Teufel to develop his bluff land. Cab would either charge an exorbitant fee for the land or extract some other kind of personal favor she didn't want to think about. The man was a shylock; he'd want his pound of flesh.

"Just . . ." she said. "Keep me posted."

Sam let her know he would.

Once everyone was finished with lunch, they returned to the field. Sam overheard Leslie remind Jules to keep an eye out—he thought, on Cab Teufel, who remained in his Lexus, windows up, car running, air blasting. Then she got back into her own truck and started off down the road, clearly concerned.

Midafternoon, Gina returned to the site. She checked in with Sam and mentioned her Wisconsin contact, herpetologist Angie McReady, only needed a piece of the snake to test for DNA. Gina had returned with the massasauga on ice, still in the cooler in her car. Before she continued searching, she also told Sam about additional massasauga research that was being done.

"There's a herpetologist in Iowa who's chipping the snakes," Gina said.

Carmel had chipped Gray. It involved placing a rice-size chip subcutaneously on the back of Gray's neck. The chip contained a number that could be read with a wand and used to ID Gray. Carmel used a small needle-like device to insert the chip. He wondered how they could insert a needle into a snake, especially when he felt certain a snake would not have Gray's sense of cooperation.

"We've used them before," Gina said. "They're getting small enough to use on reptiles, but I didn't know anyone was using chips on massasaugas."

She mentioned the researcher in Iowa, Barry Vander, bred them, chipped them, released them, and tracked them in the field.

Sam thought it sounded interesting, and so did Gina.

The Wisconsin folks weren't chipping their snakes, but Angie McReady had a wand. She checked their dead massasauga, but it wasn't chipped.

They kept searching through the rest of the afternoon. By 5:30 p.m., they'd made pretty good progress. They'd worked their way to the midpoint of the field, abreast of where their vehicles were parked beside the road. Sam finally called it off and reminded everyone they'd start again at 7:30 tomorrow morning.

Then everyone began heading back to their vehicles.

That evening, Sam waited until Gray had been fed, watered, and bedded down before he called Carmel. He was sitting in bed, propped up on pillows, ready to lay down himself.

"Howdy, handsome," she said.

Sam grinned. "How's beautiful tonight?"

"Awww. Missing you in my bed."

They spent a few minutes going back and forth with the talk of recently betrothed people.

"You're in an awfully good mood," Sam said, after the banter.

"Some of your people responded today," Carmel said.

"How many?"

"You got four, all of them coming. Holden Riggins and his girlfriend, Dean's family, Mac McCollum and his wife, and that guy from the DNR."

"Percy Evans?" Sam said.

"That's the guy."

Percy was Sam's liaison with the Minnesota DNR. A good guy. Sam was glad he'd decided to attend.

"I guess patience is a virtue," Sam said.

"I guess. Not that we've heard from everyone, but you're trending in the right direction."

Carmel asked about his day, and he told her about not finding anymore rattlesnakes. He also mentioned Gina's work and that they should know by tomorrow or Saturday about the origins of their snake. Sam still thought it was most likely a rattlesnake from Wisconsin. There was an extremely remote chance it was a genuine Minnesota rattlesnake—something not seen in the state in several decades.

Carmel sounded bored. As a veterinarian, she worked all day with animals, so she was less interested in Sam's rattlesnake perplexities than he was.

He understood and said goodnight.

"With any luck, you'll be in my bed tomorrow night," Carmel said.

Sam was looking forward to it.

CHAPTER 12

He was walking on the country road in the dark, carrying a 5-gallon bucket with a fastened-down top and a rattlesnake inside. The snake was quiet, and so was Der.

He had opened the bucket once, that afternoon, when he'd picked it up near the end of Adder Musgrave's drive. He'd watched the snake coil and rattle, defensive and defiant. And deadly. *Perfect*, Der thought, closing the lid and snapping it back in place. Then he left the envelope of money and returned to his car. He was back near Owen's Gap by late afternoon, with enough time to surreptitiously check on the progress of the snake hunters and note their location near the southern boundary.

Then he waited, hidden in the tree line across the road, until the searchers knocked off for the day.

Now it was midnight.

Der did his best thinking in the middle of the night. For many, the witching hour was peopled with bogeymen and banshees and the certainty the world was a dangerous place. But not for Der. The dark heart of the night was his finest hour. It was a time he conjured the way forward, had moments of inspiration even he didn't see coming. And he did it without illumination. He did it on instinct. His feet found their way in the dark.

His latest inspiration happened after a friend from the county told him about the Alta Vista development site. When he learned about its whereabouts, he was more than a little startled. He was, for perhaps the first time in years, alarmed. Though he did not show it.

"I thought that place was off-limits," Der said, nonchalantly.

"It was. But Leslie Warner figured out a workaround and zoning approved it."

Der shrugged. Then, "Hard to imagine a workaround when you're building that close to a 100-foot cliff."

"She got some firm from the Cities . . . some new idea about more secure footings and a clear barrier."

"You mean, a glass barrier?" Der said.

"Nah. Some kind of polymer thing."

"Plastic?" Der said, with surprise and feigned humor.

"I guess," his contact said.

Der let it go. But he felt . . . fear. He was afraid for the first time in 25 years someone might be close to finding those kids.

And then in the middle of that very night, a snake slithered into his dreams. A serpent. It crawled to the cliff edge and stared out over bluff country. Behind it, someone, unaware, stepped too close. Suddenly, the serpent coiled as tight as a closed fist and prepared to strike, its tail rattling like a bag of bones. Children's bones. And then it struck. Someone screamed and the world went dark and Der awoke, sweating.

A rattlesnake.

In the back of Der's mind, he remembered hearing about rattlesnakes in southeastern Minnesota, that they were rare. What if rattlesnakes were found on the property? If they were rare, they might be protected. And if they were protected, they couldn't be killed. And if they found them on that land, even one of them, given the tree-hugger bureaucrats running the state, wouldn't development be called off before it could be started?

That morning, Der's research uncovered the eastern massasauga rattlesnake; it was considered endangered in southeastern Minnesota. Under the Endangered Species Act, there was something called "critical habitat protection." The Center for Biological Diversity talked about key protections for endangered species that included prohibiting anything that might "adversely modify" a designated area, the ground where endangered species lived.

Der smiled. Gotta love the nature nuts.

Best of all, there were populations of the massasauga in nearby states.

And then he found the court records describing Adder Musgrave's criminal history.

God's hand was pointing the way, if you believed that kind of thing.

Now he carried his third massasauga beside him, ready to let it go where it would be easily found. The first serpent he'd managed to place inside the Bobcat. Genius. The second he'd let go in the ditch beside the trailered cat. The plan had been to find the second rattlesnake later that day, or early the next. Instead, the second snake disappeared. It had crawled out of their search area.

He needed another rattlesnake. This one he would plant where he was certain it would be found. Another rattlesnake would make clear this was no place to build, on land that needed to be protected in perpetuity because of what they were—endangered—and where they lived.

He stopped near the edge of the remote road. The night insects were screeching. The day had cooled enough so he felt certain, when he deposited his snake in the grass, it would curl up and await the warming sun.

He heard something else above the insect choir. A high motor whine. A distant engine. He listened carefully, turning his ear, and picked up the motor coming closer.

He hurried across the ditch into the trees.

This part of the remote road was county land. He knew it well. It was wooded all the way to the south end of the site, where a tree line demarcated the pasture from the woods. If needed, he could stay in the trees and reach that tree line completely hidden. But hiking through July growth in the dark was problematic. He knew these woods well enough to anticipate the scratch of blackberry vines and oak claws slowing his progress. He preferred sticking to the road.

He waited while the headlights approached. He watched an old sedan cruise by, one driver, one passenger. Probably kids heading home from a bar, maybe looking for a quiet place to fuck in the dark.

Thankfully, they kept moving, turning around the near bend and, from the sounds of it, continuing until they were out of sight.

Der returned to the road and kept walking.

It took another 15 minutes to reach the southern boundary of the development. He stepped into the ditch and entered the tree line. Now he needed the light from his phone to guide him. He would walk carefully among the trees, making sure he left minimal signs of passing. Even if they did see an errant footstep, some mottled pasture grass or a crushed plant stem, they'd figure it was left over from the surveyors who mapped the site, or a crossing white-tailed deer.

It took him another five minutes to hike 50 yards along the site's southern boundary. Then he turned into the pasture, hiking due north until he was at least 50 yards into the wild pasture. This snake wasn't going to crawl away and disappear. Moreover, he had been watching the searchers from across the road, and he knew this snake would be right in front of them when they continued their search in the morning.

After 50 yards, he paused. He shined his light in the nearby weeds and found a suitable depression in the land, just the kind of place a serpent might bed down and await the warming day. And then he carefully opened the lid to his 5-gallon pail.

The serpent was quiet in its bottom. It was dark and cool, and Der figured it was the best possible time to dump a dangerous rattlesnake into the weeds. He quickly tipped the bucket, angling it away from him, until the snake's heavy body slid out and dropped into the weeds.

Then Der jumped back.

And waited.

Nothing.

He back stepped through the pasture the way he'd come. He'd let the snake curl up. Even if the snake warmed in the morning and began exploring its new home, Der felt certain it wouldn't slither far. Eventually, it would be found.

Der returned along the tree line the way he'd stepped, carefully, along the site boundary. In 20 minutes, he was back in his car, headed home.

He hoped that fuckin' fed who stopped the development was the one who would find it. It would be doubly ironic if the rattlesnake bit him. Poisoned in his effort to save the snakes. Der smiled to imagine it.

What did they expect from a serpent?

CHAPTER 13

Friday

It was another hot, clear morning. By 7:30, Sam and Gray were pulling up to the bluff site. Everyone had already arrived, vehicles parked in the same location as yesterday. This morning, he saw Leslie Warner leaning beside her company truck, speaking with Jules.

Sam pulled up to the head of the vehicles and parked. He let Gray out to saunter into the ditch weeds to leave a calling card. Then they walked back to Gina, Rosie, and Bob.

Sam nodded, and they all said hello. Then, "Let's pick up where we left off yesterday," Sam said. "Same positions. I don't think we're going to find anymore rattlesnakes but assume we will. We need to walk slowly and pay attention. I don't want to rush anyone to the hospital for a dose of antivenom." Sam punctuated the warning by affixing an extendable leash to Gray's collar.

Deputy Rosie Miller's face paled.

"If you see a snake," Sam reminded everyone, though it was directed at the deputy, "any snake. Call me or Gina. Or Jules," Sam added, considering how comfortable Jules had been catching and holding the 4-foot garter snake, and that he would continue to be the nearest snake charmer to Rosie.

The comment didn't restore the deputy's face color.

Before Sam and Gray headed out across the field, Leslie came over to speak with him.

"I should probably mention something," Leslie said.

While Sam listened, Leslie told him she and Cab Teufel had worked together in the past, and that it had become a little more than work. By the time she got to know him, and what kind of man he was, she'd put a stop to it.

She told Sam that someone in the industry let her know Cab had bragged about their "brief relationship."

"I could never prove he said anything, but whenever I tried to hire locally, the men who applied all seemed to have hidden agendas. They'd either make a pass, or they weren't good at taking orders from a woman."

The nature of the construction industry didn't surprise Sam. He also wasn't surprised some men might try and hit on Leslie Warner. Probably a lot of men. Stupid men, Sam knew.

"For a while, it was tough getting work," she said.

She gradually worked her way out of it. She got jobs from people in Rochester. She hired from a pool of people outside of Owen's Gap. Good people, like Jules Ortega.

Sam wondered why she was telling him about the affair. "So, it's awkward to be around him?" Sam said.

She shrugged. "Nah, it's not that. We're really more competitors than anything else. I guess, what I'm saying is that he was surprised when he found out we were developing this site. That we got the county's buy-in."

"Okay," Sam said, and waited.

"Hard for me to imagine it, but it makes me wonder if he might be behind the snake. I've asked Jules to keep an eye on the guy, when he comes out. Dr. Blare, my main investor, has worked with Cab in the past. It wouldn't shock me if Cab was doing this snake thing out of spite. Or to stop a project he knows is going to be a good one. Or to try and get a piece of it by getting the site closed, and then offering his own bluff land for the development. Probably for a much higher price than he would normally get. And there would probably be strings attached.

"I know Cab Teufel well enough to know the man has a dark side. Yesterday, he mentioned his bluff land. And he also mentioned he was separated from his wife. Innocent enough but coming from Cab Teufel there's a hidden agenda. Or not so hidden."

Sam thanked her for the information and said he'd keep an eye out too. He and Jules. Then, "The best thing for all of us would be not finding anymore rattlesnakes." Sam was in the business of saving endangered species, so a part of him hoped he'd find more. But he also recognized Leslie Warner's predicament, and he had an instinctual distaste for predatory men, if what she was telling him was accurate.

The team's survey work was a repeat of the previous day, except that Sam worked through the midmorning break and then lunch, munching a sandwich, Cheetos, and an apple in the field, while he continued searching the ground. Everyone except Sam knocked off for lunch, at least long enough to sit and eat and drink, the day again being hot.

They found another garter snake at around 12:30, and then a short while later, Rosie Miller screamed as she watched a 2-foot-long snake writhe in front of her, turn over, and play dead. Everyone came running, and by the time Gina arrived, she took one look at the belly-up snake and said, "Awww," with affection. "It's a hognose snake."

Then she picked it up and held it so they could all see the slightly upturned nose that gave the snake its name.

"They mostly eat toads and frogs. Toads, up here, where there isn't any water source."

"Did I kill it?" Rosie asked.

Gina laughed. "Oh god, no. This is a defensive move. They play dead, like a possum. Like what we're supposed to do if attacked by a grizzly."

Gina's comparison didn't assuage Rosie's alarm. Neither did the hognose snake's awakening, as it suddenly began writhing in Gina's hands.

"Put it down!" Rosie said, stepping back.

Gina did, but not before Jules helped her take some measurements and she noted them in her book. Then she walked the snake 10 steps back and nestled it into the pasture grass.

"Love those hognose snakes," she said. "Even though they eat toads and frogs."

Sam remained working in the field because he hoped to finish by late afternoon. Not only had they found no more massasaugas, but they hadn't found any other signs that rattlesnakes had ever been here.

Over lunch, in the field, Sam texted Carmel. "We're not finding any more rattlesnakes. I've got to follow up on some stuff, but I'm hoping to be home for a late dinner."

Earlier, CO Bob Greene had told Sam about the local paper's coverage of trout stream kills, probably from agricultural runoff. Sam wanted to see if the reporter had received any threatening or whacko letters. And then he needed to write the report that, providing they didn't find any other rattlesnakes, would release the site for continued development. But he could do that from home over the weekend.

To Carmel, he added, "What are you making?" and sent it.

If he knew his fiancé as well as he thought he did, she'd say, "What are you picking up?"

Regardless, he was looking forward to his own bed. And the fact his partner would be in it.

They had been working their way south across the field, woods, and bluff and by around 3:00 were 50 yards short of the survey sticks and woods marking the southern site boundary. Suddenly, CO Bob Greene stopped and stood still as a statue, peering into the grass in front of him. Since it was the kind of thing all of them had been doing, given they were doing a snake survey, the others who might have seen Bob pause and stare—for more than a minute—probably figured, like Sam, that he was looking over a tangle of pasture grass to make sure it contained no snakes.

But Sam, who was keeping an occasional eye on his fellow searchers, noticed he remained still for longer than usual. He paused and looked at him and was ready to call over and ask if he was okay, when Bob looked up, directly at him, and mouthed, silently, "Come. Now. Hurry."

Gina was in the trees near the bluff. Sam and Gray were covering the ground at the tree edge, 10 to 15 yards from Gina. Bob had been making a kind of zigzag pattern over the middle of the acreage they were covering. Where he stood now, he was probably the farthest from Sam he had been—maybe 20 to 25 feet. Jules was nearer to Bob than Sam. And beyond Jules, Rosie was walking the ditch near the road.

"See something?" Sam whispered.

Jules heard Sam's comment and looked up. Then he watched Bob nod, vigorously, and then look down. Jules could tell from Bob's movement he was tracking something, because he leaned forward, slowly, and cast his glance back and forth until he focused on something. Something moving.

Jules started over to have a look.

Gina was obscured inside the trees. Sam knew she would want to know, so he called to her.

Gray, who had sensed some movement over near Bob, started walking through the tall grass toward him, the extendable leash beginning to uncoil from Sam's hand. When Sam turned toward Gina, he hadn't noticed Gray had turned and started toward Bob.

Jules and Gray arrived near Bob at about the same moment. Bob tried to tell Gray to stay back, but he was too interested. There was something alive in front of him, in the grass. He stepped forward to look, his nose extended.

Then there was a sudden, deadly trigger and the grass flicked.

Gray sprung straight into the air, like someone who had stepped on an electric plate.

Bob started screaming. "Rattlesnake, rattlesnake, rattlesnake!"

While airborne, Gray managed to twist his body so when he landed, he was out of the rattlesnake's range.

Jules came up beside Bob.

The coiled snake made another aggressive strike but wasn't near enough to hit a human or a wolf dog. Then it recoiled back into the weeds, its rattles sounding across the pasture, making an unmistakable, deadly warning.

Sam started running, pulling in slack on the leash. "Gray, Gray, Gray!"

Gray wasn't about to let the snake get away. He bent his nose down and carefully strained forward, sniffing, wanting to understand what was behind the interesting, unknown smell. And what kind of animal would strike out at a wolf dog.

Suddenly, the coiled snake struck out and Sam, now near enough to see it all, shouted. Guttural, deep-throated, and afraid.

Jules had stepped within the snake's range. Sam watched as Jules's hand darted fast as a mongoose. The moment before the snake's opened fangs struck Gray's nose, Jules swatted it aside. Rather than step away, Jules was on top of it, the snake's head pinned under his hand, the rest of its body writhing and rattling, whipping around, trying to free itself.

Jules's free hand caught the rear of the writhing snake, and he pressed both head and body to the ground.

Suddenly, the snake stopped fighting.

"Did you kill it?" Sam said.

Jules shook his head once.

By now, Gina had come up to the group. Rosie stayed near the road, wanting no part of the skirmish, especially since she'd heard it was a rattlesnake.

Gina used the flat-end hook of her snake stick to pin the snake's neck, just behind Jules's hand, to the ground. Sam guessed the snake was somewhere between 2 to 3 feet long. He used his snake stick to pin the tail end of the snake, maybe 5 inches ahead of its rattles, to the ground.

"Hold on, hold on," Gina said. Then, "Don't lift your hand until we're ready."

Jules had no intention of lifting his hand. At least until they were ready.

"Back," Sam said to Gray. "Back."

Gray understood and sat, far enough from the snake to be out of harm's way.

Neither Sam nor Gina let up on the pinned snake. Sam could see the rattlesnake's body was completely flexed. He guessed, as soon as the snake was released, it would recoil and strike again. If Gina feared the same thing, she wasn't showing it.

The rattlesnake's skin glistened where it was pinned, a beautiful black-and-gray mottled design. Alive and dangerous.

"I think I've got it pinned near enough to its head so it can't strike anyone," Gina said.

"You think?" Bob said, recognizing that if Gina was wrong, he or Jules could get bitten by a rattlesnake.

"Just," Gina said, "Jules, let us know when you're going to lift your hand. And do it fast."

"Yes," Jules said, quick, still holding on.

Gina took one more look and then yelled over to Rosie. "There's a 5-gallon bucket in the back seat of my car, Rosie. Please get it. Fast."

Rosie did. It was another minute before she stood by them. But she wouldn't come nearer than 10 feet.

"Bob," Gina said, recognizing Rosie's fear. "Bring that bucket over here."

Everyone understood why Rosie was afraid, even though the snake was pinned.

Once the bucket was beside them and its lid removed, Gina turned to Sam and Jules and said, "Ready?"

Jules nodded.

"Okay. On the count of three."

The second Gina uttered "three," Jules sprang away, fast as a cat. The rattlesnake's head tried to recoil, but it only had 3 inches of neck to maneuver. It used them to turn and hiss at the metal end of Gina's snake stick.

Gradually, Gina moved the flat end of the hook forward. She was careful to keep the snake pinned. If it wriggled free, it would be able to use most of its body to coil and turn and strike. At Gina and Sam and Jules.

She worked the hook forward until she could reach down and grab the rattlesnake's neck directly behind its head. Then with her other hand she grabbed the end of the snake's body.

"Okay," Gina said.

Sam lifted his stick, and she picked the snake up and dropped it into the bottom of the bucket, affixing the lid before the snake could react.

In the aftermath, everyone's adrenaline spiked.

"Wow," Gina said, and started laughing.

That made Sam and Jules smile and Bob start laughing. Rosie, who still stood 10 feet from the cluster of snake captors, appeared pale and said, "What's so funny?"

Rosie had the most logical response.

"I think you saved my Gray," Sam said to Jules.

Jules shrugged.

"Thank you," Sam said.

Jules nodded. "I didn't really think," he said.

"Good reactions," Sam said. "Good instincts."

"I guess," Jules said.

"Well, we found another one," Gina said.

"I guess it complicates things," Bob said.

"I guess," Sam said. Though it was going to take some time to figure out next steps. First, they needed to finish surveying the rest of the site, all the way to the boundary sticks. If they still didn't find any dens, or other massasauga sign, Sam felt comfortable relocating this snake. But he knew he'd have to get others involved. Meanwhile, the site would remain closed. At least until they could figure out next steps, and the provenance of this snake. At the very least, they would need to do another careful survey of the site, just to make sure they hadn't missed anything.

The developers, Sam knew, wouldn't be happy. Especially Leslie Warner.

And neither would Carmel.

Then, as if she'd been listening, Carmel responded to his earlier texts.

"What are you picking up?" she said.

CHAPTER 14

By around 5 p.m., they finished surveying the rest of the site, but found no other snakes or snake sign. The sun was well off the horizon and the day remained hot. It was Friday, and Sam knew everyone would want to knock off early.

The first thing he did, back at his Jeep, was text Carmel. "Gotta stay at least another day. Found another rattlesnake."

He didn't wait for a reply. He knew she'd be disappointed, as he was.

Everyone was gathered near their vehicles. Sam thanked them and asked if they'd be willing to work tomorrow. Everyone said they would, though Rosie couldn't be on the site until noon.

Sam wanted to do another survey, this one focusing on any dens or breeding habitat, as well as additional rattlesnakes, just to make sure they'd found everything. If they worked quickly, they should be able to finish by tomorrow afternoon. Then he, along with his USFW colleagues, could decide about next steps.

Sam phoned Leslie Warner and gave her the bad news. She wasn't happy and wanted to know what another rattlesnake meant. Sam told her that for the time being the site would be closed, but hopefully only for a while longer. He explained about tomorrow's survey and asked if Jules could assist, and she told Sam she would appreciate his participation, however and whenever he needed him.

Sam figured Jules would be reporting back to his boss, which was just fine with him.

Sam was hoping Gina's Wisconsin DNR contact had a way to extract DNA samples from a live snake (though Sam would watch from a distance). If the live snake was also from Wisconsin, it would mean they'd both been deposited here. Sam guessed that could mean the snakes were being used to stop the development, but it would also mean Sam could relocate this snake without fear there was any kind of resurgent population in Minnesota's bluff country.

He asked Gina if she'd stay to talk about the live snake and what they could do with it, and she agreed. Jules was nearby, looking interested, so Sam also invited him to stay. He seemed to appreciate the invite.

Sam told them he wanted Gray to sniff the live rattlesnake and then see if he could find any other snakes on the site. Sam knew there were certain scents associated with species, and that scent-tracking dogs had been used before to find a species (mostly humans) in an area. He didn't know if a rattlesnake scent was one of those a dog could use to ID other rattlesnakes in an area. But if it was possible, he suspected Gray would be able to do it. He would, of course, need to be careful with the leash.

There was still plenty of light and time for Gray to search. But Sam didn't want to presume Gina and Jules would help, given it was quitting time on Friday, after a long and eventful week.

Before he could share his idea with Gina and Jules, Gina said, "Here's what I think we should do. We head down to Owen's Gap, grab something for dinner, and then I stop at the local vet clinic. I know the vet. She could use a chip wand to wand our live snake. It's a long shot, but we can check and make sure this guy isn't chipped, given the guy from Iowa is chipping his snakes. And we can use Gray when the day gets a little quieter, and cooler. Don't scent-tracking dogs do their best work when the day starts to settle?"

"That's right," Sam said. "Gray and I need to head down to the hotel, book another night, and then I need to get dinner for both of us. What if we meet back here by 7:00?"

Gina had both snakes in the back of her car, the live one in the bucket and the dead one in the cooler.

"Want to get something to eat?" Gina said to Jules.

"Yes," Jules said.

Sam could tell she was excited. And so was Jules.

"Thanks to both of you for doing this," Sam said.

"Are you kidding?" she said. "It's been a great week, and now I get to go on another snake hunt. It doesn't get much better than that."

Jules and Sam agreed.

CHAPTER 15

On the way to the Bluff Country Inn, Sam called Carmel.

"Rivers," she answered, in a tone that told Sam she'd gotten his message about needing to stay in Owen's Gap for another night, possibly the weekend.

When Sam told her why, she said, "Who's this Gina chick?"

"She's a herpetologist for the DNR."

"She sounds a little too eager to help out on a Friday night," Carmel said.

Sam laughed. "She loves snakes. Reptiles and amphibians of all sorts. She's a herpetologist," Sam repeated.

"I like snakes too," Carmel said. "But I don't think I'd give up my Friday night plans to hunt them in the dark."

"First of all, I'm guessing she's in her late twenties and at least for tonight doesn't have any plans. And she looks kind of interested in this Jules kid."

"What does her age have to do with it?"

"I'm just saying, she's 10 years younger than me. Us," Sam said.

"Lots of men like younger women."

Sam started laughing. "Really? Is this my independent fiancé veterinarian Carmel Rodriguez? One of the strongest and most beautiful women I know?"

Silence.

"Carmel?"

"Dammit, Rivers, I was looking forward to our evening. Jennifer's at her dad's house."

That was code.

Sam explained about everything that had transpired over the day, and how important it was that he stay in Owen's Gap and finish another survey. And how they were going to use Gray this evening to do a different kind of search, just to see if he came up with anything.

"Me, Gina, and Jules." Sam said. "We're snake charmers."

"Not funny," Carmel said.

"Trust me," Sam said, laughing again. "If there was any way to come home tonight I would. But the sooner I finish, the sooner I come home."

Carmel said she understood in a way that told Sam she did but wasn't pleased about it.

And then they hung up.

Sam thought about heading home after Gray's evening hunt, if they finished early enough and found nothing. He could head home and surprise her. Then he could get up early and be back at the site by 7:30. Including *intimacy,* he'd probably get about 2 hours of sleep. It was tempting, but . . . he didn't think so.

After grabbing another sandwich, an apple, and some chips from the grocery store, and letting the motel know he would be staying another night, possibly through the weekend, it was not quite 6 p.m. Owen's Gap was small enough so that everything was close to everything else. It took Sam about 5 minutes to find the local *Gazette* offices, on Buchanan Street.

The moment he saw Mel Harken, he thought she seemed smart and tough. She was tall, angular, and, judging from the lines in her face, sixty-something. Maybe seventies. She had sandy, short hair and penetrating gray eyes. What you noticed most, after shaking her hand, was strength and intensity. Not just physical forthrightness, but a sense she could not be pushed around.

"Who did you say you were?" she said.

"Sam Rivers, special agent with the USFW."

Sam had come to ask her about the trout stream coverage and the recent unexplained fish kill.

Her eyes acknowledged him, and she said, "I was going to call you."

The front office was small and cluttered. There was a broad window that opened onto Buchanan Street with stenciled lettering. The desk, piled high with newspapers and papers of all sorts, was behind Mel, back in the corner. Now she turned to it and rummaged for a notebook and pencil, quickly flipping a page.

"You found a rattlesnake?" she said.

"Uh," Sam said. He was surprised she knew about it. He guessed it was either Leslie Warner or Sheriff Betsy Conrad. He could think of no good reason their discovery couldn't be shared.

"That's right. We actually found two, up on the Alta Vista development site, outside of town. Who told you?"

"The sheriff," she said. Then she looked at Sam and added, "Betsy and I go way back."

Sam told her what they'd found, but she already had most of the details, except for the most recent find. She was going to give it some coverage in the next issue of the paper. The paper was published twice per week, Wednesdays and Sundays. This article would probably appear on the inside pages of their Sunday issue.

"You did an article a week ago Sunday about a recent fish kill," Sam said.

"Bluff Creek," she said. "We did a couple of articles."

"Did they figure out what caused the kill?"

"Not yet. Why?"

"These massasauga rattlesnakes are so rare, especially in Minnesota, where they haven't found any in decades, I just wondered if someone put them there."

Mel was quick to understand his perspective, which interested her. Sam could understand it would make for a better story.

"You mean," she said, "you think someone could have put them there to stop the development?"

"I have no proof of that. Not yet. We're getting the dead snake tested, to see if it's from another population."

"Interesting," Mel said, taking notes.

"I think it's doubtful," Sam said. "But I wondered what kind of response you'd gotten to your coverage of the trout stream kill."

"Because you think someone could have read it and decided we need to stop all development, for the sake of the animals?"

"Something like that. Again, it's a long shot. I'm just trying to cover all the bases."

Mel finished writing and thought about it.

"Were there any letters to the editor or did you hear from anyone else who was outraged by the kill?" Sam said. "Maybe said they wanted to do something about it?"

"We don't get a lot of letters. I think in response to our coverage of Bluff Creek, there were a handful. But I knew all the writers. None of them were the type who would catch a rattlesnake, let alone drop it on a site to stop development."

"And none of the letter writers were crazy enough to . . ."

"Mr. Rivers, I've been involved with this paper since I was a kid. When I turned 22, my dad put me in charge. I know everyone in and around Owen's Gap, and I can't think of one who would catch rattlesnakes and use them to stop development. It sounds far-fetched. If it happened, it was an outsider. Maybe an environmental whacko from the Cities?"

Sam figured as much.

Mel asked if he would share information about the rattlesnake DNA when he got it. Sam didn't think that would be an issue and told her he would let her know as soon as he did.

If it turned out the rattlesnakes were from Wisconsin, it might support his theory about them being planted on the site. If they were from Wisconsin and Mel mentioned it in the article and whoever did it read the article, they might realize they needed to back off and keep a low profile.

Providing Sam didn't catch them first.

CHAPTER 16

Gina and Jules were waiting for Sam at the site by 7:00. Sam thought they both looked excited. And he didn't think it was just about hunting rattlesnakes.

"Guess what?" she said.

"Our snake is chipped?" Sam said.

"Yes!" Gina said.

"It's from the Iowa population?" Sam said.

"Wow," Gina said, impressed with Sam's guess. "Probably. They're the only ones Angie knows who are chipping massasaugas. Could be another population out East, if somebody else is doing it."

"But that wouldn't make any difference," Sam said. "If it's chipped, it's known. Did you call the Iowa guy?"

"I did. Barry Vander. I left a message with the chip number. I assume it's one of his, but we'll see."

"That's crazy," Sam said. The only logical conclusion was someone had put the snake there. Sam guessed it was conceivable that a pair of rattlesnakes had somehow hitched a ride on a vehicle coming from Iowa, but it was as crazy as the idea a rattlesnake found its way onto the Bobcat's seat. That made him think of something.

"You guys ever do any work in Iowa?" Sam said.

Jules shook his head and explained all their jobs were local.

"Somebody planted it," Gina said.

"What about that other snake?" Jules said. "The DNA?"

"We're still waiting," Sam said.

"But if it's also from Iowa," Gina said.

"Someone put them here," Sam said.

"To stop the development?" Jules said.

"We need to wait until we have all the information. But I can't think of any other reason to plant rattlesnakes." Sam didn't suggest it might be Cab Teufel, Leslie's competitor. But he thought about what Leslie told him earlier. It could also be someone who read about the fish kill and was striking out at any development, to stop it.

Sam, Gina, and Jules talked about what it meant. But until they heard from the Madison lab and Barry Vander in Iowa, it was all speculation. The one snake, the live snake, was almost certainly brought here. But by who and for what? They agreed it would help if they knew the exact provenance of both rattlesnakes. For the time being, there was nothing to do but continue working the site with Gray.

Gina turned back to her Prius and retrieved the 5-gallon bucket with the live snake.

"Jules punched some breathing holes in the top," Gina said.

"Good idea," Sam said.

The holes would also provide Gray with a way to obtain rattlesnake scent without getting bitten.

They figured it would be best to begin at the south end of the property, nearest to where they'd found the rattlesnake this afternoon. Then they could follow Gray's nose. If he didn't respond, they could continue working their way north on the site. Sam would periodically use the snake to refresh the scent. It shouldn't take more than a couple of hours, Sam guessed. By that time, it would be getting too dark to see.

The process worked the way Sam imagined. When Sam indicated they'd be playing the "find" game, Gray grew excited. He loved the game where he got to use the miracle of his nose to find stuff—usually items Sam had planted, for practice, but also real-life instances, like the scent of missing humans, or criminals on the run. Somehow, Sam thought Gray understood when he was hunting a criminal. At least, when he found them, he wasted no time bringing them to heel. He loved taking down miscreants.

It took them nearly an hour to cover two-thirds of the field, walking through its center south to north. Jules carried the bucket with the live snake, so Gray could periodically sniff it. But he only sniffed it a couple of times before he took off, working across the field, east to west, nearing the place beside the road where Jules had killed the one rattlesnake. Sam figured it was the scent remnant Gray was picking up, but he bypassed the place on the road's shoulder where the dead snake had been tossed. He stayed 10 feet east and then started looking excited, with his nose to the ground.

Gray had led them to the east-west middle of the field, near Alta Vista's northern boundary. Gina and Sam carried the snake poles with the flattened hook ends they had used earlier. With the sun just over the western horizon there was still plenty of light in the day. They were enjoying the evening and the hunt and especially the shift in Gray's excitement.

Then Gina's phone rang.

"Barry Vander," Gina said, answering.

Sam heard chatter on the other end of the line.

"Yup. We found it today, up here, near Rochester, Minnesota," Gina said. "Just a sec. Can I put you on speaker? I've got a guy here, Sam Rivers, from the USFW. I know he'll want to hear what you have to say."

Gina put him on speaker.

Barry's excited, high-pitched voice entered the evening air. "That's one of mine," he said. "It was in my lab. Someone stole it."

"Where's your lab?" Sam said.

"In McCutcheon, Iowa," Barry said. "I can't believe it's all the way up there. I didn't even know it was missing."

Barry explained that he raised eastern massasauga rattlesnakes (which he referred to as EMRs) in his lab and eventually, usually after two years, he would let them go in the field. In Iowa's Sweet Marsh, where he was trying to augment an endangered population. He chipped them two months before he let them go. He'd chipped this one on June 1.

Barry told them he had 27 cages, some containing one snake, some two. He fed them and cleaned their cages, but because he filled each cage with plenty of plant life and dark places to hide, he seldom saw his snakes. But he knew exactly where this snake was supposed to be. He was going to release it in August.

"Somebody stole it," Barry said. "And I can't tell you for sure when, because I can't remember the last time I saw it."

Sam asked if the Iowa EMR population had a distinct DNA signature.

"Absolutely," Barry said.

Sam told him about the other EMR they'd found and unfortunately killed, and Barry told Sam if they got it tested, he could tell them if it was from Iowa.

Sam wondered if he knew anyone who might steal a rattlesnake. Barry said he didn't, but he'd think about it.

"Do a lot of people know about your lab and the rattlesnakes?"

"No," Barry said. "Rural Iowans, especially from around here, aren't that interested. If they were, it would probably be to complain about spending tax money researching and propagating the snakes."

"Somebody knew about them," Sam said.

Barry agreed.

Sam told him if he thought of anyone who might steal one for money, Barry should let him know.

As the sunlight bled out of the day, they continued working their way down the site. It wasn't until they were very near the site's northern boundary that Gray's behavior grew more intense, more agitated.

"Whadya got, boy?" Sam said. "Find, find."

Gray's tail began to wag as he turned east, toward the bluff, then back west, toward the road. He took a couple of paces to the west, but seemed to come to a dead end, scent wise. Then he turned back east, toward the bluff. Then he made a bee line through the remaining 10 feet of grass, crossing the site's survey markers, heading into a copse of trees very near the bluff edge.

Sam ran after him, worried his excited nose might take him over the cliff or into the defensive strike of a rattlesnake. Gina and Jules followed.

There was a small opening in the trees about 15 or 20 feet short of the cliff edge. It was the start of a rock shelf. The limestone stretched a few feet out of the soil and then stopped in a 2-foot drop-off, still more than 10 feet from the start of the 100-foot drop. Sam was right behind Gray and watched him stop in the opening under the rock shelf. Thinking there could be a rattlesnake in the opening under the shelf, he leashed Gray before he could stick his whole nose into the area. Rocks and dirt had fallen away from the gap, leaving an opening below the shelf.

When Gina and Jules came up beside them, Sam handed Gina Gray's leash.

"Hold him back, would you? He gets excited when he finds something. And he's acting like he did."

"The EMR?" Gina said.

"He's sure acting like it."

Sam lengthened his snake pole and used its hooked end to probe the opening from a safe distance. Then something rattled.

Sam stepped back, pulling the stick out with his retreat. "You hear that?"

"That's a rattlesnake," Gina said.

"I heard it," Jules said.

"We gotta get it out of there," Gina said. She looked at the rocky area and the opening and said, "This is a perfect place for a timber rattlesnake, or even a den. The only way to know if it's our EMR is to coax it out into the open."

"Gina, can you give Gray's leash to Jules? If you can get beside me with your stick, maybe both of us can scare it into the open."

"You mean, piss it off?" Gina said.

Sam thought about it. "You got any other ideas on how to get it out here?"

"Pissing it off is a good one," Gina said.

"Okay. Be ready with your stick. If it shows itself, try and pin it to the ground."

"This isn't my first rodeo," Gina said.

Gina stood bent over to the left of Sam, ready with her stick. Sam bent down and began probing deeper into the hole. He probed until they heard the rattle again. Sam was trying to stay calm, but a rattle is a warning. He didn't know how near the rattlesnake was, but he knew it was pissed. And warning him to stay away.

He started to pull his stick out and its end caught on something. It wasn't a rock, because he could still move it. He tried moving it forward and backward, to loosen it from what he figured was a root, but it was stuck. Finally, he jerked hard and something snapped. Something big. It didn't feel like a rock. The narrow end of his curved stick was stuck in something. Carefully, holding on to the farthest end of his probe, Sam managed to drag the object out.

When it was finally in the open, Sam saw what appeared to be a kid's high-top roller skate, with something sticking out of it.

"Is that a roller skate?" Gina asked.

The tip of his curved stick had caught on the roller skate's tongue, puncturing a hole through the old leather. Once it was in the open, Sam had a clearer look at what was sticking out of it.

"Is that . . . ?" Gina started. But she didn't finish the question because both she and Jules could see exactly what it was.

"A leg bone," Sam said.

CHAPTER 17

"What the hell?" Gina said, peering at the shin bone.

"We gotta get that snake out and see what else is in there," Sam said.

Given what Sam had already found, they were all shocked. But Jules, who had set the bucket with the live snake down, was still holding Gray and keeping him at a distance. Gray was interested in the bone but appeared more interested in the small cave from which it'd come. Where they'd heard the rattle.

Sam could see Gray's interest. "Tie Gray off to one of those trees," he said, pointing to a sturdy sapling 10 yards away. "We need you here with that bucket, ready to lift the lid."

Jules understood and took a moment moving Gray and bringing the bucket close to the cave opening.

Once Sam knew Jules was ready, he returned to probing the cave.

Sensing the boot had come from the left side of the dark opening, Sam used his stick to probe right. The snake obliged with a rattle. Sam kept probing and sweeping with the end of his stick. While he probed, Gina stepped around and on top of the limestone abutment, peering over its edge, ready to pin the snake to the ground when it showed itself.

Finally, attacking or annoyed or just trying to escape, the snake's head peered out of the opening.

Gina watched it, another EMR, move 6 inches into the open, cautiously, peering ahead and to the sides. Once its head was out, Gina used her stick to pin the snake's head to the ground. The overhead assault was unexpected and the EMR fought against it, writhing and opening its jaws, its fangs extended, deadly. If it managed to wriggle free and return to the recesses of the cave, there was no telling when they might get it out. She kept the rattlesnake pinned.

Sam, also afraid the animal might writhe out from under Gina's stick and escape, reached behind the thrashing serpent and used the hooked end of his stick to pull the back end of the snake's body out of the opening.

Now Sam and Gina were both trying to maintain their holds on a pissed-off rattlesnake, without hurting it. Suddenly, Jules darted in and gripped the snake's neck directly behind its head. He dropped onto the ground and reached into the dark hole to secure the snake's body, where it was fighting to free itself from Sam's hooked end. If he was afraid of encountering a second EMR in the hole, he didn't show it. His hands moved deftly, quickly, and in a moment the snake was free, writhing in Jules's hands.

"The bucket!" Jules said.

Gina was already ahead of him. It took a moment to pop the bucket's top. She kept it centered over the 5-gallon's top, because there was already one rattlesnake laying in the bucket's bottom.

"I'll pull it away and you can drop it in," she said. "Ready?"

"Yes," Jules said, trying to keep a grip on the writhing snake, its jaws wide open, its menacing fangs at the ready.

In one quick movement she lifted the lid and Jules lowered the snake's tail until its rattle end dropped below the bucket's lip. Now the snake in the bottom of the bucket rattled. Jules, as if in answer, let the snake in his hands fall. As soon as its body dropped to the bottom, Gina shoved the lid in place.

It had all happened so quickly, instinctively, trying to secure an angry, dangerous rattlesnake, but taking care not to hurt it, that Sam wasn't sure if Jules or Gina or both had been bitten.

"You guys okay?" he said, breathless.

Jules nodded. Then he looked at Gina, who was looking at him.

"Goddamn it," she said.

And then she started laughing. Then they all started laughing, despite what they'd also found in the crevice, and the tension went out of the air.

"Goddamn it," Sam said.

Gina high-fived Jules. Even though Jules had grown up with rattlesnakes, his adrenalin had spiked, and his hands felt jittery. But he smiled.

Sam turned to both of them and said, "Stay here. Don't touch anything."

Sam had a collapsible army surplus shovel and a flashlight in his Jeep. Sam unfastened Gray from the tree and walked him back to the Jeep. Once inside, Gray peered out of the rear window, his intense, multicolored eyes accepting his fate. But his eyes betrayed his unabated interest.

"Sorry, buddy," Sam said. "It's best if you bed down for a while. But you were great."

Gray seemed to understand and appreciate the praise.

Back at the cave, Sam kneeled in front of the opening and flicked on his flashlight, peering inside.

"Looks like black plastic," Sam said. "With the rest of a knee bone sticking out of it."

"Oh god," Gina said. "How old do you think it is?"

"No idea," Sam said. "But it looks like it was stuffed here and covered over. Eventually, these rocks and the surrounding dirt came loose."

He began digging away enough dirt to widen and deepen a hole, so he could see more clearly into the opening. Once the area was widened, he carefully scraped away soil from what he thought should be the second foot and roller skate. He handed the light to Gina and asked her to keep it pointed at the end of the black plastic. He managed to scrape more plastic aside until Gina said, "It's another roller skate. And it looks like it also has a foot in it."

Sam kneeled beside her and used the flashlight to illuminate the white leather boot side. Just above its top, Sam's shovel had accidentally cut into the leathery skin, revealing more desiccated flesh and dirty bone.

Sam backed away and said, "This is a crime scene." He stood beside the grave and dialed 9-1-1.

"We don't want to do anything else without a crime scene crew up here."

Emergency dispatch answered. Sam explained who he was, where he was, and what he thought they may have found. A grave. With a body. He mentioned Deputy Rosie Miller, since he'd been working with her, and she knew how to find them. But the sheriff also knew their location. He asked to be patched through to Sheriff Betsy Conrad.

After a series of clicks, Sheriff Conrad came on the line.

"Agent Rivers," The sheriff said. "What's up?"

He explained he was on the development site. He explained about using Gray to search for more snakes and that Gray found another snake, but also something else.

"I think he found a grave," Sam said. "He uncovered a foot stuck in a roller skate. Once we thought we were digging up a body, we stopped."

"A roller skate?" the sheriff said. "You sure it's a roller skate?"

"Definitely. Looks like it was a white roller skate, with a shin bone sticking out of it."

There was silence over the phone. A long silence.

"Sheriff?" Sam said.

Then there was a confused string of expletives, followed by, "Tell me exactly what you've got and how you found it."

Sam explained about how Gray led them to a small cave near the Alta Vista site, not far from the cliff, and that they'd used poles to get the snake out; how his had hooked on something; and how, when he forced it out, the boot came with it. And the bone. When they widened the opening, Sam saw another roller skate and more bone.

"Don't touch anything else," the sheriff said.

"We stopped digging as soon as we saw more bone."

"Back off the site. Secure it, but don't touch anything."

"I know, I know. Evidence."

Sam told her they were in a stand of trees very near the cliff edge, just outside the northern boundary of the Alta Vista site. He and Gina and Jules. They'd wait for them to get here. He suggested she call up her crime scene crew, and she said, hurriedly, "They'll be there," and then hung up.

Sam stayed near the hole in the trees while Gina and Jules went up to the road to meet whoever came next.

In less than five minutes, a siren was cutting through the dusk light. It grew nearer, fast, and in a few more moments, the siren grew silent as it pulled up and parked in front of Sam's vehicle. Its engine stopped, but its lights kept flashing.

Back in the trees, Sam could see the cruiser. He heard Gina talk to a deputy and explain where Sam was and what they thought they'd found.

Then in the distance, they heard more sirens.

By the time the sheriff arrived, there were three cruisers parked by the side of the road, their lights all flashing. As the deputies arrived, each one had to come into the woods to see where Sam stood near the opening in the trees. Sam told them not to come any closer because it was a crime scene. They understood, then returned to the road.

The sheriff arrived with Deputy Rosie Miller and another deputy. Sam heard the second deputy introduced to Gina and Jules as Chief Deputy Vince Baker. The chief appeared to be about the same age as the sheriff.

The sheriff told the other three deputies to stay near their cars. And then he heard the sheriff's voice above the others. "Lead the way, Rosie."

Sam watched the beams from a pair of big flashlights come into the pasture and then into the trees; in a moment Deputy Rosie Miller appeared, accompanied by the sheriff and the chief deputy behind her.

The sheriff introduced the chief to Sam and then said, "Whaddya got?"

Sam had them shine the light onto the separated boot with the bone sticking out of it. He told them the rest of the body appeared to be stuffed into the small cave under the limestone slab. Then the sheriff cussed.

"Crime scene techs are on the way," she said. "We use the Rochester guys. Bluff County has a tenth of the population of Olmstead. We don't have much need for crime scene analysis. At least not like this, so . . ."

She uttered a few more expletives, turned, and said, "Never thought it'd come to this. I guess I always worried it might."

Suddenly Sam realized she might know who was in the grave.

"You know who this is?" Sam said.

The sheriff looked at Sam, and then realized he was an outsider and so probably didn't know. "I think it's one of the Garcia kids. I forget their names. Just kids. They went missing 25 years ago. Two years after I started as sheriff."

"Goddamn it," the chief said. "The Garcia kids. I wonder if the other one's in there."

"Rosie, can you go up to the intersection near County Road 7 and meet the techs? They aren't going to know how to get in here."

Rosie nodded and left.

"And find out their ETA," the sheriff said, calling behind her. "Tell them it's a goddamn emergency. And tell them to be sure and send Peggy. Peggy'll wanna be in on this from the start."

Sheriff Betsy Conrad looked at Sam and said, "Peggy Landrau. She's the head of the crime scene techs. Best I've ever seen at what she does."

CHAPTER 18

The sheriff, the chief deputy, and Sam returned to the road. One of the deputies had driven Deputy Rosie Miller out to the turnoff to wait for the techs. The sheriff decided one of the other two deputies should stay, just in case, and sent the other one back out on patrol.

Sam, Gina, Jules, the sheriff, the chief, and the other deputy waited nearly an hour for the crime scene techs to arrive. While they waited, Sam heard more about the disappearance of the Garcia kids, and what happened after they'd disappeared. The sheriff was the only one of the three county law enforcement officers who was on the job at the time. The others were too young, but, like Gina, they were from around here, so they remembered the incident.

"The shit hit the fan, is what happened," the sheriff said. She explained she had only been the sheriff for two years, so it was an initiation by fire. In the first month, they had more than 500 leads. They followed up on every one of them, but they were *all dead ends.*

At first, scrutiny centered around the father, Ronnie Garcia Sr. But everyone who knew him said he loved his family as much as anyone they had ever met. At least, those who knew him vouched for him. But he had a thick accent and was Mexican, so the majority of the community didn't trust him and felt certain he was involved. Because he was an outsider.

Sheriff Conrad had to look at Ronnie Sr. But she never found anything. And in retrospect, she said she should have listened to those who vouched for him, rather than the majority of the community who didn't know him and were suspicious of foreigners, especially those from south of the border. She explained that almost everyone who knew Ronnie Sr. were from the Low Valley trailer park, which the rest of the community considered dubious, at best. She was counseled not to trust the opinion of anyone who lived in the trailer park.

But she should have.

The sheriff had known Ginny Dickinson, who was 4 years behind her in the Owen's Gap public schools. She remembered there had been some controversy around Ginny, who got pregnant her senior year of high school by the handsome foreign exchange student Ronnie Garcia. Ronnie Sr. was said to come from a good family in Mexico City, but his poor language skills, or at least his accent, and the prejudice of many in the community about foreigners, prevented him from landing work on anything other than local farms, or similar kinds of occasional labor in town. Ginny got a job at the local supermarket, and the two of them—despite how they began—seemed to love each other and were making a go of it, their trailer park residence notwithstanding.

And then the kids disappeared and, the sheriff said again, "The shit hit the fan. The royal fan."

"When was it?" Sam said.

"July 17, 1998," the sheriff said. "I'll never forget it. It was a Friday."

After a month, none of their leads resulted in a thread of evidence. They had nothing. The kids had gone out roller-skating. They had told Ronnie Sr. they were heading out. He thought they were skating around the trailer park. But a neighbor saw them out on Country Road 8, right in front of the park. Then, nothing. No one had seen anything. The kids just . . . disappeared. Without a trace.

For the rest of the year, they kept investigating but never got so much as a hint of anything. Then after six months, into the new year, the leads dried up like a desert wash.

"That next year was really hard on the parents," the sheriff recalled. "You know how small towns are. Everybody knows everything about everyone. There was talk Ginny Dickinson started having an affair with some guy at the supermarket, somebody she knew in high school. Gossip," the sheriff said. "Then Ronnie Sr. started drinking. That much I saw for myself. We got him for a couple of DWIs. I was gonna revoke his license, but I decided not to, on account of the kids.

"Neighbors at the park heard some pretty loud fights. But law enforcement was never called."

The sheriff considered it mostly small-town gossip. And then one day, she learned Ronnie Sr. had left. He moved back to Mexico City.

"Guess it got to be too much for him," she said. "First, he's accused of abducting and killing his own children. Then he can't get a job. Then he starts drinking and then he's fighting with his wife." The sheriff shook her head.

For many in Owen's Gap, Ronnie's return to Mexico was an admission of guilt. They considered him a fugitive, and the sheriff was criticized for not going after the man. But after the sheriff investigated Ronnie Sr., she knew he had nothing to do with the disappearance of his kids. He had alibis for his whereabouts when the kids went missing. And it was obvious to any casual observer that the man was devastated to the point of trying to end his own life over his kids.

"Hell," the sheriff said. "He turned over every stone he could think of, looking for his kids. And then as fall came, and winter, and then the new year, and he grew more and more despondent and started drinking . . .

"That next year was an election year," the sheriff said. "I ran for re-election and almost got beat by a guy who swore he'd get to the bottom of the kids' disappearance. He was a shithead who didn't know his ass from his elbow. But he claimed I wasn't doing enough. Anyone who knew what we'd done knew we'd exhausted every lead, every theory, we'd turned over every rock. It was just . . . there was never any clue as to what happened. Nothing. We even got the FBI involved, since it was a double kidnapping. But they hit brick walls just like we did."

"And you got re-elected," Sam said.

"I'm just thankful there are more reasonable people in Bluff County than racists and rednecks without a speck of smarts in their heads."

The sheriff stared off into the western horizon, which was now almost entirely dark. There was some illumination in the distant sky, Rochester's city lights 30 miles distant.

"We'll wait until Peggy finishes," the sheriff said. "And see what we have. If there are two bodies and we think they're the kids, I'll need to get Ginny up here."

"Their mom?" Sam said.

The sheriff nodded.

"That'll be tough," Sam said.

"I see Ginny almost every week," the sheriff said. "At the HyVee or around town. I haven't thought of her kids for a long time. Except this time of year. Probably everyone does. Everyone who lived through it."

"Maybe she'll finally get some closure," Sam said.

"Maybe," the sheriff said, in a way that told Sam she wasn't looking forward to her talk with Ginny Dickinson-Garcia. She was certain it would result in more pain than closure. How could it be otherwise?

CHAPTER 19

Given that the crime scene crew had to be summoned from the other side of Rochester, and Peggy Landrau and three members of her crew needed to be called into work, Sam thought they made pretty good time.

An older woman, slightly overweight with short gray hair and serious spectacles, got out of the passenger side of the crime scene van. She moved like someone used to being in charge.

After greeting Sheriff Betsy Conrad and giving a cursory nod to the others, Peggy said, "The Garcia kids?"

"Maybe," the sheriff said.

"I can't believe it. Twenty-five years," she said, shaking her head.

She asked about how they'd been discovered, and the sheriff turned to Sam, who explained about the site, what they'd been doing, and then how he, DNR herpetologist Gina Larkspur, and Jules had been using Gray to see if he could locate other rattlesnakes when he found the narrow cave and grave. And the snake.

"Rattlesnakes?" Peggy asked.

"The eastern massasauga rattlesnake," Gina said. "It's endangered in Minnesota."

"Interesting," Peggy said. "I hope you didn't find a nest?"

"We've found three snakes," Sam said. "The first one was killed out by the road. The second we found at the other end of the development." Sam pointed south. "We think they're not from around here. If this one was dropped off by the road, it must have found its way to this cave and figured it was a good place to hole up."

"Because it's a rattlesnake," Peggy said.

Sam nodded. "They like dark places."

"Burt, make sure you bring the tape," she said behind her, to one of the other techs. "Agent Rivers, why don't you show us what you found?"

She told the rest of them, except the sheriff, to return to the road.

"It might have been 25 years," Peggy said. "But if whoever did this left anything, we'll find it."

Sam took them down to the opening in the trees. He showed them the hole, the boot, and the rest of it.

Peggy grunted. "Well, let's see what we got."

She told Burt to circle the site with the tape and to make it a big circle. To the non-crime scene techs—the sheriff, Sam, and the others by the road—she said, "Everybody stays out except us." To the sheriff, she said, "Betsy, I'm looking to you to keep people up by the road. If this is them, when others hear about this, it's gonna be a shit show. The local stations'll want to cover it. You just need to make sure and keep them away. No closer than the road," she said, looking over her spectacles to make sure Betsy understood.

"Will do, Peg," the sheriff said.

Then it was Peggy Landrau's site. The first thing her crew did, after they roped off the area with crime scene tape, was bring in lights. They had a generator in the van. They hooked up overhead intense LED lights on tripods and lit the place up like it was some kind of moon landing. Then they started working, slowly, painstakingly, careful to listen for a rattle. But none ever came.

For his part, Sam knew they'd be at it most of the night. He, Gina, and Jules were standing by the side of the road. It was after 9:00 and they had all decided to leave. There was nothing more they could do here, except wonder about what they'd found.

Then Gina's phone rang.

"It's Wisconsin," she said. "Angie?" she answered.

Angie McReady, Sam remembered. The Wisconsin herpetologist who was testing their dead snake's DNA.

"Iowa?" Gina said. "You're sure?"

The caller was.

"Okay," Gina said. "Thanks for letting us know. I know it's late."

There were a couple of other comments, and then Gina ended the call.

"Iowa?" Sam said. "The DNA from the dead snake was from the Iowa population?"

"Yes," Gina said. "And I bet the one we found at that grave site is also from Iowa."

"How certain are they?" Sam said.

"She said she has 100% confidence in the Madison lab."

"And the DNA signature is accurate?"

"That's what she says. I don't know that much about the DNA analysis, but she does, so I trust her. The dead massasauga's from Iowa."

"Somebody's putting them here."

"Three of them," Gina said.

"Somebody who wanted to stop the development," Sam said.

Then Sam looked over to the opening in the stand of trees illuminated in the hot night. They could see figures bent over the grave. Graves, he guessed.

"And now we know why," Sam said.

They chewed on that for a while. Sam knew he was going to pay Barry Vander, the Iowan herpetologist and researcher, a visit. First, they needed to use the wand to see if this snake had a chip. If it did and it was also one of Barry's, Sam would need to return both of them.

"Can you wand the EMR we found tonight?"

Gina could. It was late, but she'd call her veterinarian contact and see if they could still run the wand over it. If not, she could do it first thing in the morning.

"And can you take care of them, until we can get them back to Iowa? I can probably run them down tomorrow."

Gina could.

Even though it was starting to get late, Gina and Jules were energized by all that had happened.

"I'll call the vet. Then I think I need a drink," she said. "What about you guys?"

Sam suspected Gina was making the offer out of courtesy. At least to him. "I've gotta head back to the motel and get Gray settled down, and call Carmel."

"I could use a drink," Jules said.

Gina and Jules took off, and Sam reminded her to phone him as soon as she got word about the wand.

Before Sam left, the sheriff took him aside.

"How much longer will you be looking for rattlesnakes?" she said.

Sam brought her up to date. They'd found three, but, given that they'd probably all come from Iowa, he believed they could make an argument to open up Alta Vista sooner rather than later. Probably by Monday. Sam knew the crime scene crew should be done by then, and the bodies (if there were two) would be exhumed.

The sheriff was surprised to hear the snakes were from Iowa.

"Until now," Sam said, "I'd hoped they were indigenous to Minnesota. Maybe a new population. Once we found the chipped snake, I figured it was maybe environmental terrorists. But this," he nodded to where the techs were working in the trees, "changes things."

He waited while the sheriff considered it.

"Those snakes were meant to close down Alta Vista," Sam said. "If you knew bodies were buried nearby, and there was a chance they might be discovered, with all the digging, and with people eventually living nearby, it makes sense you'd want to stop it."

"I could use your help," she finally said.

It wasn't the response Sam expected, but he said, "Sure. Whatever you need."

"Technically, those graves, if that's what they are, are outside Alta Vista's boundaries. I don't want to get into a pissing contest with local developers about re-opening the site."

"You mean, given the rattlesnakes were planted, they'll lobby to start clearing land?"

"You don't know Cab Teufel," the sheriff said. "And Leslie's got skin in the game. They'll want to get back onto the site, sooner rather than later."

If Sam thought about it, he could see her point. But he hadn't thought about it because he figured, once they'd determined the rattlesnakes were brought here from Iowa, the USFW would let the site be reopened and development could continue. Should continue. The discovery of the graves was a complicating factor. But Sam knew they'd be done with the graves and removing the kids, if that's who it was, by morning. Or earlier.

Technically, the developers would be within their rights to ask the authorities to reopen the site for development and begin clearing land.

Sam waited for her to continue. But Sheriff Betsy Conrad stared back at him, herself waiting.

And then he thought he understood.

"You want the site to stay closed for a while?"

"I need time to think about it," the sheriff said. "There could be evidence in the pasture near the trees."

"So don't reopen it?" Sam said.

The sheriff looked back at him with another penetrating stare.

Finally, Sam said, "You'd prefer the USFW, the feds, be the ones to insist Alta Vista remained closed? For the time being."

The sheriff shrugged. "The feds have a little more sway than we do."

And she wouldn't be pissing off her constituents, Sam knew. The sheriff wanted Sam to take the heat.

"And I'm an out-of-towner," Sam said.

"You understand my position," she said.

"How long do you need?" Sam said. "A couple days?"

"That'd be enough," the sheriff said. "Once Peggy finishes, we'll have a better sense of what we're looking at. Then we can decide. But I think you should keep it closed for at least a couple more days. No longer than a week, anyway."

"They're gonna be pissed," Sam said. He remembered Leslie Warner had said she was on a tight deadline.

"But you guys are used to it," the sheriff said. "Besides, you'll be gone by the end of the week."

And the sheriff needed to live here, Sam knew. And get re-elected, if she was running again.

There were still some outstanding issues he needed to address. He would like to try and figure out who stole the snakes from Iowa. He knew wherever that trail led might also lead to whoever was responsible for the Garcia kids.

"I'll play along," Sam said. "But you'll owe me."

The sheriff grinned. It was the first time Sam had seen her smile all evening. Sam made the comment in humor, but they both knew it was true.

"Yup," she said. "Not sure you'll ever have a chance to cash it in, but I'll owe you."

CHAPTER 20

Across the gravel road from Alta Vista, a slope of wild pasture rose 50 yards to a deciduous tree edge. The edge, and the woods behind it, were filled with mostly mature oaks. It was an oak savanna that had populated much of the Driftless for tens of thousands of years. This was county land, public. It could be used for hunting and gathering, but it was too small and too near Owen's Gap and surrounding farmland to have been used for anything. A perfect place for a lookout.

Der stood behind one of the oak sentinels and peered through the dark. A pair of high-powered binoculars hung around his neck, bringing the scene across the road in close. When the sheriff had come up to the road with Sam Rivers, Der lifted the binoculars and focused.

The evening was full-on dark. The man did not worry about being seen. He worried about what was happening across the road. The intense lights lit up a section of trees the man knew well, though he had not set foot on that ground for 25 years. Now it looked like some kind of midnight movie set. He knew why they were there, and it had nothing to do with cinema.

He cursed, softly, to himself. His secret was being dug up, like a tumor being cut out of his spine.

He was a smart man. He reminded himself, he was Der Führer.

Back at the tree line, Der questioned his misfortune. For so long he had considered July 17, 1998, a day of destiny. In Der's memory, everything that happened after leaving the Golden Gar was shrouded in mysterious good fortune. He had struck the kids at sunset. It had taken him several minutes to discover them and decide what should be done. It was a lifetime, under the circumstances. But for that entire lifetime, no one drove along County Road 8. It had always been a remote, infrequently traveled road, but as Der thought of it, a divine hand stayed local traffic.

Over the years, it had been one stroke of good luck among many. The girl had not broken open and bled across the Rover's grill, leaving telltale evidence. He had a roll of black construction plastic in the Rover's rear. On his return to the farm, he'd seen no one, passed no one. Near midnight, he'd traveled side roads to the bluff site, and it felt as though the world on a Friday night in the middle of summer in and around the Hole had entered some kind of standstill, a peculiar quietude. He'd pulled to the remote side road, hustled his loads into the woods, taken a half hour to find the perfect spot—the narrow cave opening near the cliff edge. And then he hurriedly widened a hole large enough to stuff them into the rear of the cave, sealing it over with dirt and stone. He had returned to his Rover without anyone passing by.

Until Joe Smiley and his wife.

But the hick dairy farmers had paid little or no attention. Joe had slowed, Der recalled. He'd slowed down and Der thought, from where he'd been hidden inside the tree line, that the Smileys turned and looked at the Rover while he passed, but then kept driving.

It had been weeks before he saw Joe Smiley again. But the man said nothing about his Rover being stalled by the side of the road near his farm. Why would he, given that Der believed the farm couple had been struck blind by God's hand. Or providence had veiled his Rover to make it unrecognizable.

Afterward, it was as though the entire county, the entire state, had assumed the kids had been kidnapped. Like that other kid up north. Kidnapped and never found. Vanished.

Periodically, stories appeared in the local paper. Whatever happened to the Garcia kids? There'd been speculation. There'd been wild guesses. Because their father had been Mexican, there were suggestions he'd been part of a Mexican drug cartel and the kidnappings had been some kind of revenge. There'd been talk of Garcia's family back in Mexico City—they had taken the kids back to their country. There were wild opines about witches, warlocks, dark spirits, serial murderers, and others. But nothing had ever been found. The Garcia kids had just *vanished*.

Every year there was a call for new clues, for anything someone may have seen that might shed light on the disappearance. But there were only the old conjectures, guesses so far afield Der had never worried.

No one had ever come looking for Der and his Range Rover. No one had ever guessed. Even his buddy Paul, who knew he'd left the Golden Gar with a belly full of Harvey Wallbangers, had never connected the dots, never suspected it could have been him who was the grim reaper.

Good fortune. Divine fortune, Der believed. When he considered that evening, July 17, 1998, it was a turning point in his life. He'd turned tragedy into triumph. He'd gone to the University. He'd gotten his degree. He'd taken over the old man's farmhouse and property. And the Lair in the barn and everything it held.

Der had come to believe the reason God smiled upon him was because God revered what had almost been, the rise of the pure white race. God was granting favor to Der in the hopes his vision would rise again. Der believed providence intervened in the ways of man and selected some to be his instruments, his change agents. Der had been chosen to help birth purity.

But now, looking across the pasture at the intense LEDs lighting up the trees, the graves, he wondered if there was an inexplicable turn in his good fortune.

Think, he told himself, in the same way he had nearly 25 years earlier. *Think, think, think, think . . .*

His revery was startled by an engine off to his right, through the trees, where the remote road turned off the county blacktop. It ran along the southern side of the oak savanna, traveling east to west until it hit the bend in the road, a quarter mile away.

Der watched a flicker through the trees. He watched the lights turn at the bend and drive toward the vehicles parked along the road.

He'd seen that truck but couldn't recall where. It was a pickup truck. It was too dark to see the color, but there was printing on its side panel. Some kind of business. He watched the pickup truck approach the parked cars and begin to slow.

Of course, it was a spectacle. The truck would stop to look. When it came abreast of where Der was standing in the trees, he lifted his binoculars and read "Bright Horizons Dairy" along the truck's side panel.

Joe Smiley.

And then it occurred to Der with sickening awareness. What if Joe Smiley remembered seeing the Range Rover parked there 25 years ago?

He watched Joe Smiley slow. He watched the truck come abreast of the spectacle. The old farmer drove carefully, nearly coming to a full stop, surely peering at the commotion in the trees.

Der held his breath. If he stopped, and they told him what they were doing, it might trigger something in the old farmer's mind. Then a deputy waved Joe Smiley on.

The old farmer obeyed, cruising slowly past the vehicles, skirting them, clearly going slow enough so that he could take in what for now remained a mystery. He drove exactly as he had 25 years ago, when he paused to look at Der's Rover.

Once beyond the parked cars, Smiley accelerated.

Der let out a long breath. Some kind of relief.

But for how long? What would shake loose in the old farmer's mind, in his memory when he got home and told his wife about what he'd seen? That night, she'd been there too.

Over the years, when it came to the Garcia kids, Der had always considered his good fortune, guided, as he believed, by a providential consciousness.

Now he wondered.

Think . . .

He watched the red taillights of Joe Smiley's truck fade around the distant corner like a pair of devil's eyes.

Then, suddenly, the knowledge of what could be done—must be done—struck him like a thunderbolt, so bold it couldn't be anything other than divine. It was inspiration so powerful, so perfect, it startled even him.

Providence had just shown him the instrument of his salvation.

CHAPTER 21

Finally, when Sam and the sheriff were done with their discussion by the side of the road about Sam and the feds being responsible, for the time being, to keep Alta Vista closed, Sam and Gray returned to his Jeep and started down the road toward the Bluff Country Inn. It was nearly 10:00. On the way he got a text message from Gina.

"Vet used wand on EMR. It's got a chip. I called Barry. He said it was one from his lab that he had released last year in the Sweet Marsh."

That's interesting, Sam thought. The Sweet Marsh was in Northeast Iowa, at least a 2-hour drive from Owen's Gap. He used the Jeep's Bluetooth to tell her he'd gotten the message and they'd talk in the morning.

Then he called Carmel.

"Obviously you found another rattlesnake," she said, clearly irritated.

"Sorry to call so late."

"And I'm sorry you aren't lying here beside me."

"I know, I know," Sam said. "After we found that rattler this afternoon, I got Gray involved and we did another search this evening." Sam paused, still feeling what Gray found was surreal. "He found another rattlesnake and a 25-year-old grave containing two lost kids."

"What?"

Sam explained about how Gray used the live rattlesnake to sniff out another, which led him to the decomposed bodies.

While Sam explained, Carmel felt stunned. She took a moment. Sam's comments were incongruent to the purpose of his visit to the Alta Vista site. It took her a second to shift, in her mind.

"Oh my god," she finally said. "Now I remember. Owen's Gap!"

"You remember those kids?"

"Yes! Oh my god. I'd forgotten. When I was a kid. I was like 12 or something. They disappeared."

Carmel told him what she could remember, but details were spotty. The two Garcia kids had just disappeared, she said. And were never found.

"I guess it was back in 1998?" Sam said.

"Yes! In the middle of summer. Like, around now. It was a Friday."

"Good memory."

"I remember because I was supposed to go to a party and my folks wouldn't let me out of the house. Because of those kids."

Sam was up on the Iron Range back then, trying to survive his father's emotional and real blows.

"I don't remember hearing about it," Sam said. "The sheriff told me they never found anything."

"Nothing," Carmel said. "At least that I remember. They just . . . vanished."

"Until now," Sam said. "So tragic."

"It was," Carmel said. "So sad. Their photos were posted all over the papers, even up here. It was big news all over the state. At least for a few days. Then, you know, other stuff took over."

"The Garcia kids," Carmel said. "From what I remember, it sounded like somebody had just come along and kidnapped them. It was awful."

There wasn't much more to say about the kids because Carmel didn't remember much more.

As Sam told her what he knew, she began to recall more details. There was the Hispanic connection. Carmel was a Rodriguez. Her dad had emigrated from Mexico and had been challenging racism his entire life. Eventually he became a well-respected veterinarian. But because of his accent, he had always sensed prejudice in a few people.

Carmel guessed one of the reasons the Garcia kids quickly faded from the media's coverage was because they were Hispanic. And their dad was a foreigner. If they'd been white, Carmel wondered, the story might have had more staying power.

"Maybe," Sam said.

They were both quiet for a moment, thinking about it.

"For the time being, you cannot repeat this to anyone," Sam said. "The sheriff still needs to contact the mother, Ginny Dickinson-Garcia."

"Oh god," Carmel said. "I cannot imagine it."

"I know. By the time I left, they'd found them both."

"That's . . . horrific," Carmel said.

Sam agreed. "The girl was close to Jennifer's age."

"Oh," Carmel said, with a pang. "That poor woman. As a mother, I cannot imagine anything worse."

"As a human being, I cannot imagine it."

"You need to find them," Carmel said. "You need to find whoever did this. They should be crucified."

Sam had been thinking about the site and finding the Garcia kids. Leaving the grave, on his way back to the inn, he had a moment to consider it. The body had been wrapped in plastic. What looked like heavy black construction plastic. He also knew the Alta Vista site had been off limits for development until recently because of technical reasons. It had been the perfect place to bury the kids. And then there were the endangered rattlesnakes. Whoever did this knew about the development and knew dropping a few endangered species on the place would be an imaginative way to stop it. Then it occurred to Sam that whoever had done it was . . . *watching*. They'd found out the area was being developed. There couldn't have been that many who knew about Alta Vista. People from the county? Officials? It was a line of inquiry he was going to pursue. With the sheriff, who owed him. And who, if she was smart, would let him assist.

"Somebody knew the kids were there and knew the place was about to be developed," Sam said. "That means it's gotta be somebody local. Someone," Sam paused, "involved."

"You have to find them, Sam. I know you've worked on a lot of bad stuff, but this one . . ." she paused. "This is in a class by itself." After Sam shared what they had found, it was difficult trying to make small talk. Carmel told him about Jennifer's school event—she'd gone out for sixth grade basketball and Carmel wasn't sure she was cut out for the hoops. Sam asked about the RSVPs to their wedding. But it all came out wooden, given their minds were both filled with the tragic news.

"I wish you were here," Carmel finally said. "To process this. To be with me. I could use a hug."

"Me too," Sam said. "I feel so bad for her. The mother. And the father."

"Be careful," Carmel said. "Whoever did this is a monster, capable of anything."

Sam assured her he would, then hung up.

The Garcia kids disappeared in 1998, when Sam was, what, the same age as Carmel at that time, 12. He'd been living in Defiance, up on Minnesota's Iron Range, trying to navigate between an abusive father and an overprotective mother. And spending as much time in the woods as possible, to get away, to find solace, to experience whatever limited sense of grace the wilderness around Defiance provided. Enough.

He and his old buddy, Holden Riggins, had spent a lot of time in the woods, pretty much for the same reasons. They must have been in the woods when the Garcia kids went missing because Sam didn't recall anything about those kids or the town of Owen's Gap.

Carmel was raised in the Twin Cities. She was smart and a good student and conscientious—of course, she remembered it. She was probably paying attention.

He took a moment to Google the "Garcia Kids in Owen's Gap" and found an article from the local paper, the Owen's Gap *Gazette*. "Mystery of Disappearance Still Haunts Town." It was from last

Sunday's paper, which marked the 25-year anniversary of the kids' disappearance. The article talked about the kids, Ronnie Jr. and Sally, and the parents. There was a photo of them from 1998, right after the kids had disappeared. Ronnie Sr. was the epitome of "tall, dark, and handsome." Ginny looked like a homecoming queen. The two kids had inherited their parents' good looks. Beneath the sober-looking couple, Ginny Dickenson-Garcia was quoted: "Please help us find our children."

Back in 1998, a fund was set up for the parents, so they could take time off work to follow any lead, assisting the Owen's Gap police and the county sheriff's office. The fund was depleted after just two years.

Sheriff Betsy Conrad was quoted in the article: "This time of year I always think about them. Although it's been 25 years, it is still an open investigation. An active case." The sheriff said they still got leads, but fewer and fewer each year, and so far none of them had resulted in any breakthrough.

The article mentioned the parents' divorce and the father's return to Mexico. Ginny Dickinson-Garcia now managed the local HyVee. There was a picture of her in front of the store, standing with a pained smile. Her hair was cut short and wavy. It was a mix of blonde and gray and clipped enough to show her ears.

After Sam's marriage to Carmel, he was going to be a stepdad to Carmel's daughter, Jennifer, who was 12. Jennifer's father was very involved, so Sam recognized he'd have a purely supportive role, but still. The thought of Jennifer simply disappearing, never to be seen again, was beyond imagination. Sam could not begin to understand that kind of pain and loss. He reminded himself to hug Jennifer, the next time he saw her. She was young enough to appreciate a hug, but Sam knew that wouldn't last much longer.

Finally, Sam had read enough to grow tired. Tired of reading about that kind of evil in the world. In addition to everything else that was happening in the word, it wasn't the best palliative for insomnia.

Gray was curled on his dog bed beside Sam. His breathing was long and slow. He was in a deep sleep. The sign of a clear conscience. Probably dreaming of whitetail.

It was time to take a lesson from the animals, Sam thought. They didn't think about good or evil. They existed on an entirely different plane, where they paid attention to what they could control and ignored the rest.

Good lesson, Sam thought.

But not one he could abide.

CHAPTER 22

Der waited until midnight. He left home and took a long way on side roads to minimize the chance he would encounter traffic. It was Friday night in the middle of summer and people could be out. Kids. People who might recognize his car.

But he saw no one.

It took him nearly 45 minutes to reach the turnoff for Bright Horizons. He crossed by the drive and drove another 100 yards to a pullout that dead-ended in the trees.

He'd turned into state forest land. Across the road from the Bright Horizons driveway the forest spread from the bluff top down into the valley and beyond. The turnoff was a place for hunters to park before entering the trees. Now the rough road was hidden by midsummer growth, the perfect place for concealing Der's car.

He parked, cut his headlights and the engine, and waited. And listened. Out along the road, he could hear insects in the deep ditch grass, a cacophony of whirring and cutting. He paused long enough to make sure there were no cars. Then he reached into his center console, extracted a pair of white surgical gloves, and pulled them on.

Beneath his car seat, he felt for the Luger. He examined the pistol's safety to make sure it was on. Then he stepped into the dark, tucking the Luger into the space between his belt and the small of his back, blousing out his long-sleeved shirttail to conceal it.

Earlier, he had descended into his Lair. He'd used a gun cloth to wipe his prints off the Luger and seven 9mm bullets that he fit into the clip. If he had to use them, the Luger and shell casings would be clean.

Der walked out to the shoulder and started hiking back to the farm entrance.

He knew Joe Smiley's dairy farm. Four years earlier, he had visited to talk business with the man. He had met Mrs. Smiley. As he walked, he tried to recall her name, but he could not. It was an old name, and she was an old woman, he recalled. Not that it mattered. Soon enough none of it would matter . . . to the Smileys.

Der did not consider himself a murderer. He was a captain of the New Order. He was known to other enthusiasts, World War II collectors like himself. But he was careful to keep his acquaintances at arm's length. None of them knew the extent of his collection or where he lived. But they, like him, believed in purity. The world was filled with impurities, Der knew. There were races all over the world who were trying to dilute civilization with their different genealogies, customs, and beliefs.

As a captain, he did not kill people. He enforced an order he was quite certain would eventually be revealed. The Third Reich had brought it near enough to touch. Der believed we were on the cusp of a fourth empire. It only required soldiers like himself to keep vigil over the flame of truth, justice, and purity.

Twenty-five years earlier, he had not strangled the life out of the young boy. He had protected his heritage and eliminated someone who threatened to overrun it.

It took him less than five minutes to reach the drive entrance. There was a large sign to the left of the gravel, the pasture grass mowed low around it, so it would be visible to people passing by. BRIGHT HORIZONS DAIRY was painted in black, bold letters, set onto a perfectly white backboard. As Der passed it, there was enough ambient starlight to see the letters, to read them and notice the pale background.

Joe Smiley was a neat man, Der thought. That's what he remembered about Smiley's farm. Every item had its place. The small yard was neatly trimmed. A flower garden and vegetable garden sat in front of the house. The house itself was a small two-story with a peaked roof. There was no need for a picket fence, given the nearest neighbor lived more than a mile away. And yet Joe Smiley had fashioned one, with a perfectly hung gate. Within its neat confines was a crew cut lawn that looked like it had been sheared with hand scissors. Below the front windows, a mix of purple petunias and red geraniums sprang out of flower boxes.

Long ago, Joe Smiley had come from Cornwall, England. He still had a slight accent. But the English, Der knew, were in large part responsible for the outcome of WWII. What Der saw when he visited Smiley's dairy farm was the Englishman's effort to emulate the order that characterized the last world war. Now he was going to use it against him.

Dairy farming, Der knew, was a tough business. The successful local farmers, like Joe, worked from before sunup to after sundown, attending to every detail. To Der's way of thinking, they were an OCD bunch. There was always something left undone. Their cows awoke them before dawn. And they kept at it until well after dark. It was part of the reason Der felt certain his plan would work. At this hour, Joe Smiley and his wife would be asleep, knowing they had to rise before first light and tend to their cows.

Thinking about the locals and how they would feel after learning about what Joe Smiley had done, he worried those who knew them would not believe it. But Der knew there would be some who reflected on the clean dairy sign; the long, flat drive; the picket fence; and the boxes of splashed petunias and geraniums. Someone with property as neat and clean as the Smileys, some people would surmise, were hiding something. Something dark and brutal.

For those who might doubt what the Smileys had done, the evidence Der was about to create would be enough to persuade them.

As he approached, he watched the house, and then the barn full of milk cows behind it. Der walked silently to the picket fence.

The evening was in shadows. From what he could see, dimly, the place had not changed in 4 years. Before he stepped over the low fence, he extracted a thin black ski mask out of his front pocket and donned it, positioning the eye holes so he could see. Then he reached behind him and with gloved hands pulled the German Luger out of his waistband.

He planned to use Joe Smiley's gun, not the Luger. Every farmer had one. It would be the logical choice for what Der had planned. The loaded Luger was just in case, and for persuasion.

Der pulled the Luger's striker back. It made a metallic snap in the dark. Der waited to see if anything stirred, but not even the crickets abated. He again made sure the safety was on. If necessary, it would take no more than a millisecond to flip it off and fire.

He stepped over the picket fence and walked up the path to the farmhouse's front door.

Der assumed an old couple like the Smileys, old-school people, would leave their doors unlocked. They lived in Bluff County, with a low crime rate and nothing to fear since the disappearance of the kids. If the door was locked, Der had brought along tools to open it. But when he stepped to the knob and turned, it clicked, ever so lightly.

Der took off his boots. He needed to be careful. He did not want to leave a boot print on the floor, however faint, or a piece of errant gravel from the drive. After the Smileys were found, there would be investigators. Crime scene people. He wanted to make sure what they found here would be obvious.

Once inside, Der took a moment to let his eyes adjust to the interior. The house was small. Across a living and dining area, a small kitchen entryway opened off to the left. Der remembered the kitchen was in the rear left of the house, and the master bedroom in the rear right. Four years earlier, he and Joe sat at the dining room table and talked business, while the missus brought them coffee. Though nothing ever came of it.

A hallway to the right led to the bedrooms, a guest bedroom in front. The bedrooms were separated by a large farm bathroom. In the center of the dining room back wall was a door to a stairway that led to a dormer above—one large room, Der assumed. Though, for a childless couple, he guessed it was used as storage.

At his first step, the wooden floor creaked.

Der paused, listening for movement from the bedroom. He thought he heard something. He listened, his pulse quickening. Then he heard snoring.

Der glided across the rest of the floor as silently as a snake through grass.

There were two windows in the bedroom. The one in the center of the rear wall faced the barn. An overhead barn light was on, Der guessed permanently. The window was open. The insect whirr came into the room. When he followed the ambient light, he saw only one body in bed. Then it snored.

Joe Smiley alone. A problem.

Where was the missus? Maybe the other bedroom, on account of Joe's snoring. Then he heard another snore, lighter, from the front bedroom.

Goddamn it.

Der walked around the bottom of the bed to the other side. He stepped up to Joe's snoring head, pointed the Luger, and poked.

"Hey," he whispered, loud enough to wake the man.

Joe Smiley, startled out of his snore, grunted.

"Whaaat, what?"

"Don't move," Der said, brushing the barrel against the side of his head. Der could see the man was awakening to the presence of a man beside him wearing a black ski mask, holding a gun.

"You need to get your wife in here."

"What, what?"

"I want you to call your wife," Der said, firm. "Everything's going to be fine. I just need a couple things. Then I'll leave. You and your wife will be fine. Call her."

And then, from the front bedroom, the missus stirred.

"Joe," she called, groggy.

"Venita," Joe said. "Come here."

"Joe?" Venita said, awakening herself.

"Come here, Venita. Please. Now."

Venita could hear his urgency. The bed creaked and she shuffled down the short hallway to the master bedroom. As soon as she crossed the bedroom's threshold, she saw Der, masked, standing with the gun, and screamed.

Der came to the foot of the bed, raised the gun and aimed it at Venita's head.

"No, no, no," Joe said. "Don't shoot." He was on his elbows, the covers still over him.

"Venita," Der said. "No one's going to get hurt. If you do what I say. You need to get into bed next to your husband."

"Do what he says, Ven. He's not going to hurt us."

"That's right, Venita. I just need a couple things, and then I'm gone."

Venita crossed the floor, pulled back the covers, and got into bed next to Joe.

"Whatever you need, we'll give it to you," Joe said.

"That's good," Der said, watching them from the foot of the bed. "Got any guns?"

"No," Joe said. "I don't have guns."

"What kind of farmer doesn't have a gun?"

"I just," Joe said. "I've never needed one. Never believed in them."

"How do you kill rats?"

"Poison," Joe said. "Traps."

Another problem. But one he could deal with.

"Got any cash?"

"My wallet," Joe said. "On the dresser."

There was a dresser to the side of the room, near Venita's side of the bed. Der stepped to the dresser, found the wallet, and set down the gun. He opened the wallet and found several twenties, and some miscellaneous bills. He took the wad and made a show of pocketing it.

"That it?" he said.

"That's all," Joe said.

"What about a checkbook. Personal checks?"

"The dining room desk."

"You know where they are?" Der looked at Venita.

She nodded. She was terrified, Der saw. Good.

"Get the checkbook and a pen," Der said to Venita. "If you try to run or do something stupid, you won't see your husband again. And I'll come after you."

"I won't run," she said, in a high whine. Then she got out of bed.

Der moved to the foot of the bed, to let her pass. She was an older woman who moved slowly, slightly bent over. She wore blousy pajamas. She walked into the nearby dining room. Der heard a desk drawer open and, in a moment, she returned with the checkbook and a pen.

"Give them to your husband, and get back into bed," Der said. She did.

"I want you to sign a couple of blank checks for me."

Der assumed the Smileys were smart enough to know they could alert the bank as soon as he left. Der guessed they banked at the Bluff County Community Bank, in Owen's Gap. If they did, they would probably call Hank Stanslow, the president, as soon as they had a chance. But Der didn't care. He needed Joe's signature. And he knew the Smileys would play along, even if they realized the absurdity of his request. Even if they thought they recognized Der's voice and thought they knew him. In a few moments, that wouldn't matter.

He watched Joe Smiley use the ambient light from the barn to sign first one check, pulling it out of the checkbook, and then another. Der came around the bed, keeping the Luger trained on Joe while Joe handed the blank, signed checks to him.

As soon as Der held the checks, he stepped forward and fired one shot, point blank, into Joe's forehead, so the spray from the bullet would hit the wall behind him. The ejected shell flew straight into the air. Before the shell struck the bed, Der turned the Luger on Venita. She had started a scream so piercing and loud it blocked the sound of the Luger's blast. Then her head was knocked sideways, and she tumbled out of the bed onto the floor.

The partial scream, the Luger, and the commotion were clamorous. The window was open. But no one lived near enough to hear the shot or the scream. Neither would anyone driving down the gravel road, though Der hadn't heard anyone. They were alone in rural Bluff County.

But he waited, just to be sure.

The gunshots and scream silenced the insects. After a full two minutes, one or two crickets started up in the dark. And then the rest of them began calling again, just like before.

Der used his iPhone flashlight to examine the scene. He cast his light on the floor next to Joe Smiley's bed. There was the one casing from the bullet he had used on Venita. He found the other casing on the bed. The checkbook was sitting on Joe Smiley's lap, next to a limp hand. Der picked it up and examined it.

All the matter that came out of Joe's head was against the back wall, behind him. The checkbook appeared untouched.

Der returned the checkbook and pen back to the dining room drawer where Venita had retrieved them. Der flashed his light into the open drawer, found the place where the checkbook normally rested—they were an organized couple—and returned it to its place. He held onto the pen.

Back in the bedroom, Der walked to Joe's side of the bed.

Joe Smiley had signed his checks with his right hand. Der took a few moments to insert Joe's hand into the Luger's trigger guard. Once he was ready, Der aimed the Luger up near the ceiling and fired. The Luger made another loud noise but appeared to enter the wall, up near the top, making a small hole. The shell casing ejected straight into the air and landed on the blanketed bed. Der reached down and pocketed the shell.

He flicked on the bedroom light to examine the top corner near the ceiling where the bullet had entered the wall. At first, he couldn't see anything. As he moved closer, carefully, he could see a tiny hole, practically invisible unless you stared up at the cornice. But who would?

He looked back over the room before shutting off the bedroom light.

Perfect, he thought.

He doubted the authorities would notice. Joe's hand would have the telltale gunpowder residue. He set the fired Luger down beside it, in the way it would have fallen had Joe held and aimed the gun, first at his wife, and then himself.

Der unzipped his hunting vest, reached into his inside panel pocket, and pulled out a plastic-covered letter. It was a typewritten confession. Der explained everything the way it had unfolded. Joe had been driving out County Road 8. He had accidentally struck the two kids and killed them. He'd had a few drinks and didn't want to serve time for vehicular manslaughter, so he buried them, near his farm, on property he never thought would be developed. It was a terse confession.

The authorities could fill in the blanks. Joe had killed his wife because he didn't want her to learn about what he had done or live with the knowledge of who he was. Then he killed himself. Given the Smileys and the unregistered weapon and the fact it was a German Luger . . . *hell,* Der thought, *maybe they'd think he was a Nazi sympathizer. Maybe they'd think the man had been a white supremacist and that accounted for why he had the Luger.* There were lots of plausible explanations, and Der felt certain they would conjure one that suited them. And fit the evidence.

It took him a few more minutes to use Joe Smiley's pen and the signed checks to carefully trace his signature onto the paper. Then he traced the indentation in the paper, this time with ink. He'd brought two more copies of the confession just in case the first traced signature hadn't appeared good enough. But when he examined it, closely, comparing it to the signed check, it appeared perfect. Definitely good enough to pass scrutiny.

Then he folded the checks and tucked them in his back pocket. He walked back into the bedroom and returned Smiley's cash to his wallet. The scene was a murder-suicide, not a robbery.

Der backed out the way he'd come, stepping into his boots after closing the front door. He retraced his path down the curved driveway and then along the road. He hugged the edge of the trees in case any cars drove by, so he could conceal himself. But no one ever came.

He got into his car and backed out of the turnoff and was down the road, when he finally smiled. He was pretty sure the hand that fired the Luger had, once again, been guided by providence. In one bold stroke he had eliminated a loose end, given the authorities the identity of the Garcia kids' murderer, and kept his Lair secret and intact.

Der knew the world was a crazy place. But he also felt, with divine intervention, it was only a matter of time before the world was righted and the New Order was returned to the universe.

CHAPTER 23

Saturday

By 7:00 on Saturday morning, Jules was nearing the Alta Vista site. He had a slight headache from too many beers with Gina-the-snake-girl, but he smiled. He liked her. He thought she liked him. Maybe his luck was changing? He had wanted to put the death of the rattlesnake behind him, and he thought Gina had helped him do that. Besides, the no good that came from killing a snake—if he believed what his mother believed (which wasn't always the case)—had been finding the bodies of those kids.

Regardless, in the middle of their third beer, Gina had gone to the bathroom while he'd taken a call from Leslie Warner. She'd spoken with Sam Rivers. For now, and probably until the end of next week, the feds were keeping the site closed. She'd protested, but Sam claimed his hands were tied.

Jules thought he knew why Sam Rivers was keeping the site closed, but he said nothing about what they'd found. He'd been told by the sheriff, Sam, and others not to say anything about the bodies or the grave, at least until the sheriff had time to inform the mother. So, for now, he just listened to what his boss had to say.

Leslie had another development project she was starting, on the other side of Owen's Gap. It, too, required the use of the Bobcat to clear land. She told Jules that if he wanted time and a half, he could trailer their Bobcat to the new site in the morning and get to work.

Time and a half always sounded good to Jules.

"Do what you can tomorrow," Leslie had said. "I'll meet you at the new site Monday morning."

He knew he would explain it all to his boss, when the discovery of the kids became known. But he also knew she needed the new site cleared, so by 7, he turned the corner in the gravel road and approached the throng of vehicles still stationed beside the site. As he approached, he saw three trucks, a county cruiser, and the large white van with Olmstead County Sheriff's Department lettering on its side. Apparently, they had worked through the night.

A nondescript sedan was blocking the front of the Warner Construction flatbed. Jules pulled up and parked in front of the vehicles. Then he stepped out of his truck and walked back to where a deputy leaned against his cruiser. On his way, he glanced over to the trees that stood just outside the northern Alta Vista boundary markers. There were still people in the trees, beginning to dismantle huge LED lights and trailing equipment back to the truck.

"Can I help you?" the deputy said, as Jules approached.

The deputy hadn't been one of those Jules had met the previous night.

"I need to get that trailer and Bobcat," Jules said, pointing to where it sat, hemmed in by the parked cars.

He looked back at the vehicle and said, "Let me figure out who owns that car in front of you, and I'll get them to move it."

"Thank you," Jules said. He returned his gaze to the trees. People were hauling equipment out of the woods. It looked like they were finishing up.

On his return to his company pickup, Jules heard cows. Milk cows. He stopped to listen. He must have missed the sound when he first pulled to the side of the road, intent on getting the trailered Bobcat. The cows sounded like they were stressed. Jules had worked dairy long enough to recognize the agitated lowing of milk cows whose udders were distended because they hadn't been milked.

The distant clamor was coming from where Joe Smiley had told him his dairy farm was located. If it was Smiley's farm, Jules wondered if there was a problem. He didn't know Joe Smiley well, but judging from his demeanor, Jules didn't think he was the kind of farmer who would miss a milking.

The vehicle in front of the trailer pulled away from the shoulder and drove down the road to a new location, pulling over and parking.

Jules hustled back to his truck, backed it up to the trailer hitch, and took five minutes to hook up the trailer and connect the signal lights. Then he pulled away from the shoulder and headed down the road, waving thanks to the deputy.

Joe Smiley had asked Jules to visit. The Smiley farm was on his way to Winona. It was a good time to take the man up on his offer.

Nobody liked the sound of milk cows in pain.

CHAPTER 24

Early Saturday morning, Sam Rivers had just driven up to the Alta Vista site to check on progress when a call came in.

"Mr. Rivers," the man said.

"Jules?" Sam said.

"I am at Joe Smiley's farm," he blurted, in a coarse whine. "Something terrible has happened."

Jules told him about hearing the cows, then knocking at Joe Smiley's door. When there was no answer, he entered the house and found them. Both dead. Shot.

"Call 9-1-1," Sam said.

There was a pause.

Then, "Yes," Jules said.

"I'm three minutes away," Sam said. "Call 9-1-1 as soon as you hang up and don't touch anything. I'm on my way."

After Sam pulled into Smiley's drive and got out of his Jeep, the first thing he noticed was the clamor of lowing cows.

Jules was leaning near his truck, looking pale and afraid.

"Did you call 9-1-1?" Sam said.

"Yes."

"What's with the cows?" Sam said.

"They haven't been milked. It's why I came. I heard them and thought something was wrong. I knocked on Mr. Smiley's door and when no one answered I was worried. I went in. I called, but they didn't answer. And then I found them."

Sam had overheard Jules speaking with Joe Smiley about working at his dairy. And he could tell, from Jules's face and his hesitation to call 9-1-1, that he was nervous. He needed a distraction. Sam also wanted to assuage the clamor coming out of the barn.

"Can you do anything about those cows? Can you help them?"

"But you said not to touch anything," Jules said.

"I'll wait for the responders," Sam said. "I can talk to them. You didn't touch anything in the house, did you?"

"No. I saw them. And left. It was . . . horrible."

"Then you called me?"

"When I got outside. Then 9-1-1."

"For now, just do what you can with those cows. They sound like they're in pain."

Jules nodded once, quick. Then he turned and started walking toward the barn.

In the distance, Sam heard a siren. Rather than go in and disturb another crime scene, Sam figured the siren was near enough to wait. In a couple of minutes, the siren grew near, then stopped, and then Sam watched flashing cruiser lights enter the farm drive.

It was the sheriff and chief deputy again.

"What the fuck?" Sheriff Conrad said.

"I don't know," Sam said. "I haven't been inside yet. I just got here. Were you up at Alta Vista?"

"Headed that way when we got the call," the sheriff said. "What's with the cows?"

"I guess they missed a milking and they're not happy about it," Sam said. "Jules, who heard them and decided to check on it—he's the one who found the farmer. He's seeing if he can help."

"Vince and I were going to talk to Peggy Landrau," the sheriff said. "Now that she's finished. Never got a chance." She looked at the house, and said, "You follow me, Vince. Sam, you can come in behind. You know the drill. Don't touch anything and be careful where you walk."

At the front door they took off their shoes and boots. The sheriff used a hanky to turn the front doorknob. The door was unlocked. She pushed it open. Then the three of them entered the house, carefully, in single file.

It was a small house, and the front living room opened into a rear dining room—probably the largest overall room in the house. And the place was neat, clean, orderly. No dust. Nothing amiss.

There was a door in the back center of a living room and dining room. Probably to an upstairs dormer, Sam guessed. A room to the left led to a rear kitchen. And if Sam had to guess, the entry to the right led to a bathroom and two bedrooms, the master probably in back.

The deathly stillness in the house felt eerie.

They found the farmer and his wife in the master.

"God," the sheriff said. "Joe and Venita Smiley."

Mrs. Smiley was lying on the floor in a pool of nearly dried blood, most of it spread beneath her head and shoulders. Her head was turned to the side, facing the wall. A bullet hole had torn into her face and, Sam guessed, knocked her out of bed.

Joe Smiley's face didn't look much better. He was sitting in the bed, but the back of the wall was covered in blood and his forehead was misshapen from the bullet. A Luger pistol rested near Joe's right hand. There was a shell casing beside it.

The sheriff glanced at the floor on Joe's side of the bed, and said, "Another casing over here."

At the foot of the bed was a piece of paper with writing on it.

Sam, happy to have something to divert his eyes, peered at the typewritten note, without touching it. He bent over to read.

"I killed the Garcia kids. I was drinking and went down County Road 8 and hit them. I couldn't see them because of the sun. When I saw what happened I figured I would go to prison. I buried them where I thought they would never be found.

I am sorry. Please forgive me."

Beneath the note was Joe Smiley's signature.

"Murder-suicide?" Sam said.

Sheriff Conrad nodded. So did Chief Deputy Vince Baker, who read the brief note and said, "I'll be damned. I've known Joe since forever. Never saw this coming. Never would have believed it."

"Me neither," the sheriff said. "This guy was about as squeaky clean as you can get."

Sam thought about it. "You'll have the crime scene guys check it out?"

The sheriff nodded. "Of course." Then she sensed something in Sam's face. "You see something?"

Sam shrugged. "Prudent, is all. Odd someone who was going to do this would type a note."

The sheriff thought about it. "I guess."

"That looks like an older pistol," Sam said. "A German P-08 Luger. It's an odd weapon to have. It's not for hunting or shooting rodents, typically. It's more of a collector's item. You ever heard Joe Smiley talk about it?"

Both of them shook their heads no. "But it's not unusual to have an old pistol hanging around a farm," the chief deputy said. "I'd be surprised if we didn't find some others."

Sam shrugged again. "And it's an odd wound," Sam said. "Shooting yourself in the forehead."

They all thought about it.

"I don't know," Sam said. "There are probably statistics on it. But I suspect most suicides shoot themselves in the side of the head. Or put the gun in their mouth or under their chin."

"Not that you're thinking clearly when you do it," the sheriff said.

Sam agreed.

"But shooting yourself in the forehead is . . . awkward," Sam said. "And Mrs. Smiley was shot in the face. I'm assuming, given she fell out of bed, she must have been awake and sitting up, or getting up, when she was shot. If she'd been shot sleeping, she'd be shot in the side of the head and wouldn't have fallen. Hard for me to imagine a guy who had been married for as long as these two could shoot his wife point-blank in the face when she was looking at him."

"That many years is plenty of time to develop some marital baggage," the sheriff said.

Sam knew it was true, but he said, "Or come to terms with it. The long-marrieds I've known usually seem like they've found some kind of grace. They've figured it out."

They backed out the way they'd come, without touching anything. Sam walked to the end of the hallway and saw the other bed, apparently slept in.

"Odd," Sam said.

The sheriff and the chief looked in and wondered about it.

"Maybe he was snoring," the sheriff said.

"She went here and then went back to bed when he stopped?" the chief said.

"Maybe," the sheriff shrugged.

Once outside, Sam heard Sheriff Conrad call Peggy Landrau and explain they needed her.

"When it rains, it pours," the sheriff said.

Sam was standing near enough to hear Peggy Landrau say, "Fuckin'-A."

Jules had apparently settled the cows, who had gradually, one by one, ceased lowing in pain. They were still making sounds, but their clamor had died down.

Sam walked back to the barn and opened the door.

Sam didn't know dairy operations, but this one appeared state-of-the-art. Approximately 20 cows were all in small stanchions, 10 on either side. He could see Jules bending on the other side of the barn. He disappeared behind a cow at the end of the line.

The cows had quieted because they had automatic milking devices affixed to their udders. The devices flowed down to a central holding tank. Jules appeared to be working on the last cow. The milking mechanism was now almost louder than the cows. Some of the cows were still lowing, but it was a less agitated sound.

After finishing his work with the last cow, Jules came around to where Sam stood just inside the door's threshold.

"You know this stuff?" Sam said.

"I worked on this kind of operation in Texas," Jules said. "I am so sorry to see Mr. and Mrs. Smiley. Yesterday, he asked me to visit."

Sam remembered.

Jules's face blanched and he looked away. Taking care of the cows had preoccupied him, but now he was remembering the bedroom scene. The bloody chaos.

"He was such a nice man," Jules said.

"I never spoke with him, but the sheriff and chief deputy agree. It wasn't the kind of thing either of them could imagine. Out of Joe Smiley."

The two men stood in silence for a few moments. Outside, Sam heard the arrival of a truck. He glanced out to see the crime scene truck pull up, followed by two cars. The sheriff and chief deputy stepped over to meet them.

"They'll want to speak with you," Sam said.

Jules looked concerned.

They heard voices outside and Sam knew in moments they'd be re-entering the farmhouse.

"It's just routine," Sam said. "Tell them what happened. And it would help if you could mind the cows, at least until we figure out some alternative."

Jules nodded. "Of course."

Sam remembered Jules had called him instead of 9-1-1, and he now seemed to be concerned about the sheriff and chief deputy. But maybe it was just because he was a foreigner—at least by accent—and the presence of an outsider in a place like Owen's Gap might be automatically suspect. And he was the first one on the scene.

It occurred to Sam that Jules might be undocumented. But that wasn't a fair assumption, Sam knew. Besides, Leslie Warner didn't strike him as the kind who would hire undocumented workers. He'd ask her, just to be sure.

Regardless of the young man's work status, what Sam sensed from Jules was goodness. He was earnest, and from working with him the last three days, Sam could see he was an attentive, hard worker. Moreover, he was good with snakes. Or at least fast in catching them, and comfortable holding them.

Jules said he'd wait until the cows were emptied, and then he'd pull and clean the milking devices. Smiley's holding tank appeared to be refrigerated. It was a clean, well-ordered operation.

A few pairs of work boots were set inside the barn door, neatly placed on a mat. Sam guessed Joe Smiley walked to the barn each morning, stepped out of his normal footwear, and donned the boots to work in the barn. The place had that kind of orderliness, cleanliness.

He glanced through the barn's threshold and saw six people: Peggy Landrau, the sheriff, chief deputy, and three techs. Peggy's crew was still dressed in the sterile outfits they'd worn when sifting through the graves. Or they'd taken time to don new ones. Sam watched as everyone in front of the door pulled on disposable, sterile shoe coverings. Then they stepped into the house in single file.

Sam thanked Jules for helping out with the cows. He also told him not to speak of this to anyone. At least until it was public. Sam would call Leslie Warner, Jules's boss, after he was sure Ginny Dickinson had been informed. Sam would bring Leslie up to date. On the kids and on this.

CHAPTER 25

After Sheriff Conrad and the chief deputy led Peggy and her crew through the house into the rear bedroom, Peggy thanked the sheriff and told her they could take it from here. With Peggy's whole team working, she didn't think the analysis would take too long, given the nature of what she was seeing. If the sheriff wanted to stick around, that'd be good.

"While you're waiting," Peggy said, "You might call the medical examiner."

"Was she up at the grave site?"

"About 3:00 this morning, after the mom saw the kids."

The sheriff had called Ginny Dickinson-Garcia at around midnight. When she told Ginny why she was calling, Ginny said, "I'm coming," quietly.

"You don't need to," the sheriff said. "It's been 25 years, Ginny. We can ID them from DNA."

"No," she said, firm. "I want to see them."

By the time Ginny arrived, Peggy's crew had unearthed the two kids. They had laid them off to the side in a pair of zippered body bags. The techs were still searching around the site for anything they could find. Ginny arrived at around 1 a.m. The sheriff led her to the grave site, though its location was obvious from the LED lights trained on the clearing inside the trees.

The sheriff introduced her to Peggy Landrau.

"You don't need to do this," Peggy said. "I think the sheriff might have told you, we can ID them from DNA analysis."

"I want to see them."

Peggy had been through this kind of thing before. Never with children who had been buried for 25 years. But with other victims. Regardless of how gruesome, the next of kin—in this case, a mother—needed to see. Peggy understood.

The sheriff led Ginny to the edge of the grave and nodded, waiting for Peggy to unzip the bags. Peggy did, first revealing the desiccated skulls. They were hideous, Peggy knew. Ginny looked on in silence. When the bags were completely opened, Ginny could see their tattered clothing, twisted legs, and old skates. The mother focused on the skates. One pair of skates was black and smaller. The legs fitting into the white skates were horribly twisted and broken.

When she saw the clothes and skates, she said, "That's them." It came out of her in a whisper. The tears welled, and then she sobbed, moving a crumpled hand to her mouth, as though she might catch the hiccup that came out of her. "Their skates," she managed, in a crying whine. "And clothes. The ones they were wearing . . ."

Ginny Dickinson-Garcia turned away, having seen enough. Broken by it. She would never be the same because of it. You cannot unsee something like that. But she knew she had to see them. And now she knew she would never forget.

The sheriff accompanied Ginny back to the road and then to her car. The sheriff couldn't imagine how a mother could look at the illicit grave site of her vanished children after 25 years and survive seeing its grisly remnants. But what else could she do? *What else would any of us do?* the sheriff thought.

Back at Joe and Venita Smiley's farmhouse, Sam Rivers hung around long enough to speak with the sheriff, and to see if he could assist.

Once outside, the sheriff nodded to Sam and said, "Let me call the medical examiner."

Sam nodded and waited while the sheriff contacted the medical examiner and explained where she was and that her presence was needed, again.

Sam heard some kind of exclamation, and then the sheriff said, "I know. I know. But if you can be out here by," she looked at her watch. It was only 8 a.m. "By 9:00 or so, that'd be good." Then she hung up.

"Can I do anything?" Sam said.

"I don't think so," the sheriff said. "If you've got the time, you can wait with me and see what Peggy finds. Maybe she needs help with something." The sheriff shrugged.

"Sure," Sam said. "Tell me how it went last night."

The sheriff told Sam she'd hung around until well after midnight, until after Ginny Dickinson's visit.

"How did that go?" Sam said.

"About as fucked up as you can imagine," the sheriff said. She grew quiet and added, "Poor woman."

"Did she recognize anything?" Sam had to ask.

Peggy nodded. "The clothing and skates. The bodies were too decomposed to tell what they were, other than bodies. Of kids."

Sam couldn't imagine it.

"They'll confirm with DNA?" Sam said.

The sheriff nodded. "But at this point it's routine."

After nearly an hour, two crime scene techs walked out of the house. They were followed by Peggy Landrau, who paused at the door's threshold and said, "Got a minute?" to the sheriff.

"Sure." Then she looked at Sam and said, "Come on."

Sam followed her to the door, and Peggy stepped back while they covered their footwear with disposable booties.

"I just wanted to show you something," Peggy said to the sheriff.

"Sure." She turned and nodded to Sam. "Three heads are better than two."

Peggy nodded and walked into the house. The two bodies had been bagged and moved into the living room. The sheriff and Sam followed into the rear bedroom.

The German Luger was bagged and lying on the bed. The two shell casings were bagged separately, next to the Luger.

"This farmer's prints were on the gun," Peggy said. "And we checked his right hand for gunpowder residue and found it. He was the shooter. Or at least he shot the gun."

"Okay," the sheriff said.

"But I've been working this job for nearly 30 years. I've seen lots of self-inflicted gunshot wounds. In fact, I'd say that's the number one death scene I've worked on over the years. Suicide. I don't remember ever seeing anyone who shot themselves in the forehead."

"Sam said the same thing," the sheriff said.

"Couple other things," Peggy said. "This Luger has a clip. We checked the clip and the casings. Both the spent ones and the ones in the clip. None of them had prints."

"Odd," Sam said.

"You think they should have had Joe's?" the sheriff asked.

"Sure. Why not? Also, the clip. The Luger's been well oiled. It's been well taken care of. Not surprising, given how the rest of this house and the farm appears. But I'm surprised we didn't find any prints on any of that stuff."

"Maybe he'd just cleaned it," Sam said.

"Maybe. But he still would have left prints, handling the bullets and the clip. Especially given what he planned to do with it. Why would you wipe clean the clips and bullets if you intended on killing your wife and yourself?"

The sheriff shrugged. "Joe Smiley was a neatnik. Maybe he did it out of habit? Or maybe it had been loaded for a while, before the kids were found?"

Maybe, they all thought. But it was odd.

"Also, a Luger clip like this one typically holds seven shells," Peggy said. "Joe Smiley is the kind of guy who would fill the clip. But there were only six shells in the clip. Two fired and four left in the clip."

"Maybe he fired one to make sure it worked," the sheriff said.

Peggy shrugged. "Maybe. But we didn't find it."

"Also, the missus didn't appear to be killed as she slept."

"Maybe he woke her up," the sheriff said.

"Maybe. But think about it. They been married probably forever. He wakes his wife, she sits up, and he shoots her in the face?"

Sam agreed it didn't make sense. And then he thought of something, a way he could get Gray involved. Gray's nose.

When he proposed it, Peggy Landrau shrugged and said, "Couldn't hurt."

Dr. Marilyn Couch, the Bluff County medical examiner, arrived as Sam went out to get Gray from the back seat of his Jeep.

The sheriff introduced Dr. Couch to Sam. She was an older woman with a head of thick gray hair, no makeup, and wrinkles around the eyes and mouth. She had a professional demeanor Sam appreciated.

With the help of the two crime scene techs, the Smileys were put onto gurneys and transported to the medical examiner's van. Once the house was cleared, at least of bodies, Sam brought in Gray.

First, Sam lifted the bagged Luger from the bed. Then he carefully unsealed the plastic and let Gray smell the gun. Then he repeated the same process with the two spent shells.

"Find, Gray. Find."

At the familiar command, Gray perked up and his tail wagged. He began nosing around the room. First, he went to Joe's side of the bed and sniffed the floor where one of the casings had fallen.

"Good boy," Sam said, stroking Gray's head. "Keep looking. Find."

Gray's head pivoted, his nose in the air. He waved it the way a surgeon might wield a scalpel, skillfully. Sam knew Gray's nose was one of the finest, most sensitive tools on the planet—at least for locating objects by scent.

Gray paced around the bed. Sam, the sheriff, and Peggy made room for him. He went to the other side of the bed. He smelled the blood, skirted it, and then in the corner he lifted his front paws to the wall and stretched. His head arched up so he could get his nose high into the air. Stretching higher than 6 feet, given Gray's size. Clearly, Gray was interested in something up the side of the wall, higher than he could reach by stretching on two legs.

They watched as Gray came down, circled, and then repeated his trick with the hind legs, trying to get higher.

Sam was behind him with the leash. He looked up to where Gray's nose was pointing and said, "I think I see a hole up there."

Peggy Landrau came around and joined them, careful to keep from stepping in the blood. She looked.

"I think you're right," she said. "Back him off, would you? I'm going to get one of my guys to come in and have a closer look."

Sam and Gray and the sheriff stepped out of the house, and one of Peggy's younger techs came into the house to replace them, carrying a step ladder.

It took another 10 minutes, but Peggy came out holding a baggy with something inside it. Something small.

"Luger slug," she said. "Looks like it anyway. We'll do the ballistics, but judging by your dog's nose, it must have been fired from the Luger."

"Odd," Sam said, again. "If that was fired last night, where's the shell casing?"

"I got a theory, but before I get to it, I wanted to share something else with you."

She let the sheriff and Sam examine the slug. Neither of them had ever seen a Luger slug, so they had no reason to think it was anything other than what it was.

Peggy also held the plastic-enclosed confession. She waved it and said, "Here's the thing: My guys found some signatures on some documents in that living room desk. The signatures are definitely a match. But my tech examined it using a magnifier. If you look at the signature closely, there are a few places where the ink, from the pen, slips out of the signature groove on the paper."

"Signature groove?"

"The groove left when the pen pushes on the paper. You can see on the bottom of this paper, if you look closely, that the paper has been indented by the man's signature. Any writing instrument would do it if you pressed hard enough."

"So maybe he pressed hard?" the sheriff said.

"Could be. Could also be somebody traced his signature to make the indentation and then traced the groove with ink. That would account for why some of the ink appeared to be outside the traced signature grooves."

Sam looked at the signature up close but couldn't see anything.

"Gotta use a magnifier," Peggy said.

Sam nodded. Again, he had no reason to doubt her, or the tech's observation.

"Did you guys find the printer this came from?" Sam asked.

"That's the other thing. We did not."

"So maybe he printed it elsewhere?"

"Or maybe it was printed elsewhere by whoever forged his signature," Peggy said. "If it was forged."

The techs had made a cursory search of the farmhouse but found no additional weapons. While Peggy was showing the anomalies to the sheriff and Sam, the techs searched the barn. Jules helped in the search, but they found nothing.

The medical examiner had already left with the bodies by the time Sam spoke with Peggy about the absence of any weapons. No other pistols and no hunting rifles or shotguns.

"You had a theory?" Sam said to Peggy.

"It was murder," she said.

"The man murdered his wife," the sheriff said.

Sam thought he understood. "They were both murdered," he said.

Peggy nodded. "I don't think it was a murder-suicide."

Sam and the sheriff paused. They weren't sure what to think about it. The evidence for the murder was pretty thin, but . . .

"Joe's hand tested positive for gunpowder residue?" Sam said, to be sure.

Peggy nodded again. "That part could have been staged by firing that bullet we found near the ceiling."

To just about anyone other than a crime scene tech, it looked like a murder-suicide. But from another perspective, it made sense. If someone else was behind the death of the kids, nearby Joe Smiley was a convenient fall guy. He and his wife.

They needed more evidence, more information.

Sam suggested people who knew the Smileys. They needed to speak with others who knew them better than the sheriff or the chief deputy. People who might know if Joe had ever hunted, had any guns, or maybe find someone who had seen Joe Smiley's German Luger. Sam suggested Mel, the newspaper publisher. He told the sheriff he could head into town and ask the reporter about Joe Smiley and who knew him best. Small-town papers, Sam knew, were in the business of knowing the community and its citizens. If anyone knew about Joe's friends, he suspected it was the local newspaper publisher.

"What can I say about what's happened here?" Sam said to the sheriff.

"I think he had a brother in Wisconsin," the chief said. "He's also a dairy farmer. I remember seeing the two of them in town. They looked like brothers."

The sheriff thought for a minute, wondering how she could track him down. Then she thought of something.

"Venita . . . Mrs. Smiley. I know she was active in a quilting group. I know some of those women in the group. I bet one of them knows where to find the brother. Let me make a few calls. I should let the brother know before you announce anything. I'd like to speak to him anyway. You can't say anything until we notify next of kin. I'll get back to you."

"Let me know as soon as you've talked to him," Sam said. "I can't go to the publisher and ask about Smiley's friends without telling her why."

The sheriff nodded. "After we notify the brother, what are you going to say to Mel?"

"That there was an accident out at Joe Smiley's and they're dead. But it's under investigation. That she'll need to speak to you for a statement."

"That'll work," the sheriff said.

CHAPTER 26

It was a 15-minute drive from the Smiley farm to Owen's Gap. The moment Sam passed the town's sign—good eggs and a few stinkers—the sheriff called.

"Yeah," Sam said.

"News travels fast. Got a call from Mel Harken right after you left."

"She was asking about the kid's graves?"

"That's right. And now that Ginny's been notified, she has a right."

Sam thought about it. "Okay."

"I gave her a brief statement. But I told her you were stopping by and could give her more details."

The press could be useful, Sam knew. "Okay." He was surprised the sheriff was asking him to share the details, given she was a pretty good politician who undoubtedly recognized an opportunity to be quoted, for publicity.

"I'm up to my armpits in paper over the shit that's hit the fan the last few days," the sheriff said. "You'd be doing me a favor."

Sam was wary. "Okay," he said.

"Got a call coming in. I think this might be Joe Smiley's brother. Let me get back to you."

Sam hung up. He continued driving into the center of Owen's Gap. Earlier, he'd familiarized himself with the town center. In addition to the café, there was a hardware store, the *Gazette*, a small clothing shop, a knickknack shop, the post office, a coffee shop/bookstore, and a handful of other establishments. The streetlight poles were old and looked like something out of a Currier and Ives painting, with ornate frosted-glass fixtures. The parking was angled on both sides of the uber-wide street.

There was a small-town park near the main street. Sam pulled in, parked, and got Gray out to give him some water and let him walk around.

Then Sam's cell phone rang. He figured it was the sheriff, but when he looked, he saw a 319 area code. Iowa?

"Rivers," he answered.

"Agent Rivers?"

"That's right. Barry?" Sam said, thinking he recognized the man's high voice.

"Yes. You said to call."

Much had happened since speaking with Barry the previous evening. They'd found another rattlesnake and the Garcia kids and then this morning with the Smileys. He knew he needed to get those snakes back to Barry, and he'd been hoping to do it today, but now he didn't know.

"I think we found another one of your EMRs," Sam said.

"I heard. Last night. That's part of the reason I'm calling. When Gina told me, I was surprised. That one was caught on the edge of Sweet Marsh. I let it go last fall."

"Any ideas who might have caught it?"

"That was the other reason for my call."

"You have a name?"

"I do. But I didn't think of it. After your call I was racking my brain trying to figure out who could have stolen an EMR from the lab, and the others. I wasn't coming up with anyone, so I called our local conservation officer, Rich King. Do you know Rich?"

Sam didn't.

"I remembered what you said about stealing an EMR for money. Rich knows the area and would know people who would do that kind of thing."

"Good idea," Sam said. "Rich had a name?"

"Adder Musgrave," Barry said.

Sam repeated the name. He was leaning against his Jeep, keeping an eye on Gray. He turned around, opened the Jeep's door, and rummaged through the center console for a pen and paper.

"I know the guy," Barry said.

Sam wrote down the name, verifying the spelling.

"He's ... different," Barry continued. "He lives near the Sweet Marsh. Pretty remote, and the guy lives more or less off the grid, I'd say. Rich thought of him almost immediately because he's got a record. Of game violations, poaching, and theft."

Sam asked for an address, and Barry told him it was a hard place to find. If Sam wanted to speak with him, Barry could take him out there.

Sam thought about it. If Adder Musgrave was the source of the stolen massasaugas, Sam definitely wanted to speak with him. Sam knew the man wouldn't confess to crimes—especially the theft of endangered species and breaking and entering—if he was behind the theft of the snake from Barry's lab. But he also knew that if he and another law enforcement officer went out to speak with the guy, they could be intimidating. Not that they'd make him confess but, given his reaction, they might be able to determine if he was the thief. Because if this guy had acquired the snakes for money, he'd done it for someone—the person who was trying to stop the development, Sam guessed. The person who must have murdered the Garcia kids. And maybe the Smileys.

Sam asked Barry for CO Rich King's phone number. He verified McCutcheon, where Barry's lab was located, near the Sweet Marsh, was about 2 hours southwest from Owen's Gap.

"I'm going to call CO King and see if he can meet me this afternoon. Can you meet us and take us to this guy's cabin? I can bring your snakes with me."

"Yes, that'd be good," Barry said, about the return of his snakes. "I'm sure Rich knows how to get there. But sure, I could come along too."

Sam figured three was more intimidating than two.

"Do you want me to call Rich?" Barry said.

"That'd be good. I'm thinking we could meet down there around 3:00. That work?"

Barry told him it would. He gave Sam the address for his lab in McCutcheon.

When Sam got off the phone, he called out to Gray and got him back into the Jeep.

Then his phone rang. The sheriff again.

"Yeah," Sam said.

"Did you know Joe Smiley was raised a Quaker?" the sheriff said.

"Until a couple days ago, I'd never met Joe Smiley."

"Oh, yeah," the sheriff said. "Well, he was. And his brother tells me there is no way Joe Smiley killed Venita and then himself. First of all, he didn't own any guns. He wasn't a practicing Quaker, but he still kept the faith. They're pacifists. Quakers don't believe in war. They don't believe in guns. They're conscientious objectors."

Sam remembered it. "Did you tell him about the gun? A Luger?"

"No way in hell he was a gun collector," the sheriff said. "And no way in hell he would have shot Venita. He loved Venita."

"Did you tell him about the confession?"

"I did. He said it was bullshit. First, his brother has always been a teetotaler. Had been even back then, when the kids disappeared. Second, if he'd hit the kids, he would have gone straight to the authorities."

"Then the brother thinks it was murder," Sam said.

"Seems like it. And we got motive. But who did it?"

"You want me to tell the reporter we think it was a murder?"

"No," she said. "Just tell her the truth, but keep it to them having been shot and the incident is still under investigation."

"But there's no reason for the public to be afraid?" Sam said.

The sheriff thought about it. "I don't really know that. Just," she said, pausing. "Just don't go there. If she asks, the incident is still under investigation."

"The reporter's gonna ask," Sam said.

"Probably. Hell, it's Mel Harken. She'll ask. She'll want to know as much as she possibly can about the whole thing. And she's damn good at what she does, so be careful. Just stonewall her."

"'The incident is being investigated.'"

"That's it. She doesn't need to know anything else." Then, "You know, Sam, it wouldn't hurt to remind her the local sheriff has been bird-dogging the Garcia kids for 25 years, and though it sometimes takes a long time to get results, this sheriff has a 100% closure rate on county murders."

Whenever officials began referring to themselves in the third person, Sam heard political spin designed to benefit the official.

"The Smiley murders notwithstanding," Sam said.

Another pause. "That just happened," she said. "Again, if Mel asks, we don't know. Was it a murder? Or murder-suicide? All she needs to know is they died from gunshot wounds."

Sam understood, but he couldn't help but smile.

"What do you think of Mel mentioning the German Luger in the story?" Sam said.

"Why?"

"It's an odd gun to have," Sam said. "And it appeared well cared for. It might have been a collector's item. If it was murder and the guy who pulled the trigger is a collector, maybe he liked to show off his collection?"

"Or she," the sheriff said.

"I mean, 98% of murders are perpetrated by men," Sam said.

"But we don't know for sure."

"True enough," Sam said. "But it's probably a similar statistic on gun collections. Men are the collectors. We should get Mel to mention the Luger."

"Okay," the sheriff. "But Mel doesn't need to know why we're mentioning the Luger."

"You mean, be subtle about it?"

"That's right," the sheriff said.

Sam could be subtle. But it didn't come naturally.

Sam told her about the rattlesnakes being from Iowa and that he was going to speak with a guy this afternoon who might have been involved with acquiring them. The sheriff sounded interested and told him to keep her informed.

Sam walked into the *Gazette* offices in the center of Owen's Gap and greeted Mel Harken, the *Gazette's* publisher and main reporter.

Mel might have been older, but she moved with the fluidity of a young person. Maybe she was a yogi, Sam wondered. She wore khaki pants and a work shirt and had a pair of glasses hung round her neck. But her eyes were gray, clear, and intense.

"Sam Rivers," she said. "I've been doing research about you."

"I hope it wasn't all bad."

"I'd say the majority of it was good. But the only opinion that really matters around here is mine."

Sam smiled. Mel didn't.

"I want to know about those rattlesnakes and the grave site."

"Okay," Sam said. "The sheriff is really the one you should speak with. But I can give you some background."

"The sheriff told me she doesn't know squat about rattlesnakes and that I should talk to you."

Sam guessed that was true enough. "Sure," he said. "We found another eastern massasauga rattlesnake," Sam said.

"Up on the Alta Vista development site?" Mel said. "Alive?"

Sam nodded. And then he told her what he knew. He left out the provenance of the rattlesnakes, that they were from Iowa. That part of what they'd found was still under investigation.

"I understand you're keeping the site closed down?"

"That's right. At least for a couple more days. No more than a week."

"Because of the graves?"

"The graves aren't actually on the property. It's because of the rattlesnakes. The site will remain closed until we can do one more survey. I think we've found all the snakes, but I just want to be sure."

All of the preceding was really background for the main focus of her article; the discovery of the Garcia kids. It took the better part of an hour to go over all the details Sam knew, or at least the ones he was able to share. During that time, Sam referenced how the county was lucky to have a sheriff who had been around long enough to remember the event, and who had kept it open and continued to investigate, even though leads had dried up years ago.

When Sam spoke of Sheriff Betsy Conrad, Mel Harken paused in her note-taking. Sam couldn't be sure, but he thought she recognized the comment was political pandering on behalf of the sheriff, and it probably wouldn't make it into whatever she wrote. *Fair enough,* Sam thought. *And accurate.*

Then Sam explained how Gray had found them. He explained about the sheriff, crime scene techs, and the mother's post-midnight visit to examine the graves, but that she would need to speak with the sheriff about those details, since Sam wasn't there. When she asked if Sam thought the rattlesnakes and kids were somehow related, Sam shrugged.

"Don't know. We're still investigating."

"Can you say, 'maybe'?"

Sam shook his head no. "But I do have something else to share with you."

Of course, she was interested but suspicious. Mel Harken had always found law enforcement cagey. Usually, they didn't tell you anything you didn't already know. And Sam Rivers seemed like one of those officers who was both cagey and adept. Most law enforcement people hated sharing information and hated to go on record. Not Sam Rivers. But he also seemed like the type who would only tell her what he wanted her to know.

"Okay, shoot," she said. It was an unfortunate use of words, under the circumstances.

When she heard about the Smileys, she was shocked. She, of course, knew them, though not well. But she was clearly shaken by the news. At least as much as a hard-edged publisher/reporter could be.

Sam told her what he could about the Smileys and what had happened at their farm. That took another few minutes. Again, Sam was sharing some details about the Smileys, but only what he wanted her to know. For more details, he reminded the reporter, she needed to speak with the sheriff.

The one detail he was careful to insert, in passing, as though it was an afterthought, was the Luger. It was in the middle of a sentence discussing the weapon they'd found, but Sam was nonchalant about it. Still, Mel Harken didn't miss much.

"German Luger?" she said.

"Looks like it. Yes," Sam said. "An old one."

"You mean, like, from World War II?"

Sam nodded. "I guess."

"Don't you think that's important?"

Sam shrugged. "Maybe. Maybe Joe Smiley was a collector."

"Phhhtt," Mel said, doubting Sam's observation. "Joe and Venita were good people. This is a tragedy. Small-town papers can't have friends. We publishers can't be cozying up to people we might have to write about, at some point."

She looked away. Cleary, she was upset by the Smileys.

"But I never had to write about the Smileys. They were just good people. Good, hard-working people. You may not be calling this a murder. But dimes to doughnuts, that's what it is," she said.

Sam reminded her that what happened at the Smileys was still under investigation.

Mel Harken acknowledged the official line, but she had no doubt it was murder.

CHAPTER 27

The Gap Café was a few doors down from the *Gazette* offices. The café had commandeered three or four diagonal parking spaces in front and set up tables with umbrellas, providing customers with a serviceable place to eat outside. Sam was thinking about breakfast, glanced in the café's direction, and noticed Gina sitting at one of the outdoor tables. When she saw Sam, she waved him over.

They greeted each other; Sam asked about the food, and she shrugged, "Pretty good. Hard to screw up eggs, bacon, and hashbrowns."

Sam agreed.

She was finished with breakfast but still sipping coffee.

"I'm headed to Iowa later today," Sam said. "I should return those rattlesnakes to Barry."

Gina told him they were in her car, in the shade, safe and quiet. "Do you need the dead one?"

"Yes. We should return all of them."

The waitress came, refilled Gina's cup, and Sam ordered.

Sam mentioned how it had been quite a scene last night and that he appreciated her help with the rattlesnakes. Her and Jules.

"He's an interesting guy," Gina said.

"You go out for drinks?"

"We did. Sweeney's," she pointed to a bar down the street. "Closed it down."

When she smiled, Sam said, "I guess that accounts for the late breakfast."

"I guess," she said, still smiling. "Jules had some interesting comments about it all."

"What we found last night?"

"First, we couldn't imagine being the mother of those kids. Jules is close to his mom, and he got a little misty-eyed thinking about his mom having to go through it."

Sam agreed. It was hard to imagine. Impossible, really.

"But he was also talking about the rattlesnakes. He thinks the rattlesnakes were a bluff."

"You mean, a bluff like in poker?"

Gina nodded. "He thinks they were designed to make Leslie Warner fold on the site."

Sam thought about it. "I don't know if I'd put it that way. But I think he's onto something."

"He had some other pretty interesting ideas. You remember us talking about that Mayan myth?"

"Kukulkan?"

"Yes. The serpent god."

Sam remembered. Gina reminded him about Kukulkan living below the earth and being in touch with both the living and the dead. Jules had also told Sam about his mom's belief that killing a snake was a bad omen. She'd been right, if you considered the discovery of the Garcia kids an omen. One of Kukulkan's servants, the rattlesnake, led them to the place where the Garcia kids were buried.

"I can see how that sort of mystical logic works," Sam said.

"I've always believed snakes were sacred," Gina said. "It doesn't take much of a leap for me to believe this one led us to those kids."

"I believe all nature is sacred," Sam said. "But I think it was more likely this rattlesnake was searching for a place to den. We know they prefer dark holes."

"But you can see how people like Jules's mom might think Kukulkan had a hand in it, given what we found."

"There's definitely something to Mayan wisdom," Sam said. "Especially about nature. That's true with a lot of native peoples, who were close to the earth and its creatures."

"I wrote a term paper about native cultural snake beliefs," Gina said. "Some considered snakes to be a symbol of resurrection, or renewal, because snakes periodically shed their skin. They represent new beginnings, a path to healing. Now maybe their mom and the community can have some kind of closure on what happened."

"Maybe," Sam said. "When we find the killer."

Gina nodded. "But it's a step. Our snake was a messenger."

"Yup," Sam said. "Pretty deep thoughts from a DNR herpetologist."

Gina smiled and shrugged, a little embarrassed. "Hey, it wasn't only me," she said.

Sam could see Gina's interest in the serpent gods and native myths was also because of Jules. A handsome, nice, smart Mayan descendant.

"Did you have a good time?" Sam said.

"We had a few beers," Gina said.

"And . . ."

"And what? He's a nice guy. We had good conversation."

An interesting way to express it, Sam thought.

After breakfast and getting the rattlesnakes from Gina, Sam visited the sheriff's office and asked to see the files on the disappearance of the Garcia kids. Technically, the case was still active, and the paperwork describing the incident was housed in a four-drawer vertical file cabinet. Fortunately, there was a cover file summarizing the case details.

The kids were last seen on County Road 8, heading due west out of the Low Valley trailer park. Sam had driven it, and what he noticed most was the way the remote blacktop resembled a roller coaster. There were five or six hills, each followed by deep slopes. If, as the confession stated, someone even a little inebriated was driving those hills fast, into the setting sun (given the kids probably wouldn't have been roller-skating in the dark), they could have easily not seen the kids. If the kids were on the crest of a hill, or on the downward side just over the crest, anyone heading west, driving uphill, would be driving blind.

After 25 years, Sam wasn't sure forensics would be able to ascertain the way the kids died. It was obvious the girl had been struck so hard her bones were broken in several places. But the boy's body appeared intact. They'd have to wait for the coroner's report, which would take a while.

Regardless, if it had been an accident, and whoever did it was trying to cover it up, the perpetrator may have now murdered Joe and Venita Smiley.

It also seemed likely that whoever struck and killed the Garcia kids was behind the Iowa rattlesnakes. If the perp had buried the kids near the Alta Vista site years ago, placing endangered species on the site was an imaginative way to scuttle development, so no one would find the graves. A rattlesnake bluff, as it were.

Obviously, they hadn't anticipated a rattlesnake's denning instincts, the keen skillset of a wolf dog's nose, the remarkable aptitude of a DNR herpetologist, DNA analysis of isolated rattlesnake populations, or the use of implanted chips to track rattlesnake specimens. Or that an apparently forged confession might contain the details of what actually happened.

For the time being, of course, it was all conjecture.

CHAPTER 28

The small town of McCutcheon was 10 miles outside Iowa's Sweet Marsh Wildlife Management area. On the outskirts of town, Sam turned off County Road 17 into the drive and parking area in front of the University of Iowa Herpetology Lab Number 4—McCutcheon. The building was a single-story brick edifice that looked like it had once been an elementary school. The lab's sign was the newest piece of equipment on-site, at least externally.

Sam and Gray pulled up and parked next to a white Ford Taurus and a white Chevy with the green CO's shield on its side.

As Sam got out of his car, leaving Gray inside, two men, one in uniform, came out of the low brick building.

Sam introduced himself to Barry Vander and CO Rich King. Barry wore wire-rimmed round glasses that set off a round face. He was short and pudgy and energetic. He appeared to be about Sam's age. Rich King was tall and thin with graying hair and a rugged face. He was middle-aged, but he'd clearly spent a lot of time in the sun and outdoors. Both men were friendly.

Sam handed over the bucket with rattlesnakes, and the cooler with the dead EMR on ice.

"Thanks," Barry said. "I appreciate you getting them back."

"Glad to help," Sam said.

"Come on in and I'll show you around."

Sam, who had a degree in wildlife biology, had always been interested in wildlife science, especially in the work being done in labs. The most interesting parts of the McCutcheon lab were two dozen lighted cages against a back wall. They were large, boxy, aluminum cages with full glass fronts. The tops were covered with screen lids. Resting atop the lids were fluorescent bulb fixtures with cords coming out of the backside of the fixtures. The cords were plugged into timers.

"Christmas tree timers," Barry explained, about the cages, lights, and heated reptile stones. "We've repurposed them to give the rattlesnakes normal daylight and heat for this time of year. They shut off after 15 hours."

The insides of the cages were lush with growth and around 4 feet square. There were overturned sections of logs that had been hollowed out to provide a cave-like space beneath them. Between the foliage and the cave spaces, there were plenty of places to hide. The back right corner of each cage bottom had a small depression filled with water.

Sam couldn't see any snakes in any of the cages. "Are there snakes in every cage?" Sam said.

"Yup," Barry said. "Those on the left have single juveniles. The ones on the right have breeding pairs."

"I can't see any of them."

"And you won't. They like crevices and dark places. But if they see movement outside, like us, they disappear."

"That's why you didn't realize you were missing one?" Sam said.

"That's right," Barry said. He moved over to a cage on the far left. "This is the cage with the missing snake. For now, I'm going to put both these guys here."

Barry took a moment to drop both snakes into the cage, where they took a moment to recognize their surroundings and then began to move, tentatively.

The coloring on the snakes, mostly darks and grays, spread over them in elaborately designed patterns that were hard not to admire. It was as though the finest tattoo artist in the world had designed them.

Sam said what they all thought; the snakes were beautiful.

"But most people around here see these," Barry said, "and they see something they want to kill."

Sam knew it was true. But if people understood the role animals like these played in the ecology of the region, they might think differently. They were, after all, animals that kept the rodent population in check. At least in part.

Sam was curious about how a person could insert a chip into a rattlesnake without getting bitten.

Barry moved over to some equipment tables set up in the middle of the lab. He picked up a 14-inch opaque plastic tube.

"First we fit the snake into this tube," Barry said. "The tube's not too tight, but snug enough so the snake can't turn around inside it."

He placed the tube back onto the table and picked up a syringe. "This syringe has a large enough needle so the chip can pass through it. Once the rattlesnake's secured in the tube, we use this needle to insert the microchip under the skin. Usually, we glue the injection site shut using a liquid band aid. That's to prevent the chip from falling out."

Barry set down the syringe and picked up a black handled device with some buttons, a small screen, and a large loop at the end of it.

"Once we get the chip inserted and secured, we use this scanner to make sure we can read the chip. The ID number is recorded before releasing the snake. That's how I knew the snakes you found up north were mine."

Barry explained, "All snakes are handled with padded snake tongs so as not to hurt them. Rattlesnakes should never be handled with bare hands. First, it's easier to get bit. Second, reptiles and amphibians can carry salmonella, so if you do handle them with your bare hands, you should wash thoroughly afterwards."

Sam turned to CO Rich King and said, "And you thought of ... Adder Musgrave? You think he might have stolen the snakes?"

"As soon as Barry asked about it, I thought of Musgrave. He's a marsh rat. This has his handprints all over it. I've busted him three times for poaching. He's got a record that includes theft. Now I'd say it also includes breaking and entering."

"Did you dust for prints?" Sam said.

"The front door," Rich said. "We think that's the way whoever stole the snake got in. It was locked, but it's an easy lock to pick, if you know what you're doing. And Adder Musgrave does."

"What about the cage missing the snake?" Sam said.

"Dusted it too," Rich said. "But my guess is whoever did it was wearing gloves, like you would if you were trying to grab a rattlesnake."

Made sense, Sam knew.

"We can drive out to his place," Rich said.

Outside, Barry climbed into Rich's truck. Sam got into his Jeep and pulled out behind them.

Adder Musgrave lived on the southwestern side of the Sweet Marsh Wildlife Management Area. His cabin was set near a swampy stretch of the Lower Wapsipinicon River. It had a rural route number for an address. Fortunately, both CO Rich King and Barry Vander had visited Adder in the past, so they knew where they were headed.

They made a few turns down increasingly remote roads until they came to a pair of ruts that broke off the gravel and angled into a stand of trees. An old mailbox, leaning on a metal pipe pole, marked the turnoff to Adder's place.

Sam and Gray followed CO Rich King's truck, careful to stay in the narrow ruts. The driveway, if you could call it that, ran potholed and rutted an eighth of a mile through river-bottom woods of maples, boxelders, and the occasional towering cottonwood.

They drove out of the trees into a wide, mostly dirt front yard. There was a low-hung, single-story wooden-sided structure set off to the side, its front facing the dirt yard. A smaller shack, what looked like a storage shed, stood off to one side of the yard. There was a firepit in front of the shed with a worn Adirondack chair in front of it. Even though it was the middle of the afternoon, coals in the firepit sent a single column of thin gray smoke into the warm July air.

Beyond the cabin, the woods opened up into marshland, what Sam assumed was an edge to the Sweet Marsh.

The cabin and shed were both covered in weathered wood siding. Parked to the side behind the shed sat a brand-new, camo-colored four-wheeler. Its gleam appeared out of place with the rest of Adder Musgrave's property.

Sam had seen lots of off-the-grid cabins in his line of work. Adder's place, Sam thought, looked more like a rustic hunting camp than a cabin or home. But from what Rich said, this was his permanent residence.

As soon as Sam's Jeep came into the yard, Adder Musgrave stepped onto a small cabin porch. The screen door slapped back behind him. He wore faded denim coveralls over a dirty T-shirt. The coveralls were high-water, rising above a pair of laced high-top leather boots. The man's arms were ropey, tanned, and as leathery as his boots. His hair was wild on top of his head. He had a weathered face with a four-day growth Sam assumed was permanent. At least it seemed so.

Gray rode in the Jeep's back seat. Sam glanced in his rearview mirror and saw Gray stare at Adder Musgrave with unusual intensity.

"Looks like an interesting place to sniff around," Sam said.

Judging from Gray's gaze, he agreed.

Sam pulled up and parked behind Rich's official truck. Rich and Barry stepped out and started across the dirt yard toward Adder. Sam followed.

As Rich approached, he said, "Adder," nodding. "Up for a visit?"

Adder, suspicious, said, "What about?"

Rich King laughed. But Adder didn't.

"We just want to ask you some questions," Rich said.

Barry nodded hello to Adder, extending his hand. "Barry Vander," Barry said. "We've met before."

"You the snake man," Adder said.

"That's right," Barry said. "Eastern massasauga rattlesnakes. We spoke about that earlier."

Adder accepted Barry's hand without enthusiasm.

Sam couldn't read anything in Adder's countenance. For a man who was being visited by an Iowa CO, someone who had apparently busted him in the past, Adder appeared unphased. Mute, but unphased.

"And this is Sam Rivers," Rich said. "He works with the U.S. Fish & Wildlife Service."

That got the man's attention, at least enough to give Sam a once-over.

Adder accepted Sam's extended hand with a desultory grip.

"Mind if I let my dog out to stretch his legs?" Sam said.

"Go ahead," Adder said.

Sam turned back to his Jeep and let Gray out.

"That's a damn nice four-wheeler," Rich said, nodding to it.

Gray paced over to the tree edge and lifted his leg.

"I guess," Adder said.

The four-wheeler's sidewalls were mud-spattered. Rich noticed and said, "I hope you're not chewing up the marsh with that thing."

"Stickin' on trails," Adder said. "Legal trails."

"Where'd you get it?"

"Sumner," Adder said.

"Damn, Adder," Rich said. "I bet that set you back some."

Adder considered it and said, "Got it on layaway."

Rich seemed to think about it but didn't comment. Then, "Gonna use it for turtle season?"

"That's the idea," Adder said.

"Get you around in style," Rich King said.

Adder didn't respond. Then he said, "Whad'ya need?"

"Couple of our local rattlesnakes found their way up into Minnesota," Rich said.

Adder's expression didn't change.

"Know anything about that?" Rich said.

"Rattlesnakes?" Adder said.

"That's right. One of them was stolen from Barry's McCutcheon lab. And two others from the Marsh turned up near Rochester, Minnesota."

Again, Adder didn't react. The men waited until the silence grew long enough to be awkward.

"Looks like somebody picked the door lock on the lab," Barry said. "And took one of the snakes. Not sure when, but it must have been recently."

"Don't know nuthin' about rattlesnakes or your lab."

"You know about eastern massasauga rattlesnakes," Rich said.

"I know 'em. So what?"

"And you know about my lab," Barry said.

"Never been there," Adder said.

That could be true, Barry knew. When Barry had interviewed Adder the previous summer, when he'd been asking about marsh-breeding locations for the snake, Barry had told Adder about the lab and what they were doing. Adder thought it was crazy. But to the best of Barry's knowledge, Adder had never been to the lab. Though he knew it was in McCutcheon, and clearly it would have been easy to find.

"Agent Rivers thinks whoever stole the snakes might be mixed up with a guy who's in a lot of trouble," Rich said. "Up by Rochester."

Rich paused, waiting for some response. Adder didn't acknowledge anything.

"Would you know anything about that?" Rich said.

"I don't know nuthin' about nuthin'," Adder said.

"Could be if this fella near Rochester is a murderer," Rich said. "That would make whoever stole snakes for the guy, if we're right, an accessory to murder."

Adder shrugged, without enthusiasm or interest.

They waited, but no one spoke.

Gray approached and peered up at Adder, uncertain what to make of the man or his scent.

"That dog part wolf?" Adder said.

"Yes," Sam said. "Half wolf." Sam was surprised, because most people recognized Gray was an unusual animal but thought he was some kind of peculiar breed.

Adder seemed to sniff in Gray's direction. If Sam was hoping he might be able to use Gray to friendly-up the conversation, he was mistaken.

"Mind if we look around?" Rich said.

"For what?"

"Any signs of rattlesnakes."

Adder's face darkened. "Go ahead," he said. "Got nuthin' to hide."

"Thanks," Rich said. "Given your record, Adder, you can understand why you'd be a person of interest."

"Fuck that," Adder said, under his breath.

Clearly there was no love lost between Adder Musgrave and the Iowa DNR conservation corps.

Rich turned toward the shed and Barry followed him.

To the left of the cabin, there was a path leading down to the marsh.

"Mind if we check out the marsh?" Sam said, indicating the path.

"Free country," Adder said, but he was watching Barry Vander and CO Rich King.

Sam and Gray started toward the path while Barry and Rich opened the shed door and peered inside.

It took another five minutes before Sam heard CO Rich King call his name.

Sam and Gray returned up the path.

"That's a beautiful marsh," Sam said to whoever was listening.

"It is," Barry said.

Rich and Adder didn't say anything.

Sam watched Barry get into the passenger side of Rich's truck. Rich walked around the front end, nodding to Adder, who still stood in front of his porch.

"Thanks for your hospitality," Rich said.

Adder just looked on, mute.

Sam and Gray got into their Jeep, started the engine, and followed Rich King's truck up the road.

As Sam drove away from the site, he considered Adder Musgrave. Sam was familiar with people like Adder. Hunters, trappers, people who lived off the land and off the grid. If he was to guess, it was as likely as not that Adder Musgrave had something to do with the rattlesnakes. But Sam didn't know the man well enough to get any kind of reading on him. To Sam, the man seemed a little too reticent and clearly unhappy about being bothered by an Iowa conservation officer. Which would be understandable, given Rich King had arrested Adder in the past.

Sam's phone rang. A 319 number.

Sam answered and Rich King said, "The man's strange as a three-dollar bill."

"He definitely wasn't happy about our visit," Sam said.

"I think he's our guy." Rich said.

"You do?" Sam said.

"I'm not a betting man," Rich said. "But I'd put a heavy wager on Adder. He poached and stole."

"He was definitely less friendly than the last time I interviewed him," Barry said, on speaker. "About the marsh and its wildlife and where to find rattlesnakes."

"But he knew where to find them?" Sam said.

"Oh, yeah. Definitely. The man knows the marsh, and he knows eastern massasauga rattlesnakes."

"And he wouldn't have any problems breaking into your lab," Rich said.

"Wish we could tap his phone," Sam said.

"If he has one," Barry said.

"If he does, I bet the guy's calling his Rochester contact right now," Rich said. "If that pirate didn't know what he was involved with before, he sure does now. If nothing else, we might have scared him."

"Scared people make mistakes," Sam said.

"We can hope. I can tell you right now, I doubt he bought that four-wheeler on layaway. I know Reid Cummins, the owner of Sumner ATV. No way he'd let Adder Musgrave buy that four-wheeler on layaway."

"Can you check?" Sam said.

"Heading over there as soon as I drop off Barry."

They all thought for a moment, wondering if there was anything else to discuss. No one could think of anything more, so Sam asked Rich to let him know what they found out about the ATV.

"If I'm right," Rich said, "I'll surprise Adder tomorrow morning and ask him about the money. That's a lot of cash for somebody like Adder Musgrave."

"You okay visiting the guy by yourself?"

"Adder? Oh hell, yes. He's a crusty outlaw, but he's harmless. Even if we got him as an accessory to murder, from what you say, he wouldn't fight it. He's got enough sense for that."

Sam hoped so.

CHAPTER 29

Adder Musgrave watched the vehicles disappear up his drive. He waited until he could no longer hear their engines and knew for certain they were out of sight. And sound.

Then he cursed. Long and hard.

He reviewed the meeting, worried he might have said something. First, he wondered how in the hell they'd figured to visit him. He knew he had a record, but he wasn't the only poacher in these parts. That fucker Rich King had a hard-on for him. Every chance he got, King busted his balls. It was harassment, notwithstanding he *was* the person who caught the rattlesnakes in the swamp and stole the other one from that McCutcheon lab.

A few nights past, after midnight, he'd scouted the low-hung building on the outskirts of town. After parking off the road where no one would find his car, he approached the lab, a 5-gallon bucket with a lid in tow. It was a small brick building set into a stand of trees. He scanned the building from the tree edge, looking for motion sensor lights and video cameras. But there were none. Which didn't surprise him, given the building was rural and everybody knew it held rattlesnakes.

The front door might as well have been unlocked, given no sane person would break into a building filled with rattlesnakes. But Adder wasn't exactly sane. Besides, the main door lock was pickable as an apple off a tree.

It took him five minutes to get in, find a cage, lift off its lid and reach down with gloved hands to grab a sleeping rattlesnake behind the head, and then lift it out and drop it into the bucket, snapping the lid shut. Then he was out the door, locking it behind him, and walking back up the dark ditch to his truck, no one the wiser.

He'd worn thin gloves to get in, thick ones for the snake. He wasn't stupid.

He'd done the entire swipe without seeing a single car on the blacktop, either going or coming. No headlights on any of the roads around McCutcheon, since it was after midnight.

Adder thought about what he'd done, replaying it in his mind. Far as he could tell, there was no way anyone could tie him to the lab.

But murder? Was that what that prick Rich King had said?

Adder hadn't bargained on murder. The only thing Adder knew was some guy in Minnesota wanted snakes and had the money to pay for them. He couldn't figure out how murder might be involved. A rattlesnake like the kind he'd provided couldn't kill a man if it'd bit him three times. Or a woman. Make you sick, maybe. These rattlesnakes didn't grow big enough, and their venom wasn't delivered in lethal enough quantities, to kill anyone, except maybe small children.

Maybe it was just Rich King busting his balls.

Adder knew he needed to think about this. If there was a murder, and if those damn snakes were part of it, and if that fucker from Minnesota, Der, was the guy . . . that could mean Der was dangerous. If Der was a killer, Adder had to be careful. And smart.

Adder took the next half hour walking up his drive, retrieving his camouflaged game camera from where he'd secreted it among the branches of an overgrown juniper. He'd set up the game camera to trigger off movement. Not trivial movement, like leafed-out branches blowing in a breeze. But the movement of a big animal. Like whitetails, racoons, or a man.

Adder was a seasoned game camera user. He knew where to put them, how to conceal them, and how to review the images on their narrow screens. And he knew how to use a special cable to pull the images and drop 'em on an old Dell laptop he kept back at the cabin.

Looking at the small camera screen, sure enough, after watching two racoons amble down a nearby rut, he watched a man approach from the left, walking down the drive. At two-second intervals, he watched the man step down the rut until he was directly across from their trading stump. The man peered down the drive and did a 360, at one point staring straight at the camera, but not seeing it. He was searching for anyone who might be near, or any vehicles that might be passing up on the road. Or maybe even a camera.

Adder watched the sequence. The man extracted an envelope from inside the front of his pants. The envelope, Adder recognized. Then the man placed the envelope on the stump and retreated the way he'd come. Maybe 25, 30 good images. Clear images, in which the man's face and body could be seen and easily discerned. Der, whoever the fuck that was. Adder had no idea and didn't care. Der. Somebody with a hard-on for rattlesnakes and the jack to pay for them.

And a murderer, if what Rich King said was true.

Adder brought the camera back to his cabin. He spent the next 10 minutes transferring and moving the images to his laptop. Then he fished around in a knickknack drawer for the little stick he could use to store the images. He got out a piece of paper and used a pencil to write: "The guy who bought the rattlesnakes. Three of them." Then he folded the paper with the stick inside it and dropped it into an envelope, licking its seal and folding its flap down tight.

On the outside of the envelope, he penciled "Marlene," a sister who lived over near Tripoli. Tripoli had a Dollar Store he hadn't visited in a month. Time to check it out, maybe pick up some beans. Marlene and Decker lived 4 miles south of town. Adder and Marlene had never been close. But they were kin, so he could trust her.

He wouldn't trust that old pig farmer Decker to do the right thing for money. But there wasn't any money in this. It was just ... insurance, in case anything happened.

Adder was a poacher and a thief, but he wasn't stupid.

He'd head over to Marlene's and drop off the envelope and tell her, "Anything happens to me, give this to CO Rich King." Adder didn't like Rich King, but he was a bird dog for the law. If it came to it, and his sister needed to share the package, Rich King'd know what to do with the images of the man dropping off the money and picking up the container with the rattlesnake.

Marlene was surprised to see him. Adder was happy to hear Decker was out, visiting a hog buyer over near Waterloo.

When Adder explained about the package and what to do with it if something happened to him, Marlene was concerned. Not about Adder's safety but about getting involved in something "illegal."

"Whad'ya mean?" she said, her eyes magnified beneath her pink bifocals. She was short and about as wide at the hips as Adder was thin and tall. He'd sometimes wondered if she'd had a different old man, but never voiced the suspicion.

"I mean, if I end up dead," Adder said, never one to sugarcoat.

"What in the hell you got yourself into this time?" Marlene said.

"Nuthin' I can't handle."

"This gonna come back to bite me? Am I lookin' at trouble? Knowin' you it's somethin' illegal." She held the envelope up as exhibit A.

"Fuck no," Adder said. "Got nuthin' to do with you. Just . . . if anything happens, call Rich King."

Marlene knew Rich King. They'd gone to school together over in Sumner.

"What's Rich King gonna think if he gets a call from a Musgrave?"

"Never gonna happen," Adder said. "It's just . . . insurance."

"In case anything happens," Marlene said.

"That's right. But nuthin' in there's gonna come back at you. You and Decker'll be fine."

"I don't know about that," she said.

Marlene inherited their mother's sense of propriety, while Adder had been schooled by the old man.

"Look at it this way," Adder said. "If anything happens to me, you and Decker get everything I own."

"Which ain't much."

True enough, Adder knew. "I own the cabin outright," he said. "You could sell it and pocket the proceeds."

"Who's gonna buy a cabin next to that swamp?"

"Shit, Marlene. Just do this one thing."

Finally, Marlene agreed. But she told him it better damn well never be a call she needed to make, to Rich King.

Adder agreed.

"Anything new at the Dollar?" Adder said.

It was an interest they shared.

"Got some kind of shipment of canned stuff from last Thanksgiving," Marlene said. "Deck and me been eatin' it all week. It's passable."

After dropping off the package, Adder drove to the Tripoli Dollar Store. The Thanksgiving shipment had been picked over, but he found two cans of sweet potatoes at the back of a lower shelf and bought them. Cheap.

Then he drove over to the Tripoli Public Library.

He was pissed by Marlene's comments and attitude. But he knew she'd do what he asked. She was kin.

The library was an old brick building with "Carnegie" chiseled in stone over the steep front steps. The building contained four public computer terminals in study carrels set back in the stacks. Plenty of privacy. This time of day only one was occupied, with someone so intent on the screen they didn't look up.

Adder walked down to the farthest terminal, sat down, and checked his emails, which he did occasionally, today no exception. Then he glanced around to be sure he was still alone.

He searched for murders in Rochester, and it didn't take long until he found an article about the Garcia kids. And one about the Smileys. The Garcia kids had been found on a development site. A bluff. The Smileys' deaths appeared to be a murder-suicide, but it was being investigated.

Then he searched on rattlesnakes in the Rochester area and found an article in the Owen's Gap *Gazette* about rare eastern massasauga rattlesnakes being discovered on the Alta Vista site. Their appearance had temporarily closed the site to development.

He exited and closed the browser. Once he was sure it was closed, he walked out, agitated, but careful not to show it.

That fucker in Minnesota was causing more trouble than Adder'd expected. He guessed this was the universe's way of evening out his run of good luck. As he pondered his recent streak, it suddenly occurred to him how he might let the Minnesotan know about his recent troubles. He'd be warning the man—one outlaw to another. There was no honor among thieves, Adder knew. There were angles. And Adder wasn't above using one. The angle here, far as he could see, was that Adder was owed for his troubles. Der should pay. He'd be gettin' good intel, and Adder would put away a little more money for a rainy day.

As Adder thought about it, thinking the man owed him another payment, he realized it was another stroke of good luck. And good luck came in threes. He couldn't wait to see where his unexpected good fortune might take him next.

CHAPTER 30

After getting dinner and feeding and walking Gray, Sam checked his emails.

As expected, he got an email from his boss, Kay Magdalen, in the Denver office. She wanted an update. Rather, she wanted him to start "acting like a team player. You're my worst field agent for keeping me apprised of current events . . ." Her comments continued in a similar vein, like a dog with a bone. Not a dog, Sam thought. A bureaucrat focusing on something less important than poached rattlesnakes . . . or the deaths of two children . . . or the Smiley's murder-suicide (or murder).

Sam was preoccupied. Still, he recognized, despite her stinging assessment, that she had a point. Frankly, Kay's opinion wasn't much different than Carmel's, given Sam's lackluster attention to wedding details.

When Sam Rivers became immersed in a case, there was little else he thought about. Even now he sensed vague details gnawing at the corners of consciousness. He knew there was something he needed to do. Some action he needed to take that he'd forgotten. He wasn't sure what, but he could feel it.

Reluctantly, Sam took a few moments to explain "current events" to his boss. He knew she'd appreciate his trip to Iowa to interview the person they thought was responsible for the rattlesnake thefts. That trip was legit and well within the purview of his duties. Following up on poaching endangered species was exactly what he should be doing.

But he left out his assistance with the review of the murder-suicide, and his subsequent visit to the sheriff's office to review the case details surrounding the Garcia kids. Kay wouldn't appreciate what she'd consider collateral case details, even if Sam had been asked to help out. Neither would she understand how Sam had done a favor for the sheriff—taking the heat for the continued closure of the development site so the sheriff wouldn't need to. Kay would have said it was the sheriff's problem, so the sheriff, not the USFW, should take the heat. And Kay would have especially not understood the reason he'd done it—to curry favor with the sheriff so she would owe him. He had cashed in the favor immediately, using it so he could indulge his investigative fervor on cases that had little to do with poaching endangered species. So, there was nothing in Sam's status report about his preoccupation with apparent crimes not related to wildlife.

For now, Sam spent 10 minutes explaining about his trip to Iowa and their interview of the alleged rattlesnake poacher, Adder Musgrave. He padded his report with a tangent about Barry Vander's work raising eastern massasauga rattlesnakes for release in the wild, to augment the population of an endangered species. He explained how Barry inserted a rice-size tracking number in each rattlesnake, which Sam thought was incredibly fascinating, but which he knew was a detail Kay would find uninteresting and a distraction from his efforts to identify and prosecute whoever poached the snakes.

Finally, he told her that he, Gina Larkspur, Jules Ortega, and probably a deputy, if he could swing it, were going to spend Sunday morning conducting one more survey of the Alta Vista site, just to be certain there were no other signs of EMRs or other rattlesnakes. He did not expect to find any others, but they needed to be sure.

After answering his emails and spending a few minutes responding to Kay's request, he dialed Carmel. He was hoping Carmel would be more receptive to his charms than his boss.

"Sam Rivers," Carmel said, picking up. "My occasional boyfriend."

"You mean, devoted fiancé?"

"Not sure about devoted," Carmel said.

"Am I letting down all the women in my life?"

He took a few moments to explain about his recent email exchange with Kay Magdalen.

To which Carmel said, "Sounds like it."

"Anymore RSVPs come in?"

"They did, as a matter of fact. You're a lucky man."

She'd received two more affirmatives from his less-than-punctual friends.

"And don't tell me patience is a virtue," Carmel said.

"I wasn't going to say that," Sam said, though he was. "I was going to tell you how lucky I am to be your boyfriend."

"Right," Carmel said, doubtful.

Then Sam shared his day, and she shared hers. Sam asked about her clinic and a dicey operation she'd performed on a black Lab who had torn open a garbage bag and ingested a bucket full of chicken bones. A bowel obstruction.

"That must have been expensive," Sam said.

"The owner was a teacher," Carmel said. "I could tell how much she loved that dog, so I gave her a discount."

"The pet lover's discount?"

"That's right."

"I love that," Sam said.

"Probably not a model business practice, but there you have it."

When Sam told her about his sense that he was forgetting something, Carmel was surprised.

"Don't take this the wrong way," she said. "But you seldom overlook case details the way you do details about your personal life, or our relationship."

"I love you," Sam said.

"I know you love me. And I love you. That's not what I'm talking about."

Sam paused. He knew what she meant. "Here's the deal. This case involved the murder of two children and the apparent murder-suicide, possibly faked, of a dairy farmer and his wife, and the poaching of endangered species, so it's important."

"I know. And I know you know our relationship is important."

"I always take the long view with our relationship. We're going to be together for the rest of our lives. We will have many more adventures, long after the details about this case are done. It's just, I need to focus on this case."

"I know," Carmel said. "That's why I'm helping you. I know you, Rivers. When you forget something it's because your brain's register has been so overloaded with facts it's kicked out something to make space. You've forgotten something that happened that you need to remember."

"You think?" Sam said.

"I know when similar things happen, like our wedding invites, your attention gets knocked out by this case."

"You said that."

"You're not getting it," Carmel said.

"I guess not."

"In the last 24 hours you've learned about the deaths of two kids from 20-odd years ago. You've partially solved a tragic mystery that has lingered for a long time. And you found and have investigated the murder-suicide of two people. And you've gone to Iowa to confront a poacher."

"All true," Sam said.

"So, whatever you're forgetting probably happened *before* the last 24 hours. You've been so inundated with current events something you discovered early on has been forgotten."

Sam thought about it. Then suddenly he said, "My god."

"You mean, my goddess."

"You are my goddess."

Then Sam told her about the piece of plastic he'd found in the Bobcat, the first day he was on the Alta Vista site, when he'd examined the trailer and the Cat with Jules Ortega. He'd found the piece of plastic on the floor beside the chair and hadn't thought much about it. But it looked like a handle. He'd carefully bagged it, just in case. It was not an obvious part of the Cat, so it was an anomaly. He'd thought at the time that maybe he should get someone, some forensics folks, to see if they could lift anything from it. Fingerprints or DNA. And now he realized he knew some forensics folks—Peggy Landrau and her team—who could do it for him. And probably turn it around fast, if he got someone from the sheriff's office to hand-carry it to their lab. Another favor he could ask of the sheriff. She still owed him. She could run point on it.

"If I was there, I'd have you rub my feet. For payment," Carmel said.

"And I would do it. I owe you a foot rub."

"You owe me a lot more than a foot rub."

Then they spent a few minutes in suggestive conversation about who owed who what. It was banter to which Sam finally acquiesced, because he really did respect Carmel's aptitude, her brain, her instinct, her insights. She had helped him before, and he knew she would again.

Before Sam turned out his light, he phoned the sheriff's office. He left a message. He, Gina, and Jules were doing one last survey of Alta Vista, just to be sure there were no other rattlesnakes. Sam knew it was Sunday but, if possible, could she meet him at the site? It was urgent, so the earlier the better.

CHAPTER 31

The call came in after dark. Der's throw-away had been used to make calls, never to receive one. Der kept it with him, just in case. But he thought its usefulness had been spent, now that the rattlesnakes had served their purpose and the kids' bodies had still been found. He had meant to ditch the phone, preferably into the Mississippi River. But he had been so busy and preoccupied with current events he hadn't. And now it was ringing, and Der recognized the number.

What the fuck?

He picked up but didn't speak.

After a few seconds, Adder Musgrave said, "Der?"

"We're done," Der said.

"Not according to Rich King."

"Who the hell is Rich King?"

"Conservation officer. He paid me a visit this afternoon. With two other guys. Barry Vander from that lab, and some guy from up north. Rivers," Adder said, recalling the name. "Sam Rivers. From Fish & Wildlife."

Der didn't know the two Iowans, but he knew Sam Rivers.

When Der didn't say anything, Adder continued.

"They were askin' questions. About rattlesnakes."

"What did you tell them?" Der said.

"Not a goddamn thing."

"Of course you didn't. Because if you had, you'd be in jail. And I assume you were careful. You didn't leave any evidence that could tie you back to the rattlesnakes?"

"Course not," Adder said.

There was a pause. "Then, we're good," Der said. "Because you don't know anything about me except this number, which I should have thrown away and plan to as soon as we're done with this call."

"Hold on," Adder said. "They weren't just askin' about stealin' rattlesnakes."

Der waited.

"They said it was about murder."

"You and I had a brief business transaction," Der said. "And now it's finished. Or will be, as soon as I toss this burner."

"I don't know about that."

The comment caused the hair on the back of Der's neck to bristle and his stomach to churn. He wasn't sure where this was headed, but he sure as hell didn't like it. "I'm certain," he said.

"'Cause I don't like Rich King comin' around accusin' me of stuff I didn't do."

"You stole rattlesnakes. If you did it carefully, you have nothing to worry about."

"Not talkin' about rattlesnakes," Adder said.

"It's a goddamn fart in the wind, Adder. They got nuthin'."

"Got the bodies of two kids from a long time ago, and some farmer and his old lady. And from what I can tell, four bodies in a day is some kind of record in Bluff County."

Der was surprised a swamp rat from Iowa knew about his business. The rat had been doing research.

"Got nuthin' to do with me."

"They found rattlesnakes where the kids were. Some kind of bluff."

This call was going from bad to worse. Der reminded himself that Adder Musgrave was a scofflaw and a miscreant. And if he ever confessed to anything, he'd do time. And the man had nothing on him, except the number on a burner phone.

"Got nuthin' to do with me."

After a long silence, Adder said, "I know you got nuthin' to do with nuthin'. But we both know the law got a funny way of lookin' at things. Puttin' blame where it's got no right to be."

Der didn't respond, because he was pretty sure Adder Musgrave wasn't done.

After another few moments of silence, Adder said, "But those sons a' bitches got deep pockets and 'nough time to figure out how blame can be put on someone. Even when they got nothin' to do with it. Know what I mean?"

Der did, and he did not like it. "You've got nothing to worry about."

"Maybe not," Adder said. "But the way they were sniffin' around the place, I 'spect this won't be the last time they visit."

The swamp rat continued to raise his neck hairs.

"I'm thinkin' you might like to know. If they do. Visit. And what they want."

It was the first thing the idiot said that made sense. "I guess."

"I'm thinkin' I keep the intel comin'. I'm lettin' you know about this visit on account of our business."

Adder Musgrave didn't *know* Der. But he knew enough. Der could play along. "Thanks," he said.

"There'll be more questions. Nuthin' I can't handle. But they'll be back."

When Der didn't respond, Adder continued.

"You got nuthin' to worry about. Just lettin' you know."

"Okay," Der said.

After a long moment of silence, during which Adder expected Der to offer additional cash, and he didn't, Adder said, "This here is more than I 'spected from some rattlesnakes."

"I can see that," Der said.

"Given the rest of it, how it's turnin' out, the way things are goin', I'm thinkin' the money was a little thin."

There it was. Der let it sit there.

This time Adder remained silent.

After a few more moments, during which Der thought about hanging up and being done with it, done with the swamp man, he made a different decision.

"I can see how that might be the case," Der finally said. "How about another $1,500? Think that'd cover it?"

Truth is, Adder was thinking another $500. Maybe $1,000, given there could be other payments down the line, now and then, depending. "Sounds about right," Adder said.

"Tomorrow afternoon," Der said. "Same place as before. Three o'clock. On the stump."

Adder agreed and the call ended.

Der sat in the dark for a long time. The burner sat beside him, as silent now as his thoughts.

After a while, he looked at his darkened windows. The shades were up, but the night sky was obscured by clouds. He could see nothing but darkness.

He had taken the call from his bedroom. There was an easy chair next to the window, beside the bed. An end table sat to his side, between the chair and the bed. There was a reading lamp on top of the table, with a clock radio beside it. The only light in the room came from the digital clock. It read 11:38. Not long until midnight.

Der reached over, picked up the clock radio, and flung it against the wall. It crashed, shattered, and fell to the floor. Then it lay there, looking like some kind of rodent with a too-long tail. Dead now.

Events had gotten away from Der. His plans were dangerously close to unraveling. Years ago, the goddamn Garcia kids had been taken care of. Then, seemingly out of nowhere, the kids crawled out of the grave.

Der was no murderer. He got up out of his chair in the dark and thought, *fuck fuck fuck fuck*, in the exact same way he did all those years ago, kneeling beside the blacktop, thinking as the sun went down. And then again, as he watched the kids being dug up.

In every instance, as far back as he could recall, Der had been serving a higher purpose. Those kids had been impediments to the future he imagined, and he had taken care to secure it. If one of those kids had perished by his hands, it was not because Der was a murderer. The kid would have died, Der guessed. Even if the kid had survived, he would have been a cripple. The way Der saw it, he'd done the kid a favor.

And Der had served a higher purpose.

He had not wanted to kill the Smileys. But again, there were good reasons for doing what had to be done. Solid reasons. There was still much to do. He needed to continue to secure a pure future. For him, for his community, for the world. Der felt certain God had a plan that involved a pure future. Der knew it was only a matter of time before that plan was revealed, and Der would be part of it. Because Der had taken the steps to help it along. That's what these deaths had been. Steps. Like stones on a walk into a godlike future.

And now people were threatening the world as it was meant to be. The sheriff, her deputies, many of the people in Owen's Gap. Not all of them. To be sure, Der had accomplices—people who, like him, knew the world was not the way it should be. But they also knew it could be different. With reason and the right people in power. It could be. There were glimmers on the horizon. Der needed to keep his sights clear and his mind in the right place. To help it all along, when the time came.

But what to do about Adder Musgrave? Rather, he knew what to do about him. But how to do it. The man was a hunter. He could be dangerous. Der knew Adder's demands for money would not end there. If you did business with a rat, you got bitten.

He knew what had to happen. The moment Adder Musgrave called him and talked Der through his request, Der had known.

On the back wall of the Lair there was a WWII sniper rifle with a German-made scope. To be sure, it was old. But even 80 years ago, the Third Reich had excellent optics. Der would sometimes take the rifle out of its Lair, to use it and admire its superb manufacturing. Its perfect craftsmanship. It was a sleek killing machine, flawless in its design and manufacture. He would take it out and sight it to make sure that even at 100 paces, it could center a hole in a target.

It was time the sniper got out of its Lair.

Der was no murderer. He was the remover of impediments. He was the kind of man who would do what needed to be done.

For his, and everyone's, future.

CHAPTER 32

Sunday

Sam and Gray were on the Alta Vista site by 7:30. Across the northern border of the site, yellow crime scene tape was still strung among the trees, where the Garcia kids had been found. The tape remained because Peggy Landrau's team might revisit the site, just to have one last look. Like Sam, they were being thorough.

Gina pulled up and parked behind Sam. Jules pulled in behind Gina.

Coincidence? Sam wondered. *Probably not.*

"Great morning," she said, getting out of her car.

She was smiling like someone who had a recent brush with romance.

"It is," Sam said.

"Yes," Jules said, approaching. "Beautiful." He was looking at Gina.

She blushed.

The sun was well off the horizon. The day was comfortably warm. It was going to be another hot, clear sky. Perfect for snake hunting, and Sam said so.

Jules agreed.

"Do you really think we're going to find anything?" Gina said.

"Doubtful," Sam said.

Before they got started, Sheriff Betsy Conrad drove up in a cruiser and parked behind Jules's car. She wore a beige blouse, dress slacks, and flashy brown cowboy boots. It was a nice look for the sheriff.

"Heading to church?" Sam said.

"Of course. It's Sunday."

Sam glanced across the green field and said, "Who needs church when you've got a space like this to walk around in?"

"You don't have constituents who need to see you in God's house."

"My constituents are right here," Sam said.

Gina and Jules smiled.

"Why the hell did you get me out here?" the sheriff said.

Sam was going to say something about blasphemy, especially on the Sabbath, but he decided to let it go.

He walked back to his Jeep and pulled the double-bagged piece of plastic from his glove compartment. Then he explained what it was and where they'd found it and that it was not from the Bobcat. Sam thought it might be the plastic handle from a storage bin, the kind a person might use to transport a rattlesnake.

"I'm missing the early service because of this?" the sheriff said, letting the bagged piece of plastic dangle in front of her.

Sam explained how yesterday they had gotten stonewalled by the alleged poacher, Adder Musgrave. Sam and CO Rich King both felt certain Adder knew something and had probably been the one who caught and stole the rattlesnakes. But they couldn't shake anything loose. Adder claimed ignorance, an attitude that was almost convincing, until they told him whoever had taken the rattlesnakes was involved in murder. That comment seemed to pass in front of Adder like a warning shot fired off the bow of a ship. Sam had sensed alarm. But the Iowa hunter wasn't going to show fear to a representative of the US government. Especially one responsible for policing the wild.

Sam explained to the sheriff that they were, like Peggy Landrau and her crime scene crew, being thorough.

Because the sheriff had cachet with Peggy, Sam wanted the sheriff to ask her if she could fast-track the analysis.

"And you'd rather be hunting snakes than driving for the next hour," the sheriff said.

Sam shrugged. "I would take it to her, but I only met her yesterday. And we need the analysis ASAP."

The sheriff was clearly annoyed about the disruption to her Sunday morning and said so.

"If Olmstead County is like counties in the Twin Cities, they've gotten federal money to work through an enormous backlog of rape kits."

The sheriff knew it was true. Moreover, Olmstead's 24x7 operation had already resulted in three rape convictions in Bluff County.

The sheriff would take the piece of plastic over to Peggy and ask her to "fast-track" it. But she wasn't convinced it was important enough to rush the analysis.

"We know the snakes came from Iowa," Sam said. "I think that first one was placed in the Bobcat. Probably at night when it was cool, and the snake was sedentary. And if somebody put it there, they may have dropped this piece of plastic." Sam pointed to the baggy. "This looks like one of those clip-on handles. One of those plastic bins, which would have been a perfect way to transport a rattlesnake."

"Seems like whoever dropped it there wouldn't leave it as evidence," the sheriff said.

"They would if, in trying to retrieve the evidence, they'd get bit in the face by a rattlesnake."

The sheriff considered it. "It all sounds a little fanciful."

"Like I said, we're just being thorough."

"I'll call Peggy. She's an early riser but, like you, not a churchgoer. No constituents to worry about. And she loves this kind of shit."

The sheriff checked her watch.

"If I run it over now, I can be back in plenty of time to make the 10 o'clock service."

"Or you'd have a good excuse for skipping it," Sam said.

"I happen to like church," the sheriff said.

Sam, Gina, Jules, and Gray spent the morning making a thorough circuit of the Alta Vista development site. As they searched, the day grew progressively warm. It had been very pleasant at 7:30, but by 10:30, it was hot, sunny, still, and steamy. Gray was panting, a white froth hanging at the corners of his mouth. During their circuit of the site, Gray had spent some time sniffing around the two known places where EMRs had been found, in the field and in the cave. In both instances, it had taken some cajoling to convince Gray to move on.

By 11:00, they were all back at their vehicles with nothing to show for it, except two garter snakes (the pregnant female again), perspiration, and a couple of empty water bottles.

"Great way to spend a Sunday morning," Gina said.

"Yes," Jules said. "I wish there were more snakes to hunt."

"You are such a herpetologist," Sam said.

"I am."

"And I totally agree."

She smiled. Then she turned to Jules and said, "I know a place where we could cool off. It's a lake not too far from here."

"Jensen?" Jules said.

"Yeah. You know it?"

"I go there all the time. I have a swimsuit in my car."

"So do I," exclaimed Gina.

"Sam?" Gina said.

As nice as a swim in a lake sounded, right about now, Sam figured in this instance, three would be a crowd.

Then his phone rang. It was a 563 area code. Iowa. He waved Gina and Jules off and answered the call.

"Rivers."

"Hi, Sam. Rich King."

His voice sounded tense.

"Hi, Rich."

"Adder Musgrave's been shot."

"What?"

"He's dead. Shot once in the head. We're down here trying to piece it out. The sheriff's here. Far as we can tell, it happened early this morning. But we're not sure. We'll need the medical examiner to confirm."

After their meeting with Adder yesterday, Rich King, like Sam, felt pretty certain Adder was the poacher and thief who stole the EMR from Barry Vander's lab. When Adder told Rich about the ATV and that he'd gotten it on layaway, Rich was doubtful. Rich lived in Waverly. On his return home, he stopped at Sumner ATV to speak with the owner, Reid Cummins. Everyone knew everyone in this part of Iowa. Reid would have known Adder was a bad credit risk. And if that was the case, Adder had probably paid cash. And if a guy like Adder paid cash, where did he get it?

"I don't normally work on Sundays, but I kept thinking about how Musgrave lied to us about having that much cash. He told me layaway because he knew I'd wonder where he got cash. Maybe he didn't think I'd ask the owner about it. But I did, and it convinced me he was involved and probably got the money from whoever wanted the rattlesnakes.

"I thought if I confronted him Sunday morning, unexpectedly, I might startle him into making a confession. Maybe give up who he is working for."

When Rich King drove in, he expected to see Adder standing on his front porch because of the engine noise. He found him face down in the dirt, near his firepit, in the motionless posture of a corpse. Rich saw a wound in the back of his head and the ground soaked with blood. Rich checked for a pulse, the official reaction. The skin on the man's neck was cold and leathery. Adder had been dead for a while.

"It was him," Sam said. "He was the poacher and the thief."

"Gotta be," Rich agreed. "And somebody gave him cash. And I bet he called that somebody and told him about our visit."

"Maybe he tried to shake him down for more money," Sam said.

"Probably, knowing Adder Musgrave."

"And the guy figured, loose end," Sam said.

"That, and he was looking at a money pit."

Sam couldn't believe it. If Sam was right, they had been one step away from finding the person responsible for planting the EMRs on the Alta Vista site, probably the deaths of the Garcia kids, and possibly the Smileys too. And now, Adder Musgrave.

Sam felt bad for the man. He'd been a petty criminal and a wildlife abuser, but he didn't deserve to meet his end face down in the dirt.

"I assume the sheriff will turn Adder's place upside down, looking for any clues to whoever it was who paid for the EMRs."

"They've been at it all morning. But so far, nothing. Adder had a phone, but it was password protected. They're going to try and get into it, but it'll take a while. They should be able to get a record of his calls. He also had an old Dell laptop, but it, too, is password protected. Again, they'll try and get into it, but Adder didn't strike me as a heavy computer user. I'm doubtful we'll find anything, but we'll see."

"They find the bullet?"

"Not yet. Passed through his head. The forensics team thinks it was a rifle, judging from its point of entry and exit. We looked back in the woods behind Adder's house, a logical place to shoot from. But we couldn't find any sign of anyone."

Sam remembered the location. It was thickly wooded behind Adder's cabin. Someone could have easily snuck down to the edge of the woods and waited for him to appear. And then shot him. The man was so remote no one would have heard a gunshot, even the loud and distinct shot fired from a rifle.

"Did Adder have any family?" Sam asked.

Rich thought about it. "A sister, I remember from school. But Adder never married. No kids. Nothing like that."

"Girlfriends? Cousins? Anyone?"

"The man was a hermit," Rich said. "I never heard of him being with any women. I think it was just him, and maybe his sister, far as I know."

"Maybe she knows something?"

Rich said he'd try and track her down.

Sam thanked Rich King and told him to keep him posted. Rich assured him he would.

Sam stopped at the HyVee to get a sandwich, some iced tea, and a bag of Cheetos. Then he and Gray went over to the town park. There were some young people playing volleyball at a net near the edge of the park, a game Sam suspected would end soon, given the still, hot hang to the day.

Sam and Gray went to the other side of the park, found a picnic table, and sat in the shade of a huge oak tree.

Sam shared an occasional Cheeto with Gray, and part of his sandwich. The iced tea had a hint of lemon and was lightly sweetened and the perfect accompaniment to Sam's spare lunch. He was wondering about Carmel and was thinking about calling her and telling her he'd drive up for dinner, but he knew he'd need to return—he still had loose ends to tie up. He was thinking about a 4-hour round-trip when his cell phone rang.

The sheriff.

CHAPTER 33

"Peggy checked," the sheriff said. "She found some DNA. From Henry Fields, the zoning commissioner for Bluff County."

"What?" Sam said. "Are they sure?"

The sheriff related what Peggy had told her. They were able to find some small cells, probably skin cells, on the piece of plastic. You cannot pick up anything from sweat except minerals. But they found something, and they got the DNA and then they ran it against the databases they could access, looking for a match. One of those databases is DNAFamilyTree.

"It's an exact match," the sheriff said.

"So, what was Henry Fields's DNA doing in the Bobcat?"

"On the piece of plastic that you think was part of a bin carrying a rattlesnake. By the way, Peggy's crew identified that exact handle as one used to seal a plastic bin."

"Was it large enough to hold a rattlesnake?"

"Definitely," the sheriff said.

"You think Henry's our guy?"

"That's what's crazy," the sheriff said. "I know Henry Fields, at least a little bit. He lives alone. I've always thought he was . . . well . . . maybe a little peculiar, but basically harmless. He lives on a farm outside of town. He's always lived alone, like a bachelor farmer."

"Is he a loner?"

"Not exactly. Kind of quiet. Friendly enough, if you talk to him. But reserved. I think he has friends. I think he's well liked in the county. He's a little odd. I guess . . . I don't know. I don't know if Henry Fields could have done these things. But I guess you never know."

Sam and the sheriff talked about it. Was there a logical reason Henry, the county's zoning guy, was in the Bobcat? Something to do with his work? And was there a plausible reason he dropped a piece of plastic in the Cat? And left it there? Neither of them could come up with anything that made sense, except the obvious.

"He was dropping a rattlesnake on the Bobcat's seat," Sam said. "And that piece of plastic fell off the bin, and he couldn't pick it up for fear of being bit."

"He had to leave it there," the sheriff said. "God. Henry Fields."

"Let's think this through," Sam said.

Eventually, they would need to interview Henry. Where was he the night the Garcia kids disappeared? Where was he the night the Smileys were shot? They'd be asking him the kinds of questions that would get tense fast. Questions that would let Henry Fields know he was a suspect. And if he knew he was a suspect, and had anything incriminating at his farmhouse, he'd have time to get rid of it.

"But why would Henry Fields, the zoning commissioner, okay the development of a site he knew was right next to the Garcia kids?" the sheriff said.

"Maybe he didn't?" Sam said. "Maybe Leslie Warner had to argue about it, to get it approved."

"Leslie Warner would have had her ducks in a row," the sheriff said. "If she proposed the development, she would have addressed any potential issues before she went to zoning."

Sam knew they needed to speak with Leslie and Jules. They needed to see if Henry had fought against the Alta Vista development. And they needed to ask Jules if there was any reason Henry Fields might have been in their company's Bobcat.

As they talked it through, they confirmed they needed a search warrant. When they started asking questions about him, word would get around. And when they finally visited Henry's farmhouse, they wanted to surprise him, because they were going to search the place.

"Maybe we'll find more Lugers," Sam said.

The sheriff, thinking about it, said, "I'll bring the one we have bagged in evidence."

"For Gray's nose," Sam said.

The sheriff said she'd get to work on the search warrant.

"You know someone who can turn it around quickly?" Sam said.

"Beatrice Hobson," the sheriff said. "Local district court judge. She was at the 10 o'clock service."

Nothing like a small town.

Search warrants were rare in Bluff County, but the few times the sheriff had needed one, over the years, Judge Hobson had obliged. And she'd been able to respond as quickly as the sheriff needed.

"Give me a couple hours," the sheriff said.

"I'll see if I can track down Leslie and Jules and talk to them about Henry's okay of the site, and whether or not Henry would have been in their Bobcat."

"Keep in touch," the sheriff said.

CHAPTER 34

It took Sam a couple of minutes to find Leslie Warner's phone number.

She'd just gotten off the golf course and was having lunch with the rest of her foursome.

When Sam explained he wanted to revisit the zoning approval process for Alta Vista, Leslie said, "I thought you were calling to tell me we could get back to work."

"Oh," Sam said. "Not quite yet. Probably another day. I'm pretty sure you can get back on the site on Tuesday."

"Tuesday?" Leslie said.

Sam thought about it. For now, he didn't see a reason to keep the site closed. But he needed to be sure. "Unless you hear differently. Figure . . . Tuesday."

"Okay," she said.

"But I have a couple of questions about the zoning approval process," Sam said.

"Okay," Leslie said. "Why?"

"Did you work with Henry Fields on the approval?"

"I did," Leslie said.

"Were there any issues?"

"Yes. He didn't want to approve it."

"Why?"

"He claimed he needed more time to consider my proposal, on account of building so near the bluff top."

"You think there was more to it?"

"I did. I spent a lot of time on the architectural and engineering piece of the project. By the time I went to Henry it was pretty obvious we could safely build on the site. I made sure of it."

"But he was still reluctant to approve?"

"He was," Leslie said. "I suspect it was because of Cab Teufel. You didn't hear this from me, because I need to deal with the county, but those two are in cahoots. Henry has his job mostly because Cab backed him when it came time to hire. Cab wanted someone in zoning who would keep him in the loop about upcoming projects."

"And you think Cab didn't want Alta Vista to go forward?"

"He wanted a piece of it. Cab wanted to sell me bluff property he owned for the project. And then he wanted to partner on it. That's the way he works."

Sam still wondered about it.

"But eventually, Henry Fields approved it?"

"He did. But it took some threats. Henry wanted me to wait until Cab returned. I knew Cab was out of the country and couldn't be contacted, and that's why I submitted my proposal when I did. Once I submitted, Henry told me he needed time. Which was bullshit. Then he told me I should wait for Cab, that he thought Cab had some bluff property he thought would work better. Again, bullshit. Cab would have made sure the deal worked to his advantage. Cab only worries about himself."

"And you pushed back?"

"I did. I threatened to go to the city manager. That's Henry's boss. Henry doesn't like to make waves, so he finally relented and approved it."

Then Sam explained he needed to ask Leslie a question in confidence. He didn't want anyone else knowing about the question or her answer.

"Okay," Leslie said.

"Is there any reason Henry Fields would have been in your Bobcat?"

At first, Leslie didn't understand the question. "In my Bobcat? You mean, driving it?"

"Yes. Would he have gotten into it on the Alta Vista site? Or is there any reason, as maybe part of his zoning work, he would have driven it?"

"God no," Leslie said. "I don't even think Henry Fields knows how to drive a Bobcat. He's a pencil pusher. He knows construction because his family was involved in it. But I don't think he's ever built anything. He doesn't strike me as the kind of guy who likes to get his hands dirty."

"Is it worth double-checking with Jules?"

"I can call Jules," Leslie said. "But he never mentioned it to me. And given that it would be an odd thing to happen, he probably would have."

Sam asked Leslie to double-check, making sure she let Jules know it was confidential, and to let him know.

It took less than 10 minutes for Leslie to confirm it.

"Jules said no way Henry Fields ever set foot in that Bobcat," Leslie said.

But Sam knew Henry had been in it. At least sometime.

"Okay," Sam said. "Thanks."

"Do you mind telling me what this is all about?"

"We're just following up on some details," Sam said. "Right now, it's an active investigation and I can't really share more. But you've been helpful. We really appreciate it."

"Tuesday?" Leslie said, wanting to make sure Sam Rivers remembered his promise.

"Tuesday," Sam said. He wanted to add, unless you hear differently, but under the circumstances he didn't think it was a good idea.

By 4:00, Sam was on his way to Henry Fields's house, and on the phone with the sheriff. The sheriff was also in her SUV, followed by two cruisers and four deputies, all on their way to Henry's farmhouse. Sam had just explained what he'd found out from Leslie Warner.

"It's incriminating," the sheriff said. "But let's hope we find more."

"I think this is the guy," Sam said. "We've got him refusing to approve the site."

"At first," the sheriff said.

"But clearly, he didn't want it to go forward. He only relented after being threatened. That's probably when he figured out the rattlesnake angle."

It made sense, the sheriff thought. Henry would know the zoning rules and regs.

"And we have his DNA from the Bobcat," Sam said. "And Leslie Warner and Jules both confirm there was no way he would be in there. But he was. I'm guessing the night before, he put that rattlesnake on the Bobcat's seat."

"When the plastic fell off the bin and he couldn't retrieve it," the sheriff said.

"That's right."

Again, it was all plausible. Maybe even reasonable, the sheriff thought. But she knew they needed more.

"Let's see what Henry has to say," the sheriff said.

"Do we know he's there?"

"Yup. Rosie called him an hour ago, said she wanted to talk to him about county business. He said he was on his way and should be home before 4:00."

"You think he's suspicious?"

"I would be," the sheriff said. "But I don't think there's anything he can do about it. Also, if he's enroute and we get there when he does, he won't have time to hide anything."

"Like a Luger," Sam said. "Did you bring it?"

"Right here on the seat beside me. Did you bring Gray?"

"Right here on the seat beside me."

CHAPTER 35

Shortly after 4:00, the sheriff, her deputies, and Sam Rivers watched Henry Fields's black Passat turn into his drive. The sheriff's SUV, two cruisers, and Sam's Jeep followed him in.

The farmhouse sat on an expansive acreage of pasture. The pasture was surrounded by white fencing, and there were three horses in the field. The house, like the fencing, was a two-story white clapboard with two upper windows jutting out over the roof. The yard was well-trimmed and there were boxed flowers—purple-and-white petunias and red salvia—on either side of the front door.

Henry parked and got out of his car, looking perplexed.

Sheriff Betsy Conrad got out of the SUV while the others pulled up, parked, and got out of their cars.

Sam let Gray off the back seat and out into the heat of the day, waiting while Betsy approached.

"What's going on?" Henry said.

"Henry," the sheriff nodded. "We've got a search warrant to look through your house and premises."

"A warrant?"

"That's right."

"To search *my* house?" Henry said, shocked. "For what?"

"For anything having to do with the deaths of the Garcia kids, the murder of Joe and Venita Smiley, and the murder of Adder Musgrave."

Sam watched Henry's face grow stunned, as though he'd been slapped in the face.

"What the hell are you talking about?" Henry said.

The sheriff paused. "We need to search your house and barn, Henry."

"For what?" Henry repeated.

The sheriff repeated what she'd said, which didn't dent Henry's confusion.

"I have no idea what in the hell you're talking about," Henry said. "Who the hell is Adder Musgrave? I don't know any Adder . . ."

"Where were you last night?" the sheriff said.

Henry's face, already red, phased pale. "Out of town," he said.

"Can you tell us where?"

Henry hesitated. "No," he said.

"Why not?"

"It's private," Henry said. "It's . . . a private matter. And it's none of your goddamn business."

By now, four deputies and Sam were standing beside the sheriff, listening. And waiting to enter the house. And the barn.

"If you can tell us where you were and you can prove it," the sheriff said, "that might be important."

"I wasn't here," Henry said. "And I didn't have anything to do with the Garcia kids. I learned about them with everyone else."

"We need to look," the sheriff said. Then she approached him and handed him the search warrant. Henry took it and appeared to read it.

"This is outrageous," he said.

"Henry, if you can tell us about your whereabouts over the last few days, and you can prove it, that'd help."

"None of your goddamn business about my whereabouts. I was out of town. I left last Thursday. And I just got home."

"Can you give us the names of anyone who can vouch for your whereabouts?"

"No," Henry said. "Like I said, it's private."

"Henry," the sheriff said. "This is important."

"You're goddamn right it's important. My privacy is important."

There was a stonewall moment during which nobody moved. Finally, the sheriff said, "You can let us in, and we can go about our business, Henry. Probably best if you just stay in your car."

"What the hell is this about? Did someone say I was responsible? That I killed the Garcia kids? I didn't. I don't know anything about it. Or the Smileys. I thought that was murder-suicide. And it's the first I've ever heard of . . . whoever else you accuse me of knowing. Killing. Add . . ."

"Adder Musgrave," the sheriff said.

Henry Fields looked around, glanced back down at the search warrant, exhaled, sharply, looked away, and thought about it.

"This is crazy," he said.

"Sooner we go about our business, the sooner we're done," the sheriff said.

"Goddamn it!"

Finally, Henry walked to his front door and used a key to open it. Then he stepped back, walked to his car, and without looking at any of them, got back into his Passat, sitting in his seat, staring forward, and ignoring them.

Finally, the deputies began searching the house.

No one was sure what they were looking for. Some kind of evidence they thought they'd recognize when they saw it. But for the next 90 minutes they searched every part of Henry's house. They confiscated a personal computer—an old HP desktop sitting under a desk in what appeared to be Henry's study. Or home office. They left the monitor.

When Henry saw them hauling out his desktop he sprung out of the car and protested. When the sheriff told him they needed to have a look, asking him if it was password protected, he told her it was. She asked him for the password, and he said, "No! I'm not gonna give you my password. That's private. Return my desktop. Whatever's on it is my business."

"Henry, don't make this any harder than it is."

"Betsy Conrad!" he said, red-faced in a way that looked like a tomato ready to burst. "You know me. Do you think I'm a murderer?"

She paused. "I'm just trying to get to the bottom of some questions, Henry. Questions about your whereabouts and what you've been up to."

Henry, shocked and frustrated, said, "You can go fuck yourself," and got back into his car.

Sam brought Gray forward and they stepped around the SUV's other side, out of eyeshot of Henry Fields. Sam nodded to the sheriff and Sam opened the SUV and brought out the bagged Luger. He carefully unsealed the bag, opened it, and let Gray sniff the oiled weapon. Once Sam was sure Gray had gotten its scent, he said, "Find. Find, Gray."

First, Sam led Gray into the house. They spent the next 10 minutes going upstairs, then throughout the rooms on the main floor, then into the basement. It was an old, dusky, dank basement. Sam guessed the house was 100 years old. Seemed so, anyway, judging from the stone-and-mortar foundation. But there was nothing below except an ancient coal furnace next to a new HVAC furnace, and cobwebs.

Once outside Sam took Gray into the barn and they began nosing around. Thankfully, the horses were still in the pasture. There was a tack room in the rear of the barn. It was a kind of closet with a workbench and all kinds of equipment hanging from the walls—bridles, leather straps, metal bits, stirrups, and the like. Gray's nose appeared overwhelmed by the rich smells.

And then suddenly his attention turned to the far-right drawer of the workbench. He stepped across the shadowy space as Sam was searching for a light switch. Sam found one and switched on the overhead light and turned to see Gray's paws up on the workbench.

If Gray stood on his hind legs, he was nearly as tall as Sam. He was a big animal, but also heavy in the chest and shoulders. Strong. Clearly strong enough to raise his paws onto the desk, poke his nose at the drawer, sniff hard, and then paw it and whine.

Inside, Sam found a Luger, an exact replica of the one bagged in the sheriff's SUV. The sheriff was behind him.

"Look at this," Sam said.

The sheriff approached, saw the Luger, looked at Sam, and said, "Rosie, get your gloves on. There's something here we gotta bag."

Deputy Rosie Miller approached, pulling out a pair of surgical gloves. She lifted the Luger out of the drawer and gingerly turned it, finding the safety and making sure it was on. Then she placed it into a clear plastic evidence bag.

Once outside, the sheriff approached Henry Fields, still sitting in his car, looking at his phone. Henry heard the sheriff approach and looked up.

It was hot and the engine was running for the air-conditioner. Henry rolled down the window and said, "You finished?"

The sheriff held up the bag with the Luger and said, "This yours?"

Henry looked at it and said, "No."

"This was in a drawer in your barn," the sheriff said.

Henry looked surprised again. "I've never seen it before. Somebody put it there."

Sam thought he appeared believable enough. But of course, you could never tell with a murderer.

"I think you need to come with us, Henry," the sheriff said.

Again, Henry Fields looked dumbfounded. "What for?"

"For the time being, you're under arrest. While we follow up on a few things."

"What?"

"We can arrest you and hold you for 36 hours, Henry. If I were you, I'd find an attorney. Do you know any?"

"Yes, I know attorneys. Are you serious? I need to follow you?"

"We can give you a ride, Henry."

"In your squad car?"

"That's right."

Again, he was flummoxed. He seemed to gather his thoughts quickly and said, "Just . . . I cannot believe this is happening." He looked away, and then looked back and said, "Let me call Steve Powers."

"Sure," the sheriff said. "Why don't you tell him to meet us at the station?"

CHAPTER 36

After Henry Fields spoke with his attorney, Deputy Rosie Miller read him his rights, and then put him into the rear of her cruiser and drove him to the Owen's Gap station (and a holding cell).

The sheriff asked Sam if he and Gray would take another tour through the house and barn and around Henry's grounds, given that it was a large acreage, and they had found the Luger. Of course, Sam agreed. They searched through the afternoon but didn't find anything other than the incriminating weapon.

One of the last items they searched was Henry's Passat, which was still parked in front of the house. When Sam and Gray took a spin around the car, Sam noticed what appeared to be an oil change sticker in the top left windshield. He got Henry's car keys from a deputy, opened the driver's side door, sat in the car, and examined the sticker.

Henry had changed his oil a week ago Saturday. The sticker indicated the next time the oil should be changed—it was a date and/or mileage amount, whichever came first.

Sam thought about it. He started the Passat and checked the odometer. It appeared as though Henry would need an oil change in about 9,300 miles. That sounded like a lot of miles.

There was a phone number for the oil change shop on the sticker.

Sam got out of the car and took a photo of the Passat's license plate. Then he returned to the driver's seat and called the shop.

They confirmed they had changed the oil in Henry Fields's Passat the previous Saturday. They also confirmed Passats needed to change their oil once every 10,000 miles. They had the odometer reading from Henry's visit. According to the odometer's current reading, it appeared Henry had driven 696 miles over the last week.

Interesting.

Sam checked the mileage from where he was sitting in Henry's driveway to McCutcheon, Iowa. It was 106 miles, one way. If Henry had made the trip three times—maybe a couple of times to get the rattlesnakes, and a third time to kill Adder Musgrave—he would have driven more than 600 miles.

Sam called the sheriff, got her voicemail, and left a message, mentioning Henry's busy week, at least given his car's mileage.

It was getting late by the time Sam pulled into the Bluff Country Inn. He again stopped by HyVee and bought a sandwich, some chips, and some lemon tea, too tired and impatient to sit down at a restaurant. Besides, Gray was hungry too.

Back at his room, he fixed Gray's dinner and then sat down to munch on some chips, washing them down with the tea.

Then the sheriff called.

When Sam answered, the sheriff said, "Quite a day."

Sam agreed.

"We have Henry Fields's DNA in the Bobcat," the sheriff said, rattling off their evidence. "We have a weapon that's almost the exact duplicate of the one used to kill the Smileys. And by the way, it's unregistered, just like the Smiley weapon."

"Any prints?"

"Wiped clean."

"Henry claims to know nothing about it?" Sam said.

"That's affirmative. What would you expect? He's going to cop to the gun?"

"I'm hoping he eventually cops to something," Sam said.

The sheriff thought about it. "I've known Henry Fields my entire life. He's always been an odd duck. He's hiding something. Why won't he tell us where he's been since last Thursday? What's this about his car mileage?"

Sam explained about Henry's busy week, the round-trip distance to Iowa, two trips for rattlesnakes, and another to kill Musgrave.

"Hmmm..."

"Can you ask him about it?"

"I can. But as soon as Steve got here, he told him to say nothing."

"His attorney?"

"He closed him up tight as a drum. Then they went into conference."

"But he told us he was out of town since Thursday," Sam said.

"That's right. When he was still talking."

Sam thought about it. "He could have gone down last Monday and gotten a couple of rattlesnakes. He let one go in the ditch and dropped one on the Bobcat's seat. The one in the ditch goes off in search of cover and disappears into the grave with the Garcia kids and never gets found. Henry figures he needs another one to plant and goes down and gets it Wednesday, or Thursday. The third one he puts where he knows we'll find it, at the other end of the development. We find the grave in the trees Friday night. We interview Adder on Saturday. Henry gets a call from Adder Saturday afternoon."

"When he said he was still out of town," the sheriff said.

"Easy enough to check and see if he was out of the office on Thursday and Friday."

"We can do that," the sheriff said.

"Henry drives to Adder's Saturday night or early Sunday morning and shoots him. The McCutcheon County crime scene guys think Adder was shot with a rifle."

"We checked the Luger we found at his house, and it hasn't been fired."

Sam thought about it. "If he's got a solid alibi, why doesn't he tell us?"

"He claims it's private."

"Murder is definitely something you want to keep private," Sam said. "Maybe he's having an affair with a married woman?"

"Maybe a married man," the sheriff said.

"You think he's gay?"

"I have no idea. I know he's been a bachelor for forever. Never married. But I've never heard he had any interest in men. Or women, for that matter."

"Even if he was having an affair with a married man, why wouldn't he tell us? These days nobody thinks twice about someone being gay."

"Bluff County's more conservative than most places," the sheriff said. "I can see how an older guy like Henry Fields might not want his sex life known, if he is gay."

"He wouldn't have to tell anyone but you," Sam said.

"That kind of thing'd get out," the sheriff said. "I wouldn't say anything, but I'd need to tell a deputy or two."

"If he was meeting a lover, don't you think the lover would want to come forward?"

"Unless they're married."

They both thought about it, but knew they were just making guesses.

"Can you put a tracker on his Passat?" Sam said.

"You mean, if he posts bail and gets out, to track where he goes?"

"If he gets out," Sam said, "he might lead us somewhere. To wherever he was over the weekend. Or to wherever he's hiding evidence. Like the rifle that killed Adder Musgrave."

"The search warrant is broad enough to let us do that," the sheriff said. "I'll have a deputy head over and do it tonight."

Sam thought about it. "It might help you clear him or convict him."

"Maybe," the sheriff agreed. "I gotta say, he was convincing when we first asked him, about not knowing about the kids, the Smileys, and Adder Musgrave. Not knowing anything about anything."

"As a murderer would be," Sam said.

The sheriff agreed.

"We've got a hearing in the morning in front of Judge Hobson. I'll ask the judge to deny bail. But she's known Henry as long as I have. I can't see Beatrice Hobson denying Henry bail."

"Even given our evidence?"

"So far, it's circumstantial. Putting Henry in the same Bobcat that had the rattlesnake is good, but he denies it. Finding the Luger at his place is good, but it hasn't been fired and it's clean. If it's his, he wiped it down before he put it in that drawer."

Sam knew a good defense lawyer could raise enough doubt about those two pieces of evidence to make them circumspect.

"Don't forget he was reluctant to approve the Alta Vista site," Sam said. "And there's his car mileage. I think there's enough to ask for a couple million for bail."

"That's the number I was thinking," the sheriff said. "But Henry's got his entire place to put up as collateral. I suspect he'll walk as soon as he posts whatever the judge wants."

The sheriff told Sam she'd get a tracker on Henry's car, and that she'd let Sam know what happened as soon as the hearing was over. She didn't think the hearing would take more than a few minutes, so he should expect a call before 10:00.

Sam walked Gray out into the grassy area behind the motel.

Back in his room, he phoned Carmel.

"Still in Owen's Gap, I presume?" she said.

"We got a break. Sort of a break, I guess."

Sam told her about finding the DNA in the Bobcat, the match to Henry Fields, the search of his property, Gray's find of the Luger, and how Henry put 700 miles on his car over the last week—which could be trips to Iowa.

"That all sounds pretty incriminating," Carmel said.

Sam agreed.

"But you don't sound convinced," Carmel said.

"I don't know. If you would have seen Henry Fields when we asked him about some of what we've got against him. He seemed pretty genuine. And he denied knowing anything about the murders. Or Adder Musgrave."

"The Iowa snake guy?"

"That's right," Sam said. "Henry Fields just looked . . . the way you would if your house was searched when you had nothing to do with anything. And you were arrested. Total disbelief. Total shock."

"Did you think he was going to confess?"

"I thought there was a chance."

"You're such an optimist."

Sam considered himself a realist.

"I guess I was hoping he'd confess so I could come home," Sam said.

"Aww," Carmel said. "And I want you here, lying beside me. But I've got two surgeries in the morning. I need to be fresh, and you'd keep me up."

"And I've got to give Kay Magdalen an update in the morning, before she threatens me with a return to Colorado."

They were both disappointed, and they both said so, and they both knew it would mean more tension when they were finally in each other's company. Tension that would need to be snapped by the deft stroke of hands. And mouths.

Sam asked about wedding RSVPs, and Carmel told him he'd gotten two more; she was beginning to feel bad about everything she'd said about his friends.

"I told you," Sam said.

"Rivers," she said.

CHAPTER 37

Monday

Sam was awake at first light, thinking about his day. He made himself motel coffee, using two packets instead of one, hoping the double strength might provide insight.

Today marked one week in Owen's Gap and he did not know if he should go or stay. He remembered the previous evening's conversation with Carmel. The thought of her gave him a twinge of melancholy and longing, emphasis on longing. Especially because he wasn't sure when he was heading home.

Today was Monday and he had already told Leslie Warner she could resume development on Alta Vista tomorrow. Technically, his work researching and protecting an endangered rattlesnake was done, so he should probably phone her and tell her the site was open, effective immediately. Kay Magdalen would tell him he was done, even though there were still a few details he needed to address.

Sam needed to make sure the sheriff was okay with reopening the Alta Vista site. With Henry Fields in custody, he suspected the sheriff would be fine with Sam's decision.

As Sam thought about it, maybe he was wrong about Henry Fields. The circumstantial evidence was closing around Henry like a noose. And the sheriff said Henry had always been a little different. So maybe Henry would have the night to think about it and he'd walk into the morning's hearing and confess?

But Sam didn't think so.

Sam thought Henry Fields would be free on bond before noon, or earlier. But would that necessarily mean Sam couldn't be free to go himself? Given the evidence, the sheriff had current events under control. And as much as Sam would like to see Henry's conviction through to its logical conclusion, it was county business now, none of which any longer involved endangered rattlesnakes.

Sam decided to stick around to discuss reopening Alta Vista with the sheriff. He knew the sheriff would be tied up at the courthouse until 10:00. He still needed to send Kay Magdalen a summary report, but he had plenty of time to write it, pack, speak with the sheriff, and return home.

After taking a long, airing walk with Gray, Sam stopped off at the Gap Café. At this hour of the morning, around 7:30, the day was very pleasant. But with a predicted high of 92 (heat index 100) it wasn't going to last. Though it was perfect weather for rattlesnakes.

He found an outside table near the edge, so Gray wouldn't startle any of the customers.

After placing his order, Mel Harken, publisher of the *Gazette*, blew out of the café door, clearly caffeinated. She made a bee line for Sam's table.

Sam nodded, and Gray sat up on his haunches and considered the newspaper publisher, warily.

"Who's this?" Mel said.

"This is Gray, my partner. Gray, meet Mel Harken."

Mel reached out a hand and Gray sniffed it.

"He looks like quite an animal."

"He is," Sam said.

Then she turned her attention back to Sam. "I heard about Henry Fields," Mel said.

Sam wasn't sure what she'd heard, but he knew he couldn't share anything. "Okay," he said, noncommittal.

"I wonder if you could just confirm a few points for me," she said, reaching into her pocket for a small notebook. She pulled a pen from her work shirt's breast pocket.

"I don't think so, Mel."

"Pfffft," Mel said, ignoring Sam's reluctance. "So, Henry's in jail?"

"No comment," Sam said.

"Oh, come on, Rivers. These are things I can find out by walking over to the station."

"I'm not at liberty to share any details about an ongoing investigation."

"Seems to me you owe me, Rivers. A little detail about Lugers?"

Sam remembered. "I appreciate that, Mel. But why don't you just call Sheriff Conrad. You guys are friends. She'll give you the scoop."

"She's busy."

"I'll tell you this much," Sam said. "There's going to be a hearing this morning over at the courthouse. If you head over there, I'm sure you could attend it."

Sam knew the hearing would be public. He wasn't telling Mel anything she wouldn't find out on her own.

But the glare in her eyes told him she wasn't happy about his reluctance to share details.

"My hands are tied, Mel," Sam said.

"Courthouse?" she said.

"Courthouse."

Sam waited about 10 minutes for his eggs, hashbrowns, toast, and coffee. The café's coffee was decidedly weaker than the double strength he'd made back in his room, reminding him he still wasn't feeling any inspiration.

Sam was just about finished with his eggs when Cab Teufel exited the café.

Cab, like Mel, approached Sam's table.

"I saw Mel talking to you. I suspect she was asking you the same questions she was asking me."

Sam shrugged. "Maybe."

"About Henry Fields?"

"I told her I don't really know anything, and I am not authorized to talk about an ongoing investigation."

"She said Henry was arrested yesterday."

Sam didn't respond.

Cab waited, to see if Sam would say anything or if there was a change in his countenance. But Sam's face remained blank.

"Word on the street is that Henry's a suspect in the Garcia kids' disappearance."

Sam shrugged, noncommittal.

"May I remind you that as a civil servant, you basically work for the public. And since I'm a member of the public, you work for me."

Until now Sam Rivers hadn't had a strong opinion about Cab Teufel, despite what Leslie had shared with him. It was more of a shaded perspective. But the kind of assholery that had just come out of the man's mouth was making that shade darken.

Sam smiled. "I appreciate that."

"Henry's a suspect?"

"I'm not at liberty to talk about an ongoing investigation."

Cab frowned. "How much longer you gonna be around? Can you tell me that?"

"Not sure," Sam said.

"Not sure you can tell me? Or not sure how long you're going to be around?"

"Both," Sam said.

"Are you reopening the Alta Vista site?"

"Not sure," Sam said.

"For Christ's sake, Rivers."

Sam didn't say anything. The man was disrupting his last bite of eggs.

"You should tell Leslie Warner she'd be stupid to build there, next to that grave site."

"She strikes me as the type of person who can make up her own mind."

Cab Teufel realized Sam wasn't going to tell him anything or help him out with Warner Construction.

"Have a good day," Cab said. "And a safe trip back to the Cities."

Sam guessed he was annoying Cab Teufel, but he didn't really care.

By 8:30, Sam and Gray were back in their hotel room. Sam took the next half hour reading and responding to his emails. He pulled up a fresh email, addressed it to Kay Magdalen, and thought about how to begin.

He took a half hour to write a few paragraphs that told Kay about the confirmed origin of the rattlesnakes, that they'd repatriated two of them to Barry Vander and the Iowa EMR population, that they were pretty sure they'd identified the Iowa snake poacher, and that he'd been murdered by a man who was now in custody in the Bluff County jail, awaiting a bond hearing.

But from Sam's perspective, the evidence against Henry Fields was largely inconclusive.

Sam didn't say his Bluff County work was done because he hadn't yet spoken with the sheriff. He preferred to leave his options open.

He clicked send, closed down his laptop, and began packing.

Then the sheriff called. It was 9:30.

"Did the judge grant him bail?" Sam said.

"She did—$1 million dollars, though I asked for twice that."

"Does Henry Fields have that kind of money?"

"His hobby farm is worth that, at least. And he owns it outright. He put that down as collateral."

"I think I should call Leslie Warner and tell her the site can be reopened for development," Sam said.

"Why don't you come over to the station and we'll talk about it."

That surprised Sam and he said so.

"Just . . ." the sheriff said. "Come over here. Let's talk."

CHAPTER 38

When Sam arrived, he found Sheriff Betsy Conrad sitting behind her desk, staring into space.

"Come on in, Sam."

"Have you charged him?"

"Working on it."

But it didn't seem to Sam as though she was.

"I've known Henry Fields for nearly 30 years," the sheriff said. "Way back to when I was hired on as a deputy. Did I ever tell you I dream about those Garcia kids maybe once a month?"

"No."

"It started about six months after they disappeared. After it became more likely than not that we weren't going to find them. At least, alive."

"It was a tough case."

"There was a picture of them both together. The one Ginny gave us. The one we published."

Sam had seen it.

"Cute kids. But in my dreams, they'd always appear scared. Not like they did in the photos. Scared and still alive, and like they were trying to tell me something."

"Maybe they were trying to tell you something," Sam said.

Sam was a rigorous follower of evidence. But he also recognized the value of instinct. The value of the gut, and what it might be trying to say. And most especially the value of dreams.

"I thought, once the kids were found, the dreams would stop," the sheriff said.

"They didn't?"

"Had one last night. Just like the others. The kids from that photo. Looking scared, and . . ." she paused, "maybe . . . restless, disturbed?"

"The case has been open for 25 years. That kind of history gets under your skin."

The sheriff knew it was true. "I just thought the dreams would stop, once the kids were found."

"Takes time," Sam said.

"I know," she said. "It'll take time getting used to how this case turned out."

"You mean, Henry Fields?"

The sheriff nodded.

"People surprise you," Sam said.

"Don't they? If you would have told me somebody local was involved with the Garcia kids, somebody who would be willing to commit murder to cover it up, Henry Fields wouldn't have been on the list."

"But the evidence," Sam said.

"Yup. Hard to ignore."

They both sat for a moment, thinking.

Deputy Rosie Miller appeared in the doorway. Sam and the sheriff looked up.

"We're tracking Henry," she said.

Sam remembered the tracking device they'd placed on Henry's Passat.

"He went to his house and was there for about 30 minutes," Rosie said. "Then he started moving again."

"Where's he headed?"

"Out of town. Out County Road 18."

"Under the terms of his bail he can't leave the county," the sheriff said. "That road leads to Winona. Keep tracking him. Let me know the second he crosses the county line."

She told him she would and left.

"We need to talk about Alta Vista," Sam said.

"I know. I've thought about it. It's like the rest of this case. I don't feel like I'm ready to have that site reopen. I feel like there's more to find out. But I don't know what. And it's hard for me to make a case for keeping it closed."

"Leslie Warner's gonna want to get back at it."

"And I see no reason not to let her. I just wonder if there's something there we haven't found."

"The USFW is ready to give the go-ahead. We know there aren't any more rattlesnakes, and we know where the ones we found came from."

"I know. I know," the sheriff said. "And Peggy's worked over the burial site with a fine-toothed comb. Whatever evidence was there, she's found."

"And there was nothing that ties back to Henry?"

"Nothing," the sheriff said, sounding disconsolate. "But she didn't find anyone else's DNA. The site was clean."

"It's been 25 years," Sam said.

"I know."

Rosie Miller returned. "He just turned off the road and drove another quarter mile to that remote bluff about 5 miles north of town. We pulled it up on Google Maps and it looks like Cab Teufel's place?"

The sheriff knew it. "There isn't much else out that way," she said.

"That make sense?" Sam said.

"I guess," the sheriff said. "I never thought they were exactly close. I never thought Henry was close to anyone. But if he's looking for advice, Cab would be a good one to ask. At least, he knows a lot of lawyers."

"Didn't Cab help Henry get the zoning job?" Rosie said.

"That's a fact. Cab went to bat for Henry. But I think it was more about Cab needing someone in the job he could manipulate, who could keep Cab in the loop of new development projects."

They all thought about it.

Sam's phone went off. A 563 area code. Maybe Conservation Officer Rich King?

"Gotta take this," Sam said.

Sam clicked on Accept and stepped into the hallway.

"Sam?" Rich said.

"How's it going?"

"Well, it's interesting. Remember I told you Adder Musgrave had a sister?"

Sam did.

"We looked around for her, but nobody had any idea where she was, or even if she was still alive. Turns out she got married and lives over by Tripoli. Marlene. Now her last name is Winslow, which explains why we couldn't find her."

"Did she know anything?" Sam said.

"That's what's interesting. She called us. As soon as she heard about Adder's murder, she called me. Last week Adder stopped by her place and gave her a package she was to give to me, if anything happened to him. Inside, there was a flash drive with a note that said this was the guy who bought the three rattlesnakes."

This sounded like the solid evidence they needed.

"You pulled up the images?"

"We did. Lots of pictures of some guy I've never seen before. Kind of heavyset. Sandy hair."

Henry Fields. "Can you pick out a couple of the clearest and text them to me?"

"I think so. I mean, I can't, but the guy who pulled them up can."

"Do it now," Sam said. "This is big. And important."

"Gimme five minutes," Rich said, and hung up.

Sam returned to the sheriff's office and said, "I think we've got him. An image of Henry Fields picking up rattlesnakes."

The sheriff appeared startled. Rosie was still in her office. Sam told them both about the call and Rosie said, "You sure it was Henry?"

"Sounds like it," Sam said. "Short, kind of stout. Sandy hair."

"Are they sending them?"

"Texting them. Any second."

"This changes things," the sheriff said. "Check to make sure Henry hasn't moved," she said to Rosie.

Rosie nodded and left.

"First thing we do is head out to Cab's place and re-arrest Henry and return him to a cell."

Rosie returned. "Still there."

Sam's phone buzzed. He pulled up his text messages and saw another 563 area code and clicked on it.

Two images came up under the number. There was a note that said, "CO Rich King asked that I send you these, which were given to us by Marlene Winslow."

Sam, the sheriff, and Rosie stared at Sam's screen.

CHAPTER 39

"You want my help, Henry, you've gotta be straight with me. You've gotta tell me everything."

Henry Fields sat in Cab Teufel's farmhouse living room, sipping coffee and looking scared.

"I can tell you I didn't do it," Henry said. "None of it."

"They arrested you for a reason," Cab said. "They must have something."

"I think I'm being setup," Henry said, exasperated. "They found a gun at my place I've never seen before. And they found something with my DNA on it, in that Bobcat where they first found the rattlesnake. It's crazy, cuz I never set foot in that Bobcat!"

"Walk me through it, Henry. If you didn't do it, we'll get you off. Ben Crane will get you off."

"He a lawyer?"

"Best defense lawyer in the state. One of his partners handled my divorce. He told me Ben was a pit bull in the courtroom. Ben's who you want, and I can get him for you."

"I've already engaged Steve Powers."

"You can change. Not that Steve isn't a good lawyer, but he's a generalist, Henry. You need a specialist. You need a pit bull."

"Okay," Henry said, looking down.

"What kind of gun?" Cab said.

Henry let out a long sigh and said, "They found a German Luger at my place. Not mine."

"Did they check it for prints?"

"I guess," Henry said. "That's what they said. But I'd never seen the thing."

"No prints?"

"No!" Henry said.

"That's good, Henry. Reasonable doubt. All you need is reasonable doubt. What else?"

"Somebody's trying to set me up, Cab. I'm tellin' ya. They're trying to say I killed the Garcia kids and the Smileys and some guy in Iowa."

"I'd heard the Smileys were a murder-suicide?"

"That's the official determination. But there's some questions about it."

"Do you know why?" Cab said. "Do they have evidence?"

"No idea," Henry said. "But the gun Joe Smiley used to kill Venita and then himself was the same kind of gun they found in my barn."

"A German Luger?"

Henry nodded, looking away. "Yeah," he said. "But it's not mine."

"And it doesn't have your prints?"

"No!"

"Reasonable doubt," Cab said. "Remember, all you need is reasonable doubt. Weren't you out of town this weekend?"

"Since last Thursday."

"So, you got an alibi. You got someone who can vouch for your whereabouts?"

Henry looked away. "I was up in the Cities. But it's not something I can talk about."

Cab thought about it. "Have you said anything to anyone about where you were? Up in the Cities?"

Henry shook his head no. "I mean, yes, I was in the Cities, but I can't talk about it, and this person," Henry paused. "This person can't talk about it."

"You didn't say anything to anyone about where you were?"

"I can't."

Cab thought about it. Then he grinned.

"Henry Fields. You bangin' a married woman?"

Henry, startled, looked up. "This is serious," he said.

"I know. I know. Just sayin', Henry. There's somebody who will testify on your behalf if it comes to that?"

"No," Henry said. "That's what I'm saying. It's private and no one's business, and I can't bring them into it. I won't."

"What if it's between you and prison, Henry? For life? I mean, privacy is important. Your privacy is important. But just to be clear," Cab said. He stood up, walked across the living room to an oversize desk resting against the wall. Cab turned, sat against the edge of the desk, and folded his arms. "You didn't tell them about your private situation?"

"No. And I don't see how I can."

"I don't think it matters, Henry. I think we can work around it. I admit, what they have is incriminating. But I don't think any of them are deal-breakers. I'd hold your ground on the privacy thing. That's your business and you can keep it your business," Cab said. "They got anything else?"

"Any other evidence, you mean?"

"Yes. Is there anything else tying you to any of it? The Garcia kids. The Smileys? The rattlesnakes?"

"I guess they know I went somewhere last week. They don't know where I was, but they know, from the mileage on my car, I was somewhere."

"But you didn't tell them it was the Cities?"

"No," Henry said.

Cab reached over to a desk drawer and pulled it open. Henry was across the room, staring through a window into Cab Teufel's barnyard. Cab pulled a pistol out of the drawer, a Luger.

Henry Fields was still peering out the window when he heard the Luger's trigger mechanism snap back, metallic and jarring. Then he turned to see Cab Teufel pointing the pistol's barrel straight at him.

Henry, startled, stood up.

"Sit down, Henry." Cab used the pistol's barrel to motion that he wanted Henry to return to his chair.

"What are you doing?"

"I'm protecting myself, Henry. Sounds to me like you're a murderer."

"No!" Henry said. "I never murdered anyone."

"Sounds to me like there's some pretty serious evidence pointing that way."

"You know me. You know I'd never do anything like that."

"Do we really know people, Henry? I've known you for nearly 20 years. And now you're accused of murder. I thought I knew you. But maybe not. And I guess the sheriff is thinking the same thing."

Henry peered at the weapon in Cab's hand. Then he recognized it. Then he seemed to put the pieces together, at least in a way that appeared to Cab that Henry suddenly understood. At least, something.

"I'll leave," Henry said. "I can just leave."

"You can," Cab said.

Henry stood up.

"I'll walk you to your car," Cab said.

That startled Henry. Because if what he was thinking was true—that Cab was somehow involved, that Cab had planted evidence against him, that Cab had . . . murdered people—if all that was true, why would he let him go?

"Not sure I'm comfortable having someone accused of murder in my living room," Cab said, as though reading Henry's thought. "I think it's time for you to leave."

Henry's previously crimson face had turned alabaster. "But I thought you were going to help me," Henry said. He knew it was a stupid thing to say. Henry wanted to go back, to before, to when Cab was going to hire a big shot defense lawyer, to when Cab was going to help him. Because if Cab was the one who planted evidence and murdered people, Cab was going to do something else entirely.

"Time for your departure, Henry," Cab motioned with the pistol. "Time for you to go out and get in your car and leave."

"Okay," Henry said, but so softly even he could barely hear it.

"Sounds to me like you've got nothing to worry about," Cab said.

Now it was back to the old Cab. The smart one. The fixer.

Then Henry thought that if Cab was going to do something, was going to shoot Henry, he couldn't do it in the back. So, Henry did the single most impulsive thing he had ever done in his life, considering the potential consequences. Henry stood up and turned his back to Cab Teufel. And started for the door.

Cab was already standing, the Luger pointed at Henry's back.

Cab knew Henry now understood. But Cab had a plan. It involved Henry visiting Cab to settle a score. There was going to be a struggle at Henry's car. He was going to use the Luger to try and kill Cab. There would be a fight and, in the ensuing struggle, Cab would overpower Henry Fields, overpower him as he had his entire life. Cab would shoot Henry. Shoot him with the gun Henry had brought to kill Cab. It would be self-defense. Then Cab would carefully place the Luger in Henry's dead grip, so Henry's prints would be all over it. He'd fire it off into the barnyard because it needed to look realistic, as though Henry had gotten off a shot before Cab overpowered him. Gunpowder residue.

"Sorry I won't be able to help you out, Henry," Cab said, following him to the door.

But Cab wasn't sorry. He felt again blessed by divine providence, which had shown him the way.

CHAPTER 40

The sheriff's SUV turned into Cab Teufel's drive. The driveway was 200 yards of blacktop that ran in a straight line between two white fences. The house and both sides of the fence were planted in corn, which at this time of year, in this heat and growing season, was nearly 6 feet tall.

When the sheriff turned into the driveway, followed by two cruisers, she watched two figures exit Cab's farmhouse. It was 200 yards, but she was pretty sure it was Cab and Henry.

When the two in the distance heard the vehicles, they turned to look. Then stiffly, the sheriff thought, they turned around and re-entered the house.

"You see that?" the sheriff said.

"Yeah," Rosie said. "Came out and then hurried back in."

"When they saw us."

"Looked like it."

The sheriff had both hands on the wheel. Her phone was on the seat beside her.

"You got Cab Teufel or Henry Fields on your phone?"

"Cab," Rosie said. "He's a commissioner."

"Call him. Tell him I want to speak with him."

As the sheriff continued down the long drive, approaching Henry Fields's Passat, Rosie dialed. The phone rang five times before turning to voicemail.

"He didn't pick up," Rosie said.

"That's interesting. Probably thinking. You got Sam Rivers's number?"

"Calling him now," Rosie said.

After seeing the images on Sam's phone, back at her office, the sheriff thought they could put Gray's skillset to work. Sam was five minutes behind them, having stopped by the inn to retrieve his partner.

"Rivers," Sam said.

Rosie had him on speaker.

"Might have a situation here," the sheriff said. "Don't turn into the drive. What's your ETA?"

"Looks like five minutes," Sam said.

"I want you to stay on that county road. You'll see the turnoff for Cab Teufel's place. Then the road bends around. If you stay on it, you'll be able to drive down the county road and park close to Cab's farmhouse."

The sheriff entered the barnyard and parked next to Henry's Passat, the car between the SUV and Cab's front door. The two cruisers pulled in and parked, one behind Henry's car. The second cruiser angled his car at the end of the drive, blocking it. With fences on either side, they had effectively blocked off use of the driveway, or the ability for Henry Fields to enter his Passat, at least from the driver's side.

"Okay," Sam said, wondering about it.

"The farmhouse is surrounded by corn," the sheriff said. "The house faces the front yard. I have no idea what we're walking into, but if you're willing, you could walk down a corn row and be at the back of the house without being seen."

Sam was. Willing. "Okay," he said. "And we assume he's armed?"

"Probably, given recent events."

"Turning my sound off. Anything you want to share, text me."

"Will do," the sheriff said. "No heroics, Rivers. Think of it more as reconnaissance and making sure no one sneaks out the back."

"I'm no hero," Sam said.

"Press reports indicate otherwise," the sheriff said. "Just keep your head down."

Sam grinned. "Text me," he said, and hung up.

"Now we gotta try Henry," the sheriff said.

Rosie dialed, but he didn't pick up.

Inside the farmhouse, Cab was pissed. And thinking. Could his plan still work? When they'd returned to Cab's living room, he'd made Henry sit down in a corner chair. Then he'd stepped to the side of the front living room window, where he watched the sheriff and two cruisers come down the drive. He watched them block Henry's car in, then block off the driveway. But no one got out of their vehicles.

He was wondering what they knew. If they still had a hard-on for Henry—and there was no reason they shouldn't—he could shoot Henry here. But he didn't know if he had enough time to get the gun in dead Henry's hand and fire it a few times. The gunshots might keep them at bay, but now it was all fucked up. One thing he knew for certain, a live Henry would tell them what he knew, which wasn't much, but enough.

Then that voice that he had listened to so long ago returned to his head. The voice that said, *Do it. Do what needs to be done.*

Suddenly, Henry bolted out of his chair and rushed toward the front door.

Cab turned and fired. Henry let out a yip and stumbled but kept going. Cab fired again, the plaster on the living room wall behind Henry's back splintering. And then Henry was out of the living room and had disappeared beyond the wall.

Cab ran after him, determined. He rounded the corner, saw Henry's hand on the front doorknob, and raised the Luger, taking aim.

"Drop the gun!" Sam said, just inside the back door.

Cab turned the gun and fired, wildly.

Sam disappeared, while Henry burst out the front door yelling. "Don't shoot, don't shoot. He's got a gun. I'm hit."

Cab rushed to the side of his opened front door and slammed it shut. But before he did, he glimpsed the sheriff and Deputy Rosie Miller out of their SUV, the sheriff looking over the front hood, going for her sidearm. Rosie was behind the Passat, also reaching for her gun. The four deputies in the remaining two cruisers were scrambling to get behind the protection of their parked vehicles.

Cab saw it all in a flash. He turned to make sure Sam Rivers was still out of sight.

What to do, what to do.

They knew he had a gun. He'd only fired two rounds. His clip was full. Five rounds left.

Cab ran to the rear kitchen and peered out the back door. There was no sign of Sam Rivers. It was 20 yards to the wall of corn. If he could make it into the corn and run down a row, in 50 yards, he'd be at the edge of the cornfield. He could run into the bluff woods. He'd known those woods since he was a kid. He knew a place. A thicket where nobody would find him. Where he could regroup, find his way out of the woods, keep going.

He burst out the rear kitchen door, firing left, right, and in front of him. Spraying bullets to keep Sam Rivers at bay. Nearly to the edge of corn, he heard a voice to his right.

"Drop your weapon!"

Cab raised his Luger and fired at the voice. Then he was into deep green leaves and running toward the tree edge, one round left.

CHAPTER 41

"When I said don't be a hero, I meant don't get shot," the sheriff said.

Deputy Rosie Miller was bandaging Sam's left shoulder.

Earlier, Sam had positioned himself just inside the cornfield. He crouched down between two rows but was near enough to the edge to see through the leaves and stalks. That's when he heard the shots fired from inside the house. He rushed the back door, opened it, and saw Cab about to shoot Henry Fields in the back.

"Drop the gun!" Sam said. Cab had turned and fired.

Sam ducked and heard the bullet splinter the siding beside him. He figured his yell gave Henry enough time to get through the front door. He thought he heard Henry shout something on the other side of the house, but he was thinking about his own vulnerability. He was stuck in the wide open and could have been shot through the kitchen window, the door, or from somewhere upstairs, if Cab decided to hole up in the house. That's when he sprinted to the edge of the cornfield and disappeared.

The moment Sam was sure he was concealed, he dropped behind a corn row and peered out at the rear of the house. He watched Cab peek out of the back door, and then suddenly it banged open, and the man started firing.

Sam ducked, but when he saw Cab reach the cornfield edge he yelled out and a bullet nicked his shoulder.

Afterward, he realized he should have kept his mouth shut. His voice gave Cab a target and he used it.

Sam felt a searing pain, as though he'd been snakebit, and rolled farther into the corn row. Up ahead, he heard Cab stumbling, running toward the tree line, keeping low. Sam managed to rise and began running toward the sound. He ran 15 or 20 yards and then stopped to get another bearing, but by then the sound had stopped.

Sam thought he could be waiting just ahead, ready to shoot Sam as soon as he appeared. He remembered that a Luger held seven or eight rounds, depending, and he counted back the shots and realized Cab probably had at least one more bullet. He crept forward over the next 30 yards. By the time he arrived at the trees, Cab was gone.

Then Sam walked along the cornfield's edge until he found Cab's tracks and could see where he entered the woods.

Deputy Rosie Miller and another deputy came down the cornfield's edge with weapons drawn.

"He went in here," Sam said, as they approached.

They came down the row, rubbernecking as they walked, guns still out but pointing down. Rosie was holding her weapon with both hands.

When they reached Sam, he showed them the prints, and then where the underbrush was parted and slightly trampled, where Cab had entered the trees. Rosie stepped in to have a better look, but the way forward was a crisscross of weeds, brush, and branches, and it was obvious Cab had kept going. They all paused but couldn't hear anything. If he was near, they would have heard him through the trees.

"He's gone," Sam said. "At least for the moment."

"You're hit?" Rosie said, seeing Sam's bloody shoulder.

"A scratch," he said.

"I don't know about that," Rosie said, peering at the wound.

Back at the sheriff's SUV, Rosie said, "You got lucky," finishing with Sam's bandage. "Might need some stitches, but that should hold you."

"I was trying to slow him down," Sam said to the sheriff. "It was a wild shot. He got lucky."

Sam thanked the deputy. Then he turned to the sheriff and said, "We gotta go after him."

"We gotta think about it," the sheriff said. "I don't want anyone else getting shot."

"Gray and I can track him."

"I'm sure you can. But those woods are thick this late in the summer. And Cab Teufel grew up here. He knows them and you don't. And he's got a weapon."

The two cruisers had already backed out and left the barnyard. Nearby, Henry Fields was leaning on his Passat, looking pale and frightened. Henry's right side had been grazed by Cab's shot. Rosie had patched it, a graze that didn't need stitches. Sam thought the man looked like he might pass out.

"You okay?" Sam said.

"No," Henry said. "He shot me. He almost killed me."

"Good thing we put that tracker on your car, Henry," the sheriff said.

Henry shook his head. "I can't believe it. He almost killed me. Cab Teufel."

"He would have killed you," the sheriff said. "I think you were going to be his fall guy. His ultimate excuse."

"I guess he didn't know about Adder Musgrave's game camera," Sam said.

Henry had no idea what they were talking about, but he knew he didn't feel well. He was dizzy and hot and thought he might be sick. And then he bent over and retched.

Deputy Rosie Miller waited until he was done. She fetched some bottled water from her cruiser, twisted off the cap, and walked it over to Henry.

"Drink, Henry," Rosie said. And he did.

"That guy is getting away," Sam said. "And he's dangerous."

"The more I think about it, the more I think we wait," the sheriff said. "That bluff is a climb. Up top, there's a road that runs along it for a couple of miles. I've stationed deputies up there. If he keeps heading down the bluff, he'll hit a ravine in about a mile. That empties out onto the county road. I've called the highway patrol. They've already got one cruiser on site, with two more that should be here in 10 minutes. We'll have him surrounded."

"He'll wait until dark and sneak out," Sam said.

"It's Cab Teufel we're talking about. He knows those woods and the surrounding country, but he's not exactly a Navy Seal."

Sam remembered. Earlier in the week, at Alta Vista, Cab preferred to stay in his air-conditioned car rather than walk the field. And the man was carrying a few extra pounds.

"And it's hot," Rosie said. "He can't go long without water."

"Three days," Sam said, which was about as long as a human can go without it.

The sheriff seemed to think about that. But Sam knew a man like Cab Teufel, out of shape and in his fifties, would have trouble going without water until nightfall. And the idea he might outwit what was essentially a dragnet was doubtful. Maybe even ludicrous.

"Look," the sheriff said. "I know Cab Teufel. His idea of exercise is riding a lawn mower and driving to Rochester for dinner. The man gets winded climbing over a fence."

"Anyone running from the law is going to find their fifth gear," Sam said.

"Whatever that means," the sheriff said. "I'm not sure Cab has a third gear, let alone a fifth."

"I watched the guy run 50 yards through a cornfield in a matter of seconds," Sam said.

"He'll tire quickly," the sheriff said. "He won't run far."

"I agree," Sam said. "He'll stop. And probably not far. Me and Gray can at least pick up his trail and track him to wherever he holes up. I can take the tracker we put on Henry's car. You'll be able to see exactly where I am. Once I find him, I'll text you and you can follow me in."

"Once you find him, you'll get shot," the sheriff said. She turned to Rosie and said, "How accurate is the tracker we put on Henry's car?"

"To within a foot or less," Rosie said.

"You'll know exactly where I am," Sam said.

Sam could see the sheriff was thinking about it.

"That could work," Rosie said.

"It could also get you shot," the sheriff said.

"I'm not going to take unnecessary risks. Did I tell you I'm getting married in about six weeks?"

The sheriff and Rosie both looked surprised. "All the more reason you should stay put," the sheriff said. "Tell you what," she continued. "Let's spend the next 10 minutes looking around the premises for more evidence, while we think about it."

Sam figured it was worth the time, even though he didn't want to get sidetracked. He worked with Gray through the house but didn't find any additional weapons. But when they searched the barn, Gray became distracted by the floor in the rear of the building. Sam parted the hay at Gray's feet, and he uncovered the latch to a door in the floor. When he used the latch to lift open the door, a room opened up beneath them. The Lair.

"My god," the sheriff said, looking down through the hatchway into the space.

Sam was stunned. He had heard about people collecting Nazi memorabilia, but he had never actually seen a room filled with troubling—and lethal—artifacts. The fact that this was a secret room confirmed the insidiousness of what Cab had done. Cab Teufel knew his Nazi sympathies would not be well received, so he kept it hidden, in the same way he'd hidden the bodies of those children and his involvement with the murders. And he almost got away with it.

"This is really disturbing," Sam finally said.

Rosie also had a look. When she saw the Nazi flag on the wall, she gasped. "Who would have thought Cab Teufel had a room like this one? Collected insane stuff like this?"

After seeing the nature of the additional evidence, Sam felt more strongly than ever that the man needed to be hunted down and brought to justice.

"I gotta go after him," Sam said. "Me and Gray."

"I don't think your fiancé would like you tracking an armed man through the woods," the sheriff said.

"When I told my fiancé about the Garcia kids, she told me to drop everything and get whoever did it."

"I don't think she meant putting yourself in the woods with an armed madman."

But Sam wasn't sure. Besides, he knew they'd be careful. He and Gray.

"I'll keep Gray on a leash," Sam said. "I won't let him get too far ahead. Gray will tell me if we're getting close. Gray can smell it. He starts getting squirrely."

The sheriff was still against it, but while she was waiting, she got a call from one of the deputies who was in position on top of the bluff. The sheriff put him on speaker.

"We're up here," he said. "But it's a lot of road to cover."

"Spread out," the sheriff said.

"We are, sheriff. Got all four cruisers up here, spread out about 300 yards apart. Jeremy says he's hunted turkey in these woods, and they go on for a while. Somebody who knew them might be able to hike their way out. Squeeze past us."

The sheriff paused. "Just stay put and keep your eyes open," she finally said.

After the call ended, Sam looked at her and said, "I'll go get Gray, just in case." But he had a pretty good idea they were headed into the woods.

CHAPTER 42

It took Sam a few minutes to return to his Jeep. The windows were cracked open, but it was still hot. He made sure he and Gray drank plenty of water, suspecting it might take a while to track their fugitive.

When Sam and Gray came around the corner, the sheriff, Deputy Rosie Miller, and Henry Fields were waiting beside the SUV and Henry's Passat. Henry still looked pale.

"There's a chance he could circle back," Sam said.

"I hope so," the sheriff said.

"Let that sonofabitch show his face," Henry said.

It was a surprising comment from the quiet zoning commissioner, but getting shot at can change attitudes.

"I don't think Cab Teufel is that stupid," the sheriff said.

Sam agreed. "Seems to me you could use another body or two."

"I don't want to pull any of those deputies off the bluff," the sheriff said.

"I still think you should let us go in. Me and Gray."

The sheriff paused. "What makes you think you can sneak up on him?"

"I told you. Gray will let me know. It's the way he acts. He'll be able to tell when we're close. I'll pocket Henry's tracker. Did you get it?"

Rosie nodded, holding up a small disc-shaped device. She handed it to Sam.

"I'll carry it with me and once I have a location, I'll text and let you know. Otherwise, you said it yourself. Cab knows these woods and if anyone knows where to go to hike out, it's Cab."

The sheriff didn't like it, but she knew Sam had a point.

"Just . . ." she said. "Don't be a hero."

"You said that," Sam said.

"And you got yourself shot," she said.

"Really more of a graze," Sam said.

The sheriff frowned.

Sam handed Gray's leash to Rosie and entered Cab's farmhouse. He located the primary bedroom and found a walk-in clothes closet. The space was large enough for two clotheshorses, but one side of it was empty. Sam remembered Cab was either getting a divorce or already divorced. Given recent events, he thought the man's ex made a wise choice.

On the back side of the closet door hung the knit shirt Sam had seen Cab wearing earlier. Sam took it down and could tell it hadn't been washed. Then he returned to where Gray and the others waited.

"Gray can use one of Teufel's shirts for his scent," Sam said. "We'll start at the last place I saw him, near the tree edge." Sam tucked the shirt in his belt. "I'll give Gray a sniff and let him loose. But I'll be sure to keep him close."

The sheriff, Rosie, and Henry were going to stay in front of Cab's house, just to make sure he didn't circle back. From the sheriff's SUV, she could keep in touch with her deputies up top and the patrol people farther down the county road.

"I wish I had someone to go with you," the sheriff said.

"We'd make too much noise. If he is holed up somewhere, waiting until dark, we need to sneak up on him."

The sheriff knew it was true.

At the tree edge, Sam let Gray smell the shirt. Gray was a working dog and there were few activities he enjoyed more than tracking scents. Especially in the woods. It didn't matter if it was practice or for real; Gray didn't know the difference.

Sam and Gray moved into the trees, and for the next 10 minutes, they made slow progress, the scent trail shifting back and forth. Either Cab thought he was being followed and was trying to evade his trackers, or he was getting his bearings. After a short while, the scent trail seemed to straighten out and Gray quickened his pursuit.

The woods were dense, and after a quarter mile, the trail turned left, toward the bluff slope. Gray and Sam started climbing. The hillside was covered with tree vines and thick undergrowth, but it was still clear enough to enable Sam to keep up.

Halfway up the incline, Gray turned due north, suddenly, following what appeared to be an old game trail. They continued along the trail, which ran the length of the bluff, for at least a half mile.

Sam was sweating in the dense woods. He knew Gray had to be hot, but he seemed unperturbed by the heat. He was on the hunt, and from the way he began to act, the scent was getting stronger.

There was a place halfway up the bluff where the game trail continued, but Gray stopped. He'd apparently lost the scent and doubled back to where Sam followed him. Then he turned and started climbing again, this time through a denser patch of weeds, vines, and trees.

Sam peered ahead and saw the tops of trees farther up the hillside, near what he assumed was the bluff acme. The space in between looked like some kind of dense hollow, or thicket, a bowl that flattened out before the hillside climbed again.

Sam had a bad feeling about it. Gray was 4 feet in front of him, nose to the ground. Sam hurried to reach him, and just before Gray stepped up and over what appeared to be some kind of edge, he caught Gray by the hair on his back and yanked.

Startled, Gray turned.

Once Sam was certain he had Gray's attention, he turned his free hand flat in front of him, motioning down. He repeated the gesture until Gray understood and complied.

For Gray, Sam's command to lie down made no sense. But he understood and obeyed, keeping his body pointed upwards, ready to continue the track as soon as Sam released him.

After Gray settled, Sam angled the flat of his hand straight up—the "stay" command—and Gray did.

Five feet ahead, Sam could see the lip of that bowl, the edge of which was impenetrable green. The natural hollow cut into the side of the bluff, near its top, was a perfect hiding place. Especially for someone who knew about it and was waiting until dark, when they could rise to the bluff top and keep walking out of the woods. They could also keep an eye out for anyone coming up from the bluff bottom, like Sam and Gray.

Sam guessed they were more than a mile from the farmhouse. If there were three or four cruisers with deputies up top, they'd be spread thin. After dark, under cover of the trees, it'd be easy to slip across the road to more woods and wherever else Cab Teufel thought he could go. Maybe a neighbor? Maybe someone who could give him a lift? Someone who might recognize him, because everyone in the county knew him. But someone who didn't know anything about the recent change in events. And even if he found someone who knew him and knew he was wanted for murder, he had a weapon. And he was willing to use it.

The smart move was to hole up. The hollow they were about to walk into looked like great habitat for rattlesnakes, and murderers on the run.

Sam made another motion with his hand until he was certain Gray understood. *Stay here and stay down.* Then he retreated 10 feet down the hillside and recovered the game trail.

Gray watched through the trees as Sam quietly worked his way along the game trail for another 20 yards. He walked far enough to make sure the hillside rose straight to the bluff top. Then he started climbing, quietly.

Once on top, he found another trail that ran along the bluff, in a straight path through the trees. It was dense and green but easily traversable. Sam walked it until he could see he was above the hollow. Then he stepped forward and peered down into the dense thicket.

The leaves were nearly impenetrable. But as he watched, he eventually discerned the outline of a body in the center of the foliage, largely concealed in the bush. Sam was less than 5 feet from the edge and appeared to be directly above where Gray hugged the hillside below. From this vantage point Sam was almost directly above the figure, Cab. If Sam jumped, he could be on top of the unsuspecting Cab in the time it took to fall less than 10 feet through the air.

While Sam considered jumping, the body moved. Whether because Cab heard Gray or some other sound, the man moved slowly forward. Through a narrow gap in the leaves, Sam could see he held a pistol, pointed in front of him.

If Sam drew his Glock and uttered a command, Cab would fire—ahead of him or up at Sam or both, depending on his rounds. Cab could have brought bullets with him. While Sam was thinking, he watched Cab make an unexpected lunge forward.

Sam sprang off the bluff top, flying 10 feet through the air before plummeting through dense foliage and then whumping on the back of Cab's legs. The fall blew the air out of Sam's chest like a bellows, and for a moment the world was confused.

Sam's fall caused Cab to cry out in pain. But it took him only half a second to recover before he turned, gun in hand, swinging it toward Sam.

Then an enormous gray blur appeared out of nowhere, and the man screamed and fired, his shot gone awry.

Sam, catching his breath, heard the scream and the Luger fire. Gray had Cab's arm and wasn't letting go. The gun had tumbled into the dense foliage. In the struggle, Cab's free hand grabbed a hammer-size piece of limestone, and he brought it across the side of Gray's head. Once, hard. Then again. And again.

Gray made some kind of guttural whine and went down. Then Cab rolled, looked for his Luger, couldn't find it, and dropped over the hillside, recovering the game trail and sprinting through the trees.

Sam tried to grab at the fleeing Cab but was too late. Once Cab disappeared over the edge, Sam scrambled forward, fumbled over the ground, found the Luger, picked it up, and aimed it into the trees. But all he could see was green.

Gray was down, lying on his side, still as stone.

"Gray!" Sam said, breathless. "Gray!"

The wolf dog was still, but breathing. Blood was oozing from the side of his head. His fur was wet and mottled with leaf litter. Sam picked away the litter to reveal a deep gash where the stone had struck him.

"Gray."

Glancing down Gray's flank Sam verified his partner was breathing. Gray's chest rose and settled. Finally, he stirred.

"Gray."

More movement. And then his eye opened and he tried to lift his head.

"Shhh, shhh, shhh," Sam said, placing a calming hand on Gray's neck. Gray's eye closed again, and he remained still for the next couple of minutes.

Sam managed to use his cell phone to call the sheriff and tell her what happened and where he was.

"We've got your coordinates," the sheriff said. "We know where you are."

"He's around here somewhere. He couldn't have gone far."

"Stay put. The deputies are tightening their line along the road above you. He's gotta move sometime. Without water, thirst is gonna make him move."

Sam wasn't so sure.

As soon as he hung up with the sheriff, he called Carmel.

"Gray was knocked out," he said, when Carmel came on the line.

He explained what happened and Carmel's tone, her presence over the line, shifted to calm, cool, professional.

"Just settle down," she said. "Is he breathing normally? Sitting up?"

Over the next couple of minutes, Sam related Gray's vital signs.

"He's a tough animal," she said. "He's probably going to be fine. But there's a risk of a concussion, and that gash in the side of his head needs attention. I'll be down. Two hours."

"Wait," Sam said. But the idea she'd be coming made him feel instantly relieved. "Wait. What time is it?"

"If I leave in the next five minutes, I can be down there by 6:00."

"Should I move him?"

"Just watch him. If he's up to moving and walking, follow his lead. If he can make it back to the Jeep, maybe to a road where you can be picked up, that'd be good. But this is important, Sam.

Don't let him go to sleep. And let Gray take the lead. Don't force him to move."

"I know. I know. He could have complications."

"That's right. Just . . ." she said, sounding a little anxious herself, "Call me if there's any change. I'm coming."

And then she was gone.

CHAPTER 43

The sheriff, the Minnesota State Highway Patrol, and the Owen's Gap town police flooded the area of the bluff where Cab Teufel had disappeared. They scoured the hillside throughout the rest of the afternoon and evening, until dark. Then they posted patrols along the gravel road above the area, near enough so anyone trying to sneak into the forest on the other side would be spotted. But no one ever showed.

Surprisingly, Gray seemed to recover quickly. He had a nasty gash on the side of his head, and he was panting. But he'd been panting heavily before he went down, because of the heat. Gray wore a thick fur coat designed to thicken in winter and keep him warm in subzero temperatures. In the summer it thinned out, but it was still a thick hirsute wonder not designed for the July heat of southern Minnesota.

When Gray was able, they climbed the remaining few yards to the top of the bluff and made their way out to the gravel road where the sheriff and Deputy Rosie Miller met them in the sheriff's SUV. Rosie poured water into Sam's cupped hands and Gray drank. The water seemed to revive him.

On the way back to Sam's Jeep, he gave them more details about what happened. After Gray seemed to recover, the wolf dog was keen to continue searching across the hillside. But Sam knew Gray needed to rest and that he, Sam, needed to keep an eye on him. Brain swelling could be a serious side effect from a blow to the head. It could result in seizures and, if unchecked, death. Sam would need to watch Gray for at least the next 12 hours.

The sheriff explained about beefing up their patrol numbers and how she felt certain there was no way Cab Teufel could get out of the dragnet they'd managed to set up. Especially since he was without water. She predicted it was only a matter of time before he was apprehended. Probably surrendering "like a beaten pup with his tail between his legs."

After she said it, she figured it probably wasn't the right simile, but she let it pass and so did Sam. And Gray.

Before Sam got into his Jeep, the sheriff asked to have a private word. She asked Rosie to give them a second, which Rosie understood to mean make herself scarce.

Once Rosie was out of earshot, the sheriff said, "Henry's pretty sure he figured out how that piece of plastic got into the Bobcat."

"How?"

"He was touring one of Cab's sites recently and he's pretty sure he remembered picking it up and tossing it into the trash. When he was with Cab. He figures Cab fished it out and planted it."

"That makes sense," Sam said. "Did he tell you where he went when he was out of town? And how he put all those miles onto his car?"

"He did, which is why I asked Rosie to give us a moment."

Sam waited.

"I kept pressing him and pressing him and finally he told me, but said I couldn't mention it to anyone. And if I did, he'd sue me and the county and everyone in it."

"Henry?" Sam said.

"I know. Right?"

"And now you're telling me?"

"I told him that you more than anyone deserved to know."

"And he said 'okay'?"

"Not exactly. He said if it went beyond me and you and he found out about it he'd sue you, too, and the entire USFW and probably the government."

"Henry?"

"Crazy. I know."

"I can agree to silence, but only if he wasn't breaking the law."

The sheriff thought about it. "Times have changed, so no. But if it had happened 50 years ago, he might have had problems."

Then the sheriff explained that Henry Fields was involved with a married man. Henry was fine making the relationship known, but for obvious reasons the man, who was going through a divorce, needed the affair kept quiet.

"Where was he?" Sam said.

"He and his lover were having a fling in Duluth," the sheriff said.

"Which accounts for the mileage."

Both of them thought about it for a few moments.

"Poor Henry," Sam finally said. "If it comes up again just tell him I will respect his privacy and will take it to my grave."

As soon as Carmel opened the door to his room at the Bluff Country Inn, Sam felt a startling sense of relief. He was surprised. His jaw had been tense, and he'd been pacing and flexing his hands, but he hadn't noticed. Then he saw Carmel and his world shifted. Moreover, Gray's world shifted. He stood up from his bed and greeted Carmel as though she had been gone six months instead of days. His rapid tail wag made his body vibrate and he began to whine in an uncharacteristic display of emotion.

Carmel nodded to Sam, but stepped directly to where Gray met her, standing.

"How's my boy?" she said, bending over and starting an examination that would consume her next 10 minutes. Checking his eyes, feeling his pulse, talking to him. Cooing to him.

Gray lapped up the attention like a child licking an ice-cream cone.

When she was done, and Gray returned to his dog bed, she finally turned to Sam.

"He seems pretty good," she said. "I think he's gonna be okay. How's my other boy?"

Finally, she walked over to him and wrapped her arms around Sam Rivers and squeezed. Then something he'd been holding onto welled up inside him. Fear, worry, anxiety over Gray's wound, and maybe the realization of how much he loved this woman, Carmel, and what she had come to mean to him, them, over the last year.

"I'm fine now," Sam said. But it came out of him in a whisper and his eyes began to mist.

"Oh, Sam," Carmel said. And they kissed.

Her lips, Sam thought, felt more perfect than anything he could imagine or remembered. Usually kissing Carmel caused a deep stir inside him. Now it was like a balm that soothed his fears and put him in touch with his profound concern, and fear. It came out of him unexpectedly.

"He's gonna be okay," Carmel said.

And for a moment he could not speak to answer. He could only hold onto her.

Carmel, for her part, understood his perspective. She was a veterinarian who had treated countless animals, and their owners. And she knew Sam Rivers loved his wolf dog the way a father loves a son. And she loved him for it, the way we humans, when we are at our best, can love each other.

When Sam finally took off his shirt, Carmel saw his bandaged shoulder.

"Just a scratch," he said.

"Let me be the judge of that."

Carefully, with deft fingers, she removed the awkward bandage.

"Whoever cleaned it did a good job," she said.

"Rosie," Sam said.

"I'll need to thank her," Carmel said. And then she made sure the wound was clean and covered in antibiotic ointment and rebandaged. "I think I can safely say you are fit for physical activity of whatever sort you choose."

Later, naked in bed, their warm bodies sated, they talked—about the Garcia kids, the snakes, Adder Musgrave, and how they felt certain Cab would be found. It was only a matter of time. They spoke of the heat, and about the town of Owen's Gap and the Driftless and how beautiful it all was. Then they napped, briefly, making sure to keep one drowsy eye on Gray's steady and rhythmic breathing.

And then they did it again.

Finally, the day had taken its toll on Sam Rivers; lying in Carmel's warm embrace, he drifted into the first profound and untrammeled sleep he had felt in a week.

And again, he dreamed of rattlesnakes. But they were larger and somehow different than the eastern massasauga rattlers he'd been looking for over the last several days. And they were in a dark place, deep and hidden and menacing. But not to Sam Rivers. They seemed to ignore Sam. They were hunting for someone else.

CHAPTER 44

After Cab Teufel subdued Gray with the limestone club, he took off along the hillside, following a narrow, choked game trail. In moments the dense foliage concealed his escape. He kept moving carefully but hurriedly just below the bluff top, scurrying down the narrow trail, uncertain of his next move.

After what must have been a quarter mile, he stopped to listen. And waited. But there was no one following. He assumed he had at least injured the goddamn dog enough to make its owner, Sam Rivers, pause. Now he thought Sam Rivers had given up the chase, at least for the time being.

Cab Teufel, thirsty, tired, but determined, climbed carefully through the dense vegetation to the bluff top and peered through the trees at the edge of a field. Directly in front of him, the gravel road ran along the bluff, across 50 yards of field. Cab could see a sheriff's cruiser parked beside the road with a deputy sitting on the front grillwork, watching the road. When Cab glanced left, he could see another cruiser a quarter mile distant. To his right, a third cruiser.

Fuck, he thought. *Fuck, fuck, fuck.* It was going to be impossible to cut through that field in daylight and escape into the wild country on the other side. And to the one or two farmhouses he knew he could get to. He had to wait until nightfall.

He was parched and tired, and he needed a cool place to hide to wait out the rest of the day, which appeared to be at least 3 hours off. His mouth and throat were dry, and he craved water more intensely than he could ever remember. But there wasn't a goddamn thing he could do about it. Now, he had to wait. Wait for darkness.

Providence, he knew, had been good to him. He felt certain providence would not abandon him now.

He needed somewhere out of sight, preferably a place where that goddamn dog, if he came to and picked up his trail, would not be able to follow.

Cab dropped back down over the bluff top to the narrow game trail. He scrambled along it for another 100 yards, until he figured he was between the two cruisers up on the road. And then he saw a depression in the hillside, like the place where he had first hid. The depression's edge cut 5 feet above the trail and was so covered over and filled in with dense foliage it was difficult to tell it was a hollow. But Cab could see the barest edge of a limestone wall appearing to angle back into the bluff face.

If the dog followed, Cab knew, he'd use his nose.

Cab moved forward, making sure he paced heavily along the trail. After 50 yards, he found a way down the hillside and descended until he found another game trail. Then he walked along that trail for several more yards. Finally, he retraced his steps, ascending the hillside the way he'd come, carefully making his way back along the bluff top until he was standing—sweaty, tired, and thirsty—near the narrow limestone wall.

There was an opening along the wall, a gap where the ground was barren. Maybe a foot wide and nearly 5 feet away from where Cab stood on the game trail.

Cab bent and braced himself on the trail. Then he jumped and landed, awkwardly, on the narrow patch of ground. If the dog came anytime soon, Cab hoped his sucker trails would lead him astray. At least long enough so he could conceal himself until nightfall and then rise to the bluff top and cross over the road in the dark.

Now he needed to find somewhere out of sight, where his scent would be mitigated.

He stepped carefully along the limestone wall, moving deeper into the bluff face. As he came into the rear of the hollow, the ground began to open up. There was limestone rubble in front of the bluff. The overhead trees and the wall buried this area in shadow, creating a patch of barren ground. But anyone moving along the trail below might be able to see him sitting near the back of the hollow. He needed to secret himself near the ground.

Then he saw it, a low cave opening in the bluff face, directly in front of him. If he kneeled and got low, he could wiggle his way into the opening. He could conceal himself and remain cool and hidden until dark. And his scent would be enveloped by limestone and the dark earth.

He bent low to the ground and considered the opening. When he peered inside, it was dark but seemed to open up, with the wall of the crevice rising, at least enough so he could fit into the space with some overhead room to spare.

Cab Teufel got down on his hands and knees and then lay down and managed to side wiggle into the narrow opening. He had been right; the cave was narrow and dark and cool. The perfect place to await nightfall.

Providence had prevailed again.

Cab lay quietly for the next 2 hours. His sense of thirst continued to intensify, but he heard no one coming down the game trail behind him. For the moment, he felt safe and tried to rest.

Outside, he could see the woods darken. He knew the bluff faced east, so the eastern cliffside would have to darken considerably before he rose to the pasture above him. That way was west and would remain light the longest.

He waited 10 more minutes. Then he began to roll, carefully, toward the cave opening.

Suddenly, a rattle started near his feet, loud and alarming. Cab jerked his knees up and away from the sound. But his movement caused another rattle to sound, this one near his face. Startled, Cab tried to shove some limestone rubble ahead of him, toward the sound near his face. Before he could pull his wrist back, he felt a sharp sting on the lower part of his arm. An involuntary scream came out of him, and he tried to back away from the rattle and its fangs. He moved his feet, getting ready to scramble, and suddenly he felt another sting, this one at his ankle.

Cab screamed and kicked, hard, and then for a moment there was silence.

In the darkness, he heard slithering. The snakes, one by his head and one by his feet, were moving quickly across the limestone rubble in front of him.

He struggled to move away from them, the only way he could move, deeper into the cave, and then he heard a third rattle, this one behind him. He let out a scream and was bitten again. In the back of his neck.

If his terror had not completely overwhelmed reason, he might have realized he had wiggled into a rattlesnake den. But all he felt now was elemental fear. And a voice screaming, *Get out of this hole.*

He struggled forward, but more snakes were returning to their den. They had no other option but to strike at the animal that threatened them. And they did. Again, and again, striking out to dissuade the creature from moving toward them.

After a few moments of struggle, Cab Teufel grew catatonic. Then still.

CHAPTER 45

The next morning, it took Gray some time to follow the meandering trails Cab had left the previous night. He did, in fact, discover the small hollow choked with vegetation, the rear of which opened into a cave. He passed it and went another 50 yards before descending the hillside and then picking up the game trail and following it toward a dead end.

At first, the disappearance of any scent moving forward puzzled the wolf dog. But he was a determined animal, and so he followed the scent back up the hillside and back along the bluff until he returned to the small hollow.

Sam, Carmel, Gina, Jules, and Deputy Rosie Miller all followed along.

Then, at the hollow, Gray raised his nose in the air and stepped toward the limestone wall.

"Whad'ya got, buddy?" Sam said.

Gray's tail wagged excitedly, indicating he'd found more scent. He nosed around until he discovered the edge of an opening that ran between a limestone wall and dense foliage. He was just about ready to wheedle his way into it when Gina, behind Sam, said, "Wait, wait."

Sam told Gray to stay. "What is it?" he said.

"I think I see the start of a crevice back there. Maybe a little cave. And I gotta say, this place screams timber rattlesnake."

"You mean, like where they'd den up?" Sam said.

Gina nodded.

"You see any sign?" Sam said.

"I don't," Gina said. "But I feel like there are rattlesnakes nearby."

"You feel?" Sam said.

"I know. Crazy. But I think we should step carefully. I don't think you should let Gray go in there."

"I feel it too," Jules said.

Great, Sam thought. *The two purveyors of serpent-god myth stories feel rattlesnakes.*

The group was huddled in a small opening in front of the bluff-side hollow. Carmel could read Sam's look, that he was doubtful a person could feel the presence of a snake. Even a herpetologist who loved the animals, like Gina Larkspur, or someone with ancient Mayan blood coursing through his veins.

But she also knew he, like her, had respect for ancient mythologies, and believed instinct, or our sixth sense—call it whatever you want—could intuit things our more tangible senses could not.

So he held Gray back and told Carmel to keep hold of his collar.

And then he entered the dark space on his own.

Sam scooted along the limestone wall, stepping carefully through the dense plant life at his feet. The jagged limestone seemed to stretch down to the ground in a nearly straight drop. Less than 10 feet in, Sam thought he glimpsed an opening near the ground, a dark crevice. He used his right foot to move the bracken away from the wall, stepping down on it so he could see more clearly at his feet. There was definitely a crevice. And it widened as it moved farther along the wall, toward the back of the hollow.

He took two more steps forward, using his foot to move foliage to the side, watching the crevice widen into something resembling a narrow cave opening. And then he saw fingertips, from a hand.

But they weren't moving.

Then he heard a rattle.

In the end Jules was the one who pointed out that Kukulkan, the serpent-god, exacted his revenge on the killer of the Garcia kids. He led the murderer into a cave and there some of his agents wreaked vengeance that had been 25 years in the making.

Sam wasn't so sure. But he thought it was a good ending to the story.

EPILOGUE

"Didn't you just meet these people?" Carmel said.

Sam and Carmel were having breakfast and reviewing their wedding invite list. All of Carmel's invitees had responded, and most of Sam's (though he still had four or five holdouts, about which Carmel felt frustrated). And now he was adding five more people to the list. People she had only just met.

"Sam, the bride and groom invite people to the wedding they have known for a long time. Like, since childhood. Or really good, longtime friends. And family."

"I understand," Sam said. "But I don't have any family, per se. My parents were only children, and I was an only child. They're both dead. And I've invited all the childhood friends I had, which wasn't many. And the friends I've met since."

"And your boss and her husband."

"Who are coming," Sam said. "Miracle of miracles, given I've never met Kay's husband, Clarence. And she's never attended anything I've invited her to."

"We'll see," Carmel said. "And you still have some holdouts."

"Are you just trying to make me feel bad?"

"No, Sam. I mean, it's just . . . you hardly know these people."

"You don't hunt rattlesnakes and murderers for a week and not get to know people. These are good people. I told them about my wedding, and they were happy for me. For us."

"What did you say?"

"You were the best veterinarian I had ever met. That Gray loved you as much as I did. That you were smart. And beautiful. And I recognized all that the first time I met you."

"God, Rivers. You're such a liar."

"I am not," Sam said. "That's what I told them. More or less, through the week." Not exactly, Sam knew, but sort of.

"The sheriff, I guess I understand," Carmel said. "She's a professional colleague and there's a chance you may work with her again."

"And Dean Goddard is coming. Another county sheriff. They know each other."

Carmel nodded. "I get it. But Gina, Rosie, and Jules?"

"You met them," Sam said. "I couldn't very well invite the sheriff and not invite the deputy. Rosie helped me survey the site for rattlesnakes, despite having a deathly fear of snakes. Any snakes. Gina Larkspur is a kindred spirit with a profound sense of reptiles and amphibians. And Jules saved Gray from getting bit by a rattler. The kid is the epitome of grace under pressure."

Carmel appreciated all that. But she didn't think it presaged an invite to their wedding.

"You need to mail them today," Carmel said.

"Not a problem. I took a photo of the invitation and sent them an image via email. And they all said they'd love to come."

From the look on Carmel's face, Sam immediately understood he had violated protocol.

"What?" he said.

"You don't email an image of a wedding invitation," Carmel said.

Sam guessed he understood her perspective.

"Why did we spend so much time working on them. We made them so nice. We wanted people to have the invites and then mail back their RSVPs in the enclosed envelopes. They aren't coming to a high school mixer."

True enough, Sam knew. The invites were quite stylish. One of Carmel's friends, who knew about stationery, had helped them.

"But our wedding is in five weeks. I just thought this would be easier. I can still send them invites via snail mail, if you want."

Carmel bent her head forward and started rubbing her forehead with her hand. She was silent for a moment. A long moment.

Sam reached across the breakfast table.

Eventually, she took his offered hand, reluctantly.

"Rivers," she said, sounding resigned.

"Sorry," he said. "I love you and am committed to our wedding and, more importantly, to our relationship, and I promise I will do everything possible to make sure it's wonderful, which I'm sure it will be. I'll even dance."

Carmel had seen Sam dance. Three left feet on his best day. Rhythm impaired.

But she loved him. She loved everything about him. Especially that he danced on three left feet.

ACKNOWLEDGMENTS

This book would not have been possible without the gracious assistance of several people.

Early in the process of plotting, I needed to reach out to several subject-matter experts. I knew from the beginning that I wanted the snake featured in the book to be the eastern massasauga rattlesnake (EMR), a rare species about which I knew almost nothing. My research led me to Terry VanDeWalle, Senior Ecologist and Senior Principal at Stantec Consulting Services, Inc. Terry, a PhD herpetologist, not only knows just about everything there is to know about that species of rattlesnake, but he also catches them, chips them, and studies them; he includes an entire chapter on the species in his excellent book, *The Natural History of Snakes and Lizards of Iowa*. I loved this book so much, I bought a second copy for my brother, also a snake lover. At several different points in my research, I turned to Terry for his assistance. For instance, when he told me about chipping snakes, I knew I needed to include that in the book. But how in the hell do you chip a rattlesnake? Terry explained the delicate process in detail. It should be no surprise that the university scientist in the book is named Barry Vander, a nod to Terry VanDeWalle. Thank you, Terry!

Once I had the species figured out, I needed to understand how the Minnesota DNR would respond if a rare species of rattlesnake turned up in a southeast Minnesota field. My research led me to Carol Hall, a herpetologist for the Minnesota Biological Survey. Carol explained how the Minnesota DNR would likely react, describing the different roles and departments within the organization. She was also familiar with EMRs. She was the one who told me the species was extirpated from Minnesota (and she shared the link to the Federal Register notation about it—which is included in the book).

After understanding the different DNR roles, I realized I needed to speak with a DNR Conservation Officer (CO). I already knew that the COs throughout the state are regional, so I contacted Annette Kyllo, the CO for the Rochester area, in Minnesota's bluff country. She was very helpful in explaining the likely process that would occur if a rare rattlesnake was found dead on the side of a Minnesota rural road. That process is covered in the book.

When a draft of the book was finally finished, several readers reviewed and commented on it. Special thanks to Laurie and Steve Sauerbry, Heidi Hammond, Doug Johnson, Anne Torrey, Joannie Debrito, and others mentioned below.

My son Noah, the Hollywood writer, first got me interested in treatments—single-spaced, multipage recitations of what happens in a book, including themes, characters, plot, and so much more. Noah reviewed an early treatment for the book and offered numerous suggestions. Similarly, he read the prologue and said something like, "Yup. Pretty good." High praise from a writer who has waged many editorial battles and looks forward to many more.

There are edits, and then there are edits. One of the last edits was conducted by writing teacher and fellow writer Mary Logue.

Mary has written more than 20 books, including poetry, children's books, and several excellent mysteries. Her latest mystery, *The Big Sugar,* is now available in paperback. I highly recommend it. Mary worked through every word of the manuscript and sat down with me to review her sharp work. This book is much better because of her studied efforts.

The final edit was conducted by my excellent publisher, AdventureKEEN. Their editorial team—Emily Beaumont, Jenna Barron, and Holly Cross—read through every sentence and flagged several additional parts of the manuscript that needed attention and/or clarification. A huge thanks to all of them.

Others at AdventureKEEN have also been extremely helpful, including Publisher Molly Merkle for believing in and continuing to support the Sam Rivers Mysteries; Chief Product Officer Travis Bryant for his help on book covers and much more; Book Production Artist Annie Long for her design and typesetting expertise; and Senior Acquisitions Editor Brett Ortler. If you like the covers of the Sam Rivers Mysteries, thank Travis. Liliane Opsomer and Megan Wells have provided an endless stream of marketing and PR support. They do so much and are two of the people at AdventureKEEN with whom I am in contact the most. Thanks, Liliane and Megan!

Last, but certainly not least, my wife, Anna, has provided moral support and so much more. She read early drafts of the book; listened to me thinking out loud about where the book was headed; and weighed in on characters, plot points, and related content at every step of the book's process. And finally, when a draft was finished, she read and edited the entire manuscript. Without her assistance this book would not have been possible.

About Rattlesnake Bluff *and Discussion Guide*

On July 17, 1998, two kids out roller-skating on a remote country road disappear. The town of Owen's Gap, Minnesota, does everything possible to find the children. But after two decades and following every lead, their disappearance is never solved. While the mystery begins to fade, the loss hangs over Minnesota's bluff country like a dark cloud.

Southeastern Minnesota is sometimes referred to as The Driftless, an area the Ice Age glaciers left untouched. The exposed limestone substrate is marked by holes, caves, crevices, and bluffs that often have beautiful vistas overlooking the region's rich farmland. It is also home to timber rattlesnakes, Minnesota's only venomous serpent.

Present day, an Owen's Gap developer is taking advantage of one of the region's remarkable vistas and begins clearing land for a high-end townhouse complex. Before the clearing can begin, a worker is startled by a rattlesnake. He kills the viper and tosses it onto the nearby rural road.

Timber rattlesnakes are a threatened species in Minnesota. After an anonymous call to the sheriff's office, a DNR conservation officer retrieves the snake and shares it with his friend and DNR herpetologist, Gina Larkspur. Gina is stunned to discover the reptile is a rare eastern massasauga rattlesnake, an animal that has not been seen in the state in more than two decades. Since the massasauga is an endangered species, all site development is halted, at least long enough to determine if there are any more massasaugas in the neighborhood.

Sam Rivers, special agent for the U.S. Fish & Wildlife Service, is recruited to do a site survey. The site developer and the local sheriff expect the survey to be quick and to find no additional massasaugas. If so, the site can be reopened within 24 hours.

While Sam feels the political pressure, he is thorough and methodical in his search for more rare, endangered species. Moreover, he knows if more rattlesnakes are discovered, he will have no problem stopping construction, at least for the time being.

Eventually, Sam's survey uncovers more rattlesnakes . . . and something far more sinister than anyone expected. Suddenly, Sam is searching for something much more dangerous than the region's rattlesnakes. And if he does not find it soon, people could die.

1. The book is entitled *Rattlesnake Bluff*. Can you think of two reasons why that title is appropriate?

2. Was the death of the Garcia kids an accident, or murder? Explain.

3. What is the difference between an eastern massasauga rattlesnake and a timber rattlesnake? Are there populations of massasaugas elsewhere?

4. Discuss the pros and cons of threatened and endangered species laws that enable the USFW to temporarily stop work on a construction site. Are those laws warranted? Are they a good thing? Bad?

5. Worker Jules Ortega discovers the massasauga and kills it. Destroying an endangered species is a felony. Why isn't Jules prosecuted?

6. The novel's main protagonist is a white supremacist and a Nazi sympathizer. In what ways does his perspective lead to his ultimate demise?

7. Jules may be an undocumented worker. The Garcia kids were the children of a Mexican-born father and a local mother. And dairy farmer Joe Smiley is an immigrant. In what ways do their differing immigration backgrounds play out in the book?

8. Zoning Commissioner Henry Fields's whereabouts are unknown during a weekend when murders happen, making him a suspect for the crime. He claims he has a solid alibi for his disappearance but refuses to share it. Why? If you were in Henry's shoes, what would you do?

9. Sheriff Betsy Conrad's perspectives about eastern massasauga rattlesnakes evolve over time? Why?

10. In what ways does Minnesota's bluff country play a key role in the story?

ABOUT THE AUTHOR

Award-winning author Cary J. Griffith grew up among the woods, fields, and emerald waters of eastern Iowa. His childhood fostered a lifelong love of wild places.

He earned a BA in English from the University of Iowa and an MA in library science from the University of Minnesota.

Griffith's books explore the natural world. In nonfiction, he covers the borderlands between civilization and wild places. In fiction, he focuses on the ways some people use flora and fauna to commit crimes, while others with more reverence and understanding of the natural world leverage their knowledge to bring criminals to justice.

The Story of AdventureKEEN

We are an independent nature and outdoor activity publisher. Our founding dates back more than 40 years, guided then and now by our love of being in the woods and on the water, by our passion for reading and books, and by the sense of wonder and discovery made possible by spending time recreating outdoors in beautiful places.

It is our mission to share that wonder and fun with our readers, especially with those who haven't yet experienced all the physical and mental health benefits that nature and outdoor activity can bring.

In addition, we strive to teach about responsible recreation so that the natural resources and habitats we cherish and rely upon will be available for future generations.

We are a small team deeply rooted in the places where we live and work. We have been shaped by our communities of origin—primarily Birmingham, Alabama; Cincinnati, Ohio; and the northern suburbs of Minneapolis, Minnesota. Drawing on the decades of experience of our staff and our awareness of the industry, the marketplace, and the world at large, we have shaped a unique vision and mission for a company that serves our readers and authors.

We hope to meet you out on the trail someday.

#bewellbeoutdoors

READ ON FOR AN EXCERPT FROM CARY J. GRIFFITH'S NEXT NOVEL

GRIZZLY NARROWS

Praise for *Rattlesnake Bluff*

"*Rattlesnake Bluff* gave me a pit in my stomach from its tense opening pages all the way to its dramatic and terrifying finale. Whether you're an existing fan of Sam Rivers or brand-new to the series, Griffith's taut writing will keep you turning the pages. I loved it."

—Joshua Moehling, author of *And There He Kept Her* and *Where the Dead Sleep*

Adventure Publications

**AVAILABLE SUMMER 2026
WHEREVER BOOKS ARE SOLD**

CHAPTER 1

There was a metal click as Wolf Maligan's cell door was automatically unlocked. The heavy bars swung open. Wolf heard Mug's familiar boot falls start down the Blue Row, followed by Curly's quieter plods.

The Blue Row was a part of the Medawakien Security Facility outside of Athabasca Falls, Ontario. Inmates in this part of the facility wore blue jumpsuits and were considered reasonably behaved and low risk. Some of them, like Wolf, were murderers. But over four years, Wolf had learned how to get along with the guards (biding his time) and the other inmates (again, biding time).

"It's a beautiful day on the Row," Mug said, approaching Wolf's door.

Mug's given name was Johnny Valentine. He was short and squat and he had a face that was ruddy and wide, belying his last name. His face had given him his nickname, Mug—not one he liked, which hadn't helped his disposition. Mug's job as a guard gave him an unrealistic sense of his own importance, which he liked to convey to the prisoners.

"You know the drill, 773," Mug said. "Hands and feet. Nice and easy."

Technically, Wolf arrived at Medawakien four years earlier as Inmate 773. In his first week in the yard he'd heard wolves howling out of the nearby Ontario woods and answered with a howl of his own. When the pack responded, the other inmates gave Inmate 773 his nickname.

Mug never used it.

Wolf sat on his bunk and extended his arms and legs, docile as a cat. Curly stepped in and took a moment to affix chains to ankles and wrists.

Curly Cue was big as a mountain and the guard Mug brought along when there was a chance there might be trouble.

When the manacles snapped shut, they made a satisfying click. At least for Mug, who enjoyed this part of his job.

"Time to go," Mug said.

The ankle chains were wide enough to allow walking in an awkward shuffle. Wolf stood and hobbled into the walkway.

"Dead man walkin'," Mug called out.

The comment was reserved for inmates on death row. From all accounts, Medawakien was a country club compared to Minnesota's Oak Park Heights. This morning Wolf was being transferred to the maximum-security prison to serve out a life sentence for first-degree murder, no possibility of parole. Mug had already informed his Minnesota colleagues that the best way to handle 773 was an occasional blow from a steel baton, a reminder of who was master and who was dog.

As Wolf shuffled past, some of the prisoners wished him luck.

"He's gonna need it, where he's headed," Mug said. "Ain't that right, Curly Cue?"

Curly was walking behind Mug. It took him a moment, but he finally said, "Yup."

"Yup is right," Mug said. "That's what I like about you, Curly Cue. You don't say much, but you know what's what."

"I guess," Curly said.

"Fat man don't know shit," one of the prisoners down the Row said, loud enough to hear but not be recognized.

The other inmates hooted and hollered and laughed. When Wolf chuckled with them, Mug swung the steel baton across the back of Wolf's shoulders.

For the briefest second, Wolf thought about turning and with manacled hands wrenching the weapon out of Mug's puffy fist and beating him to death. But it was two against one, and Curly was a big man. Besides, in less than 30 minutes he'd be leaving Medawakien for good.

Mug shoved Wolf forward, making him stumble.

Then, to the other prisoners, Mug said, "Looks like the blue dogs might wanna skip lunch today."

Mug had the power to cancel meals, a punitive measure he enjoyed exercising.

In front of the Blue Row's steel door, Mug signaled to the guard on the other side and the bars opened. Once through the door, they made their way along hallways and through two more security doors. The three men passed through the last gate, Wolf shuffling between them. Once through, Mug approached the bullet-proof window, behind which two sitting guards looked up.

The office was bathed in bright fluorescence. Inside, there was a console to the right with a bank of cameras and a handheld microphone sitting in front of them.

One of the guards, Frank, slid open the security glass.

"Hey, Mug."

"Frank," Mug nodded. "Inmate 773, ready for his 8:30 transfer."

"I see that," Frank said, glancing at Wolf standing 5 feet back, with Curly behind him. "We got a little problem, Mug."

"That fuckin' Reggie called in sick again?"

"Newlyweds," Frank grinned.

"Fuckin' Reggie."

"Fuckin' Reggie," Frank agreed. "Least I hope he is."

The three guards laughed.

Prisoner transfers required two guards: one to drive and one to man the radios, just in case. The road south was a cellular black hole. Reggie was supposed to be Mug's eyes and ears and voice, if they needed to radio for help. But there was a labor shortage in Canada's prisons, so it wasn't unusual for transfers to be short staffed. And the road from Medawakien to Minnesota was never busy.

"You okay goin' solo?" Frank said.

Mug thought about it. "I'd be doin' the work of two men." He liked to leverage advantages, if he could. "Seems like I should at least be gettin' double time."

Now it was Frank's turn to think. Frank was a supervisor. "Tell you what, Mug. How about time and a half? And we'll throw in lunch at McCalester's down in Cayuga." Cayuga was the border town two hours south. McCalester's had the best poutine in the country. Mug was familiar with their french fries smothered in gravy and their double cheeseburgers. He thought he might have a malt too.

"Okay," Mug finally said.

Going solo violated protocol. Especially when it involved a murderer. Still, for the last four years, apart from occasional recalcitrance, Wolf had kept his mouth shut and his eyes down.

"773 will behave himself," Mug said, turning to look at the inmate.

The man's wrists and ankles were manacled, and the chains were connected by a length of steel cable. There was no chance Wolf could do anything but obey.

When Wolf didn't respond, Mug said, "chained up six ways from Sunday doesn't allow a man to get into much devilry."

"Fuckin' A," Frank agreed.

"Fuckin' A," Mug smiled.

Frank handed over the paperwork, and Mug filled out and signed the necessary blanks. In less than five minutes the last security door opened, and Mug walked through, following the shuffling Wolf. Outside, another guard waited beside the prisoner transport vehicle, a Ford van chassis outfitted with the latest technology. Mug liked the outside light options; red, white, and blue flashers on the front and back, and floods on all sides. Signage declared the van's purpose—ONTARIO PRISONER TRANSPORT—with a video eye in the O of PRISONER. There was a rear warning to follow-on vehicles—KEEP BACK. But Mug did not expect to see more than a half dozen cars before his early poutine at McCalester's, down on the border.

The van contained three secure compartments, all accessible by two-way radio and onboard video cameras. Mug opened the side door to the single prisoner compartment, a steel enclosure with locking seatbelts. There were two rear compartments that could each hold three prisoners. But the side compartment was smaller, more secure, and more likely to result in rough jostling if Mug wanted to make sharp turns and sudden brakes, just for fun.

Once belted and locked in, Wolf was chained twice—around the ankles and wrists, and around the waist and legs.

"Sit back and enjoy the ride," Mug said, and grinned. "Parts of it might get a little bumpy."

Wolf had learned to avoid eye contact with the guards, especially Mug. Eye contact intimated equality and invited retribution. Now he was careful to avert his gaze.

For more than an hour the ride south was routine. They had seen three vehicles on the road. Two traveling north. And another, a Mercedes convertible, Mug noticed, traveling south. The Mercedes pulled up behind the van, ignoring the KEEP BACK warning across the rear doors.

From Mug's front seat console, he watched the Mercedes approach and grow too close. The angle of the camera lens was elevated enough and the image clear enough so Mug could see down into the Mercedes. It was a woman. She had black hair pulled into a tight ponytail that swished back and forth in the open air like a cat's tail.

Mug watched the road but kept an eye on the rear camera.

The woman wore a red scarf around her neck and a pair of dark sunglasses. Mug could see enough to know she was a looker. What Mug noticed most was her satiny blouse. Even through the windshield the blouse showed an attractive outline of breasts.

Rich bitch, Mug thought, watching the road.

Before Mug could engage the rear speaker and tell the Mercedes to back off to at least five car lengths, she hit her turn signal, double honked a warning and sped by . . . going well over the speed limit.

He assumed she was someone's plaything. Probably a doctor's wife, out of Toronto, heading to their palatial cabin in the woods, where she'd get naked with their groundskeeper.

Mug had a pornographic imagination.

As the Mercedes rocketed by, Mug flipped her off, hoping an Ontario Provincial Patrol would pick her up for speeding. He'd love to watch her get pulled over and nailed. But given the rarity of cops patrolling this road, Mug knew it was unlikely.

The Ontario wilderness had plenty of bogs, lakes, and rivers, necessitating highway twists, turns, and bridges. Ninety minutes south he came around a sharp turn and was startled by an accident. The Mercedes was catawampus on the opposite side of the highway, facing the opposite direction. As Mug came around the corner, the transport van was practically on top of her and he braked, screeching to a halt.

The right front headlight of the Mercedes appeared crumpled. The driver's side door was flung open, and the woman lay with her torso hanging out of the car, nearly upside down. There was a red streak across her forehead and down her face, bleeding onto her blouse.

Behind the open driver's side door, he could only see the top of her torso. The air bag hadn't opened, which probably accounted for why she was bloodied.

It took a second to absorb the scene. Obviously, she'd struck the right side of the bridge with her right front fender. Probably distracted by a goddamn cell phone. The impact must have spun her car to the left, where it did a 180, crossing the highway and ending up in the opposite lane, facing the opposite direction. Now the vehicle was half off the highway. Her right arm was flung over her head, resting on the pavement. She'd been wearing a seat belt, now awkwardly wrapped around her middle, which appeared to be the only thing holding her in place. The impact must have knocked her sunglasses off. Her eyes were shut, and she was still as a corpse.

Transport protocol dictated any time the van stopped, especially for something unexpected, like an accident, he was to radio out. Then he should make sure the transport van was secure.

But the van was in a precarious spot. If another vehicle piled down the highway behind him, he'd either be rear-ended or they'd swerve to miss him and plow straight into the Mercedes. And the woman.

Across the narrow bridge the road from the south turned out of the woods and immediately entered the bridge. It was a short bridge, no longer than 50 feet across a small creek. Anyone traveling north would enter the bridge and be hard pressed to stop before hitting the car and the woman, especially if they were traveling the speed limit.

In an instant Mug understood there was no time for protocol.

He cut the engine, jumped out of the cab, and hurried across the pavement. As he approached, he could see blood on the blouse and across her face. Her right arm hung awkwardly above her, possibly broken or dislocated. The shoulder strap was across her middle. Her left side was hidden by the door. But her skirt was hiked up over a pair of bare, sculpted legs. The legs were strong and shapely and attached to what looked like a fit body, even though it was nearly upside down and bleeding.

He quickly tried to determine the blood's source and see if she was breathing. Blood trailed out of the corner of her mouth. She must have struck the steering wheel when the airbag didn't open. He couldn't tell if she was breathing.

He bent down to have a closer look. When he did, her eyes popped open. Her left hand came out from under the seat quick as a snakebite. She fired a Taser into Mug's chest.

The Taser tongs delivered a 50,000-volt charge that immobilized the startled Mug. While the charge was only five seconds, the sluggish aftermath gave the woman enough time to tumble out of the car, come up with a pair of handcuffs, yank Mug's fat wrists behind his back, and cuff him.

He moaned, starting to come out of the shock.

She picked up a roll of duct tape and wrapped his ankles four times, fast as a rodeo rider roping a calf, tearing off the end of the tape just as Mug kicked his feet out.

"What the fuck," he managed.

She jerked the Taser prongs from Mug's chest. Mug squealed as she backed up and tossed the Taser, wires, and prongs into the back seat. Then she pulled a second Taser from inside the Mercedes and fired a second charge into Mug's back.

While Mug was stunned, she dug through his pockets and found his keys. Then she hurried to the van. She sorted through the keychain and found the one for the side door and opened it.

Wolf blinked in the sunlight. He blinked and looked and saw the blood and said, "you shot?"

"Fake blood," she said. "Take care of him. Hurry."

She looked through Mug's keys until she found a pair she thought would fit his manacles and tried them. Lucky.

Wolf was free and out of the van, rubbing his wrists and walking awkwardly toward where Mug lay on the pavement, hog tied and incapacitated but coming around.

"Fuck!" Mug said, beginning to realize his arms and legs were bound.

"Got a gun?" Wolf asked the woman.

"Glove compartment. Hurry."

As Wolf moved toward the car's front seat he kicked Mug, hard. Then he popped open the glove compartment, found the weapon, a Glock 42, and backed off the seat, stepping onto the pavement next to Mug's head.

Wolf turned and kicked Mug twice, in the ribs.

"That's for the Row," Wolf said, spittle coming out with his words.

Mug screamed from the kicks and then groaned.

Wolf checked the Glock to make sure it was loaded. Then he turned it on Mug and said, "you're lucky I don't got more time," and fired, twice, point blank at the man's head.

Mug bucked and then lay still.

"Push him into the ditch," the woman said.

Wolf pocketed the Glock and hoisted Mug's boots off the pavement. He lifted the dead weight by the ankles and dragged him to the other side of the car. The road's shoulder was narrow, and after 5 feet it dropped to a swampy area filled with cattails and weeds. Wolf situated the dead man parallel to the road, on the outer edge of the shoulder. Then he pushed him, and Mug rolled down the side of the embankment into the cattail stand, the side of his head and half his body splashing into swamp water. The only way anyone would see the body was if they stopped on the shoulder and peered over the edge.

While Wolf managed Mug the woman peeled a faux crumpled right headlight and fender off her car, some kind of magnetized mess, and tossed it into the back seat of the car, returning the Mercedes to its pristine appearance.

"Take the van," she said, tossing Wolf the keys. "There's a turnoff ahead in 3 miles. Follow me."

She was in the Benz, turning over the engine long enough to accelerate forward, back around, and head south, petal to the metal.

It took Wolf seconds to cross the road and enter the van. He tossed the Glock on the passenger seat and turned over the engine.

By the time the woman was over the bridge she was going the speed limit.

Wolf was right behind her.

Three miles south he watched her signal a right turn and pull into a two-lane rut. She centered on the ruts and accelerated.

Wolf had to straddle the two ruts with the wider van chassis. But the shoulders on either side were flat and dry and after a hundred yards the ruts bent left and emptied into a weed-covered opening, what must have been an old gravel pit. A faded red F-150 pickup truck, a vintage make and model, was along the side of the opening. Mug braked.

The woman was already out of her Mercedes, standing next to the driver's side door.

As Wolf got out of the van the woman, keeping her distance, tossed him the keys.

"Looks old, but that's to keep you under the radar," she said, nodding toward the F-150. "It's been rebuilt. This'll get you down to Mexico and back, if that's where you want to go. After our business."

Wolf glanced at the truck and then considered the woman.

During the four years Wolf had been incarcerated, his only visitor had been Wilhelmina Gunn. Her gray hair was tousled around her head like a rat's nest. Her face was wrinkled as an old crone. She wore a threadbare, khaki-colored smock that hung like a tent over thin shoulders. Everything about her seemed tawdry and aged. Unless you looked carefully . . . at her hands and her intense green eyes. And when she winked. That quick eye movement caused the skin on the right side of her socket to crinkle, showing the edge of some kind of mask, which Wolf, unlike the guards, didn't miss.

Wilhelmina claimed she was Wolf's sixth grade teacher, come to visit when she heard Wolf was in a Canadian prison. Then there was a coded conversation about loving the outdoors and rivers and how you had to be careful about rivers because they had a mind of their own. Then another wink. Then Wilhelmina reminded Wolf about a bully in school named Samuel, and by then Wolf was tracking.

Over the next 15 minutes, she complained about aging, telling Wolf the worst part was the way some people, bullies, would take advantage of a single lady on a fixed income. She wished Wolf wasn't in here, she whined, and that if he was out, she knew he would help her deal with the Samuels of the world. The predators. The hunters. She told him she couldn't promise, but she was hoping to see him again, maybe when he got out? She mentioned his transfer date and where he was headed, to Minnesota, and she had a cousin in the state she'd been meaning to visit. She told him she'd be waitin' for him. Another wink.

A month later he got a letter from Wilhelmina, with more code. It included a photo of the woman now in front of him, leaning against the Benz.

"My niece Justine," the note said.

Prison security opened and read inmates' letters. But the letter was just an old lady's small talk. They saw the photo and, before returning it to the envelope, they passed it around, admiring the old crone's niece, a looker.

"Who are you?" Wolf said.

"Someone like you," the woman said. "Someone who wants Sam Rivers dead."

The name Sam Rivers flushed Wolf's face red. Rivers had killed his friends, put him in prison, and eventually got him convicted of murder and put away for life.

"What's he done to you?"

"Does it matter?"

Wolf was 62. But he was hard, tough, and mean, and for the last four years he'd been incarcerated. With men. Not only was a woman in front of him, but she was better looking than any woman Wolf had the rare luck to be with. Or had taken. And she was alone. Defenseless. In the woods. The way Wolf liked it.

He started toward her.

Her right hand reached behind her and brought out a second Glock. She lifted it in front of her and with two hands pointed it straight at Wolf's head, in a stance that told Wolf she knew how to use it.

He stopped.

When she was sure she had his attention she said, "You need to focus. As soon as someone back at Medawakien sees this truck stopped, they'll radio. Then it'll be less than an hour before the patrols come see what the fuck's going on."

Wolf listened.

"Everything you need is in the truck," she said. "New ID. Change of clothes. Money. In the next 60 seconds you need to get rid of that prison suit."

"Can't go south," Wolf said.

"You can for 15 miles. Take the road west and keep driving until you can find somewhere to pull over and use what's in the truck to finish your disguise."

"What about Rivers?"

"Rivers'll keep. Three, maybe four days, you'll have your chance. For now, you got one job. Go west. Stay north of the border. When you get to Saskatchewan, hold up. There's a phone in the truck. A burner. Know how to use one?"

Wolf nodded.

"I'll call you tomorrow. Make sure you pick up."

Wolf thought about charging her. But for the moment, the sense of her comments broke through his desire to have fun with her.

"I can hunt Rivers myself," Wolf said.

"But I'm going to make it easy for you."

She opened the driver's side of the Benz and got into her vehicle, keeping the gun pointed at him. The engine was still idling.

"Find somewhere in the woods to hole up," she said. "At least long enough to use that mirror to change the way you look. There's clippers. Shave your head and use the wig. You got ID. Just don't get caught. And don't do anything stupid."

She put the car in gear and said, "Tomorrow. Answer my call."

Then she accelerated down the ruts, turned, and disappeared.

Wolf spent two seconds watching the Benz. He wasn't the kind of man who took orders from anyone. Especially a woman. But he had to admit her plan had worked. So far.

He shed the jumpsuit and pulled on a red flannel shirt with faded coveralls. The coveralls were high water. Then he hurled his prison footwear into the nearby woods and donned a pair of work boots, scuffed and worn. They fit, which made Wolf wonder if the woman, Gunn, if that was her real name, knew his shoe size. But he didn't take too long to think about it. He was in the truck and turned over the engine with a rumble. It was loud, but typical for an aging F-150. The woman had thought of everything. Then he was down the road and turning west in a little less than 20 minutes, on his way to freedom.

And eventually, with or without help, to kill Sam Rivers.

PRAISE FOR *WOLF KILL*

"Griffith's prose makes you feel the winter chill . . . and the twisty plot delivers a chill down your spine. This is a Minnesota mystery with razor-sharp teeth."
—Brian Freeman, *New York Times* best-selling author of
The Deep, Deep Snow

"*Wolf Kill* is a terrific read! The writing is so good that you can feel the frigid winds blowing through this dark and masterfully crafted novel even as the suspense heats up. And the wolves are as magnificent and frightening as you could hope.
—David Housewright, Edgar Award–winning author of
What Doesn't Kill Us

"In northern Minnesota, winter is full of dangers that can kill: hard cold, hard men, and hungry wolves. Cary Griffith brings the menace of all three into play in his riveting new thriller. Returning to the childhood home he fled 20 years earlier, Sam Rivers finds himself battling a group of scheming reprobates and struggling against an avalanche of painful memories. Griffith's intimacy with the territory he writes about comes through in every line. I loved this novel and highly recommend it. But I suggest you enjoy it under a warm blanket. Honestly, I've never read a book that evokes the fierce winter landscape of the North Country better than *Wolf Kill*."
—William Kent Krueger, Edgar Award–winning author of
This Tender Land

"Cary J. Griffith defines the savage, howling beauty of a Northern Minnesota winter in this taut, compulsively readable mystery. I want more Sam Rivers!
—Wendy Webb, author of *The Haunting of Brynn Wilder*

PRAISE FOR *COUGAR CLAW*

"In this highly anticipated second novel in the Sam Rivers series, Cary J. Griffith delivers another finely researched and compellingly written thriller. Both the beauty and the savagery of our natural world form the heart of a Griffith story. In this case, it's the predatory habits of cougars. When the killing of a Twin Cities man in an apparent cougar attack brings Sam to the Minnesota River Valley to investigate, what follows is a gradual and fascinating revelation of not just the predatory nature of cougars, but that of humans as well."
—William Kent Krueger, Edgar Award–winning author of
This Tender Land

"*Cougar Claw*, the second installment in the Sam Rivers series, sends the U.S. Fish & Wildlife special agent to the scene of a grisly cougar killing on the outskirts of the Twin Cities. As usual in Sam Rivers's world, all is not as it seems. Griffith doubles down on his strengths in this series, giving us another vibrant cast of allies, suspects, and a misunderstood predator, while navigating a path between animal rights and human fears of the natural world. I can't wait for Sam Rivers's next assignment."
—Mindy Mejia, author of *Everything You Want Me To Be* and
Strike Me Down

"A deadly threat from the wild comes too close for comfort when an urban bicyclist is found mauled to death by a cougar. In this second book in the Sam Rivers mystery series, Cary Griffith takes us on a hair-raising hunt to find the cougar—and the truth. Mixing deep knowledge of the natural world with the twists and turns of the best suspense novels, *Cougar Claw* is a thoughtful and thrilling story."
—Mary Logue, author of *The Streel* and *The Big Sugar*

PRAISE FOR *KILLING MONARCHS*

"In *Killing Monarchs,* Cary J. Griffith combines monarch butterflies, a Mexican cartel, and compelling characters—both human and canine—to deliver a chilling thriller you won't want to put down. Sam Rivers and his wolf-dog partner, Gray, make a terrific, crime-fighting duo!"
—Margaret Mizushima, author of the award-winning
 Timber Creek K-9 Mysteries, including *Striking Range*

"What do murders disguised as overdoses, endangered monarch butterflies, and international heroin smugglers have in common? U.S. Fish & Wildlife Special Agent Sam Rivers and Gray, Sam's rescued wolf-dog hybrid with a nose for narcotics. As the bodies pile up in the Land of 10,000 Lakes, Sam and Gray are on a mission to stop the killer before he claims his next victim. A gripping thriller highlighting the ironclad bond between man and his best friend, *Killing Monarchs* had me turning pages all night long. Sam Rivers and his faithful wolf dog are my new best friends."
—Brian Malloy, author of *The Year of Ice* and *After Francesco*

"Both thriller and mystery, *Killing Monarchs* mixes an elementary-school science project with scorpions and drugs. Totally surprising is how butterflies flit into this fast-paced and tantalizing story. Cary Griffith has laid out another fabulous tale, based on solid knowledge of the natural world, with a provocative sense of the deviousness of humankind."
—Mary Logue, author of *The Streel* and *The Big Sugar*

PRAISE FOR *DEAD CATCH*

"The terrain is rough—the characters rougher—in this suspenseful mystery set in the wilds of Northern Minnesota. U.S. Fish and Wildlife Special Agent Sam Rivers must wade through turbulent waters to determine if a childhood friend is guilty of walleye poaching and murder or if, as the ex-convict insists, he was set up to take the fall. The author weaves together the rugged landscape and his knowledge of those who inhabit it to spin a tale of corruption and deceit sure to please readers who enjoy a gripping outdoors mystery."
—Lois Winston, author of the best-selling and critically acclaimed Anastasia Pollack Crafting Mysteries

"*Dead Catch* captures your attention from the opening sentence, and then, like Griffith's first victim in the poacher's net, you're caught in a trap that'll keep you flipping pages until the final twist. You'd best call in sick tomorrow, as this book will keep you up all night."
—Jeffrey B. Burton, award-winning author of *The Dead Years* and the Mace Reid K-9 Mysteries

"A fascinating and thoroughly satisfying investigation into the shadowy world of illegal fishing"
—Pamela Beason, author of the Sam Westin Wilderness Mysteries

"The first chapter of *Dead Catch* by Cary J. Griffith has everything I love in a mystery: a remote setting, wildlife facts, a life in peril, and a twisted murder. Hook, line, and sinker, I was caught."
—Sara Johnson, author of the Alexa Glock Forensics Mysteries set in New Zealand